C8000000223649

KT-445-562

)12

TIME TO KILL

Recent Titles by Brian Freemantle from Severn House

Sherlock and Sebastian Holmes

THE HOLMES INHERITANCE
THE HOLMES FACTOR

Charlie Muffin

DEAD MEN LIVING
KINGS OF MANY CASTLES

AT ANY PRICE
BETRAYALS
DEAD END
DIRTY WHITE
GOLD
HELL'S PARADISE
ICE AGE
THE IRON CAGE
THE KREMLIN CONSPIRACY
THE MARY CELESTE
O'FARRELL'S LAW
TARGET
TWO WOMEN

TIME TO KILL

Brian Freemantle

This first world edition published in Great Britain 2006 by
SEVERN HOUSE PUBLISHERS LTD of
9–15 High Street, Sutton, Surrey SM1 1DF.
This first world edition published in the USA 2007 by
SEVERN HOUSE PUBLISHERS INC of
595 Madison Avenue, New York, N.Y. 10022.

British Library Cataloguing in Publication Data

Freemantle, Brian
    Time to kill
    1.   Revenge - Fiction
    2.   Suspense - Fiction
    I.   Title
    823.9'14 [F]

    ISBN-13: 978-0-7278-6446-8   (cased)
    ISBN-10: 0-7278-6446-7   (cased)
    ISBN-13: 978-0-7278-9189-1   (paper)
    ISBN-10: 0-7278-9189-8   (paper)

All Severn House titles are printed on acid-free paper.

Typeset by Palimpsest Book Production Ltd.,
Grangemouth, Stirlingshire, Scotland.
Printed and bound in Great Britain by
MPG Books Ltd., Bodmin, Cornwall.

To Jeremy, with thanks for too many kindnesses to count

One

Jack Mason woke abruptly but without stirring, instantly aware of where he was. Knowing, too, that it was precisely 5 a.m. because he'd rigidly trained himself to awaken at that time every morning, as he had rigidly trained himself in so many other ways, in so many other things. He remained unmoving – further training – alert to the penitentiary sounds around him, listening for the unfamiliar. There was nothing but the all too familiar metal clatter and groans and snores and occasional cries from sleeping, snuffling men. Mason came down from the top bunk in one fluid, coordinated movement, landing soundlessly, animal-like, on the balls of his feet, intent upon the lower bunk. Peter Chambers slept on, undisturbed.

Mason didn't need the subdued lighting from the permanent outside illumination that silhouetted the cell bars, finding them from instinct after so long. Shrugging his back comfortably against the bars he reached up, finding the reinforcing cross strut just as easily, and slowly raised his legs until his body made the perfect L-shape for the first of the daily cell exercises. Having achieved the L-position, he held it, supported only by his hands and arms, for the self-imposed and calculated five minutes before lowering his feet to the floor. He repeated that initial process for over a full thirty minutes, without any of the stress or strain he'd suffered when he'd first initiated the exercise, many years ago. After that he performed the customary 100 press-ups using both arms, before switching to fifty on just his left arm and fifty on his right. Turning on to his back he completed 100 sit-ups using only his stomach muscles, not securing his feet or supporting his head between locked hands. There was not the slightest discomfort.

'You know what I've waited years to see? But know now

1

that I never will.' Mason gave no reaction to Chambers' sudden question from the semi-darkness of the lower bunk; never to be surprised was something else which he had coached himself.

'What?'

'Seeing you cramp up, not being able to go through one of your routines.'

'It'll never happen.'

'You really think you can keep it up when you get out?'

Mason rocked back and forth only once for the momentum to bring himself upright, without using his hands. 'Of course I will.' But making himself ready – invincible – wouldn't any longer be the priority. There'd be only one priority then. Finding Dimitri Sobell. To take, as agonizingly as possible, everything from the Russian, as Sobell had taken everything from him. Only after inflicting every imaginable hurt and loss would he finally kill Sobell, as badly and as painfully as it was possible for anyone to suffer before dying. Other training had been to study every conceivable torture to prepare himself for every option. His favourite, taken from Truman Capote's *A Handcarved Coffin*, would be to plant an amphetamine-crazed rattlesnake in the man's car, hoping that Ann would be in the vehicle, too.

'We gonna keep in touch?'

Like hell we're going to keep in touch, thought Mason. From what he'd gauged from Chambers' innuendos – sometimes coming close to outright boasts – there had been at least three million dollars more than the court had identified and traced of the twenty-million-dollar computer fraud for which Chambers had been sentenced to twenty years, matching that of his own, thankfully reduced to fifteen, as Chambers had been, for exemplary model prisoner behaviour. Mason had long ago earmarked that three million dollars to be his retirement pension: Chambers was the last on Mason's untraceable disposal list. 'We've already agreed that we will.'

'I'm never sure you mean it.'

'Stop sounding like a petulant gay.'

'Don't call me that! You know I'm not gay!'

'That's what everyone else thinks.'

'Stop it!'

Chambers wasn't gay and even if he had been there wouldn't have been any attraction, despite sex – very much

2

and very often heterosexual sex – being the basic cause of Mason's downfall. Mason hadn't known about the outstanding three million dollars when he'd first cultivated Chambers. He'd initially sought out the former bank official to learn, as he had learned, the computer expertise with which the man had stolen the twenty million, although for reasons quite different from Chambers. 'Now you *are* sounding like a petulant gay.'

There was a brief silence from the still dark cavern of the lower bunk, before Chambers said: 'You gonna stay around here, in Pennsylvania, when you get out?'

'I don't need any reminders of this place,' said Mason, who'd served his sentence in White Deer Penitentiary.

'Where you going to go?'

'I haven't decided yet.' Because I don't know where Dimitri Sobell is, buried under a new name within the Witness Protection Programme, fucking the brains out of my ex-wife, Mason thought, trying to resist the easy anger. It was time he put the electronic traps in place to discover that.

'So how we gonna keep in touch?'

'You tell me where you're going to be, when you get out. And I'll look you up. I gotta look for work. Set myself up in a place somewhere.' Like so much – virtually everything in Jack Mason's life, in fact – that was a lie. There was eight hundred thousand Russian-supplied dollars in the safe deposit box his former, inefficient CIA employers had failed to locate during their investigation into his spying for Moscow. In addition, there was another interest-earning $200,000 from the estate of his mother, who had died five years after he was jailed, unaware, because of her advanced Alzheimer's disease, of his crime or that he was in jail. Those who thought they had investigated him so thoroughly were unaware of the real treasures that were being held for his release among his mother's stored effects to which his unwitting lawyer literally held the key. But it was essential to plead needful poverty if he was ever to get close to Chambers' even greater secret financial fortune.

At last Chambers swung his legs out of the cavern, emerging into the half light. Despite the prison diet he was a fat-bodied, soft man with pale-blue eyes and receding hair whose sexuality it was easy to doubt. 'We could go into business together.'

'Doing what?'

'Combining our expertise, yours from the CIA, mine from how to make money work.'

'Which brings us to the great big question,' lured Mason. '*With* what?'

'A great big question you don't have to worry yourself about,' smirked the other man predictably.

'I'll put some thought to it,' promised Mason, impatient with the too often repeated conversation, glad of the sound further down the landing of a baton being noisily rattled along the cell bars.

'Howitt,' identified Chambers, unnecessarily.

Frank Howitt was the senior prison guard on the landing who always disturbed the convicts this way, a full thirty minutes before the wake-up bell. He didn't do it against the bars of Mason's cell, though. Howitt was a huge man, maybe 6 feet 4 inches and at least 250 pounds, his belly sagged over his inadequate uniform belt, his face mottled red from untreated blood pressure and booze.

'How you lovebirds doing?'

'Good, thank you, Mr Howitt,' replied Chambers, meekly.

'How about you, Mason?'

'Good.' The absence of any subservience was obvious.

'That's what you've got to be, very, very good so you don't fuck everything up during what little time you've got left here.'

'That's not going to happen.'

'You sure about that?'

'I'm sure about that,' mocked Mason.

It was Howitt who looked away first from the eyeballing. 'You're listed to see the warden today.'

'I know.'

'Better make sure you've got all your answers ready, as well.'

'I have.'

'You think you've got the answers to everything, Mason?'

'Enough to get by.'

'I've never agreed with remission, for guys who did what you did. I think motherfuckers like you should get that very special goodbye needle.' Executions in Pennsylvania were by lethal injection.

'You told me already, too many times.'

'So I'm telling you again.'

'Suit yourself.' Mason very positively, dismissively, turned his back on the man.

'You're not out yet, Mason.'

The former intelligence agent continued to ignore the obese chief officer, embarking on another self-invented exercise routine that involved his falling forward to take his full weight against the wall on his outstretched arms, to alternate on each, then to push himself fully upright before falling forward again.

'You be careful – very, very careful,' threatened Howitt, at last rippling his baton back and forth against the cell bars louder now than on any other cell, noisily enough to make Chambers wince.

'He's right, Jack,' said the cell mate. 'You're not out yet. He's bastard enough to catch you on some infringement to screw everything up.'

'Bastard enough but not clever enough,' dismissed Mason, breathing easily, normally, without interrupting the exercise. 'He's more frightened of me than I am of him.'

Because there had been no suggestion at his trial that Mason was dangerous or that his dealings with Russia at the height of the Cold War had involved violence, he had served his entire sentence at Pennsylvania's White Deer Penitentiary, arriving on the very same day as Howitt. Mason recognized the man from that initial day as the bully he had become over the years, intimidating everyone but Mason. The simple reason for that exception was that the first time Howitt threatened him Mason confronted the man very closely, their faces almost touching, and said, 'Fuck with me and I'll kill you. And you know that I will.' Howitt *had* known it, as everyone else over the years had come to know without Mason once having to prove it. Mason, an attentive pupil, had acquired the convincing psychology at the CIA's academy at Quantico.

'He's got authority on his side,' insisted Chambers.

'Forget it,' said Mason. He was sick to his stomach at the thought of how long he was going to have to spend outside jail with the man, until he got his hands on the three million dollars. He was, Mason decided, going to earn every cent.

They were both ready for the automatic release and retraction of their cell door, filing out with their towels and shaving packs. The twelve prisoners further back along the corridor stopped, giving Mason time and space to emerge and the four already ahead on the landing obediently stood aside for the man, with Chambers close alongside, to be in the first group into the shower room. Four more men waited against the shower wall, unchallenged by the three inside guards, leaving the usual two stalls empty for Mason and his cell mate. Mason took his time undressing, knowing everyone would be looking at his muscle-hardened body because everyone always did, and didn't hurry inside the shower, either. Two shaving basins were empty for them when they emerged. There was a gap for them at the head of the mess hall breakfast queue and two spaces at the table Mason preferred, in a corner.

'I'm going to miss this special protection,' confessed Chambers, whose release wasn't scheduled for another six months.

You probably are, thought Mason: you're going to get shit when I'm not here to protect you. 'I'll spread the word for you to be left alone.' He had three million bucks to protect, after all.

'You're going to find things a lot different outside, after fifteen years,' warned the warden, a white-haired, stick-thin career prison governor named Hubert Harrison.

'I'm sure I am, sir, although I've tried to keep up to date as much as possible,' said Mason. The warden had for a long time been the only man in the penitentiary to whom Mason showed any respect, although that was kept to the barest minimum.

'I know you have, Mason. I wish everyone here accepted their punishment as objectively as you've done, 'fessed up to the wrong and shown the determination you've demonstrated to rehabilitate.'

'Thank you, sir.'

'You got any firmed-up plans?'

If only you knew, thought Mason. 'Nothing positive. I've enjoyed running the library for these last few years. Might try something involving books.' He smiled. 'Although I don't mean trying to write one. Maybe something involving distri-bution, where I can utilize what I've learned about computers while I've been here.'

'From what I hear you could go into competition with Bill Gates and Microsoft.'

'I'm not that good.' Mason knew he was assessed to be very good indeed according to his legitimate instructors. A year earlier, using the illegal expertise he'd learned from the bank fraudster, Mason had embedded deep within his prison personnel records a 'Trojan Horse', a hacker's bug with its password and access code known only to himself in which the entire traffic in and out of those records was automatically duplicated and from which he could access everything that had preceded it, from the very moment of his sentencing. Using either the penitentiary's rehab computer training room or the dedicated station in the library in which he'd been assigned as chief librarian for the last six years, he'd taken his time to read every report, assessment or recommendation about himself. Before today's meeting with Harrison he'd gone into his Trojan Horse looking for the records of the automatic warning which he knew, from his CIA experience, was sent to everyone supposedly hidden forever in a Witness Protection Programme, of the imminent release of a felon for whose imprisonment they were responsible. He had been concerned at not finding it, as he'd failed to do every day over the preceding month. Mason had expected to find it – and everything else he needed to discover about the new life and identity of Dimitri Sobell – long before now. A change of routine was an unsettling uncertainty.

'We should hear the parole arrangement by next week. Of course, you'll be attached to DC, your last city of domicile.'

'Yes,' accepted Mason. He'd already read the exchanges between Harrison and the parole authorities and knew his exemplary record was going to cut him as much slack as he could expect. The parole restrictions were still going to be a potential irritation, although he'd already thought of some evasions.

'They could give you a steer about accommodation, if you intend to stay there.'

'I'm not sure that I do,' said Mason. 'Ann's divorced me for the Russian. And got the proceeds from the sale of our old house.'

'Thought about where you might resettle?'

'California is where the computer industry is,' Mason said,

smiling. 'And the winters are warmer there than on the East Coast.'

'And that physique you've developed will look good on Venice Beach,' smiled the warden, in return.

'I did wrong,' said Mason. 'Very wrong. When I arrived here I made myself a personal promise, not to let my body or my mind atrophy.'

'You didn't do either,' acknowledged Harrison, a reform-dedicated penologist. 'Wherever you choose to live and whatever you decide to do, I know you'll be successful.'

'I'm absolutely determined to be,' said Mason, a remark entirely for his own benefit.

Two

S o long and so well had Daniel Slater adjusted to his new life and identity that he rarely consciously thought of his previous existence. One of the few exceptions were weekends like this, when he and Ann took David into the Ridge and Valley Appalachians of Maryland to camp and for Slater to teach their son the survival tradecraft he'd learned from his geology professor father in the harshness of his native Siberia. The recollection only brought nostalgia for his father. Slater didn't miss Russia, didn't miss anything about his first twenty-six years as Dimitri Sobell, so perfect did he consider every-thing to be as Daniel Slater.

'Not one mistake so far,' said Ann, who'd automatically learned the backwoodsman techniques as Slater had taught them to their son.

'I'd have corrected him by now if there had been,' said Slater. He and Ann had let the boy lead their detour off the official trail, to choose a path upon which they would make as little sound as possible – to avoid disturbing any game or animals – and select their campsite, close enough to the tight tree clump to provide the wind break, but far enough away to avoid added precipitation if there were a storm. Another flank was protected by a natural ground bank in which David had already cut the conduit to carry away any water from where the tents were, although no rain was forecast. David's pup tent was further shielded on its third side by the separate tent Slater and his wife would occupy. The stream from which they would get their drinking and cooking water – purified by boiling on a fire for which David was at that moment preparing a rock and pebble base in the turf-removed hollow – was about ten yards from the site on its unprotected side, flowing away from them down a slope sufficient to prevent any back-up flooding. There were no animal paths or markings to indicate it was a watering hole. David used the extra rocks he had collected to seal against drafts along the edges of their tents, both of which he'd pitched with their entrances away from the already tested and determined wind direction. He'd taken that into account when positioning the fire base too, to take the smoke away from, not into, the camp. It would be blown into the high fir shield and dispersed, not form into an identifiable plume to attract a forest ranger. The guiding principle of David's backwoodsman instruction was never to cause or leave a detectable trace of their having been there. When they left, the ashes and the fire-blackened stones would be scattered into the fast moving stream and the turf replaced in the fire pit.

'You're doing fine, David,' encouraged Slater. He always called his son by his full name, never abbreviating it as his father had never abbreviated his name, not even omitting the patronymic, always Dimitri Alexeivich. His widowed father had been the icon in Slater's life, the man he admired as well as loved above anyone and anything else, the image in which he'd always worked to model himself in David's upbringing. Slater was glad his father had died before his defection. His father had been a fervent, uncompromising communist, which Slater had never been, despite his father's overwhelming influence in everything else, particularly in his joining the KGB. Slater had no doubt that had his father been alive when he defected, the man would have disowned him for abandoning his country; he would not have wept, either, at the retribution that might have been exacted had the KGB ever been able to find him. Which they hadn't, although Slater knew they would have tried because they always tried, wanting to make a physical example of what happened to those they regarded as traitors.

'Good enough to be an Indian scout?'

About to turn fourteen, David was engrossed in the exploration history of the western United States and Slater had encouraged the interest by comparing David's backwoodsman prowess against that of the earlier settler heroes whose images adorned the boy's bedroom walls, although greatly outnumbered by past and present basketball stars. David was close to being unnaturally tall for his age and was the star in his own right of both his school and youth club basketball teams.

'Almost,' said Slater.

As David hurried off to collect kindling twigs and fire-wood, Ann said, 'You're too hard on him.'

'I'm not,' denied Slater, at once. 'I praise him when it's due.'

'Not enough. You're trying to bring him up too quickly in your own image,' said Ann. She was a blonde, exercise-trim woman who believed her second life was as perfect as Slater believed his to be, although she'd never told him outright. To have done so would have inevitably taken them back to the times she wanted to exorcise: the cheating, the physical violence of times with Jack as well as his whoring and neglect and her attempted escape into the bottom of too many gin bottles.

'Would that be so bad?' There was no irritation in his voice.

'He shouldn't miss out on being a young kid.'

'He's not missing out on anything. And never will.'

They were only aware of David's return at the very last moment, so silently, despite his height, did the boy instinctively move through the wooded undergrowth. 'I've stacked up a lot of stuff lying around,' he said. 'Enough to take us through tomorrow. Big stuff from some felling over the brow.'

'About time I helped,' offered Slater.

'I can manage.'

'Together we can do it twice as quickly.'

'I should set the fire first. There's not a lot of sun left.'

'Well done!' praised Slater, looking pointedly at his wife. It had been a test. By the time they would have made another wood collection, even though it had all been assembled, there would not have been sufficient heat in the sun to start the fire through the glass scrap upon which Slater insisted. To have used ordinary, reserve-only matches represented a failure. Slater's return, laden with branches, was another test, although this one for himself. So many were supported on his outstretched arms that Slater could not see to pick his way soundlessly over the twigs and bark and branch-fallen forest floor. So he moved cautiously, feeling and assessing each step before imposing the slightest weight.

'Got you!' shouted the boy when Slater judged himself still too far away from the camp to be detected. He hadn't heard the give-away twig snap, either.

11

'Identify,' demanded Slater, going into their rehearsed routine.

'You're next to a birch sapling between two conifers,' complied the boy, coming into view. 'And you were scuffing.'

David was far better than he had been at his son's age, conceded Slater. He consoled himself with the thought that it was easier to move soundlessly over the permanently frozen tundra around Irkursk than the tinder-dry undergrowth of an early summer Maryland. These outings had an underlying reason, far beyond David becoming expert in outdoor existence and survival. They were just one of several ways Slater intended making his son as totally self-sufficient and confident as possible.

'Don't try to carry as many logs as me,' he admitted, sweating as his outstretched arms ached under the weight.

The fire was well alight and Ann had moved their equipment into their tent by the time Slater got back, letting the logs drop and supporting himself half bent, panting, with his hands against his knees.

'Why'd you try to carry so much, macho-man?' she demanded.

'I didn't realize how heavy they were,' admitted Slater. 'I'm out of shape.'

'Maybe David should start teaching you.'

'Maybe he should,' agreed Slater, as the boy re-entered the clearing, carrying without apparent effort what appeared to Slater to be practically as big a load as he had.

It took each of them two more journeys to complete their log pile, stacked as an additional wind break, Slater carrying less each time. David constructed the wood spit over the fire to grill their steaks, which he did perfectly without burning the meat or allowing the wood to catch alight from the dripping fat.

As they ate the boy announced, 'Tomorrow I'm going to try to catch some fish. I'm sure there are some, trout maybe, in the rock pool just over the rise.'

Slater considered it an unlikely location but didn't challenge the boy. 'If you're right I could teach you how to bake them in clay.'

They burned the meat debris on the fire, to prevent its lingering scent attracting forest predators, and built up the fire as a further deterrent and to warm the stream water to wash. Slater and Ann shared a double sleeping bag, both naked because their relationship was still very physical although that night neither moved to make love, contentedly tired from the climb and from their contribution to setting up the camp.

There were fish in the river pool and David caught two, not with a line but by lying trapper fashion with his hands in the icy water to snatch them out when they swam over his caressing fingers. He caught a rabbit, too, in a snare he set before he began to fish, and he skinned and gutted it for their evening meal. For most of the remaining morning and early afternoon they wandered the forest, with Slater further challenging the boy on which berries and fungi and plants were edible, against those that were not.

'Did you really do things like this with your father?'

'A lot,' said Slater, cautiously.

'How long did it take you to learn it all?' asked the tall boy, striding slightly ahead of his parents as they descended towards their camp.

'Quite a while.'

'I'd have liked to know what your father looked like – seen a photograph.'

Slater was conscious of Ann's sharp sideways look, to which he didn't respond in case David unexpectedly turned back. It had, not surprisingly, taken the untrained Ann longer than Slater to completely adopt their new CIA-guided personas. Very soon after Ann had become pregnant, they had begun devising their own legend – using the ingrained KGB credo of keeping small falsehoods and outright lies to a minimum, to avoid being caught out – to satisfy the inevitable curiosity of their then unborn child. Over the months and years they'd been confident they had prepared as effectively as possible, even to the extent of believing everything about their new, now secure identities. But increasingly there had been questions and curiosity from David they had not anticipated.

'I wish I had one to show you,' said Slater. 'But I've told you the house fire in which my mother and father died destroyed everything.'

'Wasn't there any other family, apart from you?' persisted the boy.

'You know all my mother and father's relations died in Poland in the last years of the war in Europe.' Sometimes Slater regretted the Polish invention, which had been an unnecessary CIA insistence to account for his Russian accent in an immigrant America in which foreign accents aroused little interest anyway; over the subsequent fifteen years the accent had flattened out to be virtually undetectable although there was still the Slavic flaxen hair and high cheekbones of his genuine ancestry.

'It must be awful to lose everybody and everything like that,' said David.

'It is. And it's something you're never going to know,' guaranteed Slater, working to cut off the discussion.

'I'm sorry!' apologized David, at once. 'It's just that—'

'I know,' interrupted Slater. 'Let's not think or talk about it any more.'

That night, secure in their double sleeping bag, but again not having made love despite neither of them still being tired, Ann said, 'It's not going to go away.'

'I'll handle it.'

'We're going to have to be very careful.'

'Don't worry.'

'I do worry.'

'We'll be OK. We knew it was going to happen, sooner or later. He's accepted that you were an orphan, with no known family. It's obvious he'll keep on to me.'

Ann turned away from him, to fit herself comfortably against his bent legs. 'I don't want the bubble to burst.'

'I promise you it won't.'

'Ordinary looking son of a bitch,' judged John Peebles, gazing down at the arrest file photographs of Jack Mason.

'They usually are,' said Barry Bourne. Both CIA relocation clerks assigned to the Justice Department were comfortable in their cocoons, insulated against any disruption or stress, their only responsibility to monitor and keep up to date Cold War defection and witness protection cases.

'You ever come across him before?'

'How the hell could I! It's years ago, long dead history.'

Peebles, a bespectacled, angularly featured man, flicked through the file until he came upon Dimitri Sobell's picture.

'Ordinary again, the guy next to you on the Metro.'

'If they'd had horns and tails it would have made it easier to recognize them as bad guys,' said Bourne, a fan of late-night one-liner gangster movies.

'You think guys who did what Mason did should get remission?'

'Whatever damage they caused between them, it was a long time ago,' said Bourne, shrugging. 'Damned glad I didn't work here then.'

'Guess I'd better see what the penitentiary records say about Mason. And warn Sobell he's about to be released.'

'Never understand why we bother,' said Bourne. 'There's a *Dragnet* rerun on TV tonight. You gonna watch it?'

'Hadn't thought about it.'

'You should. It's a classic.'

Three

'California!'
    'Your idea for us setting up a business together was with computers, with my security input, right? California is where the computer industry is. So that's where I told the warden I was thinking of moving to.' Having identified the West Coast to the governor as his most likely resettlement area, Mason was observing the universal intelligence mantra of preventing the accidental disclosure of any lie. It wasn't likely that Chambers would talk about their going into business, but there was no way of predicting what the fat fuck would say when he underwent his release interview. Every base had to be covered.

'I don't like California.'

'I do.'

'The computer industry isn't that centralized any more – that was years ago. It isn't like that now.'

'How the fuck do you know! You've been inside for almost fifteen years!'

'And kept in touch with the outside as much as you have.'

'I'll check out California, until your release – see what I think about the potential.' This shouldn't really be coming to him as such a surprise: hadn't he known for years of the burden Chambers was going to be?

'I was thinking of New Orleans, maybe. I like New Orleans.'

He hadn't thought this conversation through sufficiently, Mason accepted, self-critically. The admission unsettled him. Just as quickly, though, he saw the potential unconsidered benefit. Their penitentiary association would be thrown up on day one of any investigation into Chambers' killing, if there was the slightest doubt about the supposed accident Chambers' death would appear to be. And the last thing Mason intended to risk was having that association – his face and his name, even though he was shortly to discard the identity – emblazoned across every television screen in the country. Pleased with the quickness with which the complete recovery came to him, Mason said, 'Let's slow this down a little, Peter. All I told Harrison was that California might be a good place for me to look at when I got out. I didn't say anything about you and I setting up together. And I don't think you should, either. What the fuck right has anyone got to know what we're going to do! You get asked, you say New Orleans. We don't tell them anything.'

'You're right!' said the other man, with forced belligerence. 'What the fuck right do they have to know what we're going to do! We paid already.'

The totally controlled Mason kept any reaction from his face but thought how predictably like a programmed bank official the other man was; if he hadn't known – and hacked into the prison records to confirm – the countrywide scam Chambers had so brilliantly conceived, Mason wouldn't have believed it possible for such an ineffectual man to have carried it off. The fact that the man had eventually been caught proved his limitations, Mason supposed. Unlike himself. He hadn't been arrested for any mistakes he made: he'd been served up on a plate when the motherfucker Sobell defected.

'That's my boy! I stay with California, you stay with New Orleans, not a word to anyone about what we're planning. When we decide which or where we want to be, we make our own minds up. Fuck 'em.'

Chambers' bravado enthusiasm wavered. 'We can't just buck parole.'

Jesus, this wasn't going to be easy, Mason thought. 'Who said anything about bucking parole? We both chipped off five years by working the system their way. We don't dump it all down the toilet the moment we step outside the gate.'

'Whatever you say.'

That's how it was always going to be until he got his hot hands on the three million dollars, thought Mason: whatever he said, whenever he said it, however he said it. 'Which means there can't be any contact between us, once I get out. No letters, no phone calls, OK?'

'OK,' said Chambers, doubtfully.

'So I need to know where to find you.'

Chambers frowned. 'I don't have a place. Why don't I come to you?'

'Because I don't know where I'll be in six months' time, when you're released. And I just explained to you why we can't keep in touch while you're still inside.'

'What we going to do?' asked the former bank official.

Mason suppressed the sigh. 'You were living in New York when you got arrested, right?'

'Right.'

'So that's the parole board you'll have to report to, initially,' reminded Mason. 'Pick a hotel, a big one – a convention place, maybe – where we'll disappear in the crowd. You're due out when, the 26th, 27th, somewhere around then?'

'The 25th,' supplied Chambers.

'I'll call you on the 28th, after you've had time to settle in and maybe sort your parole. We'll celebrate.'

'That sounds good.'

'All you've got to decide is the hotel.' Allowing himself the irritation, Mason added, 'You got five weeks to think about it: after that, I'm gone.'

Another of Mason's self-taught disciplines was objectivity, and objectively he recognized that his irritation wasn't motivated by Chambers' vapid dependency but by there having been no CIA access to his records from which to discover Dimitri Sobell's new identity and whereabouts. With further discomforting realism Mason was increasingly coming to fear that the CIA warning system had changed and that he was not, after all, going to be able to follow the easy route to Sobell. Compounding that discomfort – discomfort wasn't sufficient: scourging, eye-tearing frustration – was his awareness that he hadn't evolved an alternative way to find the man upon whom he was going to impose every suffering.

Chambers totally missed the contempt. 'It's going to be great, you and I.'

'Great,' echoed Mason, hollowly, as an echo is a hollow sound.

Mason had not expected – nor been warned until the previous evening – that he would be taken from White Deer for his interview with the Washington DC parole board ahead of his release and was glad one of his most recent hacking expeditions had been to study the regulations governing the procedure. He became even more grateful when Frank Howitt announced that he was to be the escort for the tightly scheduled, one-day trip. It was not until Mason put on the suit in which he had been sentenced, and not worn since, that he realized how preposterously out of date he appeared: he so obviously looked like a long-term convict. The perpetual exercise, over all the years, had virtually changed his physical shape and maybe, apart from his face, his very appearance, so much so that the clothes were those of a smaller, different person. The jacket was strained across his expanded, muscled shoulders, which in turn shortened the sleeves way above his wrists, while the waistband of his trousers was too wide for his now taut waist, puddling the pant cuffs around his ankles.

The sniggering Howitt said, 'You've no idea what a fucking mess you look!'

The chief prison guard was in plainclothes, too, encased in a suit Mason judged to be only marginally better than his, looking like a chrysalis about to burst, although not to release anything of beauty. Mason said, 'I'll play Laurel to your Hardy.'

Howitt's face tightened. 'You'll jump to whatever string I pull. I'm going to enjoy myself today.'

It was a set up, Mason decided. In all his near fifteen years in a penitentiary he had never heard or known of an about-to-be-released prisoner being escorted to such a parole board interview. He needed to be extremely careful, alert to everything.

As Mason pondered this, Howitt said, 'Which arm do you want, left or right?'

'Arm?' queried Mason.

'To be cuffed. You don't think I'm going to trust you not to run, do you!'

'Don't be a cunt.'

'It's against regulations to swear at a prison officer,' seized Howitt, at once.

Mason hesitated before extending his left wrist, his face fixed against the intentional, painful tightness. Mason guessed his wrist would be chaffed raw by the time he'd gone to and from Washington DC.

'That's better,' smirked Howitt.

Maybe better for me than for you, thought Mason. His suspicion grew within minutes when they left the penitentiary without any sign-out formalities. Gerry Garson, an acolyte guard who always stayed close enough to Howitt to have his dick up the chief's ass, was at the wheel of a battered '99 Ford, in street clothes, not uniform. Mason memorized the registration. There was a sharp stab of pain in his wrist as he got awkwardly into the rear. Mason timed his move as Howitt prepared to enter, seemingly to make room for the huge man. The effect was to topple the right-handedly restricted man almost full length across the rear seat. As Howitt floundered himself upright, Mason said, 'You all right there, Frankie?'

'You fuck with me, you're going to lose,' threatened Howitt.

'Fuck with you how, Frankie? What have I done?' Mason saw Howitt twitch with the pain in his wrist, only just holding back. Garson's uncertainty was reflected in the rear-view mirror.

Howitt became aware of his colleague's reaction from the driver's seat. 'You OK about the schedule, Gerry?'

Garson moved off before replying. Even then he just said, 'Uh huh.'

'Everything on time?'

'Uh huh.'

'You OK, Gerry? You don't sound so sure,' said Mason.

'I told you to shut the fuck up!' demanded Howitt, who finally managed to cover his bruised and injured arm.

Mason looked away from the man and stared intensely at his first sight for fifteen years of the flat surrounding country-side – of anything – outside the penitentiary, having been refused compassionate release for his mother's funeral. The lifers fantasized of release being like arriving from another world, and to a degree that was how it seemed to Mason. He was instantly aware that he hadn't prepared himself by half, a quarter even, and that his minutely planned schedule needed possible readjustment. He abruptly felt a hollow emptiness like literally being an alien. He couldn't remember, couldn't think – which was fucking ridiculous – what he'd expected, apart from noise and bustle and people. Even accepting, as he did, that White Deer was isolated, there was none of that. None of anything. A few cars passed, quietly. There were cows in a distant field. Even further away, on a jagged skyline, a coalfield rig: a lot of smoke, certainly. Did smoke overhang a coalfield? Whatever it was, it was industrial. In the first one-street township – what the fuck was its name; surely he should be able to remember the nearest town! – the neon advertisements flashed and glittered their Las Vegas copy, too cluttered for any of it to be read or understood, but there still weren't the people there should have been, the noise and the activity he'd held for all these years in his mind and wanted to see, to be part of again.

Unnecessarily – disconcertingly – Howitt said, 'This is the outside, asshole: the other, real world. I wanted you to see it, to know how inadequate you're going to be out here, among it, not knowing what the fuck to do.'

Mason remained staring away, unspeaking, sure which of them was the most inadequate. It was a hell of a temptation not to put Howitt back on his personal disposal list. But he wouldn't. It would all be too easily linked, if Chambers' death and that of Dimitri Sobell ever became suspected to be anything but accidental, which he didn't intend them to be but against which he had to protect himself.

'Think about it!' demanded the man overflowing into Mason's part of the seat. 'Think what it's going to be like out there. You know any more how many cents make a dollar? How much change to expect when you buy a beer from a ten? How to fuck a woman, after fucking Chambers for so long?'

Mason turned back into the car, shifting in the overcrowded rear seat to be able to look directly at Howitt. And he just looked, saying nothing, as he'd looked and spoken when Howitt had first tried to intimidate him, which was what he knew the man was attempting now, trying as best as his pea-sized brain could manage to make up for all the years of being so openly despised and ignored. Knowing, too, that Garson was driving more with his eyes on the rear-view mirror than on the road ahead and listening to everything, and despite having his head or whatever else up Howitt's ass, would spread the word back at White Deer, because it was too good to keep to himself.

Eventually, spacing the words, Mason said, 'Remember a long time ago, Frankie? Try. Try very hard to remember what I told you when you came on to me all that long time ago. And then shut the fuck up.'

And, bully-like, Howitt did. Garson moved uncomfortably in his driver's seat.

To Mason's ear, to his imagination, the outside traffic to which he returned at last got noisier, almost deafening, the closer they got to the city and its airport. All the cars and the lorries and the air-horn bellowing rigs seemed to be travelling faster than he remembered, too, even though he knew they weren't and that it was an institutionalized, misleading impression. But after today he wouldn't be misled, just as he wouldn't, as soon as possible after his forthcoming release, be wearing an out of style suit. It was all made so much better by the irony of it being the fat asshole to whom he was tethered being the unwitting source of such early but necessary preparation. Mason looked back inside the car, although remaining expressionless.

'What!' demanded Howitt.

'Nothing.'

'Nothing what!'

'Nothing . . .'

'Careful!'

'Mr Howitt.' Using the respect made it the ultimate sneer.

As they approached the airport Howitt said to Garson, 'You keep in touch, make sure there aren't any delays on the return flight, OK?'

'OK,' said Garson.

'We'll definitely be back tonight, whatever. If there's a problem I'll call your cell phone.'

Because they had to be back within a day, to cover what he was sure was an irregular excursion, thought Mason. Or was it?

'We've been through it,' reminded Garson, with surprising impatience.

At the airport Howitt was far more careful getting out of the car than he had been getting into it, causing Mason no physical discomfort, but as soon as they entered the terminal Mason accepted it wasn't physical discomfort Howitt intended now. The towering man carried nothing to disguise their being handcuffed, actually creating space between them as they walked to the check-in for the linking chain to be obvious, even intentionally putting them in the path of people who, awkwardly and startled, needed to go around them. Howitt maintained the performance in the embarkation lounge, where he produced his ID authorization for the security official to ensure that they boarded, very publicly, ahead of everyone else. The charade went wrong when, to his immediate anger, Howitt discovered that their designations meant he had to be ushered into the inner seat for Mason to get the aisle. There was an ineffectual tug of war to be first to fasten their seat belts. Mason won, securing his ahead of the other man.

Mason waited until the moment the seat belt sign went off after departure before unbuckling his harness to turn to the chief prison guard to say, 'I need to piss.'

'Piss yourself.'

'You think the parole board would go along with you on that? I don't think they would. Or my lawyer, either.'

This time Howitt did jerk Mason's wrist, unexpectedly, to unfasten his belt but Mason didn't react. Instead he stood considerately in the aisle for the man to get out but actually led their way up to the toilets. At the toilet door Mason said, 'You think we can make it in there together?' knowing full well that they couldn't. He manoeuvred the two of them to put Howitt's back to the entire, watching cabin, so that none of the other passengers would be able to see who unlocked the handcuffs to identify who was the prisoner and who was the guard. Mason had difficulty peeing and took his time, and afterwards used all the offered astringents and soaps and colognes. He let Howitt rap on the door twice before unlocking it, keeping it open for the man to enter. Howitt hesitated but shook his head.

Back in their seats Mason said, 'You done this a lot, prisoner escort?'

'Enough.'

'Surprised you didn't assign someone else – Garson, for instance.'

'I wanted to look after you personally.'

'Thought that might be it.'

'As I'm going to,' added Howitt.

What trick was the motherfucker planning to pull? Or try to pull? It had to be something big enough, serious enough, to screw the intended remission. Which made it almost too obvious. Mason saw the stewardesses slowly approaching down the aisle with a breakfast trolley.

Probingly, he said, 'You think we need to go on being joined at the hip like this? One of us is going to get a lapful of coffee and it's your right hand that's tethered.'

'Maybe you're right.'

Too quick, too easy, thought Mason: altogether too obvious. Then he thought, surely not, surely nothing so stupid! But then Howitt *was* stupid, as institutionalized as any lifer; more institutionalized even.

Howitt released the handcuffs, dropped them into his bulged pocket and sat surreptitiously massaging his wrist until the trolley reached them. Mason waited until the other man chose and was served before ordering juice, coffee and rolls, more alert to Howitt than to the curious and attentive stewardess, all mockery abandoned.

At the pilot's announcement of their descent into Washington's Reagan airport, Mason, probing further, offered his left wrist and said, 'We going Siamese again?'

'What the hell?' said Howitt, shaking his head.

Mason was careful to block the disembarkation queue in the aisle to let Howitt precede him along the aircraft, and once they got on the ground he remained as close as Gerry Garson habitually did in the penitentiary. Inside the terminal Mason divided his concentration, aware of Howitt using the passenger bustle to change position between them but just as intently identifying police and security staff as they walked. For someone of his awkward bulk Howitt was surprisingly quick when he made the move Mason was anticipating. Mason could easily have dodged sideways behind the abruptly disappearing man if he'd wanted to. Which he didn't. Instead he went immediately to two uniformed policemen and said, 'I'm a prisoner at White Deer Penitentiary, under escort from Pennsylvania to appear before a Washington DC parole board. I've become separated from my escort, Chief Guard Frank Howitt. I want to put myself under your supervision and into your custody until he's relocated and I'm taken to where I'm expected.'

Jack Mason checked his satisfaction at outsmarting the chief prison guard – reminding himself how devastated he would have been at not outsmarting him – but objectively acknowledged that he had benefited from a lot of luck in approaching those two particular airport police officers. Neither showed any disbelief or surprise at his approach, which he reinforced by dictating his prison number the moment he was shown into an airport office. They accepted just as quickly that they should confirm his identity by telephoning White Deer and from Hubert Harrison's office obtained the direct parole board number, further to confirm his scheduled appointment. There was only a five minute delay before a parole board official called back to affirm Mason's scheduled meeting, with the request that Mason be transported into the city to be placed in federal custody. It was only when the senior of the two officers sought permission to comply with that demand from their airport commander that there was the first indication that Howitt had reported Mason's escape to the FBI, who had alerted every airport security service with the request for a perimeter cordon to be imposed around the airport as well as the grounding of every departing flight until the arrival of agents from the Bureau's Washington field office. After a further thirty minutes, during which the cordon request was cancelled and the approaching FBI team stood down by a cell phone intervention, a sweating Howitt, his normally red face now puce, arrived at the terminal office, accompanied by the commander and two unidentified assistants.

So inadequate and unconvincing was Howitt's flustered improvisation of Mason's alleged dash for freedom that the commander insisted on the two officers escorting Mason to the parole board meeting, where two FBI agents were waiting as the obvious result of an advanced account of events from the airport. One agent attended the board meeting, from which Howitt was pointedly excluded.

The official encounter, prepared and rehearsed as Mason was from every well studied and glowing account of his prison behaviour, became an anti-climax by comparison to what had preceded it. Mason recited his thought of re-locating to California and rehabilitating within the computer industry – without challenge from anyone on the board – and was introduced to his parole officer, a woman named Glynis Needham who wore a severely cut trouser suit and had a short, mannish hairstyle. In a deep voice she promised to have a list of temporary DC accommodation by the time of Mason's actual release.

'There was a situation at the airport?' questioned the chairman, after what Mason assumed to be all the formalities were completed.

'Yes, sir.'

'We'd like you to tell us what happened, as far as you are aware.'

'I'm really not sure,' said Mason. 'I was handcuffed to Chief Officer Howitt when I left White Deer and for the beginning of the flight. It was awkward, obviously, so during the flight Chief Officer Howitt took the handcuffs off. I expected them to be put back on when we got to Washington but Chief Officer Howitt didn't bother. I tried to keep very close to him when we disembarked but suddenly he disappeared. So I immediately surrendered myself to the airport police, in whose custody I remained and who brought me here, together with Chief Officer Howitt.'

'You didn't run, try to escape?'

Mason was sure he perfectly timed the apparently surprised pause at such a suggestion. 'The two airport policemen are with me, here. Please ask them what I did when Chief Officer Howitt disappeared. I know only too well how any remission would be destroyed if I had tried to escape. But why should I have tried?'

The one FBI officer escorted Mason into a side room at the chairman's announcement that they did intend to hear from the two airport officers. When they were alone the agent said, 'What the hell happened?'

'It was like I told them back there.'

'It didn't sound too good to me.'

'It was what happened!' protested Mason.

'I wasn't talking about you.'

It was thirty minutes before they were recalled to the hearing room. The chairman said, 'I think we've heard all we need to. Ms Needham will be in touch.'

'Can I make a request, sir, in the light of what happened?' asked Mason.

'What?'

'I really mean what I said about knowing full well how my situation might be affected if there were any further misunderstanding. Could there be an additional escort when I'm taken back to White Deer?'

'The decision has already been made elsewhere that there should be,' said the tribunal chairman.

The fact that Mason had not been told of the impending Washington visit until recreational lock-up the night before, and with the two intervening nights, extended by the full day in between, an almost forty-eight hour break in his routine of hacking into his computer records had been created. At the first opportunity on his return, he tried again and felt an immediate surge of total satisfaction at discovering two new entries in his file. The first was the belated although customary CIA access from which he immediately learned that Dimitri Sobell was now Daniel Slater, living at 2832 Hill Avenue SE, Frederick, Maryland. The cherry on the cupcake was to read that Frank George Howitt – who'd actually been separated from him for his handcuff-free return to White Deer the previous evening – had been suspended from duty pending an internal enquiry into the Reagan airport episode.

That same morning, although three hours earlier, the formal CIA warning of Mason's release, together with CIA contact numbers if necessary, had been in Slater's mailbox when he left his Frederick house. Apart from its almost indistinguishable Washington DC postmark there was no outward indication of its sender, so he didn't bother to open it until he got to his security consultancy office.

When he did open it Slater was engulfed by a physical coldness he hadn't known since Siberia.

Four

The sensation quickly passed but before it did Slater's immediate thought, the camping weekend still fresh in his mind, was that mentally as well as physically he was out of shape. He instantly became irritated at the doubt. The surprise, shock even, was entirely understandable; certainly not a failing or a weakness. And most definitely not the result of complacency. He hoped.

Because of the camping expedition Slater had arranged an easy, early week beginning, his diary empty and two of the three outstanding security analyses already dictated on tape, for typed-up presentation, sufficient to occupy Mary Ellen, his receptionist/aide for the morning, if not the entire day. There wasn't any curiosity when he told her to hold all his calls. After doing so, Slater locked the communicating door to the outer office against any unexpected and unwanted intrusion, wanting complete, uninterrupted isolation.

There was welcomed reassurance in the lack of any physical reaction in his hands when he smoothed the letter out before him on his desk. He searched for – demanding from himself – all the necessary KGB tradecraft in which he had once been so expert. He was sure the watermark of the paper, which he held up against the light, was genuine, but the letterheaded Justice Department box number didn't accord with any listed against the main Pennsylvania Avenue address in the DC telephone book, nor in any of the specific reference manuals, or the unlisted logs he'd compiled during the twelve years he'd run his small security consultancy agency. Neither did the contact telephone number, although it carried the 202 DC dialling prefix. The printed although undesignated sender was J Peebles – not a name or a person he knew from his induction into the Witness Protection Programme – but the scrawled signature was indecipherable. It was addressed 'Dear Sir', although his adopted name, in full, was on the envelope. At last, more intently than on his first reading, Slater studied the sterile lines:

I AM FORMALLY REQUIRED BY THE TERMS AND CONDITIONS OF THE VICTIM AND WITNESS PROTECTION ACT, 1982, AS SUBSEQUENTLY AMENDED, OF THE UNITED STATES OF AMERICA, TO ADVISE YOU OF THE IMPENDING RELEASE, UNDER REQUIREMENTS OF SENTENCING RE-MISSION, FROM WHITE DEER PENITENTIARY, PENNSYLVANIA, OF JACK CHARLES MASON, IN WHOSE PROSECUTION YOU WERE A PRIMARY PROSECUTION WITNESS ON JANUARY 10 THRU 14, 1986, CASE NUMBER 01121. IF YOU HAVE ANY CAUSE OR REASON FOR FURTHER INFOR-MATION PLEASE CONTACT THE ABOVE NUMBER BETWEEN 9 AM AND 5.30 PM, MONDAY TO FRIDAY.

It concluded, above the indecipherable signature: 'Yours faithfully'.

What was decipherable? The case number was certainly right. And the bureaucratic officialese fitted the jargon of the dozens of American government letters and documents he'd read – mostly provided by Jack Mason – during the three years he had headed the KGB's Washington *rezidentura* at the Russian embassy before defecting, because of his unsuspected love for Ann, rather than obey the statutory end-of-posting recall to Moscow. What else? There had not been any contact from the CIA or the Justice Department for years, once he'd been debriefed on the KGB's Washington operations and staffing and given his shielded, video-linked evidence against Mason. So it was hardly surprising he didn't recognize the name J Peebles. Or the telephone number or the Justice Department address: total secrecy and anonymity was the entire purpose and function of the Witness Protection Programme. At once the contradiction came up, like a halting flag. With all those provisos, why write him such an identi-fiable and identifying letter, its security guaranteed by nothing more protective than the correctly addressed envelope and the correct stamp, which wasn't any sort of security guarantee at all. Why, all those years ago, hadn't he been told there would be such a warning, as and when Mason came up for parole or release? The letter talked of conditions being amended but if the advice was an innovation after his case, he should have been told, not left all this time and then so abruptly confronted.

All the uncertainties had to be resolved, all the unanswered questions answered and those answers double-checked before disclosing the approach to Ann. Which he would do, rather than keep the letter from her. The most solemn vow each had made to the other when they had embarked upon the life they now had – after their affair had begun and Slater risked everything by confessing that he was not her husband's CIA friend but his KGB control – had been that there would never again be any secrets between them, most specifically of all about Jack Mason. And if . . . Slater refused to let the spectre form. To do so would be unprofessional. He paused at that thought, too, accepting a practical reality, not an unformed speculation. He had – briefly he hoped – to revert to what he had once been, a professional intelligence officer, believing nothing, trusting no one, confiding in no one, apart from, of course, Ann. Could he do it? This doubt unsettled Slater more than any other that morning. Of course he could do it, he told himself. He didn't have any choice. It wasn't any longer just Ann he had to protect and guard from danger. Now they had David – as precious to each of them as they were to each other – who had to be kept from all and any harm. He couldn't – wouldn't – fail either of them.

Slater's receptionist Mary Ellen Foley, a plain-featured, sheltered woman who at twenty-eight still lived with and supported her widowed mother whose hand-knitted shawls and sweaters Mary Ellen frequently wore, as she was that morning, showed no surprise at Slater's announcement that he needed to go into DC to complete the last outstanding security report. She was to log all in-coming calls with a return number, identification and full address but not disclose where he was or offer any suggestion when he might be back in the office. If there was an unannounced, unexpected visitor she was to note the time. He'd keep in touch during the day to pick up any messages, but she shouldn't wait if he hadn't returned by 5.30. For the first time in the eight years she'd worked for him, Mary Ellen's insistence upon writing down his instructions didn't seem unnecessary. Her reminder to herself about unexpected visitors would be sufficient in turn to remind himself – although with his new professional determination he wouldn't need reminders – of specific times to check the CCTV footage from the lobby, elevator and seventh floor upon which his office was located.

As he left Slater said, 'I like the sweater. Blue suits you.'

'My mother made it,' smiled the woman, gratefully.

'I guessed.'

Slater was glad that in the early months of his new identity and relocation he'd instinctively taken various precautions to thoroughly orientate himself to the geography and transportation routes of Maryland, and even into the surrounding states, although today's journey into DC scarcely needed such rehearsal. It enabled him, though, to turn off and on the interstate to avoid its traffic bottlenecks and get into the capital well before noon. He made sure to head for the car park near Union Station, not for the appropriate irony of it being where he'd often held his clandestine, document-exchanging meetings with Mason, but to be sure, in the age of cell phones, of finding coin-operated kiosks within the railway terminal itself. It only took him a further ten minutes, traversing the concourse and the upper level, buying all but one instantly discarded newspapers, as well as magazines, to obtain coins from notes for his hopefully untraceable call to the unknown J Peebles, despite that morning's letter having been delivered to his known address. Once more Slater refused to contemplate the spectral upheaval of his having, at a moment's unexplained notice, to drag Ann and David into escaping flight if he developed the slightest doubt about what was to happen.

Slater separately stacked his nickels and dimes on the convenient shelf, knowingly overpaid for the first call and then dialled the number on the letter, quickly pocketing the incriminating document.

The telephone rang twice before a voice said, 'Yes?'

Slater didn't detect the slightest blur of an accent other than American, although one word wasn't sufficient to be sure. 'I received a letter today.'

'Yes?'

'Are you J Peebles?'

'Who are you?'

Definitely no hint of a recognizable Russian accent but that meant nothing. 'The letter said I was to call this number, if I had any questions about its contents . . .' Fifteen years ago the conservative estimate had been that it took three minutes electronically to get a traceable, cross-grid reference for an incoming telephone call. From the security consultancy business he now ran Slater knew the gap had technologically narrowed to a minute and thirty seconds. A recording of the conversation would be automatic if he were connected to a CIA facility. He'd been on the phone for forty-five seconds.

'Who are you?'

'How many people would have this morning received a letter from J Peebles that might have prompted this call?'

'If you are calling from a public telephone, this conversation is not secure.'

'I know. Which is why I am going to terminate it in another sixty seconds.'

'What do you want?'

'Answers.'

'Ask your questions.'

'This conversation is not secure.'

There was a discernible sigh. 'I'll ask you again, what do you want?'

'A meeting.'

Now there was a pause. 'What for?'

'The answers.'

'I'll set one up.'

'I'll set one up,' insisted Slater.

'When?'

'Now.'

'That's not possible.'

It would take a minimum of twenty-four hours to put in place a snatch squad with any chance of success. 'Why not?'

'It . . . it isn't.'

'That's not acceptable. I still have numbers I can call, to complain.' Slater was glad he'd retrieved the ancient contact procedures from his safe before he'd left the Frederick office. From the sweep hand of his watch Slater knew he had been on the telephone for one minute, ten seconds.

'Where?'

'The Mayflower Hotel.'

'An hour then?'

'How will you recognize me?'

'I have your photograph, of course.'

Hardly the necessary reassurance that the approach was genuine. The KGB successor, the *Federalnaya Sluzhba Bezopasnosti*, would have as many photographs of him, albeit twenty years old, as the CIA. 'Describe how you're dressed: the colour of your suit, shirt and tie.'

There was yet another hesitation. 'A sport coat. Brown. Blue jeans. A polo shirt. Blue again. No tie.'

'Age?'

'Twenty-eight.'

'Hair?'

'Brown.'

'Height?'

'Six one.'

'Glasses?'

'Yes.'

'Describe them. Heavy, light, what?'

'Heavy. Black framed. Whereabouts in the Mayflower?'

'Just be there. I'll find you.'

'Jesus!' exclaimed John Peebles. 'It was Sobell or Slater or whatever he's called. You wouldn't have believed the conversation!'

'I probably would, if you'd recorded it,' said Barry Bourne.

'Shit!' said Peebles, looking down at the telephone and its connected but unactivated apparatus.

When Peebles finished recalling the conversation his partner said, 'You going to go?'

'I guess I've got to.'

'The regulations are that you get permission from Langley. And send them the recording, to verify the voiceprint,' Bourne reminded his colleague.

'Shit!' moaned Peebles again. 'He said he still had numbers he could complain to.'

'This isn't looking good.'

'I know. Fuck it!'

'What's he want?' asked Bourne.

'He wouldn't say, on an open line.'

'Proves he's professional.'

'I reminded him first,' insisted Peebles, defensively.

'You gotta go.'

'I know. But what about Langley? Oh fuck!'

'You disconnect the plug of the recording machine, disconnect one of the internal wires and then plug it back into the mains. That's why the tape didn't run. It's not your fault – the equipment is faulty.'

'That's good,' accepted Peebles.

'What about permission?'

'I don't go, he complains to whatever numbers he's got. I'm fucked either way.'

'Better you go, try to keep a lid on everything.'

'Fucking son of a bitch defector!'

'Be careful,' advised Bourne, unsympathetically.

'You wanna come along?' invited Peebles, hopefully.

'We both can't be out of the office at the same time.'

Peebles went to speak but changed his mind. Instead he thought, Asshole.

Slater went completely around the Mayflower Hotel block, finally establishing a vantage point bench on Connecticut Avenue that gave him a view of the main entrance as well as one to the side. He held up the one retained newspaper, *USA Today*, sufficiently to shield him but not high enough to obscure his observation as he looked out for a flurried group arrival of the snatch squad, his confidence growing as the time passed without his identifying one. It grew further when he identified the man he assumed to be Peebles, not emerging from the Metro, upon which he was concentrating, but coming up the avenue itself on foot from the direction of Lafayette Square. There were no telltale body movements or quick head shifting to indicate anyone else was with him. He went by the side door, hesitated at the main entrance without looking around to establish whether he might be under surveillance and then pushed inside. The man was precisely on time. Slater remained where he was, with no intention of going into the hotel, still alert for a group arrival once he had been recognized and identified by the entering man. There was nothing that aroused his suspicion.

It was forty-five minutes before the man emerged, again

through the main entrance. This time he did pause to look around, the intention obvious before he did so, enabling Slater more fully to raise his protective newspaper. Slater was on his feet, hurrying in pursuit, the moment the man turned to walk back the way he had come. Within minutes Slater was comfortably in position ten yards behind, eight people separating them as a convenient barrier if the tall man turned to check his back. He hadn't by the time they reached the grassed square, which he started to cross towards the White House and where Slater chose for them finally to meet.

'Let's sit here, on one of the benches,' said Slater, coming up from behind.

'Jesus!' exclaimed the man, visibly jumping.

'You Peebles?'

'Of course I am. What the hell's going on?'

'My being careful is what's going on.'

'I just wasted an hour back there at the hotel.'

'Forty-five minutes,' corrected Slater. 'Let's sit on the bench, like I suggested.' He waited for Peebles to lower himself before following.

'What is it you want?' demanded Peebles. He was visibly flushed, embarrassed at his startled reaction.

'Why'd you write the letter?'

'It was spelled out. It's regulations.'

'I wasn't told that – warned about any release letter – when I went into the programme.'

'That was spelled out, too. There's been a lot of amendments. Six or seven maybe, since your case. I think the warning clause was included in the Witness Protection and Interstate Relocation Act of 1997: H.R. 2181.'

'Don't you know!'

'That was the statute.'

Slater didn't believe it was; Peebles was making a wild guess. 'Mason got twenty years. It's only been fifteen.'

'He got maximum remission, apparently. A model prisoner.'

'Is he already out?'

'In four or five weeks.'

'Which penitentiary?'

'I'm not sure I'm allowed to tell you.'

'Which penitentiary?'

'Pennsylvania.'

Close, thought Slater. Almost too close. 'Where's he going?'

'How the hell do I know? If I did I certainly wouldn't tell you.'

'I don't think it was very secure, telling me in a letter like that.'

'It's the system.'

'Everyone like me get such a letter, simply sent through the mail?'

'There aren't a lot of people like you,' said Peebles, in weak sarcasm. 'Guys who've been involved in criminal cases, organized crime prosecutions, sure, all the time.'

'How many people like me have you sent such letters to?'

'If I was asked that by somebody else like you, would you want me to answer?'

'The letter said if I had any cause or reason for further information I was to call you,' reminded Slater. 'How many calls do you get from defectors?'

Peebles hesitated. 'You're the first I've had.'

'What about your department?'

'We don't share cases,' lied Peebles, his embarrassment turned to anger at believing he had been made to look stupid.

'You any reason to believe I am at any risk from Mason's release?'

Peebles looked sideways along the bench in genuine astonishment. 'Absolutely not! I told you, he's been a model prisoner. He wouldn't have got maximum remission if there was a history of threats, would he?'

'You're not operational, a field agent, are you?'

'What's that got to do with anything?'

'Maybe a lot. Perhaps we'll need to keep in touch?' suggested Slater. There'd been little to arouse any professional fear. What incongruities there had been were easily accountable by the fact that Peebles was clearly a back office clerk.

'If there is a need, let's do it properly next time, OK?'

'Very much OK,' came back Slater. 'You need to talk to me you do just that, telephone and arrange this sort of meeting. Not send a letter that could have been intercepted or mislaid and caused me all sorts of problems.'

'I don't imagine there being a need.'

'Keep in mind the approach I want if it does.'

Slater remained on the park bench, watching Peebles walk

away, not once bothering – or allowing himself – to look back. An adequate check, as far as it had gone, decided Slater. Now came the hopeful double check. Slater hailed a passing cab to take him back to the station, where once again he stacked his pocket-bulging coins on the telephone kiosk ledge, fed seventy-five cents into the box and dialled his long ago ascribed number at the CIA's Langley headquarters.

'Yes?' demanded a voice before the telephone appeared to ring.

'I want to speak to Burt Hodges.' The raw-boned, laconic-voiced Texan – certainly not this voice – had been his case officer from the moment of his defection and through the seemingly never-ending debriefing sessions.

'Who?'

'Hodges. Burt Hodges.'

'There's no one of that name here. Who is this?'

'I once had a lot of dealings with Burt Hodges. This was the number I was given to keep in touch.'

'How long ago?'

Slater swallowed. 'Fifteen years.'

'No one named Burt Hodges has worked here in the ten years I've been here. Why don't you tell me your name? Maybe I can help?'

'What about Art Cole?' He'd been Hodges' partner, a sharp-featured, critically impatient man, Slater remembered.

'Art retired maybe eight, nine years ago.'

'Can you tell me how to get in touch with him?'

'No,' refused the voice, at once. 'You give me your name, a number to reach you on, and I'll try to get a message to him.'

It had been a stupid, unprofessional attempt, Slater accepted. 'It doesn't matter.'

'Maybe it does. If you don't want to give me your name why don't we set up a meeting? It might be that I could help with whatever you wanted to talk to Burt or Art about.'

It was extremely unlikely but perhaps Jack Mason still had friends, acquaintances, within the Agency. The debriefing agents – the CIA department to which he knew he was connected – had never known his Frederick relocation. 'It doesn't matter,' repeated Slater, replacing the phone before the man at the other end could argue any further.

*   *   *

37

Mason's summons to the warden's office came two days after the parole board debacle. The only person he recognized, apart from Hubert Harrison, was Glynis Needham, whose trouser suit today was a muted brown check. There was no introduction to the other three men. A woman technician sat beside tape-recording apparatus on a separate table, a back-up notebook already open before her. Mason had expected Frank Howitt to be present, but he wasn't. The chief prison guard hadn't been on the landing in the last two days. Gerry Garson had, but studiously ignored Mason.

Harrison said, 'We'd like you to help us with what happened when you went to the Washington parole board meeting.'

'Is this an official enquiry?'

'Not yet,' said the governor. 'We're just trying to get things straight in our heads.'

'Shouldn't I be allowed legal representation?'

There was a stir among the unnamed men. One of them, a fat, white-haired man, said, 'Why should you need a lawyer?'

'I believe myself to have been the victim of a conspiracy,' declared Mason. 'I believe an attempt was made by Prison Officer Frank Howitt to have my remission revoked by staging an apparent attempt by me to escape from custody.'

There was a fresh stir throughout the room. The records clerk looked up from her scribbled notepad to check her machine.

'That's a serious accusation,' said the gruff-voiced parole officer.

'To have lost five years remission would have been very serious to me indeed,' said Mason.

'Why don't you tell us what happened?' suggested another of the unnamed men.

'I have already given an account to the parole board, which Ms Needham has heard,' said Mason. 'The parole board also heard from police officers at Reagan airport to whom I immediately surrendered, after Prison Officer Howitt vanished. I don't think it advisable for me to give any further details until I've had the opportunity to discuss everything in full with my attorney and received legal advice upon filing a civil claim upon my release.'

'A conspiracy needs the involvement of more than one person,' said the third stranger, who had so far not spoken.

'I know,' said Mason.

'Are you alleging more than one person was involved in a conspiracy against you?'

'I could be.'

'Who are they?'

'They will be named in any claim, if I am advised to make one,' said Mason.

'This threat might need to be brought before the parole board, for their consideration,' warned Glynis Needham.

'As would that threat need to be brought before a civil court, most definitely if it in any way influenced my already agreed remission,' said Mason.

The woman flushed. The white-haired man said, 'I don't think Ms Needham's remark was a threat.'

'That's reassuring,' said Mason.

'There's no cause for this meeting to degenerate into acrimony,' said the warden.

'That's reassuring, too, sir,' said Mason. 'I'd like to use this opportunity formally to request a meeting with the lawyer who represented me at my trial and who settled the estate after my mother's death.' Already knowing from his close study of his own file that it was, he added, 'I would expect the name of my attorney to be on my records. I can, of course, supply it if it's not listed.'

'That is your right,' agreed Harrison. 'There doesn't appear to be any further progress we can make here today.'

'I would like everyone here to accept and understand that this is the very last thing that I want – or wanted – to happen,' said Mason.

'An asshole!' declared John Peebles. 'Prancing about like someone out of a James Bond movie.'

'They're not worth watching,' judged Bourne, the film buff.

'He didn't put me down, though,' insisted Peebles. 'I told him not to be so fucking stupid and to scurry back into his little hidey-hole. And not to bother us again with stupid questions.'

'Well done,' said Bourne. Liar, he thought.

Five

It was gone nine by the time Slater had checked David's homework and they'd eaten supper together and settled the boy before Slater and Ann were alone. Even then Slater hesitated, briefly tempted to break the vow and not after all tell Ann of the letter, uncertain of her reaction. But he didn't, even more fearful – and professionally aware of the erosion that deception brought – of her somehow discovering that he had abandoned their solemn, mutual promise at the first moment of pressure.

Slater said, 'There's something you should see.'

Ann looked up, smiling, from her book. 'What?'

Without any preliminary explanation Slater offered her the letter, watching as the colour as well as the smile drained from Ann's face. She looked up at him and whispered, as if sharing a secret, 'Oh my God!'

'It's all right,' insisted Slater.

'How can it be all right! How can anything be all right!'

'Listen. Please listen.' Quietly, over-stressing the control, Slater recounted the Washington visit and his encounter with Peebles, at her interrupting insistence relaying word for word everything about their exchanges, as well as his assessments of them.

'You think he made up the amendment legislation!' she challenged at once.

'I thought he guessed at it,' qualified Slater. 'And I was right. When I couldn't reach the guys I originally dealt with at Langley I checked at the Library of Congress. It was a House bill in 1992 that included the release warning: it was primarily intended for organized crime witnesses within the programme.'

'Why didn't . . .?' Ann waved her arms, seeking the identity.

'Peebles,' supplied Slater.'

'Why didn't Peebles know the right statute?'

Slater shrugged. 'He's a form-filling clerk, not accustomed to being questioned or needing to show any initiative.'

'How do you know that?' demanded Ann.

'It was practically written on his forehead.'

She didn't smile. 'That's not good enough. You know that's not good enough.'

'Darling, it's OK.'

'It's not OK,' she refused. 'I said it would never go away and it never will.'

'Jack's been a model prisoner. That's why he's got his remission.'

'You don't know him. No one knows him like I do. He won't have forgotten. Or forgiven. He'll want to expose us, maybe even to the Russian embassy. Hurt us as much as he can. What would it do to David? Oh my God!'

'How can he find us?'

'I don't know,' said the woman, emptily. 'But I know that he'll try.'

'And fail. There's no way he can find us.'

'We can't be sure,' said Ann, even emptier. 'Pennsylvania's the next goddamn state!'

'That's not going to make it any easier for him. Or dangerous, for us.' Spacing the words in the hope of re-assuring her, Slater said, 'Jack Mason doesn't know where we relocated. Ann Mason and Dimitri Sobell have vanished: ceased to exist.'

'I knew it was all going to come back, one day,' she insisted, her mind blocked.

Slater hadn't expected the collapse to be as bad as this; hadn't expected a collapse at all. Until this moment he'd believed that over the years they'd laid all the threatening, haunting ghosts: talked everything out to exhaustion and satisfied each other – and themselves – that they could never be discovered for who they had once been and who they were now. He was certainly convinced that he had moved on and was disappointed to find that Ann hadn't, that in effect Ann had been deceiving him with her assurances and insistences. What else wasn't she sure about? Them maybe? If she wasn't then the deception was practically unimaginable. So why was he imagining it; raising his own, taunting ghosts? She had to love him as totally as he loved her.

He supposed on balance he had made the greater sacrifice, although he'd never considered it as such, in abandoning his very existence and his country for his love of her. But after the first few days of understandable disbelief at truly learning who he was and what his function had been, running her husband as a traitor, Ann had just as willingly stepped out into the unknown; been prepared even for the retribution from Moscow he'd honestly warned could engulf them if they were ever found, as well as enduring the humiliation and exposure of their affair at Mason's trial, although fortunately she'd been spared an actual court appearance. Never once had she questioned or complained about the surreal initial months, months that stretched into more than a year, totally stripping herself of one, albeit miserable life to adopt another. And she wasn't questioning it now. Ann was behaving like this, seeming almost immediately to crumble, *because* she'd adapted so completely and loved him so absolutely and she was terrified of losing everything they had.

He said now, 'Nothing's come back. Nothing *is* going to come back. All right, maybe I was knocked off balance when I got the letter. Which obviously I had to check out. Now that I have I'm satisfied there's nothing sinister; nothing for us to worry or panic about. We just go on as we have been doing for most of the past fifteen years, living our lives, enjoying our lives. Nothing bad is going to happen to us. I won't let anything bad happen to us.'

'You said Peebles told you Jack will be out in four or five weeks?'

Slater saw that his wife was wet-eyed, although not actually crying. 'Something like that.'

'You definitely said four or five weeks!'

'I know what I said, Ann. There's no reason for us to argue.' He couldn't remember the last time they had even squabbled.

'I'm not arguing. I just want to get things straight.'

'He said four or five weeks.'

'Where will he go?'

'Peebles said he didn't know. That he wouldn't have told me, even if he had known.'

'There has to be a reason for their warning us.'

42

Slater couldn't criticize Ann for echoing his own first thought. 'That's not so! It's a statutory obligation, a legal requirement, nothing more than that.'

'That's just what Peebles said,' insisted the woman, disbelievingly.

'It's what I checked out and confirmed at the Library of Congress.'

'Is Peebles going to keep in touch?'

'Ann, stop it! There's no reason for him or anyone else to keep in touch. Forget it.'

'How the hell can I forget it?'

'You have done, for the past fifteen years!' They were definitely arguing now.

'No I haven't,' she denied. 'I've *waited* for the past fifteen years. I think I need a drink.'

'It didn't drown anything out before.' She'd been very good at disguising it, Slater remembered. He hadn't even guessed when they'd started their affair, although they'd both had too much to drink the first time, and afterwards agreed it had been a bad mistake; Ann remorseful for cheating on a husband despite his so consistently and blatantly cheating on her, actually financing his womanizing with Moscow's money, and Slater – or Sobell as he was then – personally horrified at breaking every KGB rule as the control of a major American spy source. Neither had been drunk the second time. Or the third.

'I want a drink,' Ann demanded.

It had once been a bottle a day, Slater recalled, pouring the measure he knew Ann had liked then, adding ice, lime and tonic to the gin. He didn't make one for himself.

'Not joining me?'

'I don't need it.'

Ann remained staring at the full glass on the table between them, like a fairground fortune-teller trying to predict the future from a crystal ball, making no attempt to pick it up. Slater remained silent.

At last Ann said, 'I don't need it either. Throw it away.'

'Well done,' praised Slater, who'd only just stopped short of trying to persuade Ann to enrol in Alcoholics Anonymous all those years ago.

'There's something I do want, though.'

'What?'

'Better alarms and security.'

Slater opened his mouth to say it wasn't necessary but decided against it.

Tension remained between them. Each was aware of the other working hard to keep any indication of it from David, although Slater was discomfited driving the boy back from basketball practice when David said, 'I thought you were a bit hard on the guys tonight, Dad?'

'They weren't all trying their best,' said Slater, defensively. 'A team only works as a unit. One or two lay back and everything gets put out of synch.'

'You actually yelled at Steve and Paul.'

'Let's hope they pull their full weight next week.'

When he tried the door that night, Slater discovered Ann had put the security deadlock on – a matching deadlock she'd insisted he have installed the day after the letter arrived, on the art gallery she ran on Main Street, as well as CCTV cameras on both – and when she answered the door, after assuring herself who it was, Ann said, 'I thought you'd come in through the garage. You think it's a good idea to leave the car out?'

Saying nothing Slater went back to the car, triggered the garage door lift and put the vehicle away, entering the house through the inner connecting door. Finally inside the house he saw she'd slipped the bolts, as well as resetting the deadlock. The following morning, the episode in his mind, Slater found himself instinctively checking for surveillance as he drove into Frederick. There was a quick flare of irritation, just as quickly dispelled. What was wrong with that? he asked himself.

According to Peebles' schedule Mason would still be in the penitentiary and he genuinely believed what he'd told Ann, that there was no conceivable possibility of Mason ever locating them, even if her former husband attempted to do so, which Slater doubted just as strongly. But he'd had the specialized training and attained the expertise, an expertise he still utilized to a limited extent in the business he now ran. He'd even taken that expertise – or caution – into his business. To avoid the need for a large, potentially curious work staff Slater designed the security, but subcontracted the actual fitting and installation to others.

Why not maintain – or rather recover – all his other expertise, Slater now asked himself? There was no excuse for letting that craft wither out of shape, as he'd acknowledged from the most recent camping weekend that he'd neglected the physical fitness he'd once so strenuously kept up. Hadn't one of his personal, professional mantras been that an all important edge should be constantly honed, to remain sharp, not allowed to become blunted? It shouldn't be difficult, to bring it all back. Everything was still there, except for the back-up of the omnipotent KGB. His skills were just dormant, like a learned language was initially difficult to recall to fluency if it wasn't regularly spoken.

It wasn't a decision he'd tell Ann: wasn't sure, even, if he'd keep to it himself. Despite their solemn mutual undertaking always to be honest with each other, Ann had kept things – far more relevant things – from him: *I've waited for the past 15 years!* echoed in Slater's mind, not just the words but the virulence with which she'd said them. He wouldn't be withholding as she had withheld from him, for so many years. To tell her, to hint even, what he was only vaguely considering would cause her much greater worry than the letter had.

Hadn't he been waiting for the past fifteen years for Mason's release, complacent until now that he still had another five years to go until he needed to confront the possible repercussions? No! Slater determined at once. Mason wasn't a physically violent man. He'd looked capable of it but it had been a pretence, like so much else about Jack Mason was pretence; the way he'd convinced any woman under the age of sixty with a faint pulse that he was the stud upon whom James Bond had been modelled. At the man's trial it had emerged that almost invariably Mason intentionally let slip to any woman he was trying to seduce that he was a CIA agent who'd risked his life in Moscow and Vienna and Prague, although not that it was in the Russian capital that he'd been photographically entrapped, literally with his trousers around his ankles, by a planted KGB seductress. Nor that while he had been stationed in all three cities, he'd never been exposed to or experienced any danger. Mason's greatest intelligence coup was manoeuvring a recall from Moscow to the CIA's Russian Desk at Langley, and that was for his KGB masters.

He still might amuse himself recovering all the old, perhaps even outdated and superseded tradecraft, thought Slater. It could conceivably be a selective re-learning process from which he'd isolate things to teach David.

Jack Mason wouldn't have recognized the attorney who'd represented him at his treason trial: their association over his mother's estate had been entirely by letter. Since 1986 Patrick Bell had lost virtually all his hair, put on at least 28lbs and needed thick-lensed spectacles. His breathing was strained, too.

'Sorry I couldn't make it until now,' apologized Bell. 'I'm pretty busy.'

'Not a problem,' assured Mason, who'd actually wanted the meeting pushed back as close as possible to his release date. He looked around the interview room assigned to them and said, 'You sure this place isn't wired?'

'It's against the law,' said Bell.

'So's murder, rape and sexually molesting children. Still happens all the time.' It was irritating having to go through the prison complaint charade before getting to what was really important to him, but he'd been patient for fifteen years and the delay now was going to be about fifteen minutes.

'We're OK. Trust me. What's the complaint?'

Bell made no attempt to take notes as Mason recounted what had happened during the Washington visit. He didn't once look at Mason, either, but sat head bowed on the other side of the interview table. Nor did he interrupt.

It seemed several moments after Mason stopped before the lawyer said, 'Why should Howitt try to set you up?'

'I told you, to screw my maximum remission.'

'Why'd he want to do that?'

'Because I haven't kissed his ass, like everyone else.'

'That serious enough to him, to try a stunt like this?'

'He's a bullying bastard. Wants everyone frightened of him.'

'But you're not?'

'And he knows it. There's going to be an internal prison enquiry. It's on hold until we were able to talk like this.'

'You're alleging conspiracy. Who else was involved, apart from Howitt?'

'An ass-licking guard named Gerry Garson.'

'What producible evidence have you got?'

'I wasn't officially signed out. Which I understand I should have been, according to prison regulations. And I wasn't taken in a secure prison van, which I also understand is covered by prison regulations. I was taken to the airport in Garson's private car – I've got the number – and paraded in handcuffs until we approached Washington. They weren't put back on, definitely not on the return trip, when I was under FBI escort. Shouldn't I have been taken by the US Marshall's office?'

'Technically, perhaps.'

'That's what technicalities are for, rules to be observed.'

'The moment Howitt disappeared, you handed yourself over to airport police.'

'They could be called as witnesses. The FBI who got called in didn't believe Howitt's story. And there's to be an internal enquiry, like I told you.'

'When you went into Reagan terminal it was just the two of you – you and Howitt?'

'Yes.' Come on, let's get it over with!

'No other witnesses?'

'There's the airport policemen.'

'Who weren't involved until you went up to them? No one actually witnessed Howitt ducking away?'

'No.'

'It's your word against his. He's a senior prison guard, you're a convicted felon. I'd take a bet the records show you properly signed out.'

'Who's got maximum, good behaviour remission. Why should I risk screwing it up trying to escape less than a month before I was going to be released anyway!'

'Your release being delayed, because of what happened?'

'Not that I've been told. I think that's something you should establish.'

'At the moment you haven't lost anything?'

He could have predicted the conversation, thought Mason, who had no intention of pursuing any sort of claim to its end. 'Not for Howitt's want of trying.'

'You looking for financial compensation?'

'Don't I deserve it, having had five years of freedom put in jeopardy?'

47

'Which isn't going to be jeopardized. You beat the bastard, if indeed it was a set-up.'

'He should pay! Someone should pay.' And you're the key to a lot of money you don't even know about, thought Mason.

'It could take a long time.'

'I'm used to long times, like fifteen years within the same walls. All I'm asking you to do is look into it. Decide if there's a case.'

'I'm just pointing up practical, legal difficulties, that's all,' insisted Bell.

'Will you look into it, at least?'

'I'll look into it,' begrudged the lawyer. 'It won't be quick, though.'

The last thing he wanted was for it to be quick, thought Mason. 'I'm initially going to be under Washington parole, right on your doorstep. And we need to meet about other things, don't we?'

'Everything's in order, waiting,' assured the lawyer.

'How much money is in the account?' Bell had held power of attorney over his mother's estate for the past ten years.

'I checked before I left Washington,' said Bell. 'Your mother's house sold for $120,000 and there was $80,000 after the sale of the disposable assets and the money that was in the account. It's all been on the highest interest deposit, in the First National. In round figures you're looking at close to $300,000.'

'I'd like you to move, say, $50,000 into a checking account. And arrange a chequebook and cash card to be ready for when I get out.'

'Of course.'

Mason hesitated. 'There was a strongbox in which my mother kept things she thought important?' And which is even more important to me, he thought.

'That's in a safety deposit box, at the First National. Those were your instructions.'

'I'm hoping there'll be some things, momentos, that I'd like to have. Photographs, stuff like that.'

'I can understand,' smiled Bell.

'I'll get in touch, as soon as I get out.'

'Of course. It's going to take some getting used to.'

More than you could ever guess, thought Mason. 'I'll admit to being a little nervous.'

'It wouldn't be natural if you weren't. Everything will be ready for you.'

'And by then you'll have thought about this claim?'

'Absolutely.'

Mason hadn't expected to encounter Gerry Garson until the following morning at least but found the man at the far end of the library corridor later that afternoon when he closed up. Mason was within yards of the man before Garson saw him, immediately trying to hurry away.

'Gerry!' stopped Mason. 'There's something you need to hear. Something important.'

The prison guard halted, trying – but failing – to appear surprised at Mason being there. 'I didn't see you.'

'Good job I saw you then. I had an interview with my attorney today. You might know about that, as you know there's an internal enquiry about you and Howitt trying to pull that escape stunt. My lawyer thinks I've got a guaranteed compensation claim. Big bucks for me, goodbye job and pension for you and Frankie. I haven't decided yet whether to go ahead with it. If anything bad – anything at all – happened to Chambers after I get out it might make my mind up for me. I could call him as a witness. You tell Frankie that, OK? You let him know just how much his fat ass is on the line. And yours, too. You understand what I'm telling you, Gerry?'

'Uh huh.'

'The same problem about answering a simple question that you had driving into the airport,' reminded Mason. 'I want to hear from you loud and clear that you understand what I'm telling you. So let me hear it, Gerry. You understand everything I've said, don't you?'

'Yes, I've understood,' mumbled the man.

'And you're going to tell Howitt, make sure he understands?'

'Yes, I'm going to tell him.'

'That's good. It's important that we all completely understand each other.'

Mason waited until lock-up and the gradual although minimal quietening along the landing before telling Chambers, 'You haven't got anything to worry about after I get out.'

'You sure?'

'Positive.'

'How've you fixed it?'

'It's fixed.'

'I'm grateful.'

'You haven't told me what hotel you've chosen for us to meet at, when you get out,' prompted Mason.

'The New York Sheraton, on Seventh and 56th. Conventions all the time.'

'The 28th.'

'I'll be there, waiting.'

So will I, thought Mason. Everything was going like well-oiled clockwork.

Six

Jack Mason didn't resort to any histrionics like stopping outside White Deer to gaze up in relief at the heavens or turn back with an obscene gesture, as he'd seen and heard of other long timers doing at their moment of release. Neither was the reservation anything to do with his first experience of relative freedom for the parole hearing, although it had put the disposal of the antiquated broad-lapelled and flap-trouser cuffed suit at the top of his immediate agenda. In the lost environment of penitentiary incarceration such predictable demonstrations were the closely watched and intently discussed stuff of prison folklore and Mason had years ago determined against performing for anyone's satisfaction or benefit other than his own. He didn't have difficulty either, in preventing any surprise at seeing Glynis Needham waiting at the wheel of a macho, broad-wheeled Cherokee 4x4, appropriately dressed in jeans, check work shirt and work boots.

At the car door he said, 'I've got a travel voucher.'

'I've got wheels,' said the parole officer.

'It's a long drive to DC.'

'We've got all day and I like long drives.'

'You take this care about every parolee?' asked Mason, getting into the vehicle.

'No.'

'Why me?' asked Mason, although he believed he already knew.

'Because I felt like it. And we got things to talk about.'

To have been waiting outside this early she would have had to have driven over the previous evening and stayed somewhere, Mason calculated. 'I'm glad you did.' He wondered how long it would take for her to make her pitch? But it really was a long drive. She didn't have to hurry.

'So how's it feel to be out?' Glynis Needham asked, firing the engine.

'Good.' Which role would she play, bull or bitch? He could allow himself to think about pussy now, after subjugating what had once been a preoccupation. Her shirt was too loose to decide what sort of tits she had, even though they would be off limits to him.

'You going to miss your friend?'

'My friend?'

'Chambers.'

Did she believe like everyone else that he was gay, as she very obviously was, and that because of it there would be some bizarre empathy between them? 'Sounds like you're taking a special interest.'

'I always take a special interest. That's my job.'

'I'm grateful for how you're doing it so far.'

'What about Chambers?'

'Everyone got that wrong.' He didn't want her to have any curious recall if she heard later of Chambers' death. Why the hell had she raised it now!

'Sure,' she dismissed, just as confusingly. 'I've got you a room in a hostel.'

With sheets smelling of piss, farts and jerked-off semen, he guessed. 'I'm not staying in any hostel. If you've read my file properly you know I've got money. I was thinking of something by myself at a Guest Quarters. There's one I remember by the Watergate.'

'I don't like – or want – hostility.'

'Neither do I,' said Mason. He wasn't worried the stupid bitch didn't like being confronted. She had to agree to his staying somewhere other than in the accommodation she had selected.

'Then let's not have any.'

She'd be the bull with the strap-on dick, Mason decided. 'If you've read all my reports you know I'm not hostile and you would have known of my inheritance, while I was inside. I've got more than enough jail money until I see my lawyer and pick up the bank things he's been holding for me.'

'I do know about the inheritance,' said the woman. 'And I'll do everything I can to help you settle down.'

'Thank you. You're heading for the interstate, right?'

She chanced a sideways glance. 'Why?'

'You mind stopping at a mall, first? I want to get out of this fancy dress.'

She sniggered. 'Good idea. Difficult to believe that suit was once snappy, isn't it?'

'Maybe catch a coffee and a bagel, too?' Knowing she'd expect the remark he added, 'First food I can choose myself, now that I'm out.'

'Why not?'

The interstate was being signposted before they came to a shopping complex. It was far bigger than Mason could remember from 1985, the year he'd been arrested and held, pre-trial. He disguised any outward bewilderment at the bustle and the size, isolating almost forgotten store names. Mason was oddly glad, although he didn't know why, when the woman got out of the car to walk with him into J C Penny. He bought everything new, even underwear and loafers, bemused that the fitness regime had taken an inch off his old waist size and added two across his chest and shoulders. He bought an additional pair of jeans, three extra check sport shirts and a loose, Italian-labelled windbreak. Glynis Needham chose a soft leather grip to carry his purchases in. She also brought a large plastic shopping sack to the changing room for him to bag up all the discarded clothes, which he dumped into a waste bin directly outside the store, on their way to the nearby McDonald's. Mason, who in the penitentiary had rigidly controlled his diet as he'd controlled everything else, had a sausage and egg McMuffin breakfast, with extra hash browns and drank three cups of coffee and insisted on paying for Glynis's maple syrup waffles and coffee, as well as his own meal.

'Feel like you've never been away?' said Glynis Needham.

'Feels like I shouldn't have eaten so much.'

'You're doing good. Damned good.'

'Good?'

'I know you're nervous, getting out. But no one would know, certainly not now you're dressed properly.'

'If there's still a Guest Quarters near the Watergate, we could make a reservation from here.'

'You want me to do it for you, on my cell phone?'

Mason felt a blip of irritation, at being beholden, but said, 'If you wouldn't mind.'

'It's my job to fit you back into society,' she said, with almost mocking formality.

'You're helping a lot, this early,' said Mason, his irritation lessening at the awareness that it was he who was patronizing her rather than how she thought it to be. He watched and listened attentively, determined not to make mistakes when he got his own cell phone.

Glynis Needham made her pitch within minutes of their getting on to the interstate, tapping her fingers against the wheel to accompany the softly playing country and western for which Mason thought they were both dressed.

She said, 'I think there might have been a misunderstanding.'

'Misunderstanding?' queried Mason, genuinely confused.

'When we met at the penitentiary after that mix-up in Washington. I didn't mean it to sound like a threat when I said a compensation claim might affect your release.'

'Then it was my misunderstanding,' said Mason, in seeming apology. It was close to being amusing.

'You serious about going ahead with it?'

Mason set out automatically to use the word 'fuck', which she'd probably expect after his being institutionalized for so long in an environment in which the obscenity featured so much, but instead, maintaining the reformed persona, he said, 'Howitt tried to screw me over.'

She gave another sideways look at the restraint. 'But didn't manage it.'

'It could have cost me another five years.'

'But it didn't.'

'He still tried.'

'You properly thought about what it would mean? Headlines again, your being recognized wherever you go. You really want all that notoriety repeated?'

'I want Howitt properly punished for what he tried to do, like I was properly punished and served my time, for what I did.' It was difficult not to laugh aloud.

'I'm on the inside here, remember. I know what's already been sworn by the airport police and the FBI,' said the woman. 'Howitt will be found guilty at least of gross negligence, which will mean his being stripped of his rank and seniority.'

'He deserves to be dismissed.'

'That won't happen.'

'It will if there's a full hearing and I get compensation.'

'You really think it's worth it, put against the anonymity you'll lose? It's you and your resettlement I'm thinking about.'

Bullshit, thought Mason. She was thinking of a nice quiet, secret internal tribunal with no embarrassment to the prison service, which was what Hubert Harrison had been thinking of during their final release interview at which the warden had even used some of the same words and argument as Glynis Needham was now employing. 'I gotta go with my attorney's advice.'

'No, you don't,' insisted the woman. 'You've got to *listen* to his advice and make a decision based upon it – upon what's best for you. And I think you should balance that decision by what I've warned you you'll lose.'

'I don't know,' said Mason, choosing the moment to introduce his supposed uncertainty. 'I got to think about it, like I've got to think about a lot of other things like relocating to California . . . California and sunshine.'

'That's exactly what you've got to do,' urged the woman. 'Think long and hard about what there is to lose against what there is to gain.'

It came as a sudden, physical chill, so that Mason shivered and was surprised to find that he had his arms around himself, hugging himself, and that there was a churning sensation, physical again, deep in his stomach. He unwrapped his arms, embarrassed although he was alone in the Guest Quarters apartment but kept his hands together, driving back into himself the control that he'd always been so confident of having. Gradually the shivering stopped and the inner turmoil went. There was sound: outside traffic noise and the inevitable scream of an emergency siren; but to Mason it appeared to be – it *was* – total silence. He hadn't known such silence for years, he realized: fifteen years, longer if he included his remand custody. Or aloneness. Always the rustling, crying, shifting movement of the claustrophobic human anthill that was unrelenting, uninterrupted imprisonment.

With that awareness came another, what Glynis Needham had called his doing good. She'd called it nervousness, too, and now all alone in what he judged to be utter silence Mason accepted that she was right. From the moment of his stepping out through the penitentiary gates that morning he'd been hanging on, refusing the nervous uncertainty, refusing to admit it until now. But now, finally and unembarrassed, he did. It was more than simple nervousness. He was actually, shiveringly, frightened: frightened at the unexpected and unknown. Of how to go out and use a cell phone without making a mistake, drive a car, make a telephone reservation at a restaurant or for a show, of how to find his way around and how to talk to people without making it sound like a challenge, as it had been instinctive to confront everyone he'd been surrounded by for so long. Abruptly, angrily, Mason halted the drift. None of it was unknown. It was unaccustomed. He'd adopted another life, another way of existence. And survived by doing so: surmounted everything instead of being crushed by it. Now he had to adapt again. Become accustomed to living and behaving as he had once but hadn't needed to for too long. He had to do better than that – far better. In the penitentiary he had been the person everyone knew and was physically aware of, the hard man everyone made way for, was wary or downright frightened of. He didn't want to be – couldn't risk being – recognized like that any more. He had to become Mr Invisible, the crowd man no one saw or remembered; the crowd man two people in particular would never see, until he wanted them to see him: Mr and Mrs Daniel Slater, of 2832 Hill Avenue SE, Frederick, Maryland.

It had been a switchback time. Ann's fear had appeared gradually to subside as the days passed after Slater received Peebles' letter but noticeably mounted in the final two weeks leading up to when they understood Mason would be released. She snapped back irritably at the slightest provocation – at no provocation at all – and sought arguments in everything. It became routine for her to check every security lock and bolt and alarm after Slater nightly setting them and at the beginning of those final two weeks insisted that Slater have installed permanently operating camera monitors not only at the house but at her gallery, so that any visitor could be seen and identified before being allowed in. At the gallery Ann also demanded CCTV recording cameras. She refused to remain in the house alone but came with them on the nights Slater took David for basketball practice, ensuring they were locked into the car inside the garage before operating the automatic door opening. Their worst argument followed Slater telling Ann that David had asked if she was ill: 'Sure I'm sick. Sick with worry!' Although only slightly less serious was the row when Slater suggested they really did ask their doctor for tranquilisers. *'Here's our problem, doctor. My ex-husband, who spied within the CIA for Moscow, has just been released from jail and I'm frightened he'll try to find my current husband, who was the KGB agent who ran him before defecting. You got a pill that'll help me with that crock of shit?'*

It was in the immediate aftermath of that row that Slater held Ann in his arms until she quietened down and said, 'If we don't get this under control we're going to break up.'

Ann clung to him as she said, 'I know.'

In an irony they were never to learn, because they'd not had a specific release date, that was the night that Jack Mason sat in his hotel apartment less than 200 miles away, listing to himself all and every adjustment he needed to make to fulfil his long-planned retribution.

Seven

The eggshell-thin effort at preservation, each overcompensating and deferring to the other, lasted two days before coming close to being wrecked by another letter, which Slater opened – as he now every day opened the mail immediately upon delivery – after coming back from the first part of their newly established routine of waiting with an embarrassed and protesting David at the school bus pick-up before coming back to collect Ann for the gallery. Like every other precaution – and despite David's close-to-tears objections – the school run escort was at Ann's insistence.

'It's not from Peebles,' decided Slater at once, standing alongside the woman at the kitchen table to look down at the unopened envelope. 'It's not the same typeface.' He was sure his self-protective alertness was back to the level – better even, because of Ann's persistence – that it had been when he'd headed the KGB *rezidentura* at the Soviet Union's Washington embassy.

'Don't you think they've got more than one computer!'

Picking the envelope up again, for closer examination, Slater said, 'It's a Frederick postmark.'

'Open it.'

Slater did so, pleased as he had been before that there was no shake in his hands, although it came close as he read the letter. 'Jesus!'

'What!'

Unnecessarily handing his wife the letter, Slater said, 'It's from the school. The principal wants to see us about David. He had a knife: threatened another kid.'

'*What?*' Ann repeated, even more anguished.

'Read it!'

Ann was still doing so as Slater was connected to the principal's office, but even in that short time Slater had himself under control, biting back the angry demand to know why there hadn't been an instant, summoning telephone call instead of a sterile letter. Instead he made an appointment but remained close to the wall phone, finally looking back to Ann.

'What did the school say?'

'We're seeing the principal at two.'

'But what did he say?'

'We're going to hear all about it then.'

Slater picked Ann up from the gallery to be at the school by 1.45 p.m., both having to stand self-consciously in the outside corridor for five minutes, both unsuccessfully scanning the constant swirl and eddy of curious young faces for the one they wanted to see. The principal, Victor Spalding, was a prematurely balding, fresh-faced career educationalist who, they knew from their regularly attended PTA meetings, was considered by the governors to be one of their best – if not *the* best – appointments in recent years. He had raised the graduation standards and accompanying teacher morale of the school to its highest level ever. They declined his offer of tea or coffee, both tensed forward in their side-by-side chairs. Slater impatiently cut in with: 'What is this all about? David . . . a knife . . .? We should have been called . . . When?'

'Three days ago,' said Spalding, selecting his answers in a clipped, New England voice. 'It's thrown up a situation we didn't know – I didn't know – existed here in the school. I wrote instead of calling because it's a school regulation. And I don't need you to tell me that it's totally out of character for David. I'm as shocked and as upset as you are.'

'I doubt it,' said Slater, at once regretting the remark. 'What situation?'

'Bullying,' said Spalding, simply. 'A gang, maybe ten kids. With knives, thank God with nothing more threatening. And even more thankfully not having caused any injury with them.'

'David belongs to a gang that carry knives!' exclaimed Ann, her voice breaking.

'No, Mrs Slater,' assured the principal, reaching into a side drawer of his desk and producing a knife they both recognized. 'David confronted them. Which is why he hasn't been suspended, like the others have. But why we're having to have this meeting.'

'Oh my God,' said Ann.

'It's his hunting knife,' said Slater, emptily. 'We go hunting . . . camping . . . in the mountains.'

'David told me,' smiled the principal. 'Didn't he tell you about the bullying? What was happening . . . ?'

'No,' said Slater. 'Was there a fight? Did anyone get hurt . . . cut?'

'No. There was a lot of noise . . . bravado . . . the physics master heard it.'

'I need to get this straight,' insisted Slater. 'There's two groups of kids, confronting each other with knives?'

'No,' said Spalding again. 'There's a gang of maybe ten kids, at least some of whom carried knives they threatened to use to establish themselves in the school. And David, who tried to confront them . . . who did confront them, in fact.'

'By himself!' exclaimed Ann, horrified.

'By himself,' confirmed the principal.

'He could have been hurt – killed,' said Ann.

'A lot of them could,' agreed Spalding.

Looking between her husband and the headmaster Ann said, 'Why didn't he tell us . . . tell you?'

Slater shrugged, without an answer. Spalding said, 'I asked him. He said he didn't want to rat on anyone. That he thought he could handle it.'

Ann made a soft, groaning noise. Slater said, 'You're being vague about how many are in this gang.'

'They're refusing to rat on each other, too.'

'What's going to happen to them?'

'They're suspended, as I already told you. I'm seeing each of their parents to discuss it.'

'Are they going to be expelled?' demanded Ann, strong in voice for the first time.

'That hasn't been decided yet.'

'If they're not, David's going to become a target,' said Ann.

'No gang is going to rule any school of which I am in charge,' pledged Spalding.

'You didn't know they were trying to in the first place,' said Slater.

'But now I do. It won't be allowed to happen again. David's shown himself to be a very brave, if foolhardy, kid. He's an excellent, hard working student and he's going to do well, through junior high and higher. But of course, I'll understand if you want to pull him out . . . look at other schools.'

'That hasn't yet come into our thinking,' said Slater. 'At this moment I'm not sure what we want to do.'

'David could have been killed,' said Ann, almost to herself, her mind held by the thought.

'Is the whole thing being brought in front of the governors?' asked Slater.

'Of course.'

'What's the sequence to be, from here?' persisted Slater.

'The interviews, each child with their parents. Then a governors' meeting, at which decisions will be made.'

'They should be expelled,' insisted Ann.

'It's one option,' said Spalding.

'But they won't be, not all of them, will they?' challenged Slater.

'There's got to be a balance, between the offence and the stigma of expulsion that will follow them – damn them – in any other school,' said the principal.

'You're seeing each of the gang – at least those you know to be involved – with their parents?' said Slater. 'Why isn't David here with us?'

'Balance again,' said the other man. 'If you wish, then of course I'll bring him in. He knows I'm seeing you . . .' The man hesitated. 'Some of the other kids, some of those that were bullied, now look up to him—'

'He mustn't think he did anything to admire . . . that he's a hero,' broke in Slater.

'Exactly,' smiled Spalding. 'Thank you for understanding what I was trying to say.'

'I don't think he should be brought in,' agreed Ann. 'We'll talk to him.'

'If you decide he should stay on here, which I hope you will, I don't want him taking things into his own hands again.'

This time it was Ann who interrupted. 'I hope something like this, a gang carrying knives, won't happen again!'

'I've already given you my assurance on that,' said the principal.

*   *   *

61

They waited to take David home, driving silently for several minutes before Slater said, 'Why didn't you tell us?'

'I'm sorry.'

'You think it's some big deal, confronting people with a knife!'

'I knew they'd back down.'

'You knew nothing of the sort! You could have hurt somebody . . . killed somebody. Been hurt or killed yourself!' said Ann.

'You always told me to stand up for myself.'

'Not with a knife,' refuted Slater. 'It wasn't on impulse. You took a knife to school, in your pocket. You knew what you were going to do!'

'What did Mr Spalding say?'

'We talked about taking you away from the school,' improvised Ann.

'He's not going to expel me!'

'Do you want to change schools?' she said.

'No!'

'Why didn't you tell me what was happening?' demanded Slater, again. 'We talk to each other about everything, remember?'

'You and Mom seemed to have other things on your mind.'

The remark momentarily silenced both of them. Then Slater said, 'Nothing more important than you taking a knife to school.'

'Are you going to split up?'

Slater switched lanes to take the next turning into a side road, coasting to a halt in the nearest lay-by. Ann had already swivelled in her passenger seat by the time Slater turned to confront David. As he did so, Ann said, 'Let's hear that again!'

'I know you're fighting. I've heard you.'

'What's that – what's anything – got to do with your taking a knife to school and confronting other guys armed with knives?' demanded Slater.

David was hunched forward, refusing to let his eyes meet theirs. 'I don't know.'

'Look at me!' demanded Slater. 'I want a proper answer!'

'Nothing, I guess,' mumbled the boy.

'Look at me!' insisted Slater, again.

Slowly, reluctantly, David looked up, his eyes brimming.

Slater said, 'You're not making sense. Arming yourself with a knife doesn't make sense and imagining that your mother and I are going to split up doesn't make sense, because we're not and never will. And talking about both at the same time, as if they were connected, which they're not, doesn't make any sense. So now, right now, you tell me, me and your mother, what's going on?'

The boy began to cry, only bringing his hands up to his face when Ann offered him a handkerchief to wipe his nose as well as his eyes. Stumbling, his words broken by sobs, David said, 'I wanted to do . . . tried to do . . . thought you would do . . . stop it . . . never meant . . . not to hurt . . . frighten them like they were frightening guys . . . they would back off . . . stop you arguing. I'm sorry . . . didn't mean . . . won't . . . sorry.'

There was a shuddering intake of breath. 'They were going for Brad most of all.' Brad Hockley lived two streets away from Hill Avenue and was David's closest friend. They spent at least two evenings a week together, after homework.

'You set yourself up as Brad's protector!'

'He was scared.' David started to cry again, face hidden in the handkerchief and when Slater made to speak Ann held up her hand, shaking her head against his doing so. Instead Slater restarted the car and U-turned back on to the main highway. No one spoke until they reached the house, entering through the garage as it was their practice to do now. Still unspeaking Ann led the boy to his bedroom, shaking her head again against Slater following. It was almost an hour before she came downstairs, alone, to where Slater was sitting, staring at the returned hunting knife on the table in front of him.

She said, 'He's gone to sleep. He's exhausted. I'll check him later.'

'Can you imagine—' started Slater.

'I don't need to,' cut off Ann. 'We were lucky. Everyone was lucky. It doesn't make sense to us but it does to him. And it was us . . . our fault . . . my fault . . .'

'No one's fault,' insisted Slater. 'He got confused. Misunderstood.'

Ann shuddered. 'We let it happen. Misunderstanding ourselves.'

'Now we're not.'

'No,' she agreed. 'Not any longer.'

Jack Mason had his priorities in careful, precise order, the decision to take everything easy, to pace himself, reached months earlier and for a very particular reason. There'd been a lot of exaggeration at his trial, to make it as bad as possible for him, like the prosecutor insisting – and getting witnesses to agree – that it would take years for the CIA to recover from the damage he'd caused.

Although he considered it unlikely, his most pressing need was to establish if the Agency still retained any interest in him. It was so important for him to discover that – surprisingly – it put his ex-wife and Slater and what he intended doing to them temporarily out of his mind, which he couldn't recall having done for the past fifteen years.

On his first full day of freedom Mason shopped, spreading his on-foot excursions around Georgetown and DC to conduct every ingrained test from his CIA training to ensure that he was not under surveillance. He bought a Brooks Brothers Ivy League suit, shirt and shoes on his initial outing and on the second went into Georgetown for soft shoes, shorts and a jogging sweater at a mall on M Street. He window-shopped at a computer outlet there but returned to his Guest Quarters apartment to continue his observation monitoring. From the apartment he called Patrick Bell to fix a meeting for the following day, waiting until the afternoon to go back to Georgetown where he exhausted almost all of what was left of his jail money to buy an already selected laptop. Back at Guest Quarters for the third time that day – increasingly confident no watch had been imposed upon him – Mason accessed his undetected Trojan Horse in the penitentiary computer to check that there had been no traffic about him between the prison and the CIA. With their email addresses logged within his embedded site he extended his check to the email accounts of John Peebles and Glynis Needham, seeing where they had separately entered his records, satisfied there had been no email exchange between them and Langley either. When he was in Glynis Needham's system Mason also confirmed that so far the parole officer hadn't acted upon their discussion of his relocating to California by initiating computer correspondence with any counterpart there.

There were some files and boxes on a table to Patrick Bell's left when Mason entered the lawyer's office and Mason wondered which held the all important strongbox that he had deposited among his mother's belongings when her Alzheimer's was too advanced for her to know what he was doing: too advanced, even, for her to know him.

'How's it going?' greeted the lawyer.

'That's a question I was going to ask you,' said Mason.

'I haven't made a formal approach to the prison authorities yet,' said Bell. 'I thought I'd give you time to reflect upon what I said in the penitentiary.'

Which is the excuse, not the point of the meeting, thought Mason. 'Nothing's changed.' If he'd genuinely intended going ahead with a compensation claim he would have been pissed off at the man having done nothing.

'I have done some research, though, tried to find precedent cases. I can't find an exact comparison that might give us a judgement to base our case on.'

'I'm not really surprised, are you?'

'It would have helped.'

'Maybe we'll help some other poor bastard by establishing a precedent for them to follow.'

'So now we can get to work!' said the balding, bespectacled man, as if he were making some revelation.

'That's what I'd hoped we'd already started. And I am sorry to learn that we haven't.'

'I haven't been idle,' protested the other man, defensively. 'I've set everything up with the bank.' He went into the nearest box beside him, extracting things piece by piece and counting them out on the desk between them. 'Chequebook, bank card, deposit book, my surrender of power of attorney over the account . . .' He looked up. 'I've retained the poste restante facility, for statements and letters to continue coming to me here at this office. I don't imagine you've got a permanent place yet?'

'I haven't,' confirmed Mason. 'At the moment I'm at the Watergate Guest Quarters. And thanks for the forethought. What about formal identification? Do I need an affidavit from you? Or for you to come to the bank with me? I need to start drawing on the account right away.'

Bell went into his box again, offering a card. 'The guy with

65

whom I dealt, John Stevenson. I told him by letter you'll be taking over the account.'

'What *exactly* have you told him about me?'

'That you've been working abroad; no reason for him to know you've been in prison. None of his business.'

'Thank you again,' said Mason.

Bell indicated the other boxes. 'This is all of your mother's effects – those that you asked me to hold after the clearing and selling up of what was disposable, the house the most obvious. You gonna take it with you today?'

'Like I said, I don't have anything permanent yet. You mind going on storing it for a few more days, until I sort the bank stuff out? I'll obviously pay whatever fee there is. I'd like to look over it, though. You got a spare office I could borrow for a while?' He wasn't going to chance losing what it contained to a sudden CIA swoop.

'No problem,' smiled the man.

Mason was only interested in the mobile strongbox and found it in the second container. The memorized combination moved back and forth smoothly, although the lid wasn't initially easy to lift. Everything he needed for his carefully planned new life lay in the separate packages and envelopes in which he'd sealed them, which had to be . . .? Mason had to concentrate, to remember the preparation. Seventeen years ago, he calculated, more like eighteen. It was an indication of Mason's rigidly inculcated control that he didn't undo anything but closed and re-secured the strongbox and put it back with everything else, none of which interested him in the slightest.

When he returned to Bell's office he said, 'It's quite upsetting, seeing things you haven't seen for so long.'

'It must be,' commiserated the lawyer. 'How long you going to stay at Guest Quarters?'

'Certainly for the next week. I'll let you know if I move on.'

Mason maintained the walking regime to make sure he remained alone, believing that he did, to get to the First National Bank. John Stevenson was a tall, humourless man whose enquiries about his overseas postings rehearsed Mason for the other bank meeting that was shortly to come. Mason endured the sales pitch of the bank's services, warned he wasn't sure where he was going to settle now that he was back in America and thanked the man for the bank's care of his mother's affairs. Stevenson accompanied him to a teller's window and when Mason withdrew $6,000 said it would probably be more convenient – and certainly safer – if Mason took out a credit card, which they could organize for him. Mason said he'd think about it.

From the first day Mason had established a fitness regime, automatically awakening at his regular 5 a.m. to jog around the perimeter of The Mall, initially using the Lincoln Memorial as his starting and finishing point. He maintained it as the week progressed, all the time continuing his surveillance caution, keeping it up going to and from one-visit-only bars and restaurants in Georgetown, not wanting to become recognized or remembered in any of them. On the fourth day he went to others in DC, like the new Old Ebbitt and the open-air bar of the Washington Hotel, overlooking the Treasury Building. That night he window-shopped the familiar hooker bars along 14th Street and saw several girls he would once have chosen but for whom now there was no physical stir, reassuring himself that sex, which had once been so essential to him but suppressed for so long, was something else that couldn't be quickly recovered.

It was not until the end of the week that Mason arranged the demanded interview with Glynis Needham, whom he knew from his twice-daily computer checks had still not made contact with California, the one thing on his priority list that needed to be most carefully timed and scheduled.

'So how's it going?' greeted the woman.

'Good,' said Mason. Which it was. Even after such a short time he didn't have the apprehension at going out in public that had gripped him the night he'd arrived at Guest Quarters and he was as sure as he felt he could possibly be that he wasn't under any CIA monitor.

'Any problems?'

'Not that I can think of.'

'Thought any more about the compensation claim?'

'In the hands of my attorney.'

'So you've instructed him?'

Fuck you, thought Mason. 'He's looking into it.'

'What's his initial reaction?'

'That he needs to think about it.' It was going to be a pain

67

in the ass keeping up the pretence with this woman for as long as it was going to be necessary.

'Anything else?'

'I've pretty much made up my mind about California,' said Mason, the usefulness hardening in his mind. 'If it's all right with you I thought I might fly out for a look-see.'

'How long you planning to be away?'

'No longer than a week.'

'I could set up something in advance for you there. They might be able at least to give you a steer?'

'That might help,' said Mason. 'You're being very helpful.'

'That's what I'm here for. You'll let me know about the meeting with your attorney?'

'As soon as he can fit me in and I've made a decision,' lied Mason.

Eight

Announcing to Glynis Needham on the ride from the penitentiary that he was considering relocating to California had been little more than a throw-away line, reflecting the minimal importance he then attached to the woman beyond her immediate convenience. But over the course of the settling down week Mason isolated the potential advantages of such a move. Objectively, despite planning as far as possible, he couldn't insure against the unexpected. And from more fouled-up professional operations than he could remember, he could most definitely recall that there was always the unexpected – which dictated that there might well be the need for an alibi. And what better alibi was there than provably being 3000 miles away on America's west coast when tragedy disastrously struck the Slaters in the country's east? And who better to confirm the word of a respected parole officer than an equally respected attorney? Who anyway needed a kick in the ass to keep Howitt dangling in the wind. Added to all of which was Mason's final conviction that he wasn't being officially watched and was therefore able to collect his second and most guarded form of protection, held like a wish-granting genie not in a bottle but in the mobile strongbox.

Finally satisfied that he was not the subject of any CIA attention and despite the man's protests that there had not been any response from the prison authorities – to whom, from his monitor of the man's computer facility, Mason knew there hadn't yet been an approach – Mason fixed another appointment with Patrick Bell.

'I'm thinking of relocating,' he declared after the initial greetings.

'Relocating?' queried the lawyer. 'I thought your parole was in DC?'

'There's nothing here for me any more. I'm going to California.'

'Just like that?' questioned Bell.

'I'm a model prisoner, remember?' That was almost too glib, criticized Mason.

'What about the claim if you go to California?'

'What about the claim if I go anywhere?' demanded Mason, irritated as he knew from accessing his computer that the lawyer had done nothing since their last meeting anyway.

'I'm still not sure it's in your best interest to start an action,' cautioned Bell.

'We went through this last time. And I told you then what I wanted you to do. You know I've got money to pay you.'

'Money's not what I'm talking about!'

'It's what I'm talking about.'

'How much money – taking costs into consideration – do you think you're likely to be awarded against how much public attention you're going to attract!'

It was difficult to believe there hadn't been contact between Patrick Bell and Glynis Needham: maybe there had been, by telephone to which, frustratingly, he had no unobvious access. 'How much would I be likely to get?'

'I told you last time I can't find a statute case, for a criteria.'

'Give me a ballpark figure.'

Bell shrugged. 'Depends on the malice and intent I could prove. The internal investigation will help but that will concentrate upon negligence. Malice and intent would bring about a criminal prosecution, if I established it existed, but I can't guarantee your being sufficiently able to prove either: everyone will close up against you and you're the convicted felon, whose word is the least likely to be accepted.'

'So I could come away with nothing?' Mason was growing bored.

'Apart from a lot of costs . . .' The man raised a halting hand, against protest. 'Which I know you're not worried about, although for an action that could take a very long time you should be, because costs could swallow up most of your inheritance. More importantly, you've got to think about your loss of anonymity.'

'I won't have the bastard get away with it!' insisted Mason.

Bell sighed. 'It's your decision.'

'And I've made it.' Mason reached into his jacket. 'What I'd like to do now is pay things up to date and take all my mother's stuff away.'

Bell must have had the account prepared from the speed with which it was produced. As a secretary summoned a cab, Bell said, 'You'll let me know where you are, if you go to California? I'll need to have an address.'

'I'll keep in touch,' promised Mason.

'Think some more about it,' urged the lawyer.

'We'll talk,' said Mason.

The concern of both Slater and Ann was concentrated upon David. Over the following days they subjugated their own fears, which Slater worked equally hard when they were alone to convince Ann were unfounded and self-generated, to allay those of their son that their marriage was falling apart. And there was some recovery from the upheaval of the Peebles letter. By the end of the first week Ann agreed to David walking by himself to the school bus pick-up. Slater still emptied the mail box and read everything before going to the office, via Ann's gallery. The next improvement was Ann's acceptance that the gallery detour wasn't necessary either, going back to driving there in her own car.

Psychology had been an integral part of Slater's Russian intelligence training and he utilized it by not avoiding talk of the knife incident. What he did avoid, very determinedly, was any discussion to appear that they were proud of what David had done. Through the conversations, they learned when each member of the gang, with their parents, had been individually interviewed and that one girl had been added to the list of offenders. David assured them that he had not been subjected to any threats or intimidation. When Slater told David of him and Ann being summoned for their second meeting with the school principal, to hear the governors' decision, the boy said at once, 'What about my staying there?'

'Let's hear the governors' decision first,' said Slater.

They weren't kept waiting this time, although they still arrived early. Spalding's opening remark was: 'I hope I've got everything sorted out,' to which Ann's overly sharp retort was: 'We hope you have, too.'

The principal insisted there had been an extremely thorough

71

investigation, during which it had emerged that only four out of a total of eleven had actually carried knives. The governors had considered metal detector entry arches as well as police presence, neither of which the school had so far decided necessary. The greatest consideration, of course, had been what to do with each of the offending students. A prime concern in every case had been the stigma – and its effect upon their future education – of expulsion. Spalding, and the governors, had been impressed, and influenced, by the reaction of each parent, all of whom, without exception, had given personal assurances that their child would never again be involved in such an episode.

'So there are to be no expulsions?' anticipated Ann.

'That's the thinking at the moment,' confirmed Spalding, guardedly.

'Which leaves David a target when all the fuss has died down?'

'No,' denied the man. 'The number of counsellors is to be expanded from two to four. And every child in every class is to be told – told, not advised – to report, anonymously if they choose or on behalf of another child if they are not the victim, the very first suggestion of bullying or threatened violence. In the particular case of David, it's been made clear to the eleven involved, and agreed by each of their parents, that they are under an unlimited period of probation. If they are involved in one more incident, their expulsion will be automatic, with no appeal.'

'Is that an unequivocal decision?' asked Slater.

'Unequivocal,' guaranteed Spalding. 'It's being set out, in writing, to each of the involved parents. As it will be to you, if you choose to keep David in the school.'

'You're definitely not going to introduce metal detection or police presence?' persisted Ann.

'No,' said Spalding.

'It would seem to be a good resolution all round,' conceded Slater.

Ann looked sharply towards her husband before turning back to the principal. 'How does the ethos of not ratting fit into it all?'

'The anonymity provision is going to be stressed at every class lecture,' said the man. 'And that's what it's going to be, a positive curriculum lecture. And not just once, in this immediate aftermath. It'll be a permanent inclusion. As I told you at our earlier meeting, there is going to be no bullying, intimidation or outright violence in a school of which I am in charge.'

'You seem to have covered all the bases,' said Slater.

'Except what you're going to do with David,' reminded Spalding.

Slater looked at his wife, deferring to her. Ann hesitated before saying, 'He doesn't want to leave.'

'What do you want, as his parents?' pressed the principal.

'The best for David,' said Slater. 'Which I think you've set into place.'

'I'll not fail you,' pledged the man. 'I'll not fail any child in my charge. David will not be victimized if he remains here, neither will he be eulogized for what he did or attempted to do.'

The meeting had been in the morning, so they didn't wait to take David home. On their way to return Ann to the gallery from which he'd earlier collected her, she said, 'I'm not sure we shouldn't take David away.'

'I meant what I said back there,' insisted Slater. 'We both want what's best for David. And he wants to stay.'

'No one gets punished!'

'If I do have a reservation, it's for setting David apart. He armed himself with a goddamned knife, just like the others did.'

'To protect a friend,' reminded Ann. 'Have you given the knife back to him?'

'Not yet.'

'Are you going to?'

'The next time we go into the mountains, maybe. But with a lecture far stronger than they're going to get back there at the school.'

'We're trying to rebuild bridges, remember?'

'Which is exactly what I'm doing,' said Slater.

That night, for the first time for more than a fortnight, which was the longest interval there had been since their marriage – since the beginning of their affair, in fact – they made love. Afterwards Ann said, 'I'm glad that's another bridge we've rebuilt.'

'So am I,' said Slater.

'We couldn't, could we?'

'Couldn't what?'

'Break up.'

'Never.'

'Convince David about that, as strongly as everything else he has to believe and understand.'

In his locked and chain-secured apartment Jack Mason gazed down at the strongbox collection he had so long ago assembled for an escape if he was ever suspected of spying for Russia. He smiled at the tremor in his hands as he opened it, more easily this time than it had been in the lawyer's office; what else could he be but excited?

Mason laid each individually wrapped package upon the table before him like a Las Vegas blackjack dealer setting out a winning hand. The passport was first, before the safe deposit registrations and their authorizing code at the First National Bank in Washington DC and the Chase Manhattan bank on New York's Wall Street, as well as a Social Security record and the birth certificate in the name of Adam Peterson.

Mason savoured the moment, the first of the euphoria he knew he was going to feel over the next few months, as an afterthought flicking open the passport. Without the slightest conceit Mason decided the photograph of himself inside could have been taken yesterday. He'd even avoided, which Slater hadn't, the almost clichéd mistake of keeping the same initial letters for the new name as for the old he was abandoning.

He was going to enjoy the trip to New York to add most of his inheritance to his $850,000 stash. And now that he had an Adam Peterson driving licence he could rent a car and make his first exploratory visit to Frederick, Maryland.

It took Mason the entire following day and four separate outings to dispose of letters and photographs and memorabilia of his mother and father's existence, none of which he bothered to look at beyond checking official-looking documents to discover if they had any financial value. None did.

Nine

A sudden and entirely coincidental flurry of external happenings balanced – even put into partial perspective – the internal difficulties from which Ann and Slater were trying to recover.

Slater had months before tendered, more in hope than expectation, for security contracts for a planned mall on the outskirts of Frederick, on the Harpers Ferry road, and in the space of a week was awarded six separate design commissions, two by nationally established names. The construction of the mall was spread over six months, sufficiently spaced for Slater to work in sequence within the building programme – as usual outsourcing each installation – without needing to take on extra staff. It was the largest combined commission he had ever won and would still enable him to take on other, additional work. Slater's conservative forecast, predicated over the preceding four years' income, was a year end, pre-tax profit increase of fifty percent. From his psychology knowledge Slater knew the financial guarantee would underpin the feeling of physical security it was essential for Ann to restore.

And the good fortune continued.

Daniel Slater didn't remotely come close to being a bull or bear stock market gambler. Like thousands – millions – of Americans he studied newspaper financial sections and Internet fluctuations but his buying and selling was barely above the par of always following the favourites through a horse-race card. He didn't win big but he didn't lose big, either.

In his small time way Slater followed pharmaceuticals and long before submitting his hopeful shopping mall tenders he'd read a Forbes magazine biography of a geneticist who'd impatiently switched from pure science to establish his own genetic research company. When that fledgling, DNA-based firm offered a dollar a share rights issue Slater took his profit from his GlaxoSmithKline investment and bought $10,000 worth. Within a month the much hyped expectation of a common cold treatment by virus DNA engineering was, without any warning, dismissed by the Federal Drug Administration spokesman as impractical and overnight Slater's $10,000 share speculation was reduced to $1,500, too quick and too severe for any escape selling.

Just one day after the acceptance of his mall security tenders the FDA's licensing announcement of a successfully tested psoriasis treatment stirred the moribund portfolio. For the first time ever the already financially bolstered Slater gambled with money he believed he'd already lost, waiting until the stock rose eight points above his purchase price before selling 6,000 shares to recover most of his original investment. He sold the remaining 4,000 shares within the same week when they peaked at $4 a share, doubling his initial $10,000 stake.

That was on the Friday. On the Saturday David dropped three baskets – the last the winner – to lift his youth club team two places up the local junior league. David chose a Wendy's instead of McDonald's for the celebration hamburger supper and during the meal they talked of taking another weekend trip up into the mountains, without fixing a specific date.

Later that night, when she and Slater were alone, Ann said, 'He didn't say anything about getting his knife back?'

'I haven't told him he will get it back on the next camping trip.'

She remained silent for several minutes. 'It's all come good again, hasn't it?'

'Everything's back to normal,' agreed Slater.

'I'm sorry, for collapsing like I did.'

It was embarrassment, not regret, Slater guessed. His was the regret for never having realized how deep her fear had been. 'It's all over now – in the past.'

'It's . . .'

'Over,' he insisted, knowing that it wasn't but not wanting her to dwell upon what had eroded too much too quickly. Perhaps as the years passed she would come to accept how completely hidden and safe they were. But that's what it would take, years not months. And Ann hadn't been alone in her fear. He'd felt the uncertainty, too. It was good – reassuring

– to know that was all it had been, a blip that he could now put behind him and never think of again.

Jack Mason was in the majority of CIA officers at the height of the Cold War of the 1980s to use, without Langley's official knowledge, Agency facilities and expertise to obtain his false ID. The irony was that that majority, who anyway operated under the CIA policy of cover names, did so to protect themselves against KGB moles disclosing them to Moscow. It was during his time as a Russian spy, when he was unsuccessfully trying to uncover such protective identities, that Mason discovered and used the technique for himself.

Adam Peterson had been born on the same day, month and year as Mason in a one-street, two-store farming hamlet six miles east of Coon Rapids, Ohio. He'd attended the local school that did not aspire to a yearbook in which an identifying photograph might have appeared and did not go on to college, but left as soon as he was able to become a farm hand, like his five brothers. He'd died just short of his twentieth birthday beneath the blades of a combine harvester. Because birth and death certificates are not coordinated within the United States, it was comparatively easy, although necessarily time consuming, for Mason to obtain Peterson's birth certificate and Social Security details and substitute his own photograph and physical details for a passport, driving licence and other documentation to become, whenever he chose, Adam Peterson. The only time he'd used them was to open the about-to-be re-accessed safe deposit and banking facilities in Washington DC and New York.

Before which he put himself behind the wheel of a car for the first time in more than fifteen years, determined, as he was determined about everything, to discard any giveaway institutionalized hesitations. Mason had been caught, during his jogging and walking re-entry into Washington DC, by the compactness of automobiles, even though the era of the fin-tailed, chrome-encrusted car had been history well before his imprisonment. As observant as he'd been trained to be, he'd isolated makes and models and decided upon a Toyota Yaris that he could confidently ask for before approaching the Hertz office just off M Street. And encountered his first unanticipated challenge.

'You don't have a credit card?' frowned the clerk, curiously.

'I prefer to deal in cash. Nothing wrong with cash, is there?'

'We got your validated credit card number and rental approval, we've got something to charge against in the event of your keeping the car longer than you first thought you'd need it. Or any other problem,' said the girl.

'Like my running away with it,' sneered Mason, recovering. 'How much do you think I'm going to get trying to sell a Toyota Yaris with a Hertz insignia at the back and no ownership papers!'

'It's what the company prefer. People don't often want to rent in cash.'

'I do. And I know you have the facility for it.' It was a gamble, because Mason didn't know.

The girl's face became fixed. She took her time getting a thick regulations book from her desk drawer and even longer finding the process. Without argument Mason agreed to the $500 deposit and paid the extra for every offered insurance cover, tensed that she might want to confirm the non-existent Adam Peterson reservation at Guest Quarters, the only address he had to offer. She didn't.

Mason set out the first afternoon to confine himself to the city but after just an hour of in-town driving he felt confident enough to amuse himself by crossing the river to climb the familiar Washington Memorial Parkway and pass the tree-shrouded Langley headquarters of the Central Intelligence Agency to join the traffic-congested Beltway. The moment he began going south Mason accepted how easy it would be to reach Frederick but just as quickly dismissed the idea. By the time he did that, pacing himself still, his driving had to be as automatic as the gear box, with no distraction whatsoever from his preoccupation with the occupants of 2832, Hill Avenue SE. Mason left at the first convenient slip road to turn back north, indulging himself as he descended back into Washington by slowing once more to pass Langley before going into Georgetown over the Key Bridge. The following day he took a different route, driving through Annapolis as far as Baltimore, where he lunched overlooking the harbour and chose a different, slower route back that intentionally delayed his return until after dark for him to regain further, night-driving experience.

The next day he set out to rearrange his wrongly placed banking facilities. He drove to the First National Bank and worked his way through the various departments, restoring to himself full control of the inheritance account Patrick Bell had administered during his imprisonment, after his mother's death. It took so long to establish the briefly needed safe deposit facility that he was tempted to abandon it, but he forced the patience, knowing that it was essential he had such a hiding place for the Glock until the very moment that he needed it. After finally achieving it he withdrew all but $3,000 from the checking account, drove directly to Reagan airport, where he returned the car and recovered his full cash deposit. He recognized the two police officers to whom he'd surrendered after Howitt's abandonment as soon as he entered the concourse. Having missed his intended shuttle because of the bank delay and with time to spare before the next, Mason lingered, although keeping himself as unobtrusive as possible, and tested himself as a crowd person. Neither officer showed any recognition, not even when Mason passed within yards of them on his way to catch his plane to New York. There was no in-flight challenge when he bought his ticket in cash.

Neither was there when he presented himself at the Chase Manhattan Bank as Adam Peterson and produced his identification documents at the securities section, although there was a slight delay in locating the duplicate bank key for the double lock deposit box. There was no curiosity from the securities official at his not having accessed the facility for so long, but on their way to the vaults Mason followed Patrick Bell's lead and talked generally of being glad to be back in America after so long abroad in the Middle East and the oil fields of Uzbekistan and latterly Scotland. The bank officer dutifully smiled when Mason remarked that the Middle East was better for getting a suntan than the former Soviet republic or the north of the British Isles. There was no attempted comparison between his signature on that day's access register and the Adam Peterson documents, but Mason himself was satisfied with the match. The official's unlocking with the bank key was a second's operation but Mason patiently endured the explanation of the summoning bell for him to be escorted back up when he'd completed his business.

Alone in the locked examination room adjoining the vaults Mason felt something approaching a sexual excitement, the first he'd experienced – and welcomed – after years of monk-like abstinence, at the moment of opening the box to gaze down at its contents. Everything lay before him as he'd left it eighteen years earlier: the money neatly stacked according to its wrap-secured and identified denominations. He'd opened the deposit before the never suspected affair between Ann and Sobell, never imagining the gravy train was going to dry up even if he were suddenly re-assigned to another overseas posting. Against that possibility and his not being able to regularly travel to New York Mason had ensured there were sufficient support funds for the facility in his open Adam Peterson account, reflecting as he put in most of his withdrawn inheritance that had his sentence run its full term there would not have been sufficient to cover the regular cost. Although it was unnecessary, because he could remember to the last dollar how much was there, he still counted each wrapped and labelled bundle. Well aware, from the closeness with which he'd kept himself up to date from newspapers and television, of bank reporting requirements under anti-drug trafficking legislation, Mason divided into two piles the cash he intended taking with him, keeping that with which he was going to replenish his account just short of $750 than that which would have triggered the legal necessity.

Like a child on their birthday saving the biggest present until last to unwrap, Mason left until last the second section of the deposit box. The Glock, snug in its still oiled cloth, the eight ten-milimetre bullets separate in their glassine envelope, appeared reassuringly before him. He'd illegally obtained the Austrian-manufactured handgun during his Viennese tour and had it shipped undetected back to the United States in the embassy's diplomatic bag. It had been an absurd oversight not to have obtained more ammunition, but he'd never imagined the need for the revenge he intended. Although he fantasized about inflicting as much agony as possible upon Slater and Ann – the rattlesnake of the Capote book he'd read in the prison library remaining his favourite – Mason realistically decided that he'd have to use the handgun, for which he would have to get more shells. He'd driven the 300 miles from Washington to New York to avoid

80

any airport detection with the weapon upon his return from Vienna and recognized as well that with the anti-terrorism hysteria that gripped the country since 9/11 he was going to have to repeat the car journey eventually to get it back to Frederick. It would, Mason thought philosophically, provide further driving experience.

For the moment, though, the incriminating Glock had to remain where he'd left it, all those years ago. Until the time came to use it upon the two people he hated more than he'd imagined it possible to hate another human being.

The securities official responded at once to Mason's summons, returned with him to the vault for the box to be restored and double locked, and escorted him back to the main, public section. The service manager to whose position he was directed was a proud-busted black girl named Helene Balanda who wore her hair ethnically braided and who, like the First National official in Washington, almost at once embarked upon an unexpectedly strong sales pitch for the various customer services up to and including cheques printed not just with fine art images but photographically those of the customers themselves, an identification that Mason actually allowed himself to laugh at. Mixed with the amusing absurdity of his risking such a choice was another stir of excitement, very definitely sexual this time. He greatly expanded his foreign posting invention with accounts of having used the various banks of the countries in which he had worked, with funds still having to be transferred, and talked of continuing to bank at the Chase Manhattan, although of there being a possible branch switch because of the uncertainty after such a long time out of the country of exactly where he might permanently resettle. He expected to be living in hotels for the foreseeable future. She accepted his account refunding deposit and, visibly disappointed, promised a replacement, name-endorsed plain-paged chequebook – for which she received no commission – and bank and Visa cards within a week. Mason said that because of his uncertain accommodation he'd personally return to collect them. Within that week he might have established a Post Office box number for his mail.

His biggest hurdle surmounted without the slightest hindrance or question, Mason left the bank with the rest of the day – and the night if he chose – at his absolute choice, enjoying afresh and in a new city the still unfamiliar freedom. He took his time walking up town, via Broadway. He hesitated at 42nd Street and its sex show and hooker reminders. On impulse he turned east, disappointed that there appeared fewer erotic offerings than when he had last been in the city, and on further impulse he cut into Grand Central Station and lunched leisurely in the basement fish restaurant off oysters and soft-shelled crabs and imported Chablis.

There were a few loitering hookers hoping for afternoon business who might have stood more chance if they'd waited for the kinder street-lit darkness but within a few yards of turning up 6th Avenue, towards the park, Mason isolated a blonde so much better dressed and made-up that he wasn't absolutely sure she was a working girl. He was re-asssured when she answered his smile and further encouraged by her careful, vice squad protective approach – 'Are you a stranger, looking for directions?' – when he slowed.

'I might be.'

'Is it a hotel or an address you're looking for?'

'I don't have either. Perhaps you could recommend me?'

'There would be a finder's fee.'

'How much?'

'That would depend upon the sort of accommodation you're looking for.'

'I like everything fully appointed. Are you familiar with such accommodation?'

'Fully appointed accommodation costs $350. It comes with a complete survey.'

'I think I need to see it.'

'I think you need to, too.'

Mason liked her perfume and the name she used – Miriam – and the clean, just showered smell when they got into the cab, and that she didn't try to crawl all over him. He was glad, too, that it was an apartment, just off Columbus Circle, and not a pay by the hour professional hotel. When they got inside Mason decided it was where she lived, not her workplace. He declined her offered drink and when he handed over the four $100 bills he told her he didn't expect any change.

She said, 'Let's make it more than a pleasure to do business with you.'

'Let's,' said Mason, following her into the bedroom. It was dominated by the bed, a mirror inset in its canopy.

'You want to undress me? Or watch?'

'Watch.'

She was good, very good. Not trying to make it a gyrating striptease but neither shedding her dress, pants and bra like a discarded skin. It was the first live naked female body he had seen since he couldn't remember when and he thought she was magnificent, no sag or lines to her breasts or stomach.

'And you?'

He wasn't feeling anything: no excitement at all! 'You help.'

The girl did that well, too, stripping him with her hands on the inside, not the outside, of his clothes, so that every movement was an erotic caress. Mason still stayed flaccid, even when she knelt before him to slide off the final piece.

She nuzzled his groin, pushing him back upon the bed, and said, 'You got a favourite? Something you really like that makes it extra good? Anything at all?'

An essential for Mason's predatory sexual need had always been cunnilingus but he'd only ever practised it with trusted mistresses, not with one night stands and never with hookers and he didn't want to risk it now, desperate though he was to be aroused. 'Blow me.'

The girl had difficulty fitting the condom, so flaccid was he. She licked and sucked and he stared up into the mirror at her perfect body as she tried. He remained limp.

'Relax. Don't tense,' she murmured

Nothing.

'You want to feel? Touch me? I want you to touch me.'

Mason touched her, going into her and she splayed and said, 'Look. Really look.'

But nothing happened and finally he said, 'It's no good.'

'It will be good. It happens like this sometimes but it will be good, next time. You want my number, for next time?'

He took her card, promising to call, but didn't shower, anxious to get away. He got a cab at once and asked for La Guardia airport, eager to get back to Washington. It wasn't his fault, he told himself. Too early, after such an abstinence. Shouldn't have tried it with a hooker, either. Needed someone he could trust: whom he knew would be clean. Not his fault at all. She was right. It would be good the next time, like it always had been. But not with her. He crumpled her card into a ball and dropped it on the cab floor, wishing the frustrated anger would go away.

Ten

I t was time.

Not immediately, not today. Today began the actuality after all the deadly – literally – fantasy. There were computer snares to be put in place from what he'd discovered when he'd got back from New York the previous night and worked out now, lying there in the dawn half light. Tomorrow. He'd set everything up for tomorrow, have a car ready in the basement car park to avoid any delay. Maybe he shouldn't have waited as long as this, maybe . . . Mason brought the reflection up short, refusing it. Not refusing. Rejecting, annoyed the doubt had ever come to mind, been allowed to *enter* his mind. He hadn't unnecessarily held back from embarking upon the retribution, as if he had second thoughts: doubtful, frightened second thoughts. As if, even, at the final moment of decision that he didn't want to go through with it. To do it. That he was frightened, didn't trust himself to do it. Didn't believe that he could do it. The doubt, the unthinkable, unacceptable doubt that he was incapable of untraceably killing those he was going to kill burned through Mason – scourged through him – and he physically reared up from his bed, the fury vibrating from him and through him, as it had when he wrapped his arms around himself, astonished by whatever had caused that reaction then and what was arising within him now. Why should he – how *could* he! – have any doubt about what he was going to do! *Had* to do. At how he had to inflict all the hurt and punishment upon those who had inflicted as much hurt and punishment upon him. OK, so Peter Chambers didn't come within that justification. But what the hell did that matter? The only thing that mattered was the hidden three million dollars that was going to ensure the very full and very satisfying future life of Adam Peterson.

Forcefully, as if there were people, witnesses, to impress or convince, Mason cast aside what little remained of the bed covering and just as determinedly, anxiously, began his restricted exercises, his mind closed off against any thought other than the preparations he had to make for what inevitably was to follow, as inexorably as the night was being succeeded by day through the drawn-back drapes. With that full day before him Mason didn't cut back on the morning's run, totally encircling the Constitution Gardens and was still back at Guest Quarters before Washington DC and its commuters were properly awake and moving.

His previous night's computer discovery from his Trojan Horse bug within her website was that Glynis Needham had finally made contact with her parole officer counterpart in California. The colleague was another woman, Beverley Littlejohn, and from the tone of Glynis's email the two knew each other. It was still, though, a straightforward professional exchange. His scanned photograph and a précis of his trial and imprisonment record was an attachment to the email itself. In it Glynis Needham alerted the other woman to Mason's intended, as yet unspecified, arrival on a possible resettlement visit to California. Mason smiled at Glynis's description of him as a contrite and obviously rehabilitation-seeking offender, the judgement qualified by the recounting of the Frank Howitt episode. There was no doubt in anyone's mind that the prison officer was guilty of gross professional – even criminal – misconduct which was going to be severely punished by an internal enquiry. She was trying to dissuade Mason from pursuing compensation litigation. Such litigation, upon the evidence already assembled for the internal tribunal, would most probably be successful. She and the prison authorities feared the resulting publicity and virtual retrial of Mason's case would make impossible any chance of Mason's unrecognized re-entry into a community, quite apart from the damage it would cause to the prison service. Glynis urged the other woman to initiate a discussion and add her dissuasion to his continuing with the threatened action. Mason smiled again at the personal conclusion that Glynis Needham liked him – 'which is rare for me, as you can guess' – and wanted him to have the best possible chance to be re-absorbed, unknown, into a city or town and any re-employment he might choose. From that concluding remark Mason guessed that Beverley Littlejohn was probably gay, too, but after what had happened, or failed to happen, in New York thoughts of sex, either sex, any sex, weren't high on his agenda.

What was of primary importance was that the electronic exchange between Washington DC and California had given him Beverley Littlejohn's all-essential email address, into which had to be implanted a 'ghost server', a quantum leap improvement upon a Trojan Horse, for what he had to achieve. The Trojan Horses Mason had installed in the websites of White Deer Penitentiary, Glynis Needham and Patrick Bell gave him the undetected facility to roam – and utilize – whatever and wherever he chose within their respective sites. The effect of installing separate and unsuspected ghost servers between the two parole officers, activated by obvious but exclusive trigger words of 'mason' or 'white deer', was to suspend between them an electronic seine net in which any exchange from Washington or California would be enmeshed and stopped, without Glynis Needham or Beverley Littlejohn knowing it. And allowing him, still without either person being aware, to adjust, rewrite or respond in what would appear to both to be expected acknowledgements but with what he wanted to convey, not what they had written, one to the other.

The time difference between the east and west coasts of America, which had not been part of Mason's evasion plan, worked in his favour. From his Trojan Horse within the DC parole system Mason knew that Beverley Littlejohn had not replied to Glynis's initial message and he had his ghost server filter in place by the time she did, just after 2 p.m. East Coast time. It was a simple acknowledgement of Glynis Needham's advisory message, accompanied by assurances to do whatever she could to help Mason's resettlement and employment, the expectation of encountering a real life spy for the first time ('I think he looks closest to Sean Connery's James Bond from the photographs') and interspersed with a lot of how-are-you-I'm-fine-it-would-be-great-to-meet-up-sometime sentiments. Mason passed it on without any alteration. Once he'd read it he didn't do anything to alter Glynis Needham's return promise to alert the other woman to his California arrival details either.

It was late afternoon Washington time before Mason was satisfied that he had his other intercepting ghost servers satisfactorily in place, tempering the satisfaction with the reminder that there was no way he could insure against any of them switching from email to telephone contact.

By chance it was the same reservation clerk as before at the Hertz office just off M Street, which spared him the delaying discussion of renting in cash rather than credit card. Prompted, though, by her recognition when the essential priority was always for him to remain unrecognized, Mason told her he'd probably return the car – another Yaris – to the airport facility, as he'd done earlier, reminding himself as he did so to list from the telephone book back at Guest Quarters all the Hertz outlets in the city, as well as those of Avis and Budget. It was impossible to calculate how long he'd need to complete his necessary total surveillance of Daniel and Ann Slater, 2832 Hill Avenue SE and whatever else emerged from it. But if he were to remain invisible it was essential he never drove more than once around Frederick in the same car model, make or colour. It was the most basic rule of undetected observation always to avoid identifiable vehicles, doubly, even trebly, important when the target was another equally highly qualified intelligence officer. Mason hesitated at the reflection, wondering if it had been a precaution practised by the CIA after Slater had exposed him. Hardly necessary, he reminded himself. They'd had all the proof they'd needed of his spying, without having to gain more with prolonged stake-outs. He would, of course, have spotted it if it had been imposed, maybe even had a chance to run.

There was no possibility of his oversleeping the next morning, but Mason decided against going out for dinner that night. He limited himself to two highballs while copying out the addresses of car rental companies, watched the early evening news, and grilled some of the steak he'd bought from the basement supermarket at the Watergate, not bothering with any wine. He didn't watch television afterwards but sat, thinking about what was going to begin the following day.

It was very definitely time.

Mason was on the road by 5.30 a.m., surprised at the volume of traffic already on the roads. It got even heavier on the Beltway, the impression heightened by the constant stream of vehicles passing him contentedly enclosed in the slow lane.

Even driving unhurriedly Mason reached the outskirts of Frederick just after seven, stopping at the first McDonald's for coffee and a blueberry muffin. He considered, but quickly abandoned, the idea of asking directions to Hill Avenue. As he was approaching Frederick from the west it was unlikely any of the staff would know an address on the other side of the town and he'd attract attention if the question was passed around among them in their effort to help.

He was waiting at the door when the tourist office opened, and to fulfil his role as a vacationing visitor Mason collected some unwanted sightseeing brochures and guides as well as the town map, choosing a Main Street cafe for more coffee and its central location to orientate himself. He located Hill Avenue SE on the map and memorized a route he didn't expect to take longer than ten minutes to complete. It was very much small-town USA. There were neat buildings and stores and a rounded civic centre with its inevitable, high-poled flag set amidst methodically arranged flower beds – tulips and polyanthus and daffodils and a lot more he couldn't name, all regimented by their colours – and pattern-sculpted grass. Mason was discom-fited – unsettled – by it. It was close to being *too* small-town, a place where almost everyone knew – at least by sight – everyone else: a place in which a loitering stranger would be obvious. Noticed. Objectively, from another viewpoint, Mason conceded it to be right – the obvious protection – for someone with a new name, a new everything including a new wife, in which to hide himself. Prepare himself for the Russian retri-bution that would be inevitable, expected, if the KGB or its successor chose to hunt him down. Would Slater or Sobell have expected that? Feared that? Of course he would have done. Retribution was always exacted upon defectors by Russian intel-ligence, if the traitor could be found.

What about him? Would Sobell – or Slater as he had become – fear retribution from him? Unlikely, Mason decided; unlikely to the point of years ago having become dismissible. Deciding when – how – Slater and Ann were going to learn he was out for revenge was going to be one of the most difficult things. Mason wanted them to know, to be terrified for as long as possible, to suffer horribly, realizing they were trapped and that there was nothing they could do to prevent his revenge. But if he mistimed it by as much as a second they'd run, seek protection from the CIA or whoever it was who were now responsible for maintaining their security. Couldn't have that; risk that. If he lost them this time he wouldn't get another chance. If he got the timing wrong he could even be rearrested. Returned to the piss-stinking, ass-fucking nether world of a prison. Could never do that. Would rather kill himself than go back to that. *Would* kill himself. Not hesitate for a moment. Wouldn't happen, though. Couldn't happen. He had them at his mercy. Except there wouldn't be any mercy. Any escape. They wouldn't know it was him, not until it was too late, when they couldn't do anything about it. That's when he'd string it out, let them know it was him. Keep them prisoners maybe, to gloat over their helplessness. Ensure they couldn't escape, though. Break their legs, so they couldn't run. Their arms, as well, so they couldn't fight back, couldn't do anything.

'You want a refill?'

Mason physically, obviously, jumped at the presence beside him of the waitress, a young, blonde, milk-fed kid most likely working her way through college. 'I was thinking. Miles away. You startled me.'

'You all right?' She appeared genuinely concerned.

'Sure. Just thinking of things, like I said. A refill would be good.'

'Looking at the history?' She smiled, nodding down at the brochures on the table beside him. 'Gettysburg's worth visiting. It's quite close.'

'I might well do that.' Mason smiled back. What the fuck was he doing? He'd attracted attention to himself, losing control – forgetting where he was – and jerking up like a frightened cat at not being aware she was beside him. She'd remember it, make a story of it to other kids that night. Mason was hot with embarrassed fury, hoping he wasn't too obviously red faced.

'You sure you're OK?'

'Absolutely fine.' He had to get out, to minimize it so there was as little as possible for her to remember; certainly not enough from which to describe and identify him.

'You staying locally?' the girl persisted.

Fuck off, go bother someone else with your coffee refills! 'Don't plan to. Just passing through and thought I'd take a look-see.'

'There's some hotels, a couple of motels, if you change your mind.'

'I'll remember that.'

'Enjoy,' she said, finally moving on.

Mason forced himself to remain at the table, hunched over the unread tourist guides to obscure his face as much as possible, knowing she'd be curious if he left the coffee he'd accepted. He gestured for his check the moment he'd finished and carefully counted out a fifteen percent tip, neither too little nor too much to give her something else to remember him by.

'Maybe see you again if you decide to stay?' She smiled, as he rose to leave.

'Maybe,' Mason said. He didn't pause directly outside the cafe, striding away to get out of sight and hopefully out of her mind. Wrong to overestimate the incident, he tried to re-assure himself. From strictly professional standards – the standards he had to maintain at all times and never for a moment forget – it shouldn't have happened. But it had only been a friendly kid trying to do her job, nothing more. If it had a relevance it was as a warning against his hanging around too long in one place or getting lost in reverie again.

Out of sight of the cafe Mason curbed the impulse to continue hurrying, although he didn't linger, either. When he got into the Yaris he realized, angry again, that he'd forgotten the route to Hill Avenue and needed to consult the map again.

Like Frederick itself, the location of the house was bad for Mason's purpose but well chosen for Slater's. It was a two storey, white painted clapboard, with an attached, single-storey garage at the end of a wide drive, now empty. At that time of the morning so was the avenue itself, stretching totally straight for at least five hundred yards – maybe more – on either side of number 2832, with no intervening cross section or street offering the slightest safe place for surveillance. Slater's house stood alone on its two or three acre plot, as did every house in the street deserted even of animals. Some of the proper-ties, although not Slater's, had trees or expansive shrubs in their gardens and there were some trees at the road edge, too. There were no dropped leaves around any of them. There were a few lawn sprinklers operating, but Mason couldn't detect a single abandoned child's bicycle, buggy or toy. Every front lawn was manicured and sharply shovel-edged. As he got closer to Slater's house Mason isolated the CCTV mountings and the separate lenses at the porch and the garage entrance he guessed to be for visitor-identifying TV cameras. Mason's spirits – and his expectation – lifted at the sight of the basket-ball hoop on the side of the garage. So they had a kid, maybe more than one. Certainly a boy, because he didn't think girls played basketball. If the boy or boys played basketball they were of school age. He could hurt Slater and Ann far more than he'd first hoped, because he'd always planned that if there were kids they'd be the first to go. He didn't have to turn his head as he passed the house to count the three separate front door locks, one big enough to be a deadlock, guessing there'd be additional inner chains or maybe even bars.

Mason drove along and around four of the streets at the end of Hill Avenue without locating a school bus drop, then retraced his route down the road that ran parallel behind Slater's house, separated from its rear neighbour by a high, unbroken hedge. He located the school pick-up on the street that formed a T-junction at the bottom. Fifty yards further along that street was a small neighbourhood shopping precinct with a shaded car park behind. He checked it out to decide upon the most concealed spot for later, and bought a *Newsweek* magazine at the convenient 7-Eleven.

Mason spent a further hour thoroughly reconnoitring the entire area around Slater's house until he was satisfied he knew every approach and exit street before driving back towards the town and stopping at a tavern he'd isolated on his way out. With the coffee shop mistake still in the fore-front of his mind Mason chose what he considered the most unobtrusive booth. He took his time with a beer studying the menu and drank another with his scrod. Fish had been a rarity in the penitentiary and a preference since he'd been released.

Mason wasn't sure what time schools let out so he was back in his already chosen and fortunately near empty parking spot behind the shopping precinct by three p.m. He remained hidden beneath a tree clump and behind his magazine, alert for each and every movement on the outside street, reacting immediately when the easily identified yellow school bus finally passed. Mason was already on the cross street before the children were disgorged, in no hurry to close the gap between himself and the kids when he saw there were a few waiting mothers.

Mason pulled himself into the cover of one of the street-edged trees that never seemed to lose their leaves, straining intently to recognize Ann, trying to adjust his recollection of his former wife who had cheated and then abandoned him so many years ago, striving to imagine how she would have changed, how she might have physically altered, under cosmetic surgery even, hairstyle and colouring almost inevitably different. Mason scrutinized every waiting mother before determining that Ann was not among them.

By that time the children whose mothers were not there had moved off, either in groups or individually, in every direction. Mason was only interested in those moving in the direction of Hill Avenue SE. A group of five backpacked kids – two girls and three boys, one of the boys much taller than the rest – was headed in this direction, followed by three individual stragglers. At the junction with Hill Avenue they all paused, as Mason briefly did in the shadow of another convenient tree, for the customary pushing and shoving farewell of children in their eighth or ninth grade. Mason's hesitation was only momentary. They were still jostling when he emerged in his recovered Yaris, letting traffic he could have beaten pass in front of him while he waited for the group to break up. Only when they did, three boys and one girl turning into Hill Avenue, did Mason consider moving and then, frustratingly, not for at least five minutes because of a sudden build-up of vehicles that didn't stop to let him out. By the time he finally emerged, all the children had dispersed and none were in sight when he turned into the empty avenue on which Slater, Ann and their offspring lived. Mason felt fresh frustration until, still about three hundred yards from the marked house, the unusually tall boy he'd already identified emerged palming a basketball rapidly against the ground, his other arm arced against imaginary opponents, ducking and weaving to the hoop to do basket loops and drops.

This wasn't the only thing Mason saw. At the bottom of Slater's drive, parked to allow the boy room for his practice, was a pale green Ford Focus. Once again without showing any obvious interest, like moving his head to look pointedly at the house or the car, Mason registered the licence plate number as he passed, without slowing, easily able from his previous assimilation of the area to pick up the route back to Washington without again needing to go back along Hill Avenue SE.

Apart from the coffee shop incident, the danger of which he was already minimizing, Mason decided it had been an extremely productive and worthwhile day. He wondered what the name was of the gangling boy who was going to be the first to die.

It was another letter, to his office not their Hill Avenue home, and in no way as unsettling as the warning of Mason's release had been, but Slater knew at once the effect it would have upon Ann and tried to forestall it. He miscalculated the time difference with San Jose and had to wait a further hour before there was anyone to talk to at the corporate headquarters of the kitchen furnishing franchise who had accepted his quote for the mall development. He had a carefully rehearsed argument that they could surely discuss and refine everything by telephone, fax and FedEx, but this was interrupted by their argument that the point of the invitation for a personal meeting with their development division was not primarily concerned with the Frederick contract, which they'd already agreed, but to discuss further commissions in other, predominantly southern, states. Slater promised to call them back the following day.

Once again Slater waited until they'd eaten and David had gone to bed before disclosing the approach to Ann. She listened, head bent, until he finished before saying, 'You couldn't get to San Jose and back in one day. It would take three, at least.'

'I might be able to manage it in two,' he said.

'Three,' she insisted. 'Maybe even four.'

'There's no danger; he can't . . .'

'I know.'

'I really could do it in three days, at the outside. I've checked the flights, worked it out.'

'Why can't you do it by fax? Emailing attachments?'

'I've already told you, my darling. It isn't this contract. They want to talk about different expansions, in a lot of other states. This could be a breakthrough.'

'I didn't think we wanted a breakthrough, to get any bigger than we are already? We make enough, between the business and the gallery. You could be recognized if you got any bigger.'

Slater shook his head. 'No one's going to recognize me, after all this time. That's all over. I can't turn it down; it could guarantee things for a long time. Set us up comfortably.'

'We're already set up comfortably enough. You could turn it down if you wanted to.'

'I don't want to turn it down!' The words blurted out, too quickly – too unthinkingly loud – for Slater to bite them back.

Ann remained with her head lowered, refusing to meet his look.

Slater said, 'If I don't go – for just three days – Jack Mason will have beaten us. We got over our problems in the beginning and you came to believe, do believe now, that we wouldn't be hurt by Moscow. We built a good life – a perfect life – but made silly mistakes when we learned Mason was being released. He can't remain forever between us, eroding us until we break up, which is what you told me could have happened if we'd let it, just a few weeks ago. But we didn't let it happen then and won't let it happen now. He's out of our lives forever. Couldn't find us even if he wanted to. You hear what I'm saying? Accept what I'm saying?'

Ann remained silent, not looking at him, for a long time. Then she said, 'Three days?'

'Just three days,' promised Slater.

Eleven

S he had to be strong, Ann decided. Just as she'd decided so long ago that she had to be. Not just strong. Deceptively, overly strong, so that David didn't detect her inner, churning weakness; Daniel, either, when he called from San Jose, which he'd promised to do as often as he could, either here at the house or at the gallery during the day. It wasn't weakness, Ann argued with herself. She knew what no one else did: knew how relentless and cruel and violent – close to madness – Jack could be; had been, to her, a virtual torturer who got something like sexual pleasure he never gained in his near-rape lovemaking but instead from the beatings. She felt physically sick now at remembering his often repeated threat, his favourite: *You ever do anything to screw me, fight me back, you know what I'll do? I'll take your face right off, make you uglier than you already are. Think what that would be like, being someone with no face.* There'd been slave-like humiliations, as well. The humiliation of parading his mistresses and whores during their overseas postings in Eastern Europe – even bringing some of them to their house and making her cook and serve table to them and then dismissing her to the guest room while he slept with the other woman in their bed. She found it difficult now to believe she'd endured everything to keep intact a marriage in which Jack had been so totally disinterested, apart from the torture he could inflict. She hadn't really found escape in the bottle; no matter how drunk – drunk even to the point of unconsciousness – she'd got there'd always been a whimpering voice in her mind asking why she didn't give up. It was Jack's voice who answered that, in his bellowing, kicking, beating voice telling her that he'd kill her if she talked to a divorce lawyer or a marriage counsellor, and perhaps because he'd beaten her for so long and told her that so often – brainwashed her so completely – she still believed those words now, this night and every night since he'd been arrested and as she would every night still to come until . . . until she didn't know when.

Something else that Ann knew was that she wasn't brave. Over the years, with Daniel, she'd rationalized that, believing in his love and care and encouragement had made her stronger – strong enough to start up her own art gallery – than she had been, but deep down she feared that she would never, ever, be confrontationally brave. If she'd been brave she wouldn't have become a slave to Jack as she had. She'd have fought back, just walked away into the unknown rather than endure what she had gone through with Jack Mason after he'd declared he couldn't stand her any longer with her constant cringing, clutching humility. But she really had been the orphan David believed her to be, an abandoned-at-birth illegitimate who'd only ever known orphanages and institutions and any home, even the home with Jack, was better than the total, frightening unknown.

She wished Daniel would call, as he'd promised, immediately annoyed at the thought because from the schedule he'd carefully written out, complete with telephone numbers and addresses and hotel reservations, she knew his plane wasn't due to land in New Mexico for another two hours. She guessed it would be at least two hours – maybe three – beyond that before he would have booked into the Marriott and made his business calls and was finally able to ring her. She had to be careful nothing showed in her voice: certainly not the gin. She stirred the ice in the drink, which would be weakened when it melted. Only this one. She could easily handle just one. Destroy the lime in the disposal and have the glass washed and put away long before David got home. And she wouldn't again leave Jean by herself in the gallery all afternoon, as she had today, knowing that Daniel couldn't call when he was travelling. Just this one afternoon and just this one drink. Or maybe just one more.

Daniel was right, as he was always right. Jack would never find them: that's what the protection programme was for, to give them the new life they had and make sure no one would or could ever find them. Unlike Jack, Daniel had never cheated her, in any way. That very first night he'd told her who he really was – 'Because I love you and always want to be with you I am trusting you with my life by what I am going to tell you' – a Russian spy supervising her traitor husband, and he'd warned that the KGB would try to find and kill him for defecting. Which they hadn't been able to do. If the then biggest, most omnipotent and vengeful spy organization in existence hadn't found them, what chance did one solitary man have, no longer even with the resources of the CIA? For all his beating and punching, Jack was a soft man, a find-the-easy-way-out-of-trouble man, not able to look after himself, survive under any pressure, like Daniel. Prison would have been hell for him, the sort of unbearable hell in which she'd existed as his slave wife. Prison would have broken him, crushed out of him any thought of revenge. Ann hadn't thought of it like that before and was angry that she'd let her fear be amorphous, without properly reasoning it through. But now she had and everything made complete, logical sense, and a rarely experienced self-confidence, not something imbued by Daniel, surged through her. And it was from complete, sensible reasoning, not the gin.

She had just one more, enjoying it as a celebration, raising her glass in an imaginary toast, proud of herself for stopping then. She destroyed the lime wedge and washed and polished the tumbler before putting it away. She spent a further hour going through the schedule for the forthcoming provincial exhibition she hadn't anticipated being asked to stage of a visiting French artist who had achieved some recognition from a prestigious gallery in Manhattan. She decided to retain until its start the display advertisement she had already run for a week in the *Frederick News-Post*, stoking her wavering confidence by making a decision without discussing it with Daniel first. She had her call transferred from the advertising department to the news desk, who assured her they intended covering her show with a photographer as well as their art critic. There was a possibility they might also run a feature, showing a selection of the paintings, in their weekend supplement. And finally she cleaned her teeth for the second time and rinsed her mouth with a breath freshener.

Ann had everything already out of the refrigerator when David arrived home from school. She said, 'You're the man of the house looking after me while Dad's away and I thought the man of the house could barbecue some burgers and hot dogs.'

'You look happy,' said the boy.

'I am,' agreed Ann.

'So am I, very happy indeed,' said David.

Ann let him make a game of it, feigning irritation when David wouldn't tell her what his news was, all the while enjoying, and comparing, his laughing excitement against the sullenness of a few weeks ago, glad that had gone just as her newly rationalized fear had gone. The boy strung it out until after they'd eaten, working hard to appear cool and un-impressed when he finally announced, 'Met a guy at school today.'

'Oh yeah?' said Ann, playing cool in return, her back to him as she stacked the dishwasher.

'Someone from the university.'

'University?'

'The University of Maryland.'

Ann turned to her son, feeling the first stir of uncertainty despite that afternoon's resolution. 'Someone from the University of Maryland came to school today?'

'To see me.'

Ann was confident the principal wouldn't have allowed someone he didn't know come into the school and talk to David, certainly not after the recent upheaval. But there should have been some communication in advance. 'What about?'

The boy couldn't retain the coolness. It came out in a blurted torrent of initially unconnected words. There was a name – Jeb Stout – a black guy, played major league, snapped Achilles, became a scout, had got a recommendation, seen him play, had been impressed . . .

'Woa, woa,' stopped Ann, raising her hands, palm outwards against the rush. 'Someone called Jeb Stout, who used to play major league until he got injured, came to school today to talk to you about basketball?'

'That's what I just said,' insisted the boy. 'He said he'd watched me play. That I could be good, very good. That I could get a sports scholarship, even . . .'

'To the University of Maryland?'

'That's what he said.' At last David hurried to his backpack and offered Ann an envelope.

There were two letters, one from Victor Spalding introducing the second, which bore a university letterhead, signed by Jeb Stout and asking for a meeting with David's parents to discuss their son's sports prowess.

Ann reached out, hugged him and said, 'Wow! We could have a famous son!' Through whom she and Daniel could be recognized and identified, she immediately thought. Spalding should very definitely have asked their permission before letting David meet the scout.

'What do you think?' asked David, eagerly.

'I think we've got an awful lot to talk about and consider,' said Ann. 'You haven't even got through high school yet.'

David's face crumpled. 'You mean I can't!'

'I don't mean that at all. I mean Dad and I have got to talk about it, with you. Then we've got to talk to the principal and Jeb Stout . . .' Ann offered David the university letter. 'And after all that we've got to decide what would be the best for you. That's the only thing that really interests your dad and me – what's best, the very best, for you.'

'But you're not saying no?'

'You heard what I'm saying. I'm very proud of you and I know Dad is going to be, when we tell him later. And I guess Mr Spalding and a lot of people at school are proud of you, too.'

'I want to be a major league basketball player,' declared the boy.

Slater didn't call until after ten, Eastern time and Ann let their son take the phone in another eruption of disconnected words that took as much time as before to link together. Throughout the to and fro Ann sat studying the child she'd never thought capable of conceiving, after the gynaecologist's prognosis following the miscarriage caused by Mason's beating, feeling the pride and love and satisfaction and other emotions she couldn't identify move through her.

When she finally regained the phone Slater said, 'What about this then?'

Conscious of David's attention Ann said, 'Isn't it exciting!'

'Unbelievable! You OK?'

'Fine. Why'd you ask?'

'I phoned the gallery from the plane, just before I landed. Jean said you'd taken the afternoon off.'

So little had they travelled by air that Ann had forgotten about in-flight telephone facilities. 'It was quiet and I wanted to concentrate upon the exhibition,' said Ann, easily recovering. 'I've decided to extend the advertising until the opening. The *News-Post* are going to cover it. Maybe do something in their weekend edition as well.'

Ann sounded all right, Slater thought. 'So that was all it was?'

'What else could it have been!' She'd checked the house CCTV playback but not that at the gallery because she'd left early, she suddenly remembered. She'd have to do it first thing tomorrow.

His had been a careless question, conceded Slater. 'Just wanted to make sure everything was all right.'

'Fixed your meetings?'

'Starting with breakfast at eight tomorrow.'

'So you might . . .' started Ann but stopped. That wasn't important any longer: she had everything sorted out, everything in proportion.

'Might what?'

'Get a good idea of what the contracts could be worth?' Ann finished.

'A ballpark figure,' agreed Slater, deciding it would be a mistake to press any further. 'What do you think about David's news?'

'There's a lot for us to talk about, think about.'

'It could be a hell of an opportunity for him.'

'I know. We'll go through it all when you get back.'

'It sounds good about your exhibition, too.'

'I hope so,' said Ann.

'Everything's on the up, like I told you it was going to be.'

'Right!' agreed Ann, believing it. 'Everything's on the up.'

Which was what Jack Mason was thinking, although not in those precise words. He'd achieved far more than he'd imagined possible in such a short time, most of it through his own clever, well-trained determination. Some of this was due to luck, that he felt he deserved, and this luck had held, ensuring everything he'd planned hadn't been destroyed by an accident he couldn't possibly have anticipated or prevented. In fact everything was on the plus side, nothing on the loss.

After only two days he knew every route into and away from 2832 Hill Avenue SE. He knew every outside precaution and protection Slater had installed, from which he could devise an entry if he decided upon one, which so far he hadn't. But that if he did, the approach couldn't be from the rear because the hedge separating Slater's house from its rear neighbour was too high and too thick. He knew that Slater and Ann had just one child, much taller for his age than any other kid in his class, who Mason estimated from seeing him get off the school bus to be either in the eighth or ninth grade. The kid obviously liked sport, basketball particularly, which was scarcely surprising considering his height. From that day's extended surveillance Mason knew the location of the school and all its approaches and the exact time the kid got on and off the school bus. And from his telephone check of the licence plate on the light green Ford, purporting to be an aggrieved driver with whom it had been involved in a minor, unreported car park knock, he knew it to be registered to Ann Slater, which told him he still had Slater's vehicle to identify. And he knew, from studying the tourist office brochures and reading that day's edition of the *Frederick News-Post* when he'd got back to Guest Quarters, how incredibly lucky he'd been not to have come face to face with his former wife.

He'd flicked through the brochures first, his initial celebratory highball at hand, not immediately registering the art exhibition flyer beyond the purple, yellow and orange daubs of the chosen illustration which was reproduced in the newspaper advertisement. It was only when he idly went back to the better reproduction of the glossier flyer that Ann's name, as the gallery proprietor, glared out at him, as well as the Main Street address. And from its number he realized that he'd walked by it twice, on his way to and from the cafe in which he'd had the unsettling coffee refill episode. All it would have needed for everything to go wrong would have been for

Ann to have been looking out of the gallery window on either occasion.

And then he remembered – or thought he remembered – a CCTV pod.

Twelve

It hadn't been a mistaken recollection: what it was, could far too easily become, was a disaster of his own unthinking stupidity. He'd been too concerned about an unimportant upset, again of his own stupid creation, over an inconsequential encounter with a college kid waitress, which meant he hadn't bothered – hadn't thought! – to check the security precautions in the town, which he should have, at all times and in each and every circumstance, considered to be enemy territory. It didn't matter – wasn't an escape or an excuse – that he hadn't known at the time that his former wife was now the proprietor of an art gallery. Hadn't he thought of Frederick – in which he *knew* Slater and Ann were living – to be a small town in which everyone knew everyone else? Shouldn't he therefore have taken every conceivable, professional precaution to avoid being technically, forensically, identified?

There were two easily visible CCTV monitors expertly positioned to scan not just everyone passing in either direction in front of Ann's gallery but also angled to picture passing vehicles and pedestrians going in both directions on the other side of Main Street. Mason, now – too late – well out of range, felt a sink of despair. What would be the loop length of the constantly revolving recording tape? One day? Mason wasn't sure but he didn't think current technology went longer than twenty-four hours before being wiped, by re-recording. It was an immaterial question. His image, front and back, would have been registered from a proximity too close to be anything but pin sharp. What about the possibility of being obstructed by the people around him? He couldn't remember, not sufficiently to believe there could be any doubt. It had been comparatively early mid-morning when he got to the town, not a lot of people on the sidewalk. More later, when he'd hurried out, anxious to get away. Less visibly obvious then. Perhaps. Perhaps not. He was clutching at straws – less than straws, threads – to hope that either Ann or Slater, the two people who probably knew him better than any other living person, wouldn't instantly identify him.

Caught by the thought, Mason looked hurriedly around for stake-out cars or obvious groups maintaining protective surveillance, but saw nothing that alarmed him, just as quickly accepting another stupidity. Why would there have been protective surveillance? He wasn't committing any offence, being in the same town as his ex-wife and her new husband, a former KGB officer. No one knew – could even suspect – that he had any way of knowing where they had been relocated, although his being in the same town stretched coincidence almost beyond breaking point. Which didn't matter. There was no proof that he was aware of it being their hometown.

However, he was suddenly aware of a serious contradiction to this thinking: he'd saved on his laptop back at Guest Quarters the illegal codes and passwords that gave him access to the websites of White Deer, the two parole officers and their ghost servers, and the lawyer, Patrick Bell. And even if he wiped them an expert computer technician would be easily able to recover it all from his hard drive. The pendulum swung again. But there was no legal justification for seizing that laptop and testing it, although from his years within the CIA Mason knew that legal justification wouldn't be a barrier if Langley chose to search his equipment. But why should they? He continued to try to reassure himself. This prompted another question: assuming – as he logically had to assume – that he would undoubtedly have been recognized by Slater and Ann, what would they do? Run to someone in authority, obviously. But who? Mason knew he'd done very well – very well indeed – discovering as much as he had through his computer infiltration, but it hadn't provided any indication of Slater still having a case officer at the CIA. Yes it had, came another quick contradiction. The approach to White Deer from someone named J. Peebles, with a Justice Department cover, had to be some sort of CIA link. Could he risk trying to hack in to Peebles' website? It would very definitely be a risk. Even when he'd been a serving agent the CIA had taken every precaution against being

electronically penetrated, not just erecting supposedly impass-
able firewalls but setting up tracer traps through which they
could track and identify anyone trying to get into their systems,
even trying to piggyback the entry through an unsuspecting
'cut-out' system into which he could initially hack. Too great
a risk at this stage, Mason decided. But there could be another
way. Glynis Needham would more than likely be brought in
if Slater scuttled to his new masters for help. He'd confirmed
what he'd needed to confirm here in Frederick, at least for the
time being. Now he had more important things to do – certainly
things hopefully to discover or from which to get guidance –
back in Washington DC.

Despite his anxiety Mason still detoured to drive along Hill
Avenue, which was still as immaculately sterile as on all his
previous journeys up and down. There were no cars in the
driveway of the Slaters' house. Before he actually passed in
front Mason lowered both sun visors of the car – today a
black Ford – and at the moment of doing so averted his face
as far away from the CCTV cameras as he considered it safe
to do. He checked the two adjacent streets as well, satisfying
himself that there was no guarding surveillance.

He chose the Beltway, which was a mistake because it was
clogged with a mid-morning build-up that twice brought him
to an irritating standstill, and it was well past noon by the
time he reached Guest Quarters.

As he walked into the lobby the receptionist said, 'You just
missed a call,' and handed over the message slip that she had
been writing.

Glynis Needham's number was written on it. There was a
tick in the 'call back' box.

It was impossible for Mason to set all the intrusion traps he
would have liked because there was a daily maid and linen
change service to the apartment, but from the moment of his
arrival he'd imposed as many as were feasible, arranging the
cooking utensils and crockery in such a way that he would
have instantly known if they'd been disturbed and since
acquiring the laptop he'd left it suspended by its carrying-case
strap in a specific, half-secured manner in the clothes closet
with the additional precaution of a cotton wisp trapped in its
zipper and another on a specific page in the unnecessary instruction manual.

Nothing had been moved or disturbed.

On the drive back from Frederick, Mason had mentally planned the precautions he had to take, which the parole officer's attempted approach didn't in any way affect; rather it increased the need for him checking his schedule before returning her call. He accessed his Trojan Horse within Glynis Needham's computer system and double-checked every communication that had passed through it since his release. There was nothing he had not already read. Neither was there in his other cyberspace stables at the penitentiary; John Peebles' personal record request was still the only item from anyone who could have any conceivable link with Langley; and nothing from Patrick Bell. Nor was there anything new or alarming ensnared in either of the ghost server filters between the two parole sites in DC or California.

During this check, Mason split his concentration, intent as he worked to assess his own physical and mental reactions; he was encouraged by what he gauged from both. He was understandably – properly – worried, but by no means panicked by the uncertainties crowding in upon him. It was time to try to remove at least one of those uncertainties.

The parole officer picked up her receiver on his second ring with a curt 'Needham' identification. He hadn't intended any suggestion of mockery in responding 'Mason' but realized too late it could have been construed as such.

'Thought you might have called,' she said.

'We're not due to meet until Friday.' It was scheduled for the morning, early enough for him to make the New York shuttle for the afternoon collection of the Adam Peterson chequebook, bank and Visa cards.

'What about the compensation claim?'

Was that all her call was about, the fucking empty threat against Frank Howitt! 'That's between me and my lawyer.'

'Jack! What more can there possibly be between you and your lawyer that you haven't talked about and decided already?'

'I've had an idea, from when we last talked.' Which wasn't a lie. It occurred to him at that very moment and he could string things out for as long as it took for Chambers to get out of prison. It was satisfying – very satisfying indeed – to think on his feet like this, as quickly as this, with the CCTV problem still unresolved.

'What's the idea?'

'I need to talk to my lawyer. Get his opinion. It's all got to be official.'

'Jack, you're not just jerking my chain here, are you? Prolonging things just to be difficult?'

'I'm considering suing the penitentiary, not you. How are you involved?'

Glynis Needham paused, her awareness of her mistake obvious. 'I'm responsible for your complete rehabilitation. I've told you how that's likely to be affected by your decision.'

'I'll see what my lawyer says.'

'What have you been doing with yourself?' asked the woman, anxious to move on.

Mason easily avoided the instinctive retort that he'd just been driving around; as far as Glynis Needham knew he didn't possess a driving licence. 'Breathing a lot of fresh air. Eating decent food.'

'What about California?'

'That's for us to talk about on Friday.'

'I've already talked to someone there.'

I know, thought Mason. 'That's good. I appreciate it.'

'Until Friday then?'

'I look forward to it,' said Mason, honestly.

When Mason called Patrick Bell the lawyer suggested a Friday meeting but agreed to bring it forward upon Mason's assurance it wouldn't take long. Although he was sure he'd memorized the code and passwords to get into his illegal Trojan Horses, Mason copied them all on a piece of paper before deleting them from his laptop. He zipped the *Frederick News-Post* and the collected brochures and flyers inside the laptop case and carried it with him to return the Ford to the Budget outlet on Wisconsin Avenue. He walked back into Georgetown, disposing of the newspaper and brochures in separate street garbage bins. He was tensed for a challenge, his story of taking a wrong turn already prepared, even though the waste ground near the canoe club appeared deserted. None came. He waited in the shadow of the Key Bridge for several minutes, assuring himself he really was alone, before hurling the computer beneath the bridge, grateful for the overhead rumble of traffic that drowned the sound of the splash. He remained where he was for several more minutes, checking everything around him, before hurrying back the way he had come. He stuffed the empty computer case into another bin just before regaining M Street. He took his time with another highball in a bar he hadn't yet used on Jefferson Drive before going back to the mall on M Street to buy another laptop identical to the one he'd bought there earlier and just thrown into the Potomac.

All he had to do now if he were questioned about his having been in Frederick was to lie and plead ignorance of his ever having been there and Mason knew himself to be an expert in doing both.

Daniel Slater was sure from his intelligence career psychology instruction that he was making a good impression. The breakfast meeting had very obviously been a filtering process, testing his technical expertise, which he knew he'd passed when it concluded with his being asked to attend a fuller, until then unannounced meeting that same afternoon. There he was introduced to the technical resources manager and two assistants and shown the provisional plans for developments under consideration during the next two years in San Diego, Dallas Fort Worth and Austin. The detailed discussions ran over two hours; Slater aware throughout that there was still an overnight flight he could get, but which he decided against when the department head invited him to dinner. Slater didn't want his assurances of regular on-site supervision at every intended expansion put into question by refusing because he wanted to return to Frederick as soon as possible.

Slater had called Ann before the breakfast meeting and knew from the tone of her voice then that she didn't feel herself under any pressure but he wasn't so sure when he telephoned that evening, before the dinner.

'Is there a problem?' he demanded.

'Of course not. Why should there be?'

'Just thought you sounded a little different.'

'It's been a long day,' said Ann, prepared if he pressed. 'Don't forget the time it is here.'

'Why a long day?'

'The exhibition, of course!' She hadn't intended the sharpness and regretted it.

'I'm sorry.' Was her explanation sufficient? 'How's David?'

'Good. I took him to basketball practice.'

'How was it?'

'OK, as far as I could tell. He's in bed, asleep already. All he can talk about is us seeing this guy from Maryland University.'

'I want to talk it through with Spalding first. Call the school for me, will you? Set up a meeting.'

'When for?'

'Any time after tomorrow.'

'I'll call first thing. How did it go there?'

'Better than I could have hoped. I guess there are others being considered but we've gone pretty deeply into things: discussed plans and dates, stuff like that . . .' Slater hesitated before adding, 'We've even talked of my doing some on-site supervision.'

'Going away, you mean?'

'Only for a day or two. This could be big for us.'

'That's good.'

'You and David could maybe come with me if it coincides with school vacations. Jean can handle things at the gallery by herself for a couple of days, can't she?'

'I guess.'

'I thought you'd be more excited. We're talking a comfortable future here.'

'I'm pleased, really. Very pleased. I'm tired.'

'I was thinking about vacations today, even before the meeting. We could easily afford somewhere.'

'Where?'

'Anywhere. Disney Land, Disney World, Yellowstone. Spread our wings a little. Tell David it was his reward for the basketball approach.'

'We'll talk about it when you get back. It'll be tomorrow, won't it?'

'First available flight. I'll be back by mid-afternoon.'

'That's good.'

Slater wished she'd stop saying everything was good. 'You sure you're OK? You're not upset about anything?'

'I told you I'm fine.' Too sharp again, she thought, hearing her own voice.

'I'll look in at the office on my way home. Mary Ellen says

everything's quiet, which is good.' Now he was using the damned word!

'Best of luck for tonight.'

'I might even hear something.'

'I look forward to your telling me all about it tomorrow.'

Ann had taken the call in Slater's den and stayed there, feeling safe because there weren't any outside windows, although she'd got over the fear during the day, hunched during most of it in her equally windowless gallery office after trying, unaccustomed to the system and how to operate it, to run back the CCTV loop. She was looking for excuses, saying she was unaccustomed to it, Ann forced herself to admit. She'd let the reel run too long by not checking it before taking the previous afternoon off, so a lot had been wiped off due to the automatic rewind and the first of the surviving images that had initially frozen her with fear had been partially lost, too indistinct for her to be positive.

But a lot of what she had seen reminded her of Jack.

At first sight – and during the several repeated playbacks – Ann had been totally convinced that it was her former husband and that he'd been there, directly outside the gallery. But then she'd imposed the control, that all too easily fluctuating control, and looked several times more and a lot closer and accepted that it couldn't be. The picture was of the back of a man walking past the gallery, nothing of his face visible at all. He'd been wearing jeans and a windbreaker and his head was slightly hunched forward, as if he were in a hurry. The shape was definitely wrong for it to have been Jack. The image on the film was of someone far thinner, more obviously fitter, than Jack had ever been and the man's shoulders were far broader. The hair was shorter, too, and lighter, although because the film was black and white she couldn't determine whether it was grey or blonde. What she had determined, during the course of an unsettled day, was that it was a remarkable resemblance, but nothing more – nothing to cause her the initial terror – than that.

It certainly wasn't anything to talk to Daniel about. She'd recovered her composure now – and the conviction that there was no way her former husband could ever find her – and she didn't want Daniel to think she could collapse as easily as she'd collapsed before the moment he was away on a trip.

And he might go away again. She also didn't want him to know that after demanding all the security devices, she'd carelessly – stupidly – forgotten to check them.

She wouldn't forget again, though, neither here nor at the gallery. A lot of her newly recovered confidence came from having followed the resolution that evening. There'd been nothing whatsoever suspicious anywhere around the house; she'd only counted a total of ten cars going up and down Hill Avenue the entire day.

Ann decided to have just one more drink before going to bed. It would only be her third and she was still in complete control. She'd better buy a replacement bottle of gin to prevent Daniel noticing that the level of the one in the house for guests had gone down.

Thirteen

S later spent a long time with Mary Ellen – wearing yet another home-knit sweater and making side notes to herself to avoid mistakes – dictating the first draft of his memorandum to the San Jose kitchen furnishing chain confirming all that had been agreed during his visit, correcting and rephrasing it before he was finally satisfied that nothing had been overlooked. On his way in from the airport the previous afternoon he'd picked up the two enquiries that had come in while he had been away and went through them overnight. Sure he could fulfil both without any conflict with those he'd already accepted, Slater quoted for those as well but was still able to cross town to meet Ann for lunch before their scheduled meeting with the school principal. David had become subdued at dinner the previous night when he'd realized the Maryland sports coach wasn't being included and after they had ordered their lunch Ann said, 'He doesn't think we're going to go along with it.'

'I told him that wasn't so, that we were working through it properly.' Slater had been very alert to Ann's mood the previous night, deciding that he'd misjudged her tone on the telephone from New Mexico, but had been surprised five minutes earlier when she'd ordered gin and tonic with her club sandwich and that her glass was already half empty. She'd only ever drunk hard booze with a meal when she was in a mess with Jack.

'I know,' said Ann. 'He wants to be a sports star. It's the only thing he's thinking about.'

'What's he going to do when he's thirty-five and his legs have gone?'

'He's just fourteen and can't imagine what it's going to be like to be thirty-five.' She sipped her drink.

'I'll talk him through it.'

'I think he expected to be included in this afternoon's meeting, too.'

'He's just fourteen,' echoed Slater. 'He'll be included if and when it's right for him to be, not before.'

'We mustn't forget what happened. How he misunderstood and was stupid and could have got himself stabbed . . . killed even.'

'I'm not forgetting anything,' insisted Slater. 'Certainly nothing to do with the knife. Nor will I use it – will we use it – to provide excuses.'

'I think we should be careful with him.'

Slater hadn't expected the conversation to be as intense. 'We'll discuss it all,' he promised. 'I won't do anything – make any decision – without talking it through with you first. We'll bring up David as we've always done, together.'

'I don't want to tilt him off balance.'

When the waitress brought their sandwiches Ann ordered another drink. Slater stayed with his one glass of Chardonnay, which he'd scarcely touched. He said, 'So there were no problems when I was away?'

'None,' said Ann, shortly. She'd considered telling him about the sighting of the man with the similarity to Mason the previous evening but decided against it. She wished that she hadn't ordered the second drink but it was too late now.

Slater hesitated, undecided. Then he said, 'You didn't have any problems with the CCTV?'

'Why do you ask that?'

'It's a system you're not familiar with.'

'I got on OK,' said Ann, unable to remember the last time she'd consciously lied to him. The second gin tasted weaker than the first. It was an old bartender's trick to make the first one strong for the taste and strength to become assimilated and then short-measure after that.

'So you felt comfortable with my being away?'

'No,' denied Ann, positively. 'I told you I was OK.'

Slater determinedly steered the conversation on to the forthcoming exhibition, listening to Ann's plans to employ caterers and a publicist for the opening night. 'And I thought you could help with some physical security. Not personally, I don't mean. There must be a local firm that could supply guards.'

The remark reminded Slater that as soon as he got a response from San Jose he needed to set things up with the installers to whom he sub-contracted the actual fitting, to ensure they had people available when the work came on stream. One of the San Jose insistences had been stringent penalty clauses against delays. 'You think that's necessary?'

'Andre Worlack is a minimalist who paints under some magnification system to achieve postage stamp detail. That's what's attracted all the attention in New York and why his work is fetching up to a thousand and more for each canvas . . . each or any of which could be fitted into a coat pocket.'

'Sounds like you could do with some more internal camera security as well?'

'I think I could. I'm seeing an insurance assessor soon, to discuss temporarily increasing my cover. Extra cameras might be an insistence.'

Was that what she really meant? Or a need she'd felt while he'd been away that had hardened in her mind when he'd told her he'd have to make other trips? 'I'll have the assessor's meeting with you, to sort it all out at the time,' Slater suggested.

Ann had finished eating but was looking at her empty glass and Slater was sure she was debating whether to order a third.

'I'd hoped you would,' she replied.

Why hadn't she simply asked him? 'You want some coffee? We've got time.'

Ann looked away from her glass. 'Sure.'

As Slater gestured for their waitress Ann said, 'I think we might have a problem.'

At last, thought Slater. 'What?'

'I had a call from Worlack's publicist, asking if I'd sent invites to New York, to internationally based critics and media there. When I said no, that I didn't imagine any of them would come out into the boondocks, he said Worlack was going to try out a lot of new work, like an out of town run that would attract attention and that he'd already spread the word around, not just in Manhattan but in Washington, too. He thought *The New York Times* as well as the *Washington Post* might come. Television maybe.'

Slater thought at last he understood Ann's need for the two gins. Tentatively he said, 'So what's the problem?'

She snorted a disbelieving laugh at the question, her coffee cup between both hands. 'You don't think there's still a Russian intelligence set-up in the Washington embassy that wouldn't recognize your photograph! That Jack wouldn't, now that he's out?'

'I think the chance is remote,' said Slater, which was an exaggeration. Why hadn't she told him last night; while he was still in San Jose even?

'Do you want to take that chance?'

'I'll stay away from the opening. The whole exhibition, if that would make you feel more comfortable.'

'I can't,' reminded Ann. 'I'm hosting the whole thing.'

It all came back to her former husband and the damned release letter, Slater decided. 'You think Jack reads art columns and magazines?'

'I don't know what the fuck Jack reads . . . what he does. I never did, remember?'

Slater was undecided what to say. He didn't want to frighten her any more than she already was; as he was and always had been of Jack Mason, a secret he'd never admitted to anyone, scarcely even to himself. 'They're going to want to photograph and talk to Worlack. You're going to have to stay out of the pictures.'

'Mine is the first provincial gallery for his first out-of-town exhibition and I'm supposed to refuse to be photographed with the most exciting, up-and-coming artist who's chosen me for that honour!' Ann realized she was talking too loudly and looked around the restaurant, embarrassed.

'I won't be there, not at all. You weren't photographed a lot during the trial; nothing will remain on any embassy intelligence file after all this time, believe me. I was the guy who ran it, knows the system. And I know there's no cross-referencing system. Why should there be? And I handled Jack, don't forget. The pictures he likes looking at don't qualify as modern art, more like gynaecological textbook illustrations.' Slater regretted the sneer as soon as he uttered it. He'd never ever taken cheap shots at her former husband's sexual abandonment of Ann.

'If that's meant to reassure me, it doesn't.'

'It's the reality of the situation.'

'It's a danger – a risk – I don't want.'

Slater decided he didn't want Ann's up-and-down uncertainties taking her back into a gin bottle, either.

They drove unspeaking to the school and this time weren't kept waiting. Victor Spalding greeted them effusively and didn't sit formally behind his desk, as he had before, but perched himself on its edge fronting them. He said, 'I think this is very exciting, don't you?'

'David does,' said Slater. 'There's a lot more we need to know.'

'I thought I explained it in my letter,' said the principal, frowning. 'As had Jeb Stout in his that I sent with mine.'

'What affect would it have on David's schooling?' demanded Ann.

The man's frown remained. 'By which you obviously mean bad affect. I don't see why it should have any: he's virtually being offered a place at the university.'

'To play basketball and then most likely go on to become a professional,' said Ann. 'What proper academic teaching is going to be fitted in with all the training and travelling there's going to be? We don't want a son washed up at age forty mumbling that he could have been a contender.'

Slater wished Ann hadn't been so vehement, knowing the remark was an unconnected overhang from their lunchtime confrontation, and was relieved when Spalding smiled, un-offended. 'We're talking about basketball, not boxing, Mrs Slater. And I don't think David's going to end up punch-drunk. You'll need to talk in much more detail with Jeb Stout about the academic structure, but I know there is one and that it's strictly adhered to. As well as I know – as you do because I've told you every time we've met to talk about David's schooling – that academically he's very bright. He could very easily – *will* very easily, if you agree to the Maryland approach – be able to handle a full academic schedule in conjunction with whatever additional sports training and competition play there might be.'

'Is the approach known about here in the school?' asked Slater.

'There's been no official announcement,' said Spalding. 'You haven't told me yet that you want to go ahead with it. But it's not a secret. I guess David's talked about it to his friends.'

'What about the previous situation that brought us together last time?' persisted Slater. 'He's got a long way to go educa-tionally before he'll even get to the university, if we do

117

agree. What sort of jealousy pressure is he likely to come under?'

'None,' insisted the other man, adamantly. 'When we were last together I set out everything we'd put in place to prevent any reoccurrence of gangs or bullying or pressure. Unless David's told you something he hasn't told any of the counsellors or his teachers, I believe it's working. Has he complained to you about anything he hasn't told anyone here?'

'Not as far as I am aware,' admitted Slater, feeling inadequate.

Spalding smiled again. 'I think you're right to be as careful as you are being: wanting to know everything. And that it's important to get everything right from the beginning.'

'That's what we're going to do,' insisted Ann. 'Get everything right from the start.'

'To ensure which I think you should speak to the Maryland coach,' said Spalding. 'He's called me already. Wanted to know if I'd got any reaction from you yet. Told me he's very willing to come here again.'

'I think we should meet him, too,' said Slater. 'But without any commitment.'

On their way back to the gallery Ann said, 'There's too much happening. Everything's too busy. Too uncertain. I want it to be quiet again.'

Mason accessed the websites periodically every day – always from his memorized codes and passwords, never his back-up copies – and remained alert to everything and everyone around him during his daily fitness schedule, switching routes and directions more than usual to defeat any vehicle surveillance. He consequently became increasingly sure no alert had been raised from his being picked up on the CCTV cameras outside Ann's art gallery. He still decided against returning to Frederick, though, until after doing all that he planned in California.

With an intervening day before his appointment with the lawyer, Mason arranged his bill settlement at Guest Quarters, which had been extremely convenient but to which he didn't think he could return, made his travel arrangements and indulged himself by buying another Brooks Brothers suit, which he wore for his meeting with Patrick Bell.

118

'So you've decided?' greeted the lawyer.

'If you think it's a good idea,' countered Mason. Nowhere on any of his email interception had there been a single approach to the lawyer from Glynis Needham – which would probably have constituted illegal interference, he supposed – so he didn't think there was a possible risk but it still might be a sensible precaution to put up a ghost server barrier on Bell's system. It was something to think about.

'What is it?'

'I've got a case, right?'

Bell made a rocking motion with his hand. 'Fifty-fifty.'

'I think it's better than that, in my favour,' insisted Mason. 'So do you.'

'With all the caveats,' warned the other man.

'Which is what I've taken into consideration,' came back Mason. 'OK, I've got a lot to lose by a full court hearing: too much, maybe. So why don't you approach the appropriate authority? Invite a compensation offer with the clear and obvious implication that if it's not made we'll go on with a full claim?'

'They'll never go for it; recognize it as a bluff,' dismissed the attorney.

'Then we'll call it if they turn us down,' said Mason. 'We'll issue a writ and see what balls they've got. Throw in a little pressure by talking about prison overcrowding that makes it necessary to share cells, which I believe to be against the penitentiary code.' Mason thought it could delay things almost until Chambers' release.

'You got this much money?'

'You settled my mother's estate,' reminded Mason. He offered the already prepared card. 'I'm going to open a PO box in California for mail.' He spoke as the idea came to him, recognizing both the alibi and potential disappearing advantage.

'You really going to go ahead?'

'Let's see what their reaction is.'

'You're determined to make this guy sweat, aren't you?'

'You bet your ass,' said Mason. Other guys, too, he thought. What the hell had happened about that CCTV? Could it be that there wasn't a protective back-up, no one to whom Slater and Ann could go for help, and just be huddled there in

119

Frederick, too shit-scared to move, to do anything? The balloon of satisfaction popped before it inflated; he'd never imagined Sobell – Slater, he corrected himself – sitting around frightened, waiting for the inevitable. That's why he had always to be so careful until he decided that they should know he'd found them. And then even more careful afterwards.

'They might go for it,' conceded Bell, reluctantly.

'That's what I think,' said Mason, with the benefit of having read Glynis Needham's email.

'I'll give it a shot,' accepted the lawyer. 'But if they reject it you want me to go ahead with the claim?'

'Absolutely,' said Mason. 'Then they'll know we're serious.'

'And still might settle?' smiled Bell.

'And *will* settle,' insisted Mason. It felt good to be in total control, ahead of everyone else's thinking.

'You've decided upon California?' said Glynis Needham. As usual she was wearing a mannishly cut trouser suit

'I've decided to take the trip and see what it's like,' qualified Mason.

'When?'

'Tonight, arriving tomorrow,' said Mason. 'San Francisco. That's where the computer industry is, in Silicon Valley.'

The woman shook her head. 'There are reporting restrictions governing your parole and I'm responsible for them. I can't have you wandering about the country, not knowing where you are.'

Mason felt a lurch of uncertainty. 'I just told you where I'm going to be. And you told me you've already been in touch with people out there. You know my record, for Christ's sake! You know I'm not going to risk anything by going AWOL . . . do anything stupid.'

'Don't get spiky,' the woman warned at once.

'I'm not getting spiky,' refuted Mason. 'I've told you all along, from the day you picked me up outside the prison, what I was thinking of doing. Suddenly you're objecting.'

'I'm not objecting. I'm reminding you of your parole conditions.'

'I'll make contact with whoever I've got to connect with as soon as I get there. All I need is a name and a contact number.'

120

'You're asking for a lot of trust.'

'I earned a lot of trust, over fifteen years. And even more when I was given the chance to run by that asshole guard Howitt.'

'We should have worked it out together. I need an address, to know where you're going to be. Beverley needs to know.'

'Beverley?' queried Mason, almost too late.

'Beverley Littlejohn. She's the parole officer I've spoken to, who's going to look after you.'

'So speak to her again, now. She gets me somewhere to stay, that's where I'll be while I look around. From where I'll make contact, the moment I get there.'

'We should have worked it out before now,' persisted the woman.

'Why didn't you tell me before now?' She'd been lax and she knew it, Mason guessed. As long as he judged it carefully he could go on playing hardball, pressuring her.

'I thought you were dealing with the compensation.'

'Which I am and which is quite separate from anything between you and I. We discussed that already.' He hoped the pinpricks of colour that came to her face were embarrassment, not anger. To ease it, if it were – as well as maintaining the pressure – he said, 'My lawyer is writing to the penitentiary, maybe the Pennsylvania prison authorities, too. I don't need to be here while that's going on. What I need to do is get myself settled. Which is what I am trying to do. All I need is somewhere to stay, if you need to know before I leave.'

'I'm going to take a chance with you, Jack. I shouldn't but I will because of your record and because you deserve the trust. I'm going to tell Beverley that you're coming but if you don't make contact by tomorrow I'm going to set off alarms and you'll be back in White Deer before the weekend's over.'

It was the only threat she could make, Mason accepted. 'You know that won't happen.'

'You make sure it doesn't.'

It only took thirty minutes and a telephone call each way between Washington DC and the Californian parole office in San Francisco to fix a hotel at the bottom of Nob Hill which Mason reminded Glynis Needham he could afford from his mother's inheritance. Mason's satisfaction at knowing she was pissed off by the ease of it all was tempered by the thought that she might now rely more upon telephone than by the email to which he had unimpeded access.

He made Reagan airport in time for an earlier shuttle than he'd intended but didn't this time isolate the two police officers to whom he'd surrendered. He got into Manhattan just as smoothly and waved to Helene Balanda at the Chase Manhattan bank on his way to the securities desk. Mason was recognized there, too, although there was still the insistence upon the necessary identification formalities.

Ever since he'd downloaded the Trojan Horse and set up the ghost server accesses, Mason had carried them with him at all times, even when he'd jogged, and there was a lift of relief when he finally put them into the Adam Peterson deposit box. He hesitated, looking down at the hoarded money, thinking that he was shortly collecting from the girl upstairs the Visa card that was going to be automatically settled each month from his supplemented account. Mason counted out another £10,000 to divide, part in cash to take with him, the remainder just under the legal amount to deposit in the account.

'How's it going, settling back after such a long time away, Mr Peterson?' asked Helene Balanda when he reached her desk.

'Like starting a new life,' said Mason, handing over the cash and deposit slip in return for his new banking and charging facilities. Which was exactly what he was doing, thought Mason, about to start a new life as a new person. The farm boy whose name and identity he was taking would have probably never imagined there was so much money in the entire world. One day he might even put flowers on the kid's grave.

Fourteen

The hotel was called the Halcyon Bay, although it wasn't possible to see the harbour from his sixth-floor room, but at least Mason could make out the upper super-structure of the Golden Gate Bridge. The hotel was better than Mason had expected but he still preferred Washington's Guest Quarters. As he'd promised Glynis Needham, he immediately telephoned the new parole officer to report his arrival. Beverley Litttlejohn responded at once to her direct line and gave him the San Francisco address and said she expected him at three. She had the details of four advertised vacancies at three separate computer firms in Silicon Valley and another across the bridge in Oaklands. Mason said he was looking forward to their meeting, which he was, curious to discover if she'd already made preliminary enquiries on his behalf and if there were any obvious sexual similarities between her and Glynis Needham.

Mason had slept sufficiently on the overnight flight from Washington DC to embark upon his mentally prepared schedule directly after unpacking, showering and setting his intrusion traps for when he left his room. There had been a lot of psychological indicators to show Glynis Needham's anger at Mason obviously outsmarting her in her own fiefdom, aside from the tightness with which she had relayed to the Californian parole officer his wish for an hotel rather than an hostel: 'he has a substantial financial inheritance'. The most obvious was her repeated, threatening insistences to the woman at the other end of the telephone that if there was no immediate contact upon his San Francisco arrival she'd at once initiate a disappearance alert.

Which had established a time frame in which Mason, still anxious that the two women might switch from email to telephone communication, knew he had to work. From his laptop

123

Mason entered the ghost servers of both, as well as his hacked-in Trojan Horses, once more from memory. He didn't have to wait long. Within ten minutes of his speaking to her, Beverley Littlejohn's message to Washington was intercepted by his barriers. Beverley provided not only the precise time of Mason's call but its duration. She wrote of the computer industry vacancies she had already assembled and added that she was looking forward to the afternoon meeting 'with my first spook and spy'. Mason let the intercepted message continue unchanged to its intended recipient. The Washington parole officer's equally prompt reply showed the woman's continuing irritation. Glynis Needham warned of Mason's remarkably quick adjustment from an institutionalized environment, to which his inherited financial independence obviously greatly contributed, and warned against Beverley Littlejohn being 'snowed by bullshit'. Mason wasn't ever to be allowed to forget his continued freedom depended upon him observing every parole condition and restriction. Mason very briefly considered editing the note but decided against doing so, passing it on untouched, relieved that both had reverted to email.

It took Mason a further hour to install a ghost server into Patrick Bell's already known and therefore accessible main frame, using his surname and words 'penitentiary' and 'White Deer' as the activating triggers. He found nothing new when he rode his already installed Trojan Horse into his existing file on the lawyer's computer.

On a San Francisco tourist street map he'd picked up on his way through the airport, Mason discovered that the address that Beverley Littlejohn had given for their meeting was conveniently just off Union Square, which gave him almost three hours to spare. He caught a trolley car up and over Nob Hill, staying on until its harbour terminal and then leisurely wandered the length of the pier, choosing a seafood restaurant at random for king prawns and Napa Valley Chablis, buying peppermints and breath fresheners from a kiosk as he continued on to take any smell from his breath. At the pier end he stood gazing out towards Alcatraz, remembering the penitentiary folklore of escapes, despite official insistences that none ever succeeded, that persisted in White Deer even when he'd arrived more than twenty years after Alcatraz's closure. He'd go on a tourist visit, Mason decided, see how it compared to White Deer, which was considered a modern federal penitentiary. He had to find some way to fill the time before disappearing as all the prisoners who'd ever tried to escape were supposed to have disappeared in the currents of the bay, their bodies never found.

Beverley Littlejohn didn't bear any butch resemblance to her Washington colleague. The powder-blue V-necked sweater showed an enticing valley to explore and the darker blue tight skirt – short enough to confirm legs that went on forever – didn't show underwear lines to suggest she was wearing anything more substantial than a thong. She was full lipped – blowing lips was Mason's instinctive thought – and the blonde hair looped close to her shoulders. She was, in every way and appearance, exactly the type of woman upon whom Mason had preyed, and he thought that if she were gay mankind had been cheated. He might have failed with the 6th Avenue hooker – an admission he'd studiously exorcised from his mind – but he was sure he wouldn't have had any problems with Beverley, given the chance. It could still be a jerk-off fantasy, which was all he could achieve at the moment and only then with a porn offering on the computer screen to help. He really did have a lot still to plan and put in place but it was important as well to get himself properly laid; Beverley Littlejohn's unexpected attractiveness was an unnecessary – even unwelcomed – reminder of what he could no longer do but desperately wanted to do, had to be *able* to do, to restore his overly long suppressed manhood. He had to be able to get it up again, like he'd always been able to, whenever he'd wanted to, however he'd wanted to. He couldn't – wouldn't – become a dead-dick cripple. He was going to get everything back; everything and more.

Aware from the emails of what had passed between the two women – 'I can't wait to meet my first spook and spy' – Mason determinedly set out to undermine whatever adverse preconceptions Glynis Needham might have implanted in Beverley Littlejohn's mind, just as determinedly testing to establish that the dossier that the woman had on the desk between them contained all his records that Glynis Needham had promised to exchange.

Mason layered charm upon self-effacement, easily slipping into the rarely failed pussy-pounce of the intended conquest at which he'd once been so adept. He stopped just short of taking the flattery too far, sure he was getting the occasional faint flush of response but confirming even more satisfactorily that the file in front of her was his in its entirety and that she'd studied it. Her immediate acceptance of his feigned remorse and serious-faced insistence of how eager he was to reassimilate into a law-abiding society came unquestioned from Beverley – whom he doubted to be more than thirty – with the eye-holding assurance that she'd do everything she could to help if he decided to settle in California.

'Glynis has promised very much the same,' probed Mason, enjoying himself.

'She takes her job very seriously.'

'As you obviously do,' Mason continued to compliment.

'Thank you.'

'You know Glynis well?'

'Not well. She lectured at a training seminar I was at. She looked me up later when she came out here on vacation.'

Could he risk going closer than an inch? Of course not, it would be ridiculous. But hadn't there been another White Deer folklore – a legend that extended to other penitentiaries in the retelling – of prisoners forming associations with female rehabilitation workers, of women actually being turned on – seeking to marry during imprisonment even – by rapists and murderers on death row, with no chance of reprieve, let alone getting into the sack together?

'You must have got to know each other pretty well if you vacationed together.'

'We didn't vacation *together*,' insisted Beverley, stiffly. 'She came out on a trip and looked me up. We had dinner a couple of times. A few drinks.'

Had 'don't be snowed by bullshit' really been irritation? Or potential jealousy? A too long forgotten – and so far impossible to retrieve – feeling warmed through Mason. 'Still good to have an apartment to use as a base rather than an hotel.'

'Glynis did not use my apartment as a base.' The denial, the words spaced for emphasis, came with more eye-holding insistence.

Back off time, judged Mason. 'I really do appreciate you looking out the job vacancies for me.'

Beverley's face relaxed into a half smile. 'That's an essential part of the job.'

'I'm very, although sadly, lucky,' said Mason, the awkwardness intentional, the words halting. 'My mother, whom I loved very much, left me everything when she died, while I was in prison. It's not urgent that I get a job right away. I will, of course. I've wasted enough of my life already to think of wasting any more.' Soap-opera dialogue, he thought.

'That's good to hear.'

'How do I account for the last fifteen years, if I get an interview?'

'The place in Oakland is a computer refurbishing outlet. They've taken two guys with prison histories before.'

'For things like I did?'

The smile came again. 'You're a first, for what you did.'

And could be again, although first in a way she didn't imagine, he thought. They really were fantastic tits. 'Oakland's the obvious. I don't have transport. I'll have to work out how to get down to the valley.'

'You make the appointments – all spread over the same day if you can – and I'll run you there in my car. I need to know you're genuinely exploring possibilities. It's one of the conditions.'

Fuck, thought Mason, who hadn't intended bothering to apply for any of the vacancies, just officially establish his presence in San Francisco after Washington DC before vanishing from both, leaving each probation official believing he'd settled within the responsibility of the other. 'I can't impose upon you like that!'

'It isn't an imposition. It's all part of the service.'

Could he really fantasise about her performing another? he wondered, idly. 'You're quite sure?'

'Quite sure.'

'I'll set things up as soon as I can.'

'What do you think of California so far?'

'I haven't seen enough of anywhere to decide,' said Mason, hoping to sound encouraging.

'Maybe there'll be the chance to see something of the place when we're driving up and down the coast?' Beverley suggested.

He was going to have his head between those gorgeous legs, Mason guessed: it was virtually a foregone conclusion, ahead of other conclusions.

Daniel Slater was glad he hadn't questioned the lunchtime gin drinking because as far as he was aware – and for which he remained alert – there was no repetition after that one episode. He got the San Jose contractual confirmation four days after despatching his memorandum of agreement, which he judged to be practically by return of post, and began negotiations with his subcontracting installers at once, more immediately having them fit CCTV monitors in the four gallery rooms in which the Worlack work was to be displayed. He also had noise alarms connected to the actual hanging hooks, once their positioning had been agreed with Worlack's exhibition designer, to sound the moment a canvas was lifted from any of them. Slater devised a secondary, linked system that automatically locked every door and emergency exit. The day before the combined meeting between himself and Ann, Worlack's designer and the insurance assessor, Slater arranged to have fitted to every hanging chain a miniature sensor that would trigger a separate sound alarm if it passed in front of detector boxes at every door, exit and window.

At the meeting the designer, a gesticulating man named Chernot, who talked as much with his hands as he did in a thick French accent, said, 'It is magnificent! Far better than I've known in some major galleries, not just here but in Europe, as well.'

'I agree, as far as America is concerned,' said the assessor.

Both left personal cards and promised to talk to Slater in the future about other exhibitions. The assessor only imposed a three percent increase on Ann's temporary additional cover.

When the meeting ended Ann said, 'You made an impression! They're going to use you for other things.'

'Maybe,' said Slater, modestly, thinking the same thing.

Ann got acceptances from *The New York Times* and the *Washington Post*, as well as from virtually every arts publication to which she'd sent invitations, in addition to two television stations with nationwide syndication links to cultural arts programmes. Slater remained in Frederick finalizing the employment of security guards while Ann flew up to New York for her first face-to-face meeting with Andre Worlack. She refused to stay overnight but returned on a late shuttle more excited – but more importantly carefree – than Slater could remember for a long time.

She said, 'They actually talked of this exhibition establishing me as one of the most important provincial galleries!'

The following day they finally met the University of Maryland sports coach. They hadn't been able to make Jeb Stout's first suggested date because of the commitments to the exhibition and their proposed alternative hadn't worked for him. Ann and Slater had then both become aware of David withdrawing within himself in the belief that they weren't going to meet with the scout, despite Slater explaining the problems. The obvious benefit from the delay was that it gave Slater and Ann time to decide upon every reassurance they'd need before accepting the scholarship offer.

Stout was already in the school principal's office when they arrived. Slater had expected the black former basketball player to be big but not to be as tall as he was and hoped David didn't grow to rival him in height. Slater guessed the man to be at least 6' 8", maybe even taller.

'Vic's told me of your reservations,' greeted the man at once. 'I hope I can reassure you.'

'We hope so too,' said Ann.

'David's got a talent,' declared Stout. 'Two, in fact. He's outstanding at his chosen sport and from what Vic Spalding's told me and the grade assessments I've seen, David is a bright student, too. And you've got my specific assurance that the first isn't going in any way to damage or affect the second. Not a single item on his curriculum here or in high school, or when he gets to university, is going to be neglected or sacrificed. If there is going to be a sacrifice, it's the spare time – evenings and weekends – when he'll have to practice and train and I doubt he'll consider that a sacrifice at all—'

'What about the homework and additional study in the evenings and weekends?' interrupted Ann.

'Again, not neglected or sacrificed,' assured Stout. 'No training on school-work nights, everything coordinated at weekends.'

'I get the impression of a pretty tight schedule,' said Slater. 'What time's he got to be a kid and do kids' things?

'All the time he needs,' said Stout. 'At the age he is now it's virtually nursery training: you'll hardly notice any change to what he already does. The only difference is that we'll train him and not you, as you additionally do at present. We want to develop his talent, not burn it out. And health is something I need to tell you about. David will get regular health checks and medical examinations, to ensure he's not strained or over-stretched.'

'How good – really – is David?' asked Slater.

'You give him the additional training at the moment. What do you think?'

'I've never thought him good enough to be a professional.'

'He's not, not yet. How could he be? But he's got the potential.'

'What about if we moved?' demanded Ann, suddenly. 'Move somewhere else in the country. You're talking of spending a lot of time and effort and I guess money. Does this offer come with any conditions on your part?'

Slater, as well as Stout and the school principal, looked at the woman. The sports scout said, 'Are you thinking of moving, Mrs Slater?'

'I'm just trying to cover everything,' said Ann, colouring slightly.

'David won't come to us under contract,' Stout replied, smiling. 'If something comes up and you have to move away, it'll be our loss. At university he'd be able to live on campus, wherever you lived.'

'Moving's not high on our priority list,' said Slater.

'I said I was just covering everything,' repeated Ann.

'We'd obviously like you to come to the university. Look over the campus and see our facilities,' invited Stout. 'With David as well, of course, if you consider taking up the offer. And if there aren't any more questions.'

Slater looked enquiringly at Ann, who shook her head. He said, 'I think you've answered everything we wanted to know. We've naturally discussed it a lot between ourselves. And I think we're going to take up your offer.'

'Excellent!' said Stout.

'You've made the right decision,' said Spalding. 'Shouldn't we let David know now?'

When they did the boy burst into embarrassed tears, laughing

130

at the same time, and kept saying that he was sorry. They arranged the campus visit after the exhibition and they celebrated at the same Wendy's as before.

In bed that night Slater said, 'It's a hell of an opportunity for him, isn't it?'

'I hope so.'

'You surprised me with that remark about moving.'

'I told you why.'

'Everything's perfect for us here; even more so now.'

'You never know when things might change.'

They never would for Ann, Slater thought, sadly.

Mason turned it into a game, at times even a childish one, just as going through the charade of job interviews was nothing more than an amusement. He had Beverley come with him to open a San Francisco PO box – phoning the number and address to Patrick Bell – and to extend his time with her he spread the Silicon Valley appointments over two days – always in the afternoons so that they finished too late for her to go back to the office – and fixed the interview for the third there, late again. He played at the job encounters, too, knowing he easily qualified for every one, sure he was better than every supposed expert who tested and questioned him; every mistake or implied limitation was intentional, all the vagueness calculated to disqualify himself. At each he volunteered his imprisonment, although not for spying for Russia, insisting it was unjust and that the computer fraud for which he had been convicted was committed by another unknown technician who had framed him. After each session Mason told Beverley he knew he'd done well and was confident of getting an offer.

He was careful but deliberate with the moves he made upon the woman, their initial physical contacts fleetingly brief and easily misconstrued or explained away as politeness, helping her in and out of the car or into buildings or seats, the brushing of his hand against hers or guiding her bare arm; nothing more than gestures of attentiveness. The sexual *double entendres* were just as carefully introduced, stopped well short of offence, never amounting to risqué banter. Mason worked the hardest at making her laugh with anecdotes of intelligence operation screw ups, the basis of most of them genuine or at least half true, always balanced with even more extravagant improvization of potentially dangerous, even life-threatening, episodes he'd experienced or knew about in Moscow and Vienna and Poland, before his reassignment to Washington DC on the CIA's Russian desk. He was positive by the second day that he had her hooked.

That was the day, drinking coffee in a diner between job interviews, when she said, 'It really does sound like James Bond!' to his immediate: 'I never once got seduced by a beautiful provocateur,' to her smiled, eye-holding reply: 'For the first time I don't believe you!' Which was prescient because that was how he'd been willingly recruited by the KGB. That was also the day he was aware of her hand brushing his, her arm ready, expectantly, to be held and when, after the second intentionally flunked interview she proposed that they look at Carmel. She accepted immediately his complementary suggestion of an early dinner and said that as far as she was aware nothing in his parole conditions precluded alcohol and that she preferred French to Californian wine. There was nothing accidental in their physical contact or touching in the restaurant booth overlooking the ocean and when they got into her car Mason asked if there was anything in his parole restrictions precluding his kissing her and she said most definitely not.

Her apartment, coincidentally just three blocks from the Oakland computer refurbishing outlet in which his interview was fixed the following day, was haphazard and they added to the clutter undressing each other on their way to the bedroom for what Mason judged the best and most successfully repeated series of fucks he'd ever managed. During one brief interval Beverley said, 'I'm sure as hell getting the benefit of fifteen years of abstinence, aren't I?'

Mason said, 'I never thought rehabilitation would be as good as this,' and for the first time since their meeting truly meant something he'd told her.

Beverley said, 'I don't care that I could lose my job over this.'

I know you could, thought Mason. It was something to keep in mind.

Mason was confident his ghost servers would block any email exchange between the two parole officers but made twice-daily checks. Beverley made her approach to Washington

132

while he was knowingly destroying any chance of employment at the Oakland plant, after the night of frantic, un-
inhibited lovemaking. He let through unaltered Beverley's
email stating that she was sure he'd succeed in getting one if
not more offers from his series of interviews, just as she was
sure he was going to make an excellent parolee who would cause
her no difficulties whatsoever and that she was looking forward
to working extremely closely with him. There was no reason,
either, to interfere with Glynis Needham's return message that
she was glad to hear things were going so well. That was the
day Mason received the first of his four anticipated rejections.

He and Beverley spent the weekend in a rented chalet overlooking the ocean just outside Santa Barbara, grocery and
wine shopping on their way down from San Francisco on the
Friday, so there was no need to emerge that night or on the
Saturday. They scarcely left their bed that day, lying naked
and uncovered as they drank their wine and Beverley said, 'I
really don't know what this is all about but I don't want it to
stop, ever. End, ever.'

Mason said, 'If I get a job, it won't have to.' Very briefly
he thought of dragging the nonsense out, because the sex was
so good, and he was enjoying moving people around like
someone directing a play, but reluctantly he decided he had
to move on.

He collected his final rejection from his PO box on the
Tuesday. He set out each letter in Beverley's Oakland apartment that night. She cried and said it didn't matter, that there
would be other openings and she'd call in all the favours she
was owed and she had a lot outstanding. But Mason soothed
and quietened her, reminded her that he'd only been allowed
to leave DC temporarily and that he had strictly to adhere to
his parole restrictions by returning to the East Coast. He'd
keep in constant touch with her from there – although at that
precise moment he didn't have a definite location – and come
back out as soon as he could. She was to advise Glynis
Needham of the setback, which was all it was, as nothing was
going to permanently separate them, and look out for more
vacancies and wait.

'I don't think I can wait, not for very long,' she said.

Mason's ghost servers worked perfectly and precisely as
he'd intended. That which he had installed on Glynis

Needham's system blocked Beverley's information of his return to her supervision and needed no rewriting, just deletions, to make it read that he'd been successful in filling a vacancy and would continue under Beverley's control. Glynis Needham emailed back that she was very pleased with Mason's relocation, that she'd officially record the transfer and that she hoped she and Beverley might work together again as successfully in the future; she might even come out west again for another vacation. It was more difficult to edit but Mason succeeded in changing it to read that she was awaiting his call upon his Washington return and was trying to get him back into the same accommodation as before.

Mason booked his return flight east in the name of Adam Peterson, to establish the disappearance of Jack Mason on the West Coast when the inevitable search was initiated. He reckoned with his intercepting ghost servers and the bullshit he could dump on Beverley he could delay for months any positive alert of his disappearance from the parole system.

By which time Ann, Slater and their gangling son would be dead. As would Peter Chambers. And Jack Mason, although only officially. Adam Peterson, on the other hand, would be living very happily on a close to $4,000,000 fortune somewhere warm in Europe.

Fifteen

At what he guessed to be halfway across the American continent, probably over Des Moines, at 35,000 feet Jack Mason suddenly decided that this was to be the day and New York to be the place for his final, untraceable disappearance and rebirth as Adam Peterson. This then marked the irrevocable beginning of the long-planned retribution. He came to this sudden decision in the sleeping aircraft after a mental argument with himself prompted by the recurring self-accusation that his trip to California had been a further postponement – a chickening-out excuse – of his dedicated commitment. Which it wasn't. California had been absolutely necessary; quite apart from him achieving his full and essential sexual recovery, he had also removed himself as far as arguably possible from where he might have been recorded on the gallery's CCTV. Mason's concern had subsided, now no more than a nagging uncertainty he accepted wouldn't ever be resolved. One of the tenets of his intelligence indoctrination was that there were never answers to everything, which the Frederick blunder proved. It having occurred, Mason was determined it wouldn't be repeated, although by contrast in California he'd made no attempt to hide his presence, positioning himself in full view of each and every security lens, anxious to establish his whereabouts there.

On his journey east, however, as he needed it to appear that he remained 3,000 miles from where he might have been filmed, Mason rented a car, as Adam Peterson, and drove the 400 miles south from San Francisco to Los Angeles, not on the scenic coast route but on the inner, wind farm and cattle-shit-stinking inner highway, bill-capped, nose blowing, sun-glassed and crowd-immersed, studiously avoiding every prying-eyed security monitor. This was a precaution he continued to adopt – successfully he was sure – upon his arrival at La Guardia.

He travelled by crowded airport bus into Manhattan and, because it would feature, albeit briefly, in his re-acquaintance with the unsuspecting Peter Chambers and he wanted to be thoroughly familiar with everything about it, Mason checked into the Sheraton Hotel on Seventh Avenue – still alert to every electronic eye – hating the convention-cluttered, jostling lobby and bars and public rooms at the same time as recognizing how perfect their concealment was going to be.

Despite his rebirth, Mason held back from anything as naively symbolic as destroying his genuine identification documentation. He remained in the murmuring human beehive only long enough to set his room-intrusion traps, then walked to the Chase Manhattan on Wall Street to store everything of his Jack Mason persona in the safe deposit box, hesitating at the Glock and its limited ammunition. He decided against removing it until the following day, after hiring the car for the drive south. He was at his most exposed with the gun in his possession.

Two days before leaving San Francisco Mason had accessed his file in Patrick Bell's computer system and found the copy of Bell's carefully phrased preliminary letter to the Pennsylvania State prison authorities inviting their response to the formal complaint against Frank Howitt, with the reminder that he was already aware of the internal enquiry and Howitt's suspension from duty. Back in the Seventh Avenue hotel Mason checked again to discover there had been no response in the intervening four days. Neither was there any email traffic between the two parole officers. Anxious to avoid any unsupervised telephone contact between the women for as long as possible, Mason called Beverley at her San Francisco office, the approach rehearsed.

He told her he was looking into a couple of possibilities – that day he was actually in New York for a meeting – but as she knew there wasn't any financial necessity for his rushing into anything on the East Coast, just a condition of his parole he had to obey. He knew he could trust her not to discuss it with Glynis Needham, but he'd decided to do little more than go through the motions with anything the woman suggested. He had one or two things to sort out involving his mother's estate – she knew, too, that he'd been in prison when she'd died – but he hoped to get back to California within a month, to be with her again. She wasn't to think of vacancies before then but in the meantime he was going to register with computer employment agencies in Sacramento, Los Angeles and San Diego, to give himself as broad an opportunity spread as possible.

'You really mean it, that you're coming back for good?' Beverley asked, eagerly.

'What's it sound like?' He'd recovered everything, Mason decided, even how to manipulate women supposedly more intelligent or professionally streetwise not to be sucked into what Glynis quite rightly labelled bullshit.

'It sounds wonderful.'

'Don't say anything about it to Glynis, though. Not yet.'

'She'll have to know sometime. She's your primary case officer.'

'When it's all fixed up. I don't want anything to go wrong.'

'Neither do I. I won't say anything. And you're right, you know you can trust me.'

'When I come out I thought we might rent that chalet in Santa Barbara again,' said Mason, as an idea began to grow in his mind.

'That would be wonderful, too. Missing me?'

'Like hell. Missing me?'

'Like hell. I don't have a number to call you?'

'I'm moving around. I'll call you when I get a base.'

'You OK?'

'Sure. Why'd you ask?'

'You sound . . . oh, I don't know. Too far away, I guess.'

'Not for long.'

'I hope not.'

'Don't do anything, say anything, to Glynis, until I get back.'

'Call me in between!'

'Of course I'll call you in between. I've got to go now, to my meeting.'

'Don't accept an offer if you're made one!'

'I promise I won't,' laughed Mason, although not for the reason Beverley assumed.

The idea that had surfaced talking of renting the Santa Barbara chalet again was a good one, Mason determined, and he started on it immediately, searching out the websites of local newspapers around Chesapeake Bay. He quickly became disappointed at the apparent lack of what he specifically needed, which wasn't just to disappear but to become invisible, seen by no one, remembered by no one, identifiable by no one. He isolated a too limited selection of possibilities, none ideal, and worked his way through rentals at Annapolis and Lexington Park, touring as many as he could on virtual reality computer links. The viewing facility wasn't available for the fishing cottage he finally decided upon, actually on the shoreline about five miles outside Lexington Park, which was further away from Frederick than he wanted but according to the listed particulars stood totally alone, without any neighbouring properties. Mason fixed a viewing with the Lexington realtor-associated property management consultant, who assured him he had at least two other similar rentals on his books if the first choice didn't work out.

With the drive south ahead of him Mason rented his largest car so far, a Lexus, collected the Glock and ammunition from the Chase within thirty minutes of its opening and was on the road by 10.30 a.m. He observed every speed limit and road restriction, conscious of the danger of driving with an unlicensed weapon and realized he could not reach DC in time to put the gun in the waiting safe deposit box at the First National. Adjusting his schedule he got off the interstate as quickly as he could after crossing the New Jersey state line, tensed at the significance of the immediate sight of a parked Highway Patrol car. He lunched leisurely at a roadside tavern, disdaining any alcohol. By 5 p.m. he was on the outskirts of DC and stopped at the first Howard Johnson hotel he came to, settling everything in advance for an early departure the following morning. The realtor was still at his office and Mason confirmed the Lexington Park viewing appointment for four the next afternoon.

He bought a plastic carry bag to hold the gun and ammunition and kept it tightly by his side when he ate at the coffee shop and beneath the adjoining pillow when he slept. As he had been the previous day in New York, Mason was on the steps of his second bank in DC when it opened, the tension easing from him as he deposited the gun and ammunition. He bypassed Frederick on his way to Lexington Park, acknowledging that he had a further and very necessary reconnoitre

138

to complete to locate a dumping place for the gun and laptop immediately after killing Slater and Ann.

Mason found the cottage ahead of being shown it by the realtor. It looked ramshackle but Mason drove for more than a mile along every approach road before coming upon another building and that looked deserted. The shoreline, a mixture of foot-dragging shingle and sand, was perfect for the resumption of his neglected fitness regime. When he returned with the realtor for the official inspection Mason found the cottage was better inside than it appeared from outside, well furnished and equipped and altogether fitted for his needs. Mason cut short the room-by-room tour and the effusive rental advantages pitch and said he'd take it for three weeks, with the possibility of extending for longer, unsure how long it would take him to isolate the boy, as an innocent, unsuspecting calf was isolated from its herd by a hunting predator. Mason was ferried back to Lexington to make out separate Adam Peterson cheques for the full rental and inventory deposit and a third, provisionally for $100, against electricity and phone charges, although he had no intention of creating an automatic number-logged telephone account. He did all his grocery and supplies shopping on that one trip and before nightfall was settled into the cottage, everything stored away, a wood fire kindled in the open hearth and all his illegal computer websites visited, with no fresh communications between any of them.

Standing at the window, gazing out over the wind-rippled bay, Mason decided that the only thing missing was a woman. But he needed to concentrate now, he reminded himself, with no time for distractions or interference. He had the first of his several perfect murders to refine and he was looking forward to it. There had, though, to be an interval for Slater and Ann to suffer the loss of the kid. That would be the time to relax by going back, as promised, to California and spend a week – or as long as he chose – fucking Beverley Littlejohn's brains out.

It hadn't been holding back – chickening out – not to have fully planned his first killing. He hadn't known, until his initial surveillance, that there was a kid – destroying whom was going to make the personal redress that much more satisfying – and the California episode *had* been necessary. Now was precisely the right time. It was disappointing that Slater and his whore wouldn't know from the very beginning what was inevitably happening to them, but as far as the official investigation was concerned the kid's death had to appear an accident. Which limited him to something involving a vehicle. Which, limiting again, wasn't guaranteed to kill. What about *not* killing? What about maiming instead, sentencing them to a lifetime of drudgery and care, as he had been sentenced to close to a lifetime of incarceration? If he didn't succeed – if the boy survived but was crippled, for instance – that initially might be sufficient, stretching out their suffering, but eventually the kid had to die, depriving Ann of the child she'd always craved. But he didn't have that much time. It would be more difficult – impossible maybe – to get to the boy a second time and if Slater and Ann died as well, as they were going to die, it really would be impossible for all three to be accepted as accidental. There was also the additional complication that very shortly – almost too shortly – Peter Chambers was going to be released and there couldn't be any delay or distraction between the first killings and separating Chambers from his stashed-away three million dollars before he died, too. Suddenly, although briefly, Mason felt overwhelmed by what he had to do in so little time. But he could do it. *Would* do it. Do it all. And very definitely start tomorrow. That was when Ann's art exhibition opened, he remembered from the discarded advertising flyer.

Slater spent the day at the gallery ahead of the evening's opening reception checking both the existing and new security installations and briefing the hired guards, all of whose references he'd thoroughly confirmed. Ann was as excited as she had been on her return from her first meeting with Andre Worlack in New York, positioning and repositioning the floral displays in the reception area, ensuring the caterers had forgotten nothing and that the wine was being chilled and was ever present at the designer's side during the hanging of each canvas. Her mood only dipped with the arrival of the first New York television crew.

As they began to set up she crossed over to Slater and said, 'The rest of the media will be arriving soon. It's time you went.'

'I'd like to stay.'

'You can't!'

'I know.'

'It's good David won't be by himself.'

'Everything's going to go great.'

'Thanks, for all you've done.'

'Call, if anything comes up.'

A local television crew came through the door, looking around enquiringly. As she moved off to greet them Ann said, 'Nothing will. Please get going.'

Slater hung back until all the crew were inside before leaving, making no farewell gesture to Ann, glad of the build up of cars which initially made it difficult for him to move up Main Street and indicated a popular first night.

David was practising baskets when Slater arrived back in Hill Avenue, stopping for the car to be driven into the garage.

'You think they'll expect me to drop a few when we go to the campus?' the boy asked, when Slater emerged from the garage. The university and sports facility visit was scheduled for the Wednesday of the next but one week.

'I doubt it. They know what you can do.'

'I need to practise some distance shots. I'm too close here.'

'You got Jeb and a lot of other people to tell you what you need to practise.'

'I want to be as good as they expect me to be.'

'You are as good as they expect you to be. That's why they made the offer. Let Jeb and the coach set the schedule. Don't try to anticipate them.'

Slater stayed outside with his son for a further thirty minutes before saying, 'I'm going to fix dinner. It's meat loaf.'

'Then going back to the exhibition?' anticipated the boy.

'No. I'm staying here.'

David again stopped playing. 'You're not going back to be with Mom?'

'Sometime whilst it's on, maybe. Tonight's her party.'

'She'll want you to be there. Expect it,' insisted the boy.

'She doesn't. We talked about it.'

'I'll be OK by myself. Maybe hang out with Brad for a while.'

'It's nothing to do with leaving you. Of course you'll be OK by yourself. And don't you have homework?'

'Nothing that's going to take long.'

'Homework first, before you go around to Brad's. We made a deal, remember?'

'It's an easy set. Half an hour tops. Then I can go over to Brad's?'

'Let's see how it goes.'

Slater set the table and put the meat loaf in the oven, able to see David sinking baskets on the visitor-checking TV monitor at the side of the porch. That was how he saw David re-open the garage, take out his bicycle and prop it up on its stand. There was only one subject of conversation over dinner, with David doing most of the talking and Slater contributing the odd remark or agreement. At one stage, leaving his plate with half a slice of meat loaf uneaten, David supposed that his training would include a diet that he would have to strictly observe. Slater was amused, although he didn't show it, at his son's intensity and suggested it was something David might ask on their impending visit.

'I meant what I said,' announced David, suddenly. 'I won't lay back on my schoolwork. I'll go on getting straight As, I promise.'

'I know you will,' said Slater. 'We never got around to that camping trip, did we?'

'A lot came up.'

'Maybe we can fit it in when things settle down.'

'Don't you think it would be an idea to surprise Mom at the exhibition?' David suggested.

'No,' said Slater, positively. 'I think it would be a good idea to do the work you brought home, go over to Brad's to hang out for an hour and then be back in time to hear all about what's happened at the gallery from Mom when she gets back.'

'She going to be there all the time this week? Nights as well as days?'

'I guess so.'

'Why don't we both surprise her one night, go over together?'

'That's what we'll do,' agreed Slater. 'One night towards the end of the show.' When all the media had finally gone, he thought.

'I won't be late back,' said David.

142

'Ride carefully.'

'I always do.'

Mason had wondered how he would feel at his first sight of
Daniel Slater, whom he still instinctively thought of as Dimitri
Sobell, but he hadn't expected it to be like this, sick to his
stomach, so bad in the first few minutes that he'd actually,
physically, retched. He still felt sick at the missed opportuni-
ties, taking a long time to calm down and rationalize that there
was no way he could have prepared as carefully as it was essential to prepare, not snatching at the first unexpected possibility.

He'd set off that day with little positive intention beyond
timing the drive from Chesapeake to Frederick. It was only
when he got to the town that he decided to watch the gallery,
sure of his concealment in a car park just off Main Street.
He'd watched for quite a long time, seeing the arrival of the
television vans, suddenly jerking forward when he identified
the man he hated enough to kill. Mason fought against his
need to vomit, swallowing and coughing against throwing up,
forcing the control into himself.

The feeling went beyond being physical. Mason would have
recognized Sobell of course: *had* recognized him, at once. But
the Russian had changed. Got bigger, fatter: more American.
The hair was much thinner and the whole ambience was
relaxed, laid back, none of the quick-moving jerkiness of their
remembered encounters. Mason wasn't immediately aware of
starting the hire car, only realizing he was moving when he
began edging the car out on to a surprisingly busy Main Street.
The delay was sufficient to get two cars between him and
Slater and he should have obviously turned off as soon as he
could, at the next intersection, but he didn't. Using the traffic
build-up for further protection and managing to stay amongst
it all the way back to Hill Avenue, he was able to stop with
Slater's house in view and see the boy at the basketball hoop.
He stayed there watching the kid practise in front of his father
and continue on when Slater went inside the house. Mason
finally turned into the avenue and was actually passing the
house when the boy came out of the garage with a bicycle,
which he put up on its rest. Sure of his geography, Mason
looped back in a square, returning close to where he'd first
stopped, looking at the waiting bicycle. It was more than an

hour, completely dark, before the boy re-emerged, got on the bicycle and passed within a yard of where Mason sat, unseen.

When would there be such another easy chance? wondered Mason, as he picked up the road back to Chesapeake. Whenever it came he'd be well and truly ready.

Sixteen

A nn had worked as hard as she knew how to make the
exhibition a success and Slater had done everything he
could think of to support her and make it happen, but neither
of them imagined in their wildest dreams that it would turn
out quite as it did.

The New York Times and the *Washington Post* both carried
stories beyond their arts sections, each declaring the exhibition the best ever of Andre Worlack's unique work. Each
carried photographs of Ann with the artist. So did every television station, as well as separate interviews with Ann, which
brought more television coverage. NBC were filming when a
New York based, Emmy-nominated star of a TV rate-topping
soap made an unannounced visit on the second day and spent
$50,000 on one miniature canvas and the publicity from that
sale prompted a procession of *People*-featured celebrities.
CBS vacillated before deciding to film the following week,
on condition that Worlack would be there. In several interviews Worlack described Ann's gallery as the most important
provincial venue he had encountered and announced it would
be the location of his next try-out exhibition. The *Frederick
News-Post* carried daily stories concluding with an editorial
asserting that Ann Slater had put the town on the national arts
culture map.

And Ann's concern at the publicity potentially identifying
them grew to encompass Slater, as well as herself. On the
first full day after the opening reception, Ann called the exhibition a terrible mistake she should never have contemplated
and positively refused three approaches, one from a local television station, for personalized features about her and her
family. The University of Maryland confirmed their approach
to David, obviously leaked by the school, which brought fresh
approaches from the local media, but they still refused to do

any personality profiles; they were now being referred to as 'the golden family'. Jeb Stout was quoted that David was going to be a major sports star of the future. The photograph of David was a bad one, making him look ungainly.

The day that the golden family description was first used Ann said, 'What are we going to do?'

'Front it out,' said Slater. He wished it hadn't happened – the first advice given them upon going into the Witness Protection Programme had been never, ever, to attract attention to themselves – but they couldn't reverse it now.

'I'm sorry. So very, very sorry. It's a nightmare,' apologized Ann.

'There's nothing to be sorry for,' refused Slater. 'And it's not a nightmare. It's your success story.' Which it was and should have infused her with the confidence she'd never had, not further despair.

'I won't agree to other exhibitions, of course.'

'There's no reason to refuse anything. It won't be like this next time. The next time we'll know what to expect, if they turn out like this one has. Know how to handle it.'

'I'm frightened, Dan.'

'The personality stuff is local and it's about you and David. I haven't been photographed or identified, called nothing more than a businessman. The week after next it'll all be forgotten.' He wouldn't go as far as admitting to being frightened, Slater decided, but he was definitely uncomfortable. But it had to be kept in perspective. It was unthinkable that he would be remembered after fifteen years; more than fifteen years if he included the trial and he hadn't been photographed giving evidence there, either. The photograph of him that had been used had been blurred and out of focus, from a Russian embassy reception.

'I'd like to believe it but I don't,' refuted Ann. 'I had two more exhibition approaches today, after what Andre said about the importance of the gallery. I wasn't even going to bother to tell you because I'm going to turn them both down.'

'Don't!' urged Slater. 'This is what you want to do. What you wanted the gallery to be recognized as. And it's worked.'

'It's not what I want to do, not put everything we have at risk!'

'We'll just ride it out,' persisted Slater. 'No harm's been done.'

146

'You don't know that! You won't know that until it's too late!'

'The Cold War's over. Has been for years. Everything's changed.'

'Jack's out, that's what's changed!'

'And he can't find us.'

'You don't know that, either!' She should have told him about the man so much like Jack on the CCTV!

'I *do* know!'

'What you don't . . .' Ann began, stopping in time.

'What?'

'Nothing.' He'd think she was paranoid or hysterical if she announced it this late; making it up to support her argument.

Slater looked at her curiously across the breakfast table. 'You were going to say something?'

'It's not important . . . doesn't mean anything.'

'You sure?'

'I'm sure. Like I'm sure it was a mistake to get into the whole damned thing in the first place.'

'It's too late to do anything about it now. And I don't want you turning down other things, either.'

Ann looked into her coffee cup, saying nothing.

'You sorry you took the chance?'

'What?'

'Took the chance of marrying me?' elaborated Slater.

Yes, thought Ann, and at once wished she hadn't, because it wasn't true. She was sorry she'd staged the exhibition, although deep down – unaware of Slater's thinking – she'd seen it as something to establish herself, prove herself capable of doing after being told for so long and so violently by Jack that she wasn't capable of anything. But she didn't regret committing herself to being with Daniel Slater. 'No, darling. I'm not sorry now and haven't been since the moment I said yes.' Why had she thought, even for a second, the opposite?

'You going to go back to the others who approached you?' asked Slater.

'We'll see.'

'What's to see?'

'This one has got a long way to go yet. Let's continue on taking it a step at a time.'

147

The following day the insurance assessor called Slater and asked to meet him on-site in Washington DC with another client staging a jewellery exhibition. The only day available was the following Wednesday.

By the third day of the exhibition Jack Mason had established a regular commute, which was to confirm David's routine as much as he could. He knew precisely the time the boy left for the school bus pick-up, not going directly to the stop but calling first at a house two streets away to collect a friend, an overweight, fair-haired boy Mason guessed to be in David's class. He'd learned the name of Slater's son was David, and of the sports scholarship, from the local newspaper profile, and discovered from the reporting of other media coverage of the exhibition's national success. For David there seemed to be no positive homecoming pattern; sometimes he went directly to Hill Avenue to practise baskets, as he had the first time Mason had followed him, but on other afternoons he stopped at the home of his fair-haired friend, although never staying longer than fifteen minutes. On the days David came directly home from the school-drop he bicycled back to his friend's house, although on one occasion the overweight boy rode to Hill Avenue. On the Wednesday of the first week David didn't come home on the school bus but arrived in Slater's blue Honda two hours later than normal carrying a sports bag, from which Mason assumed he'd stayed on, presumably at school, for after-hours training.

Mason's mind blocked when he searched for a method more likely to succeed in killing David than an apparent traffic accident. Mason recognized that his only chance would be on one of David's evening bicycle trips to the friend's house. But these were unpredictable, almost invariably in daylight – barely dusk at the very best – covered a distance of just two streets of mostly occupied houses and allowed him virtually no time to prepare, once he realized that the boy was on the move.

Compounding all these problems was the obvious need for the intended crash vehicle to be stolen, exposing him to detection and arrest throughout the time he was at the wheel until he could dispose of it. On the first evening of his resumed surveillance, before establishing as much as he finally did of David's movements, Mason began his search for a potential vehicle, starting almost casually in the shopping precinct car park from which he waited for the arrival of the homecoming school bus. There was an obvious familiarity in the way the battered, mud-splattered green Cherokee 4x4 was driven into the lot and headed for an expected space by a far wall. The driver, a young Latino, emerged with a briefcase and a rolled up newspaper, locked the off-road car and went out through the car park exit, not going in to any of the store rear entrances. Mason guessed that a second vehicle, a Volkswagen whose driver left the same way, was another regular overnight parker. When the bus arrived, Mason followed the boy as he had on the first occasion and watched from his established vantage point for more than an hour. Both cars remained where they had been left when he drove by, on his way back to Chesapeake. The following evening both were parked again, in precisely the same places, fifteen minutes before the arrival of the bus, and were there when he checked on his way back to the cottage.

Mason maintained the protection of switching identifiable cars, choosing a Hertz outlet in Annapolis and staying in the town long enough to locate a hardware store to buy a two inch length of hollow piping and some latex gloves at a supermarket before continuing on to Frederick. That was the day he read in the *Frederick News-Post* of David's scholarship. The Cherokee and the Beetle arrived with clockwork timing that afternoon and were still in their regular slots when he passed on his way back to the cottage. He decided he didn't need to look elsewhere. When he made his regular computer checks that night Mason discovered the Pennsylvania State prison authority's reply to Patrick Bell's exploratory letter and realized the following day was going to be very busy, although he had no way then of knowing just how busy.

'It was the assessor,' identified Slater, returning to the dinner table. 'Tomorrow's meeting is postponed until five.'

'What about picking David up from practice?' demanded Ann, at once. It was the first night she'd got back in time to eat with them since the exhibition opened.

'I can probably get back in time,' said Slater.

'Why don't I ride to school tomorrow?' asked the boy. 'I've done it before.'

'You've got too much stuff to carry,' refused Ann. 'I'll get away from the gallery early again.'

'Worlack agreed to the CBS interview here tomorrow night so that the gallery will be featured,' reminded Slater. Because of the continuing publicity he hadn't yet risked the planned surprise visit with David.

'They don't need me there.'

'Of course you've got to be there,' insisted Slater. 'I told you, I'll get back in time.'

'I really don't see what the problem is,' protested David. 'Practice is geared around schoolwork, because it's arranged that way. So I don't have that much to take with me tomorrow. I can easily get my gear into my backpack.'

'It'll be dark coming home,' objected Ann.

'Not properly,' argued David. 'And I've got lights. How come I could do it before but not now?'

'I don't like you riding around at night,' said Ann, inadequately.

'I don't see it as a problem,' said Slater.

'You don't!' challenged Ann, looking directly across the dinner table at him as she had at their earlier breakfast dispute.

'No, I don't!' echoed Slater, facing her just as determinedly. He was totally aware of Ann's fear – just as he was totally aware she would never be able to lose it – but if it went unchecked or unopposed it would grow and become worse.

'What's the matter? I don't understand!' protested the boy, looking anxiously between his parents.

'Nothing's the matter!' said Slater, just as urgently, remembering the nonsense of David imagining he and Ann might be breaking up. 'As you said the other night, there's a lot happening . . . a lot your mom and I have to fit in at the moment.'

David continued to look doubtfully between his mother and father. 'It all just comes down to my taking my bike to practice tomorrow, so you can both get on with what else you both have to do.'

'It does,' agreed Ann, with the same belated recall as Slater.

'So it's fixed then!' persisted David.

'Unless I can get there in time to pick you up; fit your bike in the trunk,' capitulated Ann. 'If I don't, you call me at the gallery, the moment you get home, OK?'

'I'll do better than that,' grinned David. 'I want to see what all the big deal is about; why we're suddenly famous. I'll stop by the gallery on my way back. How's that?'

'Perfect!' accepted Ann.

Which was exactly the word Mason muttered aloud to himself the following morning when he saw David leave home not to collect his friend and catch the school bus but on his bicycle, hunched beneath his backpack. It was Wednesday, Mason realized. Most probably after-school practice night.

Seventeen

Jack Mason's knuckles stretched white with the force with which he had to grip the steering wheel to stop the sudden shaking in his hands. His left leg began to pump up and down as well and he needed to use his trembling left hand to press down to stop that, too. He was glad he hadn't tried immediately to drive away. It took several minutes for the tremors to stop – in his leg first – but he remained hunched forward, holding on, to make sure they didn't erupt again. He wasn't frightened, he told himself; not too nervous, unable to do it. Ridiculous to have thought it. It was anticipation: excited anticipation. Better now. Had to think now. Plan everything in sequence. And he had all day in which to do it. All day to put everything in place and make sure nothing went wrong.

Mason watched his hand, reaching out to the ignition. Steady as a rock. Everything was all right now, he decided, picking up the road back to Chesapeake, his mind clear, mentally ticking off what he had to do and the order in which he had to do it. First rule before initiating any intelligence operation was to guarantee an escape. So he had to be ready, no loose ends left dangling, the moment he made the hit. Which remained an uncertainty. The shaking – anticipation, not nervousness, he told himself again – had been a fucking nuisance. If there hadn't been that reaction he could have followed the kid, ensuring that he really was cycling to school. Too late now. Now he had to stay with the assumption that it was going to be another delayed return home, possibly involving training indicated by last week's sports bag and that for some reason his father couldn't that night pick him up. Assumption after assumption, Mason recognized. Second rule before initiating an intelligence operation: assume as little as possible, confirm as much as possible. Nothing he could do about that, either. It looked like his best shot and he had to go with it. But be ready to abort, at the first indication of danger.

Mason's mind jumped forward at the word, at the thought of what would be the most dangerous moment for him afterwards, glad he hadn't cleared the town but wishing he'd begun to look earlier, at the first thought of escape. Mason forced himself to remain calm, which became even more difficult after he detoured to pick up David's obvious and most direct route between the school and Hill Avenue and failed to find anything remotely suitable within the necessary walking distance of the shopping precinct. He was luckier retracing the parallel routes, isolating a ramp to an overpass that in turn led on to the interstate link, again curbing his impatience at the necessity to park and examine its possibilities on foot. In the cavern created beneath the ramp was the predictable bedstead and old chair dumping place, additionally littered with the empty bottles and several identifiable syringes and cooking spoons of an improvised shelter and shooting gallery for druggies and winos, although at that moment it was empty. It stank of stale piss. Mason estimated that the search had delayed him by forty-five minutes and decided against looking any further, adding more unpredictability to his list.

He'd hardly bothered to unpack and needed less than five minutes to clear the fishing cottage, leaving his laptop as the last item to go into the car's trunk so he could access his monitoring sites. Nothing had been added to the correspondence he'd already read, the letter to Patrick Bell the only one outstanding. The letting agent was in his office when Mason stopped to return the key with a story of his sudden and unexpected recall to New York. With only four days to go before the expiry of the three-week rental he didn't, of course, expect any refund adjustment. The only telephone calls had been incoming, so the utilities deposit would be more than adequate but if it wasn't any extra could be deducted from the inventory down payment. He'd call to tell the man where to send any balance, with no intention of doing so or expecting it; whatever the amount was – $450 maybe – was a lost business expenditure. The realtor said he hoped Mr Peterson had enjoyed himself sufficiently to visit again and offered his card and Mason said he might well do that.

Mason stayed in Lexington Park long enough to buy six

plastic jerry cans at a supermarket, as well as an almost forgotten but necessary copy of the *Frederick News-Post*, but he only stopped twice on his way to Annapolis, limiting himself to just one gallon of petrol at each gas station to avoid attracting attention by bulk buying. He still arrived before noon, so sure he was well up to schedule that he allowed an hour for lunch, not sure when he'd be able to eat again. He found a store selling phone cards for the necessary untraceable calls he had to make on the same street as an American Express travel office and bought one to the value of fifty dollars. At the travel office he booked another 'red eye' flight to San Francisco, the last out that night from Washington's Dulles airport.

He decided to use the card from the main post office in Annapolis and made his first call to Patrick Bell, prepared for the conversation by having read the Pennsylvania Prison authority response the previous night but more intent upon establishing a double insurance alibi for what was to happen later that day. He was sure there was no way he could be linked to David Slater but the one unanswered, hovering question was whether he had been picked up on the CCTV.

'Sorry I haven't been in touch before,' Mason opened. 'I'm calling from the West Coast. San Francisco.'

'What are you doing there?'

'Job hunting. I'm thinking of relocating, like I told you. The parole authority know all about it. They think it's a good idea.' Caught by an after-thought Mason added hurriedly, 'I haven't even had time to check my Post Office box.'

'Any luck?'

So he hadn't missed a letter, Mason realized, relieved. 'It's looking good but nothing definite. What about the compensation claim?'

'They're offering a non-liability payment of $5,000,' said the lawyer.

'They can stick it up their ass!' dismissed Mason, his reply ready.

'That's what I thought you'd say.'

'By making the offer they're actually admitting liability, aren't they?' Mason had expected the approach to be rejected outright.

'I think so,' agreed the attorney.

'So it's a bluff. And a cheap one at that,' said Mason. 'So we call it, like we've already agreed.'

'If those are your instructions,' accepted Bell.

'They are.'

'What sort of figure will you accept?' asked the lawyer.

'Their best,' said Mason. 'We'll talk about it when we see their response to the threat of a court case.' And which I'll read before I telephone you, he thought.

It was ten thirty in the morning, California time, when Mason made the call to Beverley Littlejohn's San Francisco office. 'Where have you *been*?' she gushed, the moment she recognized his voice. 'I didn't know what was happening!'

'Legal things, my mother's estate,' said Mason. 'I'm coming back out.'

'When?'

'Tonight. You want to see if Santa Barbara is vacant? We could go down late on Friday.'

'If I took Friday off we could go down late tomorrow . . . if you wouldn't be too tired, that is.'

'I won't be too tired, not until after I've said hello,' promised Mason, heavily. 'I've fixed it with Glynis, so there's no need to talk to her, OK?' He was glad this was the last time they were going to be together. She had her use as a good fuck but he didn't like the claustrophobic cloying.

'You sure?'

'Of course I'm sure!'

'OK. Please don't get angry.'

Shut up, for Christ's sake, Mason thought. Aloud, softly, he said, 'I'm not angry. I'll see you tomorrow. I'll come to the apartment.'

'I'll be there.'

Mason made four separate gas station stops on his way back to Frederick, only just able to close the trunk after the last petrol can. A feeling of sickening emptiness, as if he needed to eat, settled in his stomach as he got close to the town and he gripped the wheel more tightly, but there was thankfully no repetition of that morning's shaking. He drove up Hill Avenue and past Slater's seemingly deserted house to loop on to the cross street and get the space next to the corner slot in which the 4x4 was customarily left. The Cherokee swept in

155

precisely on time, the Latino owner walking immediately away without glancing at the car next to him. By the time the Volkswagen arrived Mason had established that there was no telltale alarm light flashing on the Cherokee's dashboard and that there was a lot of encouraging rust, particularly around the door lock and sill.

Mason remained where he was for a further fifteen minutes, psyching himself up as he pulled on the latex gloves, waiting for the school bus to arrive. David wasn't among those who disembarked, although the overweight friend was. Mason wished the empty hollowness would go but it didn't. He'd positioned the car perfectly to hide what he was doing when he thrust the door open. The rusted door lock collapsed inwardly at the first thrust of the hollow pipe against it. There was no scream from a disturbed alarm. It took him just minutes to transfer the petrol cans between the two vehicles, still hidden by the open door. The Cherokee ignition caved in after two heavy jabs from the pipe and fired the moment he crossed the wires behind the automatic steering wheel lock, which released immediately.

As he drove, unchallenged, out on to the highway Mason wrinkled his nose at the stink of cat's piss, worse than the smell beneath the road ramp. It had to be that making him feel sick, not the empty sensation in his stomach.

'I'm not going to make it,' said Slater. 'The assessor's been delayed. We haven't properly started yet.'

'Neither am I,' said Ann. 'I phoned the school. Got a message to David about him stopping off at the gallery. I wish I could have got there.'

'It'll be all right.'

'I know,' said the woman. 'It's just . . .'

'I can't see my getting home much before eight.'

'I guess I'll be about the same time. I'll phone the house later and tell David, if he doesn't stop by. Maybe he could eat with Brad. I might suggest that to him and then call Cathy to see if it would be all right. I should have thought about it last night.'

'That's a good idea. How's Andre?'

'Very flattering. They want me to go on camera with him at the end. It's embarrassing.'

She hadn't refused, Slater recognized; that was a good sign. 'I don't think it's embarrassing. Go for it.'

'You think you're going to get the contract?'

'The guy's talking as if it's part of the assessor agreeing the extra cover . . . he's just walked through the door! I've got to go. Tell David I want to hear what it's like to be trained by a professional instead of me.'

'I'll see you about eight.'

'I love you.'

'I love you too.'

Mason didn't want to turn the engine off. How to hot-wire a car in an escape emergency, which he'd remembered perfectly, had been part of a CIA training session, coupled with the warning that a constantly running engine attracts attention. What he couldn't recall was if an engine would start a second time if it were turned off. He could only guess – wildly – at when David would emerge, although there were several obvious parent-collecting cars around the immediate entrance, from which Mason was parked at least twenty-five yards away. Mason let the engine idle for ten minutes before abruptly disconnecting the wires. He was at his most exposed, at the wheel of a stolen vehicle, loaded with six gallons of petrol and with the break-in equipment on the seat beside him; avoiding attention or curiosity from the other waiting vehicles, from anyone, was more important than the expected opportunity. If it wasn't possible it had to be aborted, some other way of attack found. His stomach was in turmoil, his mouth clamped tight against the need to throw up, his hands occasionally twitching, although not enough to hinder him making tapers from the local newspaper. Two waiting parents, a man and a woman, were talking by their cars, appearing to look directly at him. Mason didn't have any lights on, and was sure they wouldn't be able to see him or make out the mud-smeared registration. No way they could have heard the vehicle was stolen. The smell of cat's piss was stuck in his throat, in his mouth, and he retched, the sound coming out like a belch. His mouth was sour, filthy. He could do it. Had to do it. Couldn't back off now. Come on, you long-legged little asshole! For Christ's sake come on! Where was the brat?

There he was! From his height Mason instantly recognized David among the group of kids, humped by the backpack, wheeling the bicycle with those who were walking towards the waiting cars, high-fiving and gesturing as they parted, the boy actually waiting until the cars drove off.

Tentatively, the shake in his hands making it difficult at the first attempt, Mason rejoined the ignition contacts. The engine fired. Mason put on the low sidelights and pulled out in pursuit. There was too much traffic, in the opposite direction and in front – shielding him – and behind. He'd never get away after running the kid down. He'd be chased, rammed to a halt or stopped by police to whom the number would be immediately reported. It wouldn't work. Everything planned, in place, and it wasn't going to fucking work! Mason belched, sour again. There was so much to reverse: too much. He didn't even have a place to run, to hide.

Beyond the two intervening cars in front Mason suddenly saw David turn off the expected, most direct route. There wasn't any attracting blast of protest when Mason made his following turn without any signal, keeping his lights low but still easily able to see David about twenty yards ahead. It was much better, far fewer cars in either direction and lower, side-street illumination, although there were lights from most of the houses. Because of David's height his saddle had to be high, hunching the boy low over the handlebars. He was riding well, keeping a straight line, not wobbling from side to side. The road turned, straightening into a direct parallel to the main highway they'd just left. As he took the turn Mason saw from his rear-view mirror that there was nothing behind him and that the road in front was empty, too, no indication of approaching headlights.

Now! It had to be now! Mason plunged down on the accelerator, surging the car forward so abruptly the wheels squealed. He had the brief impression of David trying to look behind at the noise, for the first time wobbling. Mason hit. There seemed to be no sound, just the faintest scrape of metal against metal before David and the machine disappeared underneath. The jeep rose up over the obstruction and the scraping got louder with the bicycle and rider trapped and dragged along beneath. The obstruction pulled Mason sideways, on to the sidewalk, so that he had to brake to avoid colliding with a low garden wall. He threw the Cherokee into reverse, backing

158

off, bumping backwards over what was underneath. On the road again he accelerated although without any squeal this time. In his rear-view mirror he couldn't distinguish between the boy and the bicycle. Nothing moved. There was no sudden burst of light from any of the bordering houses.

He'd done it! thought Mason. Begun the revenge he'd thought about – lived off – for fifteen years. Their suffering began now but it was only the very beginning. It was going to get much worse, as bad as he could make it. He didn't any longer feel sick, didn't have any discomfort at all.

It was almost completely dark by the time Mason reached the viaduct den and he had his full headlights on. There was no sign or sound of anyone already being there, even when he drove more deeply in than he'd explored that morning. Mason left the lights on and the doors open, for extra illumination, to see what he was doing, upending two of the petrol cans for their contents to gush out and splashing the rest around the cab to soak the seats. He had intended to remove the petrol cap to use one of the prepared tapers as a wick but forgot that it would be locked. Instead he put it in the last full can, which he wedged beneath the Cherokee's petrol tank. He lit his other tapers from that, throwing them as well as the discarded latex gloves into the car as he ran. The explosion almost knocked him off his feet, making him stagger, but he didn't fall. He didn't look back, either, running until he got into the cross street. Then he did look, surprised at the glow showing above the intervening houses.

The hire car remained where he'd left it, in the half deserted car park. The smell in the car now was not of cat's piss but petrol, where it had splashed over him, and he drove with all the windows down to blow it away, welcoming the coolness of the night air. He was sure all the smell had gone by the time he reached Dulles but he still had three hours before the San Francisco flight, more than enough time to thoroughly wash in a rest room and afterwards savour a settling martini, although his hands weren't shaking any more and he didn't feel sick.

The bulky, bald-headed man who slumped into the seat beside him when boarding was almost completed said, 'Don't you just hate these red-eye flights?'

'Sometimes they're convenient,' said Mason.

* * *

159

'I'm still at the gallery,' Ann told Cathy Hockley. 'David was supposed to stop by after practice but he didn't. So he should have been home an hour ago but he's not answering the phone. Is he with Brad?'

'No,' said the other mother. 'I haven't seen him all evening.'

Eighteen

There appeared to be no part of David's body that was not connected to a sustaining tube or tethered to monitoring screens across which spires peaked and fell or registered fluctuating numbers. David's chest did not seem to rise or fall in time with the expanding and deflating soft-sighing bellows of a life support machine linked by a tracheotomy line. The boy's throat was heavily bandaged around the entry incision. There was further bandaging across the right side of his face, covering his eye, and a separate dressing completely turbaned his head. The bed covering was tented over where his legs would have been but where Slater and Ann knew they were no longer. Neither looked at the other, hunched on either side of the bed. Ann's eyes were actually closed, her lips moving imperceptibly. Each held the clammily cold, unmoving hand laid out towards them between both of theirs, careful not to disturb the drips and feeds strapped into both of their son's arms from frame-suspended bottles. What was visible of David's face was shiny, a wax-white frozen mask. There was no flicker from his closed left eyes, either.

A pent-up sigh whimpered from Ann, loud enough to startle them both, and at last their eyes met.

'He's going to be all right,' insisted Ann, in a fierce whisper.

'Yes.' From the initial, numbing conversation with the surgeon Slater could only remember that as well as losing both legs David's skull was fractured and there were a lot of other injuries.

'It's going to be very different, though.'

'Yes.'

'A lot of adjustments, changes.'

'A lot,' Slater went along with her.

'I want him to wake up!'

'Let him sleep. It was . . .' Slater just stopped short of saying

161

it had been a long operation to do all of what had been done. But it wasn't one operation; several. 'He needs to sleep, to get better.'

'I want him to know we're here, with him.'

'He'll know.'

'They should have arrested them by now. Whoever did it. The police . . .' Ann trailed off, swallowing tight lipped to hold back the nausea welling up inside her.

As if on cue the door behind them opened, a nurse nodding towards the unseen corridor outside. 'There's an officer . . . ?'

Slater eased his hands from David's without disturbing the drips. To Ann, unnecessarily, he said, 'You stay here.'

The uniformed traffic sergeant was different from the officer to whom Slater had earlier given David's identification details. This one had an expression of professional sympathy and the sagging belly of a man who'd spent a lot of time sitting in a patrol car. He introduced himself as Michael Hannigan and said at once they were looking into a possible connection between the accident and the torching of a stolen 4x4 about three miles away from the scene. The timing fitted with that of their only witness who'd seen an off-road vehicle driving away from where within little more than seconds he'd discovered David and the crushed bicycle.

'What, exactly, did he see?'

The policeman shook his head. 'It's not good. He first saw the car, reversing, when he turned off the main highway. That was all he saw, a 4x4. In the darkness he can't even give us a colour or any description at all of its occupants, whether there was one or more than one.'

'Reversing?' challenged Slater, at once.

'Our accident guys have gone over it pretty thoroughly now. Seems the car hit David from behind and carried him and the bike up on to the sidewalk. From the road markings they think both were jammed under the vehicle, which had to reverse to get off them and drive away as it did.'

'So David was driven over twice?'

'That's the way it looks, Mr Slater.'

'Deliberately?'

The officer frowned. 'We don't often get deliberate hit and runs . . . you're getting into criminal intent, murder even, with a question like that . . .'

'What about skid marks . . . something from which you can get tyre treads?'

Hannigan pulled his lower lip between his teeth. 'That's an astute question but then my officer told me you're a security consultant. There weren't any skid marks.'

Hannigan's remark abruptly registered with Slater, who until that moment hadn't considered any implications from this encounter with officialdom and his being a defecting Russian hidden in a Witness Protection Programme. There'd been very specific instructions about it, when they were being coached for entry, though. The inviolable rule was always to maintain their cover identities, never at any stage or for any reason to disclose anything of their past. Forcing himself on Slater said, 'You often get hit and runs without skid marks?'

'It's not unusual, Mr Slater. A guy doesn't see something, he hits it. Then runs. Why do you think someone would want intentionally to run your son down?'

'I don't,' denied Slater, quickly. 'I'm just trying to find out everything I can about what happened.' He was aware of the surgeon whom he'd briefly met earlier outside the operating theatre going into David's room. To the traffic officer he said, 'Is this going to take much longer?'

'I'm just trying to keep you up to speed . . .' The man stopped, embarrassed at the word in the circumstances. 'Sorry, Mr Slater. I mean, to tell you everything that we think we've found out so far . . .' Hannigan shook his head. 'Which I'm sorry to say isn't very much. Why don't we close it down right now?'

'My wife and I won't be leaving here, if you want me again.'

'I don't imagine that we will, not immediately. We've already got all your numbers.'

'I want to know the moment you get the son of a bitch who did this!'

'I know. We'll keep in touch. I hope everything works out OK.'

Slater confronted Ann and the surgeon coming out of David's room as he turned towards it, realizing he couldn't remember the surgeon's name. The man was still in his theatre scrubs, which momentarily surprised Slater until he reminded himself that David was probably not the only emergency in the hospital.

The man said, 'I think we need to talk, that's why I've asked your wife to come with us. My room's just along the hall.'

'Who's looking after David?' demanded Ann.

'We are, Mrs Slater,' said the man, gently. 'The nurse is staying in the room with him.'

'I don't want to leave him for long.'

'We need to talk,' insisted the surgeon.

The room into which he led them was obviously his personal quarters in the hospital. There was a family photograph on the desk, the man and his wife and two boys – one about David's age – embraced and laughing on a cabin cruiser. The nameplate on the desk reminded Slater of the forgotten name, Peter Denting. He showed them to seats before slumping behind the desk, knuckling his eyes. As if there had been no interruption in the conversation he said, 'And I wish we didn't have to talk about it.'

'What?' instantly demanded Ann.

Denting breathed in deeply before saying, 'I do not believe – neither does the neurosurgeon who also operated on him before I unsuccessfully tried to save David's legs – that David can survive.'

'He has survived!' insisted Ann.

Denting leaned forward on to his desk, a calculated gesture enabling him to turn the back of the desk photograph against them. 'Mrs Slater, David is being kept alive artificially. He's suffered a massive, multiple and continuing trauma. The shock factor is enormous. He has undergone a double leg amputation but the possibility of gangrene or blood poisoning is still there. The neurosurgeon has only been able partially to relieve two separate brain depressions from the skull fracture, which has also destroyed the optic nerves to his right eye. His spleen is irreparably ruptured, his liver is severely bruised and the right rib fractures have punctured his right lung, effectively collapsing it . . .' The surgeon paused, shaking his head in what Slater couldn't decide was a gesture of despair or apology. 'I am consciously setting out the injuries he's suffered to make it as clear as I possibly can to you that there is no chance of David recovering. He is already clinically dead.'

'He's breathing!' said Ann, jagged-voiced.

'The life support machine is breathing for him,' contradicted Denting.

164

'What are you telling us?' said Slater, who already knew.

'I am *advising* you,' qualified the surgeon, 'that there is no possibility whatsoever of David ever regaining consciousness, let alone recovering. I am inviting you to tell us to turn off the life support machine.'

'NO!' screamed Ann. 'He's going to be crippled but he's going to live and I'm going to look after him . . . he's going to be all right.'

'He's not, Mrs Slater,' persisted Denting, although still gently. 'I won't repeat myself about David's injuries. But you have to understand, accept, that they are fatal. To keep him on the life machine will at best – and it's very definitely not the best – keep David in a permanent vegetative state.'

'There's medical improvements, breakthroughs, all the time!' implored Ann. 'There could be something you don't know about.'

'I know that we can't bring someone who's clinically dead back to life. Nor will we ever be able to.'

Slater spoke just ahead of his wife, reaching sideways to stop her. 'My wife and I have to talk about it.'

'Of course,' accepted Denting. 'I'm very, very sorry.'

'There's nothing to talk about!' burst out Ann.

'Let's go back to David,' said Slater, still holding Ann's hand.

She came up at once, turning away from the surgeon. Slater released her hand, looking down at the man. 'Thank you.'

Denting made another gesture, this time more easily recognizable as haplessness. 'I just wish . . .'

They sat as they had before, in their same chairs on their same sides of the bed, each of David's cold hands cupped between theirs, Ann's eyes again closed in silent although lip-moving prayer. From the way his arm was positioned to hold David's hand, Slater saw it was almost eleven, for the first time becoming aware that beyond Ann there was daylight through the window, people walking, sitting on benches, cars passing, an ordinary day. He wasn't sure what time he'd arrived the previous night after Ann's panicked cell phone message but they had to have been in the hospital for more than sixteen hours. This time yesterday David had been alive, a whole person in a whole body. Now he was clinically dead, no longer whole. Couldn't be re-made or restored to being a whole person. There weren't going to be any more camping trips, David leading the way. David wasn't going to go to college, wasn't going to become a basketball star, maybe even a famous professional which he'd been so positive that he would become. Slater could hear the words, David's excited, laughing voice, in his mind: *I'm going to make you proud of me, Dad. You just wait. Have my picture in all the sports magazines. Slater the Slayer! How's that sound? I think it sounds right.*

'Nothing's being turned off!' Ann wasn't whispering, although she wasn't speaking loudly.

'He can't be gotten better.'

'I'll make him better. Stay with him all the time.'

'Not now, not here like this. We'll talk about it somewhere else.'

'There's nothing to talk about,' she insisted again. 'And I'm not going anywhere else until he comes round.'

'Somewhere else,' repeated Slater. How long would it take for Ann to accept? How long would it take for him to accept? He didn't expect either of them would, not completely.

'Have the police got who did it?' she suddenly demanded.

'Not yet.'

'Why not?'

'They've only got one witness, who scarcely saw anything. There's something about a stolen car being torched.' The car that ran David down and then reversed over him a second time and didn't leave skid marks, Slater thought on. It wouldn't help to tell Ann that now.

'What's that mean?'

'We didn't talk it through. I guess they think the thief burned it out to destroy any evidence. It was an off-road vehicle, the sort the witness saw driving away from where he found David.'

'Someone's going to be arrested, though, aren't they? They've got to be!' The indignation sounded odd, although Slater couldn't work out why it should. How difficult was it to burn a vehicle so completely that any evidence was destroyed? It had never been part of any training he'd undergone.

'The officer in charge is keeping in touch.' Twice, as they'd talked, Ann had jerked her head up against letting her eyes droop into sleep. Slater said, 'You need to rest. We both do.'

'I'm not leaving!'

'I'm not suggesting we leave. I'll fix something here . . .' To forestall any further refusal Slater said, 'If you go to sleep like that you'll fall over David. You could hurt him more, pull a drip out.'

Ann nodded but didn't speak.

The hospital had overnight relative facilities on the same floor. They only removed their shoes and jackets, otherwise lying fully dressed on top of their single cots. Slater didn't expect to drop off and only realized he had when he came jerkily awake at the sound of Ann's sobbing, although she didn't wake up. He stayed alert to comfort her if she did, but she didn't, just sobbed on. And then Slater started to cry and couldn't stop, his mouth clamped against any sound.

The love-fest was better than the first time – better, in fact, than any in which Mason could ever remember being involved or fanaticizing about – and satiated to the point of sexual exhaustion they actually left the chalet on the Saturday night to walk, with some difficulty and therefore briefly, along the beach before with relief finding an inn overlooking the ocean more for rest than for dinner. Mason had exaggerated intelligence anecdotes ready to maintain the lightness of their previous encounter, but Beverley was on this occasion more serious and Mason recognized the familiar sign. Beverley Littlejohn very obviously considered herself to be involved in a meaningful, maybe even permanent, long-term relationship.

Over their seafood platters she insisted upon telling him of her marriage to an accountant that had lasted three years before her discovery that he was bisexual – too belatedly accepting that she should not have been as devastated as she had been in the homosexual Mecca of San Francisco – and how Glynis Needham had so very determinedly hit upon her that she'd come close to being virtually raped by the woman whom she'd foolishly agreed to let stay during Glynis's San Francisco visit.

'I like sex, OK? So why do I attract those who like it differently from me?'

'I'm not sure how to take that!' said Mason, still trying to keep it light. But very positively not dismissing her outpourings – as absurd as they were – as had been his first instinctive reaction. And he waited.

Predictably Beverley gushed, 'No, darling! I didn't mean that. God how I didn't mean that! What I'm trying to say is that this time it's right! We couldn't be more right together and I couldn't be happier. Or more satisfied. And I don't mean just sexually. I mean I couldn't be surer than I am about anyone.'

Mason toyed with the lobster tail on his plate, stretching the moment to think. His alibi of being in California when he'd hit the kid didn't work if the timings were too deeply and properly investigated, despite his second Californian flight being booked in his new, untraceable name. But it did if the Californian probation officer under whose control he'd been transferred from Washington DC testified that he had definitely been 3000 miles away at the time and date of David Slater's accident. And Mason didn't imagine from the way she was babbling on from the other side of their booth – '*I'm not getting heavy here . . . I didn't mean things to come out like this, not this soon. Help me here, Jack, with a funny story, any story . . .*' – that it would be at all difficult to persuade Beverley to swear just such a statement.

Picking up on her last remark, Mason said, 'Maybe the only story I have matches the one you've just told.'

'You want to spell that out a little better than I just did?'

'I wish I could.'

'You're confusing me even more.'

'You're a probation officer. I'm an ex-con, a traitor to his country. What chance does that story have!'

'As much as we want it to have.'

'You're the one who said you could lose your job over this.'

'I don't give a fuck.'

'You think I want that to happen to you?' Mason pushed his plate away, as if the conversation had taken away his appetite.

'I just told you I don't give a fuck.'

'And I've just told you that I do give a fuck. I've hurt enough people, upset enough lives. I'm not going to do it one more time.'

'So what are you saying?'

'Just that. No more hurt to anyone.' He was in California, with Hollywood just down the road! Why didn't he make a career change and become an actor; this was Oscar material.

168

Because there was more money in the career he'd already chosen, came the immediate answer.

'Do you wonder why I've fallen in love with you?' asked Beverley.

Back off time now that he'd got her to say it, judged Mason. 'And do you wonder why I'm saying what I'm saying? Why, for once in my life, I don't want to risk something as important as we are becoming to each other!'

'Do you really mean that?'

'You know I mean it. Just as you know I love you so completely that I'm prepared to walk away to avoid causing you any harm.'

'I didn't expect tonight to turn out like this but I'm glad it has,' said Beverley, smiling. 'I want to go home now and stop talking.'

Thank Christ for that, thought Mason. He hadn't expected it to turn out like this either, but he was glad it had. Everything was turning out just fine, in fact. He was anxious now to return to San Francisco, where she could get back to work and he could get back to his computer and find out what was happening in Frederick, Maryland.

Beverley didn't set out to continue the restaurant conversation during the rest of the weekend nor did she object to Mason's suggestion that they drive back up to San Francisco earlier than they had from their previous excursion to Santa Barbara to beat the returning Sunday traffic build-up. During the drive Mason expanded his earlier lie about registering with computer employment agencies, both to spare himself from her irritating, job-seeking intrusion on his behalf as well as to test how far he could manipulate and control her.

'When I make the choice I want it to be right: I don't want to go into something, find out too late that I've made a mistake and have to start all over again. I want to settle down and become a pipe and slippers man.'

'I don't see you as a pipe and slippers man.'

'You know what I mean.'

'What do we do if the job you decide on is in somewhere like San Diego?'

'They got a parole office there?'

Beverley nodded.

'Would it be a problem to get a transfer?'

169

'I wouldn't know until I tried.'

'It's not something we can talk properly about until I find something and make sure it's the right one, is it?' said Mason.

'Don't get mad at me if I say something, will you?'

'What?' demanded Mason, turning towards her. Believing that he didn't hold a licence, Beverley always had to drive.

'It's an unusual situation, your not needing financially to get a job. But you've got to, according to the terms of your early release. I've got to make reports and I can't let the job hunting drift on indefinitely.'

Mason decided upon silence, actually turning away from her to look out of the car.

'Jack!'

'What?'

'I asked you not to get mad at me.'

'I'm not mad at you.'

'I know you are.'

'Let me ask you something,' insisted Mason, still not looking back into the car. 'Do you think I would do anything – allow anything – to cause you an official problem?'

'I know you well enough by now to be quite sure that you wouldn't,' pleaded Beverley, risking a smiled look across at him, wishing he would meet her.

'Then why are we having this conversation?'

'Please, Jack!'

'I thought you, of all people, would have known me well enough and trusted me well enough to see and understand the point of what I'm trying to say,' insisted Mason. 'I don't want to be – *won't* be – a fly-by-night, jumping from job to job. I told you that already! How's my work record going to look attached to one of your goddamned official reports showing that I can't hold a job down longer than a few weeks.'

'Jack, this is getting out of control! I trust you and I love you and I know you would never do anything to hurt me or cause me a difficulty. I was just telling you what I have offi- cially to do, as your case officer.'

'Let's forget it.'

'I don't want to forget anything,' refused Beverley, with a determination that surprised and unsettled Mason. 'If we're going to make a go of this, which is what I thought we had decided back in Santa Barbara, we shouldn't let silly misunderstandings build up into something more than they are. Which is what this is doing. I'm not hassling you. I just don't want anything to get in the way, put anything at risk. That's the only reason I mentioned having to file progress reports, OK?'

He'd almost pushed too hard, Mason acknowledged. 'OK.'

'You're not mad?'

'No, I'm not mad. I don't want anything to get in the way between us, either. I'll start setting things up first thing tomorrow.'

Which Mason did, although not in the sequence Beverley inferred. To guard against a sudden, unexpected return Mason curbed his impatience for a full thirty minutes after Beverley left her apartment before turning on his laptop and accessing the website of the *Frederick News-Post*. The newspaper had led its front page on the first available edition with the running down of David Slater. There were two photographs accompanying the story which turned on to an inside page to include the background account of the boy's selection for a sports scholarship at the University of Maryland, from which a spokesman described the incident as an 'appalling tragedy'. There was also a photograph of Ann on that inside page, taken at the gallery exhibition but not one of Slater. David's injuries were listed, as well as him being on a life support machine. His condition was stated to be grave by a hospital spokesperson. A police source said the hit and run was the subject of a criminal investigation 'with a particular aspect' of forensic evidence that was not being disclosed. There was a separate but connected account of the burning to death of an unnamed, unidentified man found close to the totally destroyed wreckage of a stolen 4x4 similar to that seen by a witness driving away from where David was found. The place where the man died was beneath a connecting interstate link commonly used by itinerant alcoholics and drug users. If the dead man were one of the frequent users of the area it would make identifying the badly burned body extremely difficult. It had not been ruled out that the dead man had been the driver of the vehicle but it was considered unlikely and the death was being treated as a criminal investigation.

Mason scrolled anxiously through the follow-up stories in subsequent editions of the newspaper for an explanation of the 'particular aspect' of forensic evidence but couldn't find it. But he was reassured by the repetition in those subsequent stories and police spokesmen quotes that the official investigation was very obviously stalled. The story in that day's edition was reduced to a single column of little more than two inches. David's condition was reported as unchanged. No identity had been established for the man who had been burned to death. Nowhere in anything Mason read was there reference to Daniel Slater being a defecting KGB colonel that almost inevitably would have resulted in his being named.

There was nothing new involving or about him on any of his illegal, unsuspected computer 'cuckoo' sites but there was a Chase Manhattan sales pitch for an investment portfolio in his PO box. Mason occupied the rest of the morning registering at two computer industry employment agencies, giving the box number for mail and promising to supply fuller CVs later and in the afternoon made the much delayed tourist visit to Alcatraz, thinking that if he'd had to serve his sentence there and not White Deer he probably would have risked being drowned by the bay currents and tried to escape.

Mason was irritated by the uncertainty of the undisclosed forensic discovery in the burned out 4x4, as he continued to be by his stupid CCTV mistake at Ann's gallery, but objectively he decided he was doing well, reassuring himself that there would almost certainly have been a reference to him in Glynis Needham's computer system if there had been any official interest in him.

There was still no cause to hurry back east. David Slater still had to die. Mason was enjoying himself.

Nineteen

A nn stayed constantly at David's bedside, quitting the room only when doctors or nurses needed to change either dressings, drips or the comatose boy himself, and briefly to sleep on her hospital cot. Slater left once, on the first day to collect changes of underwear for them both from Hill Avenue, each uncaring of their outward appearance. Slater spoke morning and afternoon with Mary Ellen, relieved there was no immediately impending work, otherwise leaving her to run the office with instructions to refuse any new orders or enquiries. He also talked daily with Jean at the Main Street gallery, relaying Ann's disinterested direction on how and in what order to close down the Worlack exhibition and to reject any fresh approaches that might have resulted from its success. Ann was an irregular worshipper but literally embraced the consoling offer from the hospital-attached vicar, praying with him daily with David's hand still clasped between hers, her eyes fervently clamped shut in her desperation for divine intervention. Slater, who had no belief, prayed with them too, dismissing the hypocrisy. When they remembered or were urged by nurses, they ate off trays.

And throughout David remained artificially alive.

On the fifth day, after the unanswered prayers, Ann abruptly blurted out, 'Why hasn't he woken up?'

Slater was startled by the demand: it had become a vigil without words. He said, 'He's too ill.'

'I want him to wake up!' Ann's voice was slurred, as it had been when she was drinking.

Slater remained silent.

'We should get specialists. Better people than here! Why haven't you got specialists in? Had David transferred?'

'Are you ready to talk?'

'No!' refused Ann, knowing what he meant.

'We have to talk.'

'No.'

'It's no good, Ann.'

She lowered her head until it rested on her hands that were holding David's. 'He's so cold! He needs more blankets. Get some more blankets.' She looked up as she spoke, her hair matted and straggled around a face wet and streaked by tears.

'God can't bring David back to life. No doctors, no specialists, can bring him back to life. We've got to let him go.'

'No!' she said, but for the first time her voice was softer, the resignation gradually evident.

'There's nothing we can do . . . nothing anyone can do.'

'Another day. Just one more day, please.'

'One more day,' Slater agreed.

'Just in case.'

'I'll tell them . . . make arrangements. I need to make arrangements.'

'Yes, you do that. Leave me here.'

Peter Denting was in his room, wearing street clothes, and rose at once from his desk when Slater entered. Slater said, 'We've decided.' His voice broke and he coughed and said it again.

Denting said, 'I'm glad you have. It must . . . it's the only decision you could have made . . .'

'But Ann wants one more day.'

The surgeon hesitated. 'All right.'

'And I have to make arrangements.'

'We have grief counsellors who can help, afterwards.'

Psychiatrically trained counsellors who would want background his-tories, thought Slater at once. 'Thank you. But we'll be all right.'

'They're very good. I recommend you talk with them. And with the vicar. I know he's been visiting daily.'

'We'll see,' avoided Slater.

'You're going to need a lot of help,' insisted Denting. 'Your wife particularly.'

The man was right, Slater accepted. 'I'll talk to her about it when it's over. Let's get it over first.' He was talking about his son, Slater realized, talking about letting his son die.

'And speak to your own physician,' advised Denting.

174

'There's medication, safe things, that can be prescribed. I can get something for you here, right away, if you think she'd take it. '

Ann was already hollowed out, Slater thought. How much worse was she going to be later? 'I'll think about it . . . see how she is.'

'What about you?' pressed the surgeon.

'I'll be OK.'

Denting's internal telephone sounded. The man responded looking at Slater during the short exchange and when he put the telephone down he said, 'The policeman, Hannigan, is looking for you. I'll let people know what you've decided about David . . .' The man hesitated. 'You're doing the only thing you can.'

The traffic sergeant was waiting by the nurse's station, his uniform strained around him. There was another man with him, in plainclothes. Both rose at Slater's approach. Hannigan said, 'This is Homicide Detective John Stone.'

'Homicide!' echoed Slater, at once. 'You got who killed David?'

'We didn't know David had died?' frowned Stone. He was a short, slim, unprepossessing man in a conservative, waist-coated suit.

'At the moment clinically. We're going to turn off the life support machine,' declared Slater, his voice catching as he finished.

'We're sorry to hear that,' said Hannigan, professionally sympathetic.

'Why is a homicide detective involved?' said Slater, recovering.

'You been reading the papers, Mr Slater?' asked Stone.

'No?' said Slater, questioningly.

'Forensics have come up with something . . . something we're not releasing to the media at the moment. And can't understand.'

'What?' asked Slater, holding back the irritation at not being told outright if whatever it was had something to do with David.

'The 4x4 that was torched?' picked up Hannigan. 'The inside was saturated with petrol. And although they're melted out of obvious recognition, our scientific guys think they found

175

the plastic containers in which the gas was carried. At least five. And as I already told you someone was burned to death where it was dumped and set alight.'

'Intentionally?'

Hannigan gave a gesture of uncertainty. 'And as I also told you, where it was dumped is a hang-out for winos and druggies. We haven't identified the dead guy . . .' He hesitated. 'And then I remembered when we talked that you thought someone might have deliberately run David down . . .'

'And I thought I should come and talk to you about that,' finished Stone. 'You have any cause to think your son was deliberately run down?'

Slater didn't reply at once. Never disclose yourself to be in a Witness Protection Programme or the reason for it, he remembered. It was inconceivable that Mason could have found them and in some way be involved, that he would run a child down. There'd inevitably be publicity if he told them who he was; create a situation in which Mason really could find them, from the media reports. If he was identified, he and Ann would have to run, start all over again. Start all over again without David. Ann couldn't stand that sort of upheaval, after what had happened to David. Slater didn't think he could, either. He shrugged. 'It was instinctive . . . I wasn't thinking. You working the theory that the dead man was murdered?'

'At the moment we don't have a theory, just some things that don't fit together,' said Hannigan. 'There wasn't enough time between when your son was hit and the fire for whoever stole the 4x4 to stop and stock up with gas for a long journey. And he couldn't have refuelled anyway, although he wouldn't have known that. The cap to the gas tank was locked and the owner still had the key, so it was obviously hot-wired.'

Slater stood looking steadily between the two police officers. 'Whoever ran David down bought at least five cans of gas – gas he couldn't use to refuel the vehicle – *before* he stole it?'

'That's how it looks,' agreed Hannigan. 'Preparing to destroy any evidence.'

'Evidence of what?' persisted Slater.

'Something else we haven't got around to answering, unless it was just traces of the thief when he finished with the car.'

'How many cases have you ever come across of something like that being done?'

'None,' admitted Hannigan. 'Stolen cars torched, certainly. Happens all the time. But not having the gas already in the vehicle, ready. Normally it's just using what's already in the tank.'

'Where was the body, inside or outside the car?'

'You ever been involved in detective work, Mr Slater?' asked Stone. 'You kinda think like a cop.'

'I'm a security consultant.' Was he being asked to explain himself?

'I know. That didn't answer my question.'

'No, I've never been a cop,' said Slater, his voice rising with his anger.

'How'd you get into security?'

Slater wasn't sure whether the heat he felt was anger or apprehension. He hoped it wasn't showing on his face. There was no reason to become uneasy about his being properly identified. There'd been protective provisions built into the creation of his new life. 'Drifted into it, really, after the marines. Did some embassy security work and decided to stick with it.' The government was responsible for military and diplomatic employment, as they were with the CIA, making it easy to fabricate official although false biographies for people they were protecting.

'Where'd you serve?' persisted Stone.

Enough, decided Slater. 'At the US embassies in Paris and Rome,' he recited, letting his voice rise again and knowing there were entries confirming that on army records. 'But what the hell has my army service and my job got to do with the running down of my son and the burning to death of some guy in a wino dump – both presumably by a guy you're nowhere near catching!'

'Absolutely nothing,' said Hannigan, hurriedly.

'We asked ourselves the same question, about whether the body was in or out of the car,' said Stone. 'If the body, already dead, was inside along with all that gas, torching the car would be a good way of disposing of it, wouldn't it?'

'And David?' demanded Slater, still loud voiced.

'A complicating accident. If the guy's killed somebody he's hyper, wanting to get rid of the body, driving badly. He can't stop, after hitting your son, can he, not with the cargo he's already carrying? That's why he drives away. If he's decided how he's going to dispose of the body he's also chosen where to do it. Which is another inconsistency because it's part of a traffic system, not somewhere you'd easily find, in the dark. He leaves David, without even stopping to see what he's done, goes to his pre-arranged spot and torches the vehicle.'

'So the body was inside the car?' pressed Slater. If the scenario was as they were describing it there couldn't be any possible connection with Jack Mason.

Hannigan shook his head. 'Impossible to determine. It was found *outside* the wreck. But it blew up when the heat got to the gas that was in the tank – the owner had just filled it up. The body could have been inside but blown out. There were some physical fractures as well as burns.'

'I don't see how I can help you,' said Slater, suddenly caught by the unreality of discussing hypothetical murder just yards from where David lay, murdered very much in reality if not by technical definition.

'We're sorry to have troubled you,' said Stone, without any regret in his voice. 'And I'm sorry if I upset you with some of my questions.'

'And we are very sorry about your son.'

'You're not even close to an arrest, are you?' challenged Slater. 'Whoever killed David isn't going to be caught, is he?'

'The case is very far from being closed,' insisted Stone.

'It's never going to be, for my wife and I,' said Slater, turning away from both men. 'I've got a funeral to arrange.'

Jack Mason let two days go by after picking up the Pennsylvania prison authority's dismissal of his civil action threat from Patrick Bell's computer, patiently letting the lawyer read to him over the telephone what he'd already seen on his illegal entry. When Bell finished Mason said, 'So, it's who blinks first?'

'You want me formally to file?'

'You know I do.'

'The State's got more money than you. They want to string it along, they can clean you out with potential costs before it ever gets to court. It's the oldest ploy in the book.'

Peter Chambers was being released in six weeks, thought Mason; everything was working out just fine. 'Can't we file for a stipulated hearing time?'

'That shows our hand, as far as costs are concerned.'

'Doesn't it show our determination, too?'

Instead of directly answering Bell said, 'How's the job hunting going out there?'

'Moving along. One or two possibilities,' lied Mason, easily.

'Another defensive ploy is their knowing that your anonymity is blown when – and if – we get to court.'

'We've been this way already!'

'And I want to go this way again. You think you could keep a job if you hit the headlines like you did before?'

'That's intimidation!'

'That's reality. Which I want you to face.'

'Whose side you on?'

'Yours. And don't be offensive, Jack.'

'I can use my inheritance.'

'I know what your inheritance was. You going to put all that at risk, all that and a hell of a lot more, public notoriety all over again as well as the financial cost if we lose!'

'We can't lose. Everything's stacked in my favour.' For the first time Mason fully realized what he was going to achieve. The prison authorities were going to rack up a big bunch of costs, which he wasn't going to be around to pay because he wasn't Jack Mason any more. OK, it wasn't going to be a financial penalty Frank Howitt was going to have to pay but the motherfucker would pay in every other way.

'I told you before, you're starting from the back. No matter how justified you might be in court you're the ex-con and traitor to this country.'

'Go ahead and initiate proceedings,' insisted Mason. 'And send your bill to the PO box you've got.'

'You don't have anything permanent yet?'

'Still moving around. You can send any papers I need to sign to the box number, too.'

'I've got a responsibility to give you my best advice. And my best advice is to accept the offer they've already made and move on.'

'Issue whatever you've got to issue,' instructed Mason.

'Let's see what balls they've got.' And lose yours in the process, he thought.

Beverley arrived back at the apartment by 5.30, as she had done every day since his return to San Francisco to live with her, and as he had done every one of those working days, he greeted her in an immaculate apartment ('You must have thought I was a total slut when you first walked in!') with a table and chairs set out in readiness on the minuscule balcony. While she showered he mixed the martinis, the glasses frosted, for when she came out on to the balcony which still had a better view of the bay and the Golden Gate bridge than his original hotel. It had become another ritual for her to be naked beneath the thin shift in which she emerged, bare foot.

'How's your day been?'

'Slow,' he said, as always prepared. 'There was a lot of stuff waiting for me at the post office and I managed to track down some employment outlets in Los Angeles and San Diego. I thought I might make a quick trip to register. If I caught the first flight I could probably cover San Diego and Los Angeles in one long day.' He did have the names and addresses but no intention of bothering with any of them.

'What about the agency here?'

'I checked today, of course. There's nothing.'

She sat opposite, her nakedness obvious through the thin material as she knew he liked. This time, however, she was not looking directly, invitingly, at him as she usually did, but studying the glass in front of her. 'I've got to make my first report soon. I'm going to need names, stuff like that. And I had a call today from Glynis, asking how things were going.'

'Call?' queried Mason, who'd checked for email exchanges less than an hour before Beverley's arrival home. He didn't for one minute like the idea of their changing the way they communicated.

'She's thinking of another trip out here.'

Keep it easy and cool, Mason decided. There hadn't been any reference to David Slater in the *Frederick News-Post* in the past three days from which to decide his return east, to finish what he'd started. Which wasn't really a serious obstacle to his moving on. 'She's determined to get you between the sheets, isn't she?'

'Don't talk like that, darling.'

'When's she coming?'

'She didn't say. It was just a casual conversation.'

'I'd have to move out while she was here, wouldn't I?'

'I wouldn't let her come here.'

Mason shook his head. 'We couldn't take that chance. I could use the time going down to San Diego and Los Angeles.'

She looked down again into her almost empty glass. 'I've got to make that report in the next few days. Glynis isn't coming that soon.'

Mason got up, took the pitcher from the refrigerator and replenished both their glasses. 'We'll work it out. But talking about Glynis reminds me. I owe you some money. I spent a while on the phone – your phone – myself today, talking to my lawyer about the compensation claim.'

'Glynis asked me about that,' disclosed Beverley. 'Asked me if I knew what was happening.'

The walls were definitely closing in, thought Mason. 'Why did she ask you that, as if she knew we've come as close as we have?'

'I raised it with her,' admitted Beverley. 'Asked her if she knew what was happening about it back there.'

Mason sipped his drink, to gain time. 'Why did you do that?'

'Because it could affect us. I don't want anything to affect us.'

'What did she say?'

'That the prison authority is going to face you down, make you back off.'

Beverley Littlejohn would definitely lie and cheat for him if he asked her, Mason decided. He really had to think this through, maybe even change his mind about walking away from her as he'd originally intended. Whacking the kid had been easy. Whacking Slater and Ann wasn't going to be and there was no way he could anticipate the alibi he might need. 'That's what my lawyer told me.'

'Back off then!' pleaded Beverley, urgently, coming up from her drink. 'What's more important, you and I and what we could have together? Or screwing an asshole of a prison guard and his employers by getting a few bucks?'

Three million dollars was hardly a few bucks, thought Mason. 'Put like that there really isn't a choice.'

'You going to do it then?' Beverley asked, anxiously. 'You going to abandon the whole thing?'

Why was it so important both to Beverley and the dyke in Washington to know whether he was going to pursue his civil action? wondered Mason. 'I'd do anything for you. Anything and everything,' tested Mason.

'And I'd do anything and everything for you . . . for us,' said Beverley.

'I need time to think . . . work things out,' said Mason. Most importantly of all to work out the benefits of keeping you on the leash you've put around your own neck, he thought.

'One more day!' she pleaded.

'No, Ann.'

'Just one more day!'

'We decided. You've talked to Denting. To the vicar. You know.'

'I want to be with him, when it's done.'

'We'll both be with him.'

Slater waited for her to break down but she didn't. She said, 'Tell them we're ready.'

Twenty

A nn leaned, stumbling, upon him so heavily that Slater was practically carrying her, one arm supportively tight around her shoulders, his other hand cupping her nearest elbow to keep her as close as possible and to remain upright. Ann was entirely in black, her face completely covered by an encompassing black veil into which Slater hunched, because he had not only to prevent her collapsing, but also to use as much of the veil's shadowing concealment against the cameras he hadn't anticipated, local television as well as press photographers. There was a lot Slater hadn't expected. Jeb Stout was there representing the University of Maryland – their wreath a basketball-sized sphere describing David as a star – along with Victor Spalding and two other teachers from David's school. So was Peter Denting with the two nurses permanently assigned to David throughout his hospitalization. Andre Worlack's exhibition designer came down from New York and there was a wreath from the San Jose company with which Slater had negotiated the large contract. Slater wasn't aware of the homicide detective John Stone until they left the church at its rear. Throughout the service, conducted by the hospital vicar, Ann still needed Slater's supportive arm around her shoulders, rising and sitting at Slater's urging, unable to sing – unable even to hold a prayer or hymn book – and seemingly oblivious to the sermon or to the eulogy in which David was referred to as a sports prodigy and an outstanding scholar, emptily embellished with phrases about God's mysteries and brilliant, short-lived blazing comets.

At the graveside Slater needed the help of Mary Ellen Foley to keep Ann upright. As the coffin was lowered, Ann emitted a wail more animal than human. There was no reception wake. Mary Ellen rode home with them in the funeral car and helped Ann immediately to undress and settle in bed, although she refused the sedative that the doctor had prescribed. When Jean arrived to drive Mary Ellen home, Slater told her to keep the gallery closed for the rest of the week and that he'd call at the weekend to tell her if Ann intended opening the following week, doubting that she would. He warned Mary Ellen he wasn't sure when he'd be returning to the office, either. Finally alone, he checked every hour upon Ann, who remained unmoving as she'd settled in their bed, apparently asleep. In between he drank two very large brandies, without their having the slightest effect before impulsively packing all David's clothes and belongings, including his basketball, belatedly sorry that he hadn't included the ball in the burial coffin, cumbersome – maybe even unacceptable – though the gesture might have been. He thought, inappropriate though it also might have been, that he should have included David's hunting knife: it had epitomized the camping weekends that there would no longer be. And Slater cried, abruptly at different memories and reminders, sometimes as loudly and unrestrained as Ann had wailed at the graveside.

Slater came awake slumped sideways on the couch upon which he'd finally sat after packing David's things. The lounge was in complete darkness but he knew at once that he was not alone in the room. As he straightened, sticky-eyed, aching and cold, he blurted, 'Who is it . . .? Where . . .?' There was the shift of somebody moving. 'Ann?'

There was no reply but Slater became vaguely aware of a figure sitting on the facing couch and leaned sideways again to snap on the table lamp. Ann wore a housecoat but it was open over the nightdress into which Mary Ellen had helped her. She was staring directly ahead, unfocused, holding between both hands a tall tumbler Slater knew would be gin, already half drunk. 'Ann?'

'David's gone,' she announced, no emotion in her voice.

'Yes.'

'We won't see him. Never again.'

'No.'

Like an automaton she lifted her glass, drank deeply, and lowered it back to her lap. 'He was killed. Murdered.'

'Yes.'

Ann moved, only slightly, looking properly at him for the first time. 'You know?'

184

'Of course I know, darling. He was run down . . . a car that didn't stop.'

'No!' she contradicted, louder than before, indignantly. 'He was killed by Jack. Jack ran him down. Killed him.' She drank again, robot-like.

Their doctor had warned Ann's reaction might be unpredictable. 'The police are going to find who did it. There's a detective working on the case now. I've spoken to him.'

'Jack did it. Tell him that Jack did it.'

'I will,' said Slater. 'I'll call him tomorrow.'

'You're not listening to me . . . believing me . . .' Indignant again.

'I am, darling. I'll tell him tomorrow.'

'Listen to me!' Ann insisted. 'I've seen Jack . . . know he's here. That he's found us. Wants to hurt us.'

'It's late, Ann. Let's go back to bed. I'll get you the medicine the doctor prescribed.'

Ann finished her drink in a gulp, at once offering her glass. 'Get me another. Don't water it down with too much ice. I want to taste the gin.'

Slater hesitated, knowing from the accompanying pamphlet that alcohol was not recommended with the medication she'd been prescribed, but then took the glass to the kitchen where the rarely used drinks were. She was rambling, in shock, but nowhere near drunk. He wouldn't let her have another, after this.

'Thank you,' she said, accepting the drink when he returned.

'We'll go to bed after this.' He considered having another brandy but decided against it. His mouth tasted sour from what he'd already drunk.

'When you went to San Jose,' she started again. 'When I took that afternoon off from the gallery . . .' Ann stopped, looking at her glass as if in memory. 'I didn't check the CCTV. I wasn't there. A lot had been overrun when I did look, the following day. That's when I saw him. He'd gone past the gallery. He doesn't look quite the same. He seems broader, but I know it was him.' She was talking quite ordinarily, her voice flat, conversational.

Slater sat gazing at his wife, unspeaking, unsure. It had to be a fantasy. *Had* to be. Maybe it was more than shock, a nervous breakdown even, brought on by grief. 'What did you

185

do with the tape, Ann? Have you kept it, for me to see? Changed it for one of the spares I gave you?'

Ann shook her head. 'We'd talked about it, remember? Decided there was no way he could find us. He didn't look quite the same, like I said. I thought I was imagining it. Now I know I wasn't.'

It just wasn't possible, couldn't be possible! 'You saw his face?'

She shook her head again. 'He'd gone past. It was his back. His face would have been on it if I'd looked at it earlier, as I should have done.' Ann took a deep gulp. 'I'm sorry. It's my fault David is dead. All my fault.'

'Stop it, Ann! It's not your fault. Nothing's your fault.'

'He'll come after us now. You know that's what he'll do, don't you? I know Jack. I know that's what he'll do.'

He'd have to get Ann psychiatric help, Slater decided. Were psychiatrists bound by the same Hippocratic oath as medical doctors, forbidden by confidentiality against disclosing to whom Ann had been first married and the fact that he was a defecting Russian? He'd have to check. It didn't matter if they weren't. He had to get Ann well.

'You'll have to kill him, of course,' said Ann, no tone to her voice. 'Kill him before he kills us. That's what he'll try to do, after what he did to David.' She drank again.

'Ann, we're going to have to help each other. We're going to go to bed now. I want you to take what the doctor gave you. You have to get some sleep.'

'You don't believe me, do you!' she accused again. 'You think I'm mad.'

'No, darling. I don't think you're mad. We need help, both of us. We've got to learn how to cope.'

Ann came forward on her seat, looking fixedly at him. 'You've got to believe Jack has found us, stop him doing to us what he did to David. Get a gun. Whatever. Something to protect us.'

'I will. I'll get a gun tomorrow. Today, rather. I won't let anything happen to you.'

'Don't patronize me! *Believe* me! I want another drink.'

'No, Ann. No more drink. We're going to bed now and you're going to take what the doctor gave us.'

'You locked up? Set the alarms? Checked the CCTV?'

He hadn't done any of it, Slater realized. 'I'll do it now.'

'He could have got into the house already. Be hiding somewhere.'

'He's not in the house, Ann. No one's in the house except you and me. And you're safe. Nothing is going to happen to you, I promise.'

'I want another drink.'

'I'll lock up.'

Slater went from room to room, securing the doors where he had to and checking the window bolts. Before setting the individual room alarms he fast forwarded most of that day's CCTV loop, most of which was empty even of passing cars. The only people on the tape were the funeral people who'd collected and returned them, he and Ann, Mary Ellen Foley and Jean. He saw, as he watched, that he'd left his car outside in the drive instead of putting it away in the garage as he had done in the first week or two of learning of Jack Mason's release. To do it now would mean unlocking at least three doors and turning off and resetting as many alarms and Slater decided not to bother. When he got back to the lounge he saw that Ann had made herself another drink.

He said, 'We're all locked up. And I've checked the CCTV.'

'I'm not ready yet.'

'I'm very tired, after today. And I've got a lot to do in the morning, after what you've told me.'

'I need a gun, too. We both do.'

'I need to go to bed now if I am going to be able to do everything that I have to do in the morning.'

'I'll take my drink with me.'

'All right.'

Ann rose without his having to help her and walked unaided to their bedroom, not needing the handrail to climb the stairs. She took the prescribed tranquillisers without argument, although with the gin she carried, not water.

'I told you he'd find us, didn't I?' she said.

'Yes, you told me.'

'And I was right.'

Slater decided their doctor had to be his first call in the morning. He needed a recommendation to a psychiatrist as soon as possible.

* * *

187

Jack Mason squinted close to his computer screen illustrating the funeral photograph in the *Frederick News-Post*, wishing the definition were clearer and acknowledging that Daniel Slater was good, appearing to have forgotten nothing of his ingrained tradecraft. So cleverly had Slater hunched himself into Ann's shrouding black veil that, had he not already made the identification and known the assumed identity, he would never have recognized the man who'd been his control for three years, after his re-assignment to CIA headquarters from Moscow. It could be a misconception from how Slater had been holding himself to support Ann but the photograph seemed to confirm Mason's impression from his brief sighting outside the gallery that physically Slater was slightly heavier from how he remembered the man from their monthly contact meetings. The hairstyle had definitely been changed, worn shorter and with the parting on the side opposite from how he'd once combed it. Slater had never worn double-breasted suits, either; there'd been a threadbare joke about his not wanting to look like someone from the Soviet *Praesidium*, each of whom always seemed to dress like that. It was impossible to make out Ann's features beneath the veil or to determine how much, if at all, she had physically changed. If she still drank as much as she once had the need would have been for Slater to hold her up from collapsing into a drunken heap rather than because she had been overcome by grief at the boy's burial.

Mason read the accompanying story with as much attention as he had devoted to the photograph. For the first time there was reference to a homicide investigation, although not into the killing of the boy but into the circumstances surrounding the death of the man who had been found close to the burned-out 4x4. The body still hadn't been identified and there was insufficient orthodontic work to canvas dentists, the usual method followed to trace people so badly disfigured by fire. Mason sniggered at the police spokesperson's insistence that the investigation was ongoing, initially deciding that they still weren't making any progress, before balancing the dismissal with the thought that the killing of Ann and Slater – even if it could be manoeuvred into appearing accidental which he increasingly doubted – could instantly escalate the police probe to a federal level. But that was predictable anyway after David's death. An already suspected homicide would actually increase the obvious existing confusion, more to his advantage than endangering him.

His difficulties were far closer to home, Mason decided; or to where he'd chosen to make his very convenient and sexually satisfying home. Now – immediately – was the time to go back and deal with Slater and Ann, when they were still locked into shock and grief and wouldn't be thinking about anything other than the loss of their kid, whose killing had been easy, a presented opportunity he'd grabbed and successfully used. He wasn't likely to get another, Mason realistically accepted. On this occasion he'd have to plan far more carefully, ensuring every precaution; 'never initiate an operation until establishing a guaranteed escape' echoed in his mind, the universal intelligence mantra. Which took time, potentially a lot of time. Creating an absence that had to be accounted for and accepted by the so far trusting Beverley Littlejohn if she was to be kept as a potential alibi – his best and most guaranteed escape, in fact.

Mason spent the remainder of the day trying to evolve a convincing story, picking at the too obvious flaws that she might isolate, not completely satisfied with his final resolve but unable to improve upon it. Whether he succeeded in convincing her came down to his already self-admired acting ability. Even if he did, his schedule would still be limited and if it wasn't sufficient Beverley and her usefulness would have to be discarded, which she was eventually going to be in any case.

Mason had the apartment immaculate and the drinks prepared as usual for Beverley's return, waiting for her on the balcony while she completed her homecoming ritual; the diaphanous shift that evening a pale yellow silk.

'So how was your day?' she asked.

'Decisive,' replied Mason, his script already prepared.

'You've got an interview!' she anticipated at once.

'I've been making decisions.'

Beverley sat regarding him seriously. 'What's that mean?'

'That I've acknowledged – realized – that I haven't been fair to you.'

Her second pause was longer than the first. 'What does *that* mean?'

'You're out on a limb with me. Getting involved like you have, risking everything. And I've been taking advantage of it, moving in like I have, not yet going down the coast to register with other agencies because I don't need the money . . . not thinking of what you've got to do, making out reports, stuff like that. It isn't right and it isn't fair and — '

'Stop, darling! Please stop! I've become involved with you because I *want* to become involved. I've told you already that I don't give a damn about any risks and I don't think you're for a moment, in any way, taking advantage of me. I *want* you to be here, living with me. And I know you'll get a job and I think you're being sensible not rushing it, snatching at the first thing that comes along.'

Mason shook his head in apparent refusal. 'I spoke to Patrick Bell today, too. Told him I didn't want to go on with the compensation claim. I can't risk the publicity, can't risk how it would affect us. I'll take their crap offer, close everything down.'

Beverley smiled, faintly. 'I'm so glad . . . about the publicity, I mean. That wouldn't have been a good idea, would it?'

'I have to go back east,' Mason declared. 'Bell says he's initiated a lot of legal things that have got to be unravelled now that I'm not going to proceed. The quickest way to do that will be for me to go back because I want everything to be settled quickly, once and for all, so that we can properly settle down – everything quick, sorted out and finalized. That's why I'm building in the trip to Los Angeles and San Diego.'

'You're losing me along the way here,' protested Beverley. 'Let's take it a little slower.'

Mason refilled both their glasses. 'I'll go back east tomorrow. Sort all that needs to be sorted out with Bell – with luck the shitty first offer will just about cover my costs but it doesn't matter if it doesn't. The only thing that matters now is you and I. When I'm done, I'll fly back to Los Angeles or San Diego – whichever is the most convenient but do both to complete all the formalities – and then come back here.'

'How long's that likely to take?'

Mason shrugged. 'As long as it takes. And I've got two things to ask you and if you don't like either I'll understand – be very disappointed but I'll understand because I'm an ex-con and you're a law officer according to the definition of your job.'

Beverley sat on the opposite side of the tiny balcony, her drink forgotten on the separating table. 'What?'

'You're going to have to cover for me in that first report you've got to submit – exaggerate a little on how hard I'm trying to rehabilitate and settle down.'

'I've already realized that.'

'As I said, it's your choice.'

There was a brief, hovering silence.

Mason said, 'So what is it?'

'You know damned well what it is.'

Mason smiled. 'You've no idea how much I'd hoped that's what you'd say. And something else that's just occurred to me. We've got to keep Glynis out of this. We both know how much she wants to get into your pants. You any idea how she'd react, if she found out – suspected even – what was going on between us!'

'I'm not going to talk to Glynis about anything,' insisted Beverley. 'You said there was something else?'

'There is. Will you marry me?' That hadn't been rehearsed but he decided it was brilliant and that he had the most guaranteed escape alibi he could possibly have.

Twenty-One

When he didn't produce the demanded handgun but instead, as gently as he could, suggested they see a specialist doctor, Slater expected the indignant outbursts – near hysteria even – with which Ann had greeted his doubt that she'd seen Mason on the gallery CCTV.

Instead, quite composed and without any resentment, she said, 'A psychiatrist, you mean?'

'Yes,' said Slater. There was nothing to gain from trying to avoid or sweeten what he was attempting to do to make her well again; he was obviously going to be as supportive and loving as was possible but Ann would despise him if he lied. Her very calmness had to confirm that he was right, that Ann was suffering from delusion and possibly a nervous breakdown. She'd been more agitated earlier, telephoning Jean to keep the gallery closed and telling him she was going to set all the house alarms and locks the moment he left and not answer the telephone or open the doors until she saw from the porch TV it was him at the door, even after he'd put the car in the garage. She made him immobilize the entry into the house from the garage, declaring it susceptible to electronic interference.

'So you think I'm mad; that I'm making it all up?'

'I think we need help.' Slater fell back upon already established reasoning. 'Both of us.' Another surprise was that she was very evidently stone-cold sober. He'd risked one scotch and water after leaving the office, from which he'd had his conversation with their family doctor, Herbert Mills.

'I knew this was what you'd want. I want it, too. I want it because you've got to believe me, as quickly as possible. So that we can do what we've got to do to take care of ourselves. And you won't do that, believe me, and start protecting us until you know I am not mentally ill. That's right, isn't it?'

'Yes,' said Slater, uneasily. 'I spoke to Dr Mills. He's given me a name of someone who's very good.'

'Do we tell him everything?'

'Psychiatrists are bound by the same oath of confidentiality as doctors of medicine. I checked that with Dr Mills, too.'

'You told him about us? Who we really are?'

'No.'

'He wasn't curious why you asked?'

Slater's uncertainty grew at her complete composure. What if she were right and Jack Mason had, in some inexplicable way, found them! Quite apart from his personal and moral failings, Jack Mason had been a far above average, even outstanding, intelligence officer, singled out for fast track promotion by the CIA. His unquestioned ability had actually been brought out at his trial, under attempted mitigating cross-examination of CIA executives. 'Mills might have been but he didn't ask.'

'You called him, the psychiatrist? Made an appointment?'

Slater shook his head. 'I waited to talk to you first.'

'Thinking I'd refuse? Make a drunken scene?'

'Yes. And it's a woman, not a man. Hillary Nelson.' This was unreal.

Ann gestured towards the telephone. 'Call her right now. It's still only four. There's no point in wasting time.'

Slater hesitated, caught by the further unreality that it was Ann who was patronizing him, as if he had some mental difficulty in understanding. He hadn't anticipated speaking to the psychiatrist herself when he made the call, surprised to be put through when he identified himself. In a slow southern accent Hillary Nelson told him Dr Mills had already warned he might call and had outlined the tragedy he and Ann had suffered. So much for professional confidentiality, Slater thought, before accepting that the man obviously thought Ann's need stemmed from David's death. He made a joint appointment for the following afternoon.

The unreality that evening stretched into the surreal. Ann talked matter-of-factly, as if there were no doubt of their discovery by Jack Mason, of their not being able to disclose who they were to the police and of their having to kill the man before he killed them, as if there were no doubt that was what Slater would do. It became increasingly difficult for Slater to contribute anything to such an already self-convinced and determined Ann. Her words were so absolute that, despite his disbelief, he found himself thinking back to his encounter with the ineffectual John Peebles and unnamed telephone respondents at the ancient CIA emergency numbers. Thinking, too, that they might still provide spider web safety nets to call upon and utilize. Ann's continued demeanour compounded his bewilderment; everything they discussed – or rather Ann's monologue – was conducted without any argument or anger or raised voices. Most surprising of all was that there was no demand – not even a hint – from Ann to have a drink.

Hillary Nelson was a neglectfully fat, middle-aged woman who hadn't bothered to colour the early whiteness of her hair or applied any make-up, and who wore the sort of hand-knitted, wrong-buttoned cardigan that reminded Slater of Mary Ellen Foley. The psychiatrist seated them side by side in front of her desk, lounged back behind it in her own vast chair and explained that she wouldn't take notes but would rely upon the tape recording she intended to take of every exchange between them.

'Herb Mills told me you asked about confidentiality. Don't worry about it. Nothing we talk about will go beyond these four walls. Like he told you, I'm bound by the same professional rules.'

Slater was aware of the sharp look from Ann, whom he hadn't told of their doctor's contact with the psychiatrist, in advance of the meeting. He didn't respond to it. Instead he said, 'To understand what this is all about, there are things you've got to be told that you won't expect.'

'So tell me,' invited the woman.

Daniel Slater began imagining that there was a lot to disclose and that it would take a long time, increasingly aware as he talked that it really wasn't after all a convoluted or confusing story to recount. Throughout the psychiatrist did not once interrupt or show any facial or physical reaction, head mostly on an expansive chest as if she were disinterested, dozing even. She still didn't speak when Slater finished and at last Ann said, 'Daniel thinks I imagined it all but I've not . . . I didn't. It was definitely Jack.'

At last Hillary Nelson stirred, holding up a halting hand.

'I can very easily understand your concern about confidentiality. You told Herb Mills all this?'

'No,' said Slater. Abruptly he thought that the woman might think the whole thing – of his being a defecting Russian and Mason, Ann's former husband, a CIA traitor – a total fantasy, so he hurriedly recited trial dates and full names and said, 'It'll all be on archival websites. Photographs, too.'

The psychiatrist smiled. 'And I'll access them. But I did – do – believe you. It would be a hell of a story to make up.'

'And I'm not making up seeing Jack,' chipped in Ann, at once.

'I also accept the strain that's been put upon you, living as you have done for all these years, learning of Jack Mason's release and then losing David the way you did,' said Hillary Nelson, not responding to Ann's interjection. 'It's right, useful, for me to have seen you together like this. But from here on I need to see you separately. You first, Ann . . .' To Slater she said, 'You want to come back and see me tomorrow, maybe? Or wait outside until I'm through talking to Ann?'

'We don't have time to stretch this out!' insisted Ann, talking more to her husband than to the other woman.

'I'll wait,' said Slater.

Jack Mason decided that proposing marriage to Beverley Littlejohn had been an inspiration of genius and that investing $8,000 the day after the proposal on an engagement ring put the cherry on the cupcake; she'd even, appropriately, chosen a cherry red ruby for the centrepiece of her diamond-surrounded ring.

The day after the ring purchase, Mason set out to make the final, protective alibi moves before flying back east. Beverley accepted without question that he couldn't estimate how long it would take him to set up things in Los Angeles and San Diego before his Washington flight, asking only that he keep in touch from wherever he was, with a telephone number if he were going to be there for more than twenty-four hours, and get back as soon as he could. She asked if she could start planning the wedding and Mason said of course she could, but that she shouldn't tell anyone what his background was and risk driving away friends and family. Beverley insisted none of her friends or family – which came down to a cousin

– would react against him and Mason, savouring the irony, told her that despite the job she did and the training she'd undergone to qualify, she didn't know people at all.

Mason called Patrick Bell from Beverley's apartment to announce he was abandoning the compensation claim, calculating that the delayed internal penitentiary enquiry and whatever penalty was imposed upon Frank Howitt wouldn't be completed in the time left before Peter Chambers' release, reflecting as he talked to the lawyer that he was under a self-imposed time limit if he were to hit Slater and Ann before his scheduled reunion with the bank fraudster, which was the timing he determined upon.

'You could have saved us all a lot of time, effort and expense taking my advice in the first place!' complained Bell.

'You're being paid for your time and effort, aren't you?' retorted Mason. 'I still expect to get the out-of-court settlement they originally offered.' It could actually go a long way towards covering the cost of the engagement ring, he thought, idly.

'Let's not get tetchy,' said the lawyer.

'I'm not getting tetchy. How long do you think it'll take?'

'I don't know. Two or three weeks maybe. I'll need your written authority, of course. I can't do anything until I get that.'

'I'll send it today, recorded delivery.' Bell's written acceptance response would provide further dated documentary evidence of his Californian domicile.

'You've definitely decided to stay out there, then?' said Bell.

'It's great.'

'You want everything sent to the box number?'

'The box number. I still don't have a permanent place here.'

Slater wrote and recorded his authorization to abandon the claim to the lawyer – saving the letter on his hard disc – and recorded its delivery from the main San Francisco post office. From its long-distance public telephone facility he called the Lexington Park agency from which he'd rented the fishing cottage on Chesapeake Bay and was remembered the moment he used the Adam Peterson name. That cottage wasn't available, apologized the man, but there was another practically identical one about two miles away. Mason made the viewing appointment and assured the man he was as pleased as the letting manager to be doing business again so soon. He bought the direct, one-way flight ticket to Washington DC in the name of Adam Peterson from the already chosen American Express office on Jackson Street and waited until he crossed the bridge back to Oakland to book separate flights the following day to Los Angeles and San Diego in the name of Jack Mason at another already selected travel agency in Oakland. When he got back to Beverley's apartment, in good time for her home-coming ritual, he left the Los Angeles and San Diego air tickets on the bedroom bureau.

As they sipped their balcony drinks Mason said, 'I made the reservations today.'

'I saw the tickets in the bedroom.'

'And for tonight, for a farewell dinner.'

'Where?'

'The Captain's Cabin at Trader Vic's.'

'It's not farewell, though, is it?'

'You know it's not.'

'I don't know what I'd do without you, not now,' said Beverley.

'You're never going to have to find out.' It was going to be good, a relief, to get away. It was necessary – sensible – to have taken the alibi precautions, but he hoped he didn't have to use them.

'How did it go?' demanded Slater, looking up as the psych-iatrist escorted Ann from her office.

Hillary Nelson smiled at Slater's eagerness. 'Confidentiality extends to husband and wife.'

'How do we go forward?' asked Slater.

'Easy,' said the woman. 'Now it's your turn to come into the office.'

Twenty-Two

'Jack Mason betrayed his country?' opened the psychiatrist.
'Yes,' said Slater.

'As you did yours?'

'Yes.' This was quite different from what Slater had expected; but then he hadn't known what to expect.

'Do you feel any guilt about that?'

'No.'

'Did you ever?'

'Not that I remember.'

'You didn't feel any allegiance to your country? Swear an oath of loyalty?'

'I swore an oath of loyalty when I was admitted to the KGB. It was routine. I don't think anyone took it seriously.'

'What about the family you left in Russia?'

'There wasn't any family.'

'None at all?'

'None of whom I was aware.' Slater couldn't see the point of the questioning, how this was helping Ann, although he accepted that he had to co-operate in every way demanded of him.

'Tell me how it happened, how you came to defect, why you defected, how difficult it was for you to adjust to a permanent life in America. Don't try to get anything in order. Just talk as it comes into your head.'

Slater hesitated, despite what the woman said. 'Ann and I were involved, as she's probably told you. I got my recall instructions from Moscow ... no one is allowed to remain on overseas station too long – I'd been in Washington for almost five years, which was actually longer than normal. I had nothing to go back for. Or to. No family, as I've just told you. I didn't want to leave Ann. I told Ann who I was ... not Jack's CIA colleague, which she thought I was ...'

'That was a hell of a risk, wasn't it! You'd fallen in love with Ann, hoped she'd fallen in love with you, and out of the blue you tell her that everything she believed about you was a lie?'

'She'd told me how things were between her and Jack. I didn't just come out with everything as bluntly as that, out of the blue as you say.'

'How did you come out with it?'

Slater hesitated again, genuinely having to try to remember. 'I think I asked her if she would divorce Jack.'

'What did she say to that?'

'That she wanted to. But that she was frightened of what he might do to her if she said it outright.'

'Still deceiving her?'

'I suppose I was. It didn't seem like that.'

'Then what did she say?'

'That she needed to think about it.'

'She'd told you how things were between her and Jack but she still needed to think about it when you asked her to leave him and marry you?'

'I'm not sure I said I wanted to marry her, not the first time.'

'Go on.'

'When we talked about it the next time, that's when I told her I wanted to marry her.'

'What did she say then?'

'That she still wanted to think about it.'

'Didn't that worry you . . . make you think that she might not love you after all and would go to the authorities instead, turn you in?'

'I don't think I'd told her who I really was at that time. I don't remember ever thinking she'd turn me in.'

'What did you think?'

'Ann had had a pretty shitty life. She'd thought marrying Jack was her best chance to make things better, which it hadn't turned out to be. I thought she was frightened of making the decision – that it might turn out bad again.'

'Go on,' repeated the woman.

Slater wasn't sure how to. Uncertainly he said, 'One night she was beaten up. She said Jack did it and that she didn't want to be with him any more. That she would leave him for me.'

'That was when you told her who you really were? What Jack was, as well as being a wife beater?'

'I think so, yes.'

'How did she react?'

Slater sniggered an uneasy laugh. 'I think she cried a lot more.'

'You were totally exposed. You'd told her you were a Russian spy and that her violent husband was spying, was an informant, for Russia too. Didn't you think then she might turn you both in and get rid of both of you?'

'No,' said Slater at once.

'Why not? After the shitty life you've told me she'd had, before marrying Jack, it would have been the easiest way of getting out of the shit she suddenly found herself in again.'

'I just told you I didn't think she'd turn me in.'

'Was that the way a Russian spymaster was supposed to think?'

'Nothing I did or thought was supposed to be the way a Russian spymaster was supposed to do or think. And I never regarded myself as that anyway.'

'What did you regard yourself to be?'

A question he'd always avoided, Slater acknowledged; Hillary Nelson was as good as Dr Mills had described her to be, although Slater wasn't sure in which direction she was taking the conversation. 'At the time we're talking about I regarded myself as an impending traitor.'

'But you still didn't feel any guilt?'

'No.'

'How would you have thought of yourself if you hadn't met, become involved with, Ann?'

Slater shrugged. 'How can I answer that? I *was* involved with Ann. It was the only way I could think.'

'Were you disillusioned with what you did?'

It was another unsettling question, Slater recognized. 'I think I was, yes.'

'So Ann was an excuse?'

'No!' denied Slater, loudly. 'You're twisting this and I can't see the point of what we've discussed so far. Ann was never the excuse for anything. I'd fallen in love with her and made the choice, between her and going back.'

'What would you have done if she'd said no? Defected anyway or gone back to Moscow?'

'I wouldn't have defected,' said Slater, without hesitation.

'Why not? You've already told me you were disillusioned with what you were doing and had no reason to go back to Russia.'

'I wouldn't have been accepted as a defector unless I told the CIA and the FBI everything. Which would have still got Mason the sentence he received. And caused God knows what harm to Ann, however bad her life already was.'

'But she said yes, that she would leave Jack and marry you?'

The swerve in the discussion almost off-balanced him. 'Yes.'

'Did you warn her what the upheaval would be like?'

'I didn't know what the upheaval would be like myself. I told her it wouldn't be easy, the trial particularly.'

'How bad was it?'

Slater's hesitation this time was longer than any of his hesitations before. 'It's funny, now I come to think back upon it. I don't recall it as being bad at all. We were kind of caught up in things that happened but which we were separate from. We were physically separated for a long time, as well – didn't see or speak to each other. I didn't like that because I didn't know what was happening to Ann. How she was standing up to it all. They told me she was being looked after, protected, but I didn't know—'

'Did you ever think you'd made a mistake?' broke in Hillary Nelson.

'Yes,' admitted Slater, caught by her prescience. 'At one stage I refused to co-operate until I talked to her. Knew for myself, from her, that she was OK.'

'And she was?'

'She was managing. She was committed by then, like I was.'

'What about that time, that moment? Did you have any regrets then, any second thoughts?'

'I wished – hoped – that it wouldn't be too much for her.'

'What about you? Wasn't it too much for you?'

'I was trained. Ann wasn't.'

'Was it too much for her?'

'I didn't think so, not then.'

'I don't understand what you've just told me.'

'I thought Ann had come through it OK, even that we had

the perfect life. Now I know how brave she's really been, all these years. She's been frightened, all the time, without my knowing it. Terrified, for all those years, that Jack would find us.'

'What do you think? Do you think he's found you? Is stalking you and that he killed David?'

Slater didn't answer, slumped with his head on his chest as she had been when he had first recounted their story.

'Daniel?' she prompted.

'He can't have found us.'

'Ann told me you installed a lot of extra security when you first heard Jack was being released ahead of when you both expected. That you even went into Washington to speak to the man who wrote the warning letter?'

Slater nodded. 'It was a hell of a surprise . . . a shock, I guess. Over the years his release had gone out of my mind . . .' Slater paused once more. 'My mind, certainly. I now know it had never gone out of Ann's mind, not for a moment. Then we were suddenly confronted by it. And yes, I guess you could say I panicked, before I thought properly about it. I hoped Ann would be reassured, by all the extra stuff I installed.'

'Weren't you reassured?'

'By the time it was all done I'd calmed down – knew it was unnecessary.'

'Do you still think that?'

'Yes.' Did he? Slater asked himself.

'What about what happened to David?'

'It's got to be a coincidence. A terrible, dreadful coincidence from which neither of us is ever going properly to recover. I just hope that we can stay together, that it doesn't destroy us. David was our life – without him I'm not sure what life we've got left.'

'A lot of people suffer the sort of tragedy you and Ann have suffered.'

'Not against our sort of background.' Had she been as forthright, as brutal, with Ann? Ann hadn't seemed upset when they'd swopped rooms.

'True,' the psychiatrist conceded.

'Is Ann going to be all right?'

'Do you think you are going to be all right?'

202

Slater looked curiously at her across the desk. 'I didn't think we were here to talk about me.'

'We're here to talk about everything and everyone,' said Hillary Nelson. 'And I think we've done enough of both for one day. Ann's told me she can come back again tomorrow. Can you?'

'If it will help.'

'I wouldn't have suggested it, if I hadn't thought it would help.'

'What's today achieved?' demanded Slater.

'I needed to decide whether you're both telling the truth,' declared the woman. 'I think you both are.'

'You mean you believe Ann *did* see Jack Mason!'

'I haven't yet got that far with Ann.'

'I was trained to lie,' reminded Slater, not knowing why he said it.

'I was trained to spot lies. And liars.'

Jack Mason's re-encounter with the Lexington Park rental manager was, predictably, a virtual repeat of their first meeting and as they toured the second property – the location and remoteness of which Mason had already checked out after driving direct from Dulles airport – he decided that his first visit had been a very necessary orientational rehearsal. Prompted by that thought Mason took the cottage for a full month, knowing he could quit sooner, as he had before, if he got lucky with Slater and Ann. Objectively though, as he had been after running their son down, Mason accepted it would be a miracle if he got lucky a second time; he might need much longer, even having to break away to set up some sort of stalling situation with Peter Chambers, which would be an irritating but necessary interruption.

As he had before, Mason shopped after completing all the formalities with the realtor, deciding as he packed his groceries and wine away that he actually preferred this new place to that which he had rented before. Everything was in a much better, newer condition and the shoreline longer which would enable him to resume his now too long neglected fitness regime. He tried it out that late afternoon and calculated that by running its full length, during which he isolated only one other cottage and that too far away for anyone in it to be able to properly see or later identify him, and then back again, he'd covered at least two miles. His legs and shoulders ached, reminding him how out of shape he'd become since his release from White Deer. Before making dinner Mason carried out his daily computer trawl through all his emplaced sites and found nothing new, ate early, and slept a full uninterrupted, dreamless nine hours' sleep to fully recover, in one session, from the effect of the overnight red eye from California. At no time, since leaving the West Coast, had Mason once thought of Beverley Littlejohn.

From his initial surveillance Mason knew how heavily protected both 2832 Hill Avenue SE and Ann's Main Street gallery were by CCTV, which logically dictated there would be matching internal alarms and precautions that precluded both from a direct, burglary-disguised approach; even if he evolved a way to override or sabotage their operating electricity source they would automatically revert to battery supply. If he had been supervising an authorized CIA assassination there would have been contaminating poisons or explosives, in both of which he had been schooled after his recall to Washington from his Moscow entrapment. Sabotaging their separate cars, both of which he already knew, was far more feasible when Ann's was parked behind the gallery and Slater's in the communal car park at the rear of the shared high rise in which he had his office, but again Mason had no access to technical resources in order to absolutely guarantee their deaths, nor a way to ensure that their killing would be simultaneous. He had not completely discarded the idea of killing just Slater – who after all had been directly responsible for his arrest and imprisonment – and leaving Ann bereft of both husband and son to sink back into gin-sodden despair. But at this stage of initial planning his intention remained to kill her, too, wipe the slate clean and move on. Mason had learned the unimaginative title of Slater's company – Slater's Securities – from the local newspaper's coverage of David's hit and run and looked upon that as another possible focus, although again limiting his target to just Slater alone. What other locations were there where he could get them both together and hit them both together? Mason demanded of himself, in impatient irritation.

David's grave!

Frustration at once turned to a warmth of satisfaction at the obvious, fulfilling, beckoning answer. Where else would grieving parents go together to mourn but to the grave of their tragically killed son; the grave easy to locate at the church named in the *Frederick News-Post* coverage, the grave at which Slater and Ann had been photographed together, supporting each other together, consoling each other together! Mason sniggered. Where they could be killed together. Bleed together.

'What did she say?' demanded Ann, as Slater started the car.

'She asked a lot of questions, about guilt and whether I hadn't been frightened that you'd turn me in when I told you who I really was.'

'I thought about it.'

Slater looked sharply across the car. 'I never knew that! You never told me!'

'It never came up.'

'Why didn't you?' It was an automatic, unthinking question. Slater was confused, unable to believe Ann had never told him.

Ann shrugged. 'I don't know. I guess at first I thought it was my duty but then I changed my mind.'

'Even though you loved me!'

'I don't think I was sure then that I did. I'm glad now that I didn't.'

Slater drove on for several minutes in bewildered silence. 'So am I,' he said, finally. 'She asked if I felt any guilt. And if I was worried about how you'd get through it all.'

'Were you? Worried, I mean?'

It was as if they were strangers, thought Slater. 'Yes. I thought it might have been too much for you.'

'My recollection was that it didn't seem real ... didn't seem to be happening. Are you coming tomorrow?'

'Of course!' said Slater, further surprised. 'How could you think I wouldn't!'

Ann shrugged again, as if it weren't important. 'I don't know.'

Surely this odd conversation, her strange almost unnatural calmness, was proof that Ann had a problem? He'd have to remember as much of it as possible to tell Hillary Nelson tomorrow. 'Are you glad we're seeing her?'

'I will be, if you believe that Jack has found us. And start doing something about it. Did she tell you she wants to hypnotize me?'

'No!'

'She does. I said I was quite happy for her to do so. What do you think?'

'I think she should have told me. That we should have talked about it.'

'That's what we are doing, right now. So what do you think?'

'I meant Hillary and I should have talked about it.'

'You haven't told me what you think!' she demanded.

'I want to know why she wants to do it.'

'What are you frightened of?'

'I'm not frightened of anything! I just don't want her playing tricks with you.'

'There's no need to shout. And I don't think she's playing tricks with me.'

'I wasn't shouting,' denied Slater.

'I want to stop on the way home.'

'All right,' agreed Slater, without needing to be told where.

'And thank you.'

'What for?'

'Checking in the mirrors as much as you've been doing, while we're driving. Looking for him'

'I always check the mirrors when I'm driving.'

'Thank you,' she said again.

Twenty-Three

The routine was the same as the previous day: Ann invited to begin the session by Hillary Nelson, but before his wife could enter the psychiatrist's room Slater said, 'You didn't tell me you wanted to hypnotize Ann today?'

'It was a question for Ann. *To* Ann.'

'Without involving me?'

'Without involving you,' confirmed the psychiatrist. 'Ann involved you, which is good.'

'Why?'

'I told you we wouldn't do joint sessions. I'd like to talk to Ann now.'

The curt dismissal was rude, decided Slater. Hillary hadn't given any indication yesterday, but it was possible that she despised him for who he was and what he had done. To feel which, he supposed, she had every right by whatever standards she chose. He certainly didn't intend losing his temper over it. 'I'll wait.'

'We'll be a while, if you've anything else to do.'

'You'd like me to be here, wouldn't you?' Slater asked his wife.

'Yes,' said Ann, at once. 'I want you to be right outside the door.'

Slater wondered if he'd misjudged the psychiatrist: decided too soon how good she was? She was certainly a good interrogator but upon careful reconsideration of every exchange the previous day – or as much of the exchanges as he could remember, which he decided was a lot – he couldn't see what practical benefit it had been to Ann. Which was the entire purpose – the *only* purpose – of their consulting the woman. Ann's demeanour totally bewildered him, convinced as she appeared to be that they were under imminent and deadly threat from her ex-husband, insisting upon every precaution and protection, but at the same time appearing ephemerally suspended from reality. The only occasions upon which her demeanour changed, when Ann became someone he thought he knew and could recognize, were their nightly visits to David's grave when, almost as if she were discarding a disguise, she reverted to being the weeping, grieving mother as he unashamedly collapsed into being the loss-racked father. They both had to recover – adjust – from that, Slater determined, positively. Not yet. It was far too soon yet even to contemplate their not going as often as Ann chose – nightly, as she was choosing now – to mourn at David's graveside. But he shouldn't – wouldn't – allow it to become a maudlin, emotionally corrosive habit. Maybe it was something he should discuss with Hillary Nelson, despite his belated uncertainty of her methodology and ability.

'I'm sorry if we've been too long,' apologized the psychiatrist as she emerged behind Ann; Slater realized, surprised, that Ann's second treatment had stretched over two hours. Ann was smiling, quite relaxed.

'However long it takes,' dismissed Slater, starting to following Hillary Nelson back into her rooms. He stopped at the door, looking between the two women. To Ann he said, 'You going to be all right, waiting so long?'

'I'm certainly not going home by myself,' said Ann, no longer smiling.

'I didn't mean . . .' started Slater, before tailing off.

'Maybe we won't be that long,' said Hillary.

There was only one chair directly in front of her desk today but there was a rumpled rug on a chaise longue he had been unaware of the previous day. Seeing Slater looking at it the psychiatrist said, 'How would you feel about being hypnotized?'

'I'm relaxed enough.'

'That wasn't what I asked you. I asked how you'd *feel* about being hypnotized.'

'Would it help what we're trying to do for Ann?' Slater was uncomfortable at the idea, frightened of losing control and telling her how frightened he'd been of Mason.

'I wasn't talking about helping Ann, either. I was thinking about you.'

'I thought we decided yesterday I didn't need help.'

'You may have decided that. I didn't say I had.'

'I don't need any help.'

'You think you could kill Jack Mason?'

'What?' demanded Slater, startled by the switch.

'That's what Ann tells me you've got to do. Kill him before he kills you.'

'You really believe she did see him? That he has found us?'

'I'm telling you what Ann thinks you've got to do. Could you?'

'This is ridiculous!' protested Slater.

'No, it's not. If you thought Mason would try to kill Ann, and you, as he might have killed David, could you kill him first?'

'Yes,' said Slater at once. 'I'd *want* to kill him.'

'How well do you believe you got to know him when you were handling him?'

Slater shifted, uneasily. 'Pretty well. As much – maybe more – through Ann than through our direct contact.'

'Did you like him?'

'Definitely not.'

'Because of the way he ill-treated Ann?'

'No. Because he was a traitor.'

Hillary didn't try to prevent the disbelieving laugh. 'But that's what you wanted him to be! What your job was, in Washington! Handling – managing – a traitor.'

Slater shook his head. 'I know what my job was, running Mason. That, as well as other things, was my profession. But no professional intelligence officer *likes* another professional officer who goes over to the other side. I know it sounds illogical, to anyone else, but that's how it is. It's an expedient act as I told you yesterday, I was trained to lie and deceive. That was my job, my profession. I knew, for every hour of every day after I defected and went through all the debriefings, that every other intelligence officer who dealt with me and got everything they could out of me despised me as they did so.'

'Did you despise yourself?'

Slater considered the question. 'Yes. Again, as I told you yesterday, I don't remember feeling any guilt but I despised myself. Which is different.'

'Why is it different?'

'I stayed honest to myself.'

'Do you think Mason despised himself?'

'No,' said Slater, immediately. 'I think Mason enjoyed being turned. I think he despised everyone else at Langley, thought they were inferior to him for not knowing what fools he was making of them. And I think he probably despised me, too.'

'I looked up the archival material last night, as you suggested. At the trial he was described as an outstanding intelligence officer.'

'He was,' agreed Slater, at once. 'Again, as I told you yesterday, I had to be trained to lie. I don't believe Mason needed that training. Lying came naturally to him. He was *born* to be a spy, for whatever, and whoever was prepared to pay him. Jack Mason had only two interests: money and women.'

'Was he born to be a killer?'

'I don't think so. Almost everything came easy to him; he was one of those sort of guys. But I never thought of him as someone who could kill . . .' Slater paused. 'Every national intelligence agency has those types of people. They're attached to specialized divisions, those people who don't have any problem killing someone they're ordered to assassinate. They're psychologically trained, brainwashed, if you like, that their victims are enemies of the state and that their deaths are justified. The KGB called authorized killings "wet jobs". The CIA referred to them as "terminating with extreme prejudice". But you'd surely know better than me that a person would need a special mentality, a twisted, psychotic mentality, to kill to order.'

'Ann thinks he'd be capable of killing.'

'He certainly physically attacked her,' conceded Slater. 'But hitting a woman is surely different from finding it easy to kill!'

'And he'd have a reason – a self-justification – to attack her and you again after all that you made happen to him, wouldn't he? You told me, less than an hour ago and without needing to think about it, that *you* could kill *him*. Does that mean you think you're a killer?'

She'd out-argued him, Slater accepted. 'It would be self-protection. Doesn't the law allow someone to protect themselves?'

'But you don't think he's a killer – capable of being a killer?'

She was tying him up with his own words. 'If I'm wrong and he tried to harm Ann or myself, I'd kill him.' He wasn't being honest, Slater admitted to himself. He did think Mason would be capable of killing him and Ann if he found them. How else was he not being honest? By not admitting at last, now, that he'd always been terrified of Mason, he answered himself.

'Are you going to buy a handgun? Ann tells me she wants you to.'

'If I thought there was a need.'

'For self-protection?'

'Only for self-protection,' insisted Slater, exasperated.

'Ann told me she wants a handgun, too. Are you going to get her one?'

'I haven't decided the need, not yet.'

Slater sat regarding the psychiatrist steadily, wanting to twist her reasoning as she was twisting his. 'Do you believe that Ann saw Jack Mason outside her gallery?'

'I believe that *Ann* believes she saw him.'

'So, she has a problem?'

'I didn't say that,' denied the woman. 'I have found nothing, not even under hypnosis, that gives me any cause to think or diagnose that Ann is suffering any sort of mental difficulty. Most certainly she does not have, in my opinion, any hallucinatory difficulty. After the life she led with Jack, and after that going into a protection programme with you, and then suffering the trauma of David's death, in my professional opinion it's quite remarkable that she's as stable as she is.'

'She's different from how she used to be,' insisted Slater. 'She seems . . .' He stopped, groping for the words to express himself. 'She seems to be floating above everything.'

'It's her way of coping. She surely deserves that?'

'She drinks!'

'No, she doesn't, not unless you can convince me otherwise. She drank when she was with Jack. She's been quite honest with me about that. It was another way of coping with the circumstances in which she found herself. And she had *a* drink or two, when you got the letter about Jack. She's been quite honest about that, too, even admitted that's how she came to miss most of what she says was on the CCTV loop. But she hasn't drunk since. Or has she?'

'No,' admitted Slater. He came forward in his chair, towards the woman. 'I do need your help. I need you to tell me what to do about Ann, about her thinking, *believing*, that she saw Jack.'

Hillary's shoulders rose and fell in a gesture of helplessness. 'I've gone through all the logic with her, after speaking to you. Talked about how secure Witness Protection Programmes are supposed to be and how unlikely it is that Jack would have been able to find you, particularly as I understand it was so soon after being released from a penitentiary. She's still adamant it was him.'

'What can I do?' pleaded Slater.

'You went to Washington, to see the man who wrote you the letter about Jack. Couldn't you find out Jack's whereabouts from him? If Jack's on the other side of the country – not *in* the country even – that could possibly reassure her. So might buying her a handgun.'

'You're actually suggesting I buy her a gun!' exclaimed Slater.

'It's not against the law. And if you're right she's never going to have to use it, is she? If she had a gun and learned how to use it, it would give her more reassurance, wouldn't it?'

'I'm not sure,' said Slater, perfectly describing his mindset. Was it he who needed the help that Hillary Nelson had consistently offered? According to the psychiatrist, Ann was suffering no mental imbalance, but was convinced beyond persuasion to the contrary that she had definitely seen her ex-husband just yards from her gallery within days of his release from a reduced twenty-year imprisonment, and that he should try to discover from God knows who – the CIA, presumably – Jack Mason's whereabouts, and in the meantime buy her and have her trained in the use of a gun!

'You don't think I have been – am being – much help, do you?' openly challenged the woman.

'No, I don't,' agreed Slater, at once, angrily. Still held by the anger, he went on, 'I came to you for help, about Ann's illness, her delusions. And got nothing!'

Spacing her words, as if doubting Slater's comprehension, Hillary Nelson said, 'Ann doesn't have a mental illness! I've told you she's remarkably, surprisingly, stable. It's you who is insisting she's deluded about seeing Jack. I'm not going to tell you that she's deluded. I've no way of deciding if she is or if she isn't, apart from taking your word, and to take your word that Jack hasn't found you I'd need some proof to the contrary – and I don't have it any more than you do. I've given you all the advice and help I can. Bizarre though it might be, like a lot about this is bizarre. You want recommendations to other psychiatrists, I can give you as many as you need. I can't do any more, suggest or advise any more.'

'I'm sorry,' apologized Slater. 'I didn't mean to be rude. It's just . . .' He broke off again, searching for the words. 'I don't know what to do . . .'

The woman stared at him across her desk, waiting. When he didn't continue she said, 'I think Ann should come back in, don't you?

Slater shrugged. 'If you say so.'

As the psychiatrist talked, encapsulating her opinions, Slater acknowledged that she was summing up their sessions and their conversations with complete, objective honesty and total impartiality. She described both of them as being remarkable and insisted it was a natural reaction that they should both feel the need to visit David's grave as often as they were doing, which reminded Slater he'd forgotten to mention it to the woman. He presumed Ann had. Ann's only objection came when the psychiatrist gently pressed her to accept she might have been mistaken if it were proven that Mason was nowhere in the vicinity of Frederick when she'd believed she'd seen him on the CCTV loop.

'What would you accept as positive proof?' Ann demanded suspiciously, speaking for the first time since she had joined them.

'That's more a question for you to answer,' replied Hillary, still gently. 'But Daniel's going back to the man who wrote you the release letter, people he's still got numbers for at Langley, aren't you Daniel?'

He'd been manoeuvred into attempting the reassurances the psychiatrist had suggested, Slater realized, unoffended. The more he digested Hillary Nelson's insistence upon Ann's mental stability, the more he acknowledged that he'd welcome the reassurance, too. He said, 'Yes, that's what I'm going to do.'

'When?' asked Ann, at once.

'Tomorrow,' promised Slater. 'Tomorrow if I can set up a meeting. I'll try to do that later today.'

'What about the handguns?' persisted Ann.

'I'll look into it,' said Slater.

'I want a promise from both of you,' said Hillary Nelson. 'I want you both to keep in the closest touch. I want to know that you stay OK.'

Jack Mason realized the limitations of the cemetery as the double murder location, just as easily – and quickly – as he had first thought it perfect.

Drawing upon his professional training – 'Do everything you can to vanish into every environment' – Mason entered the graveyard wearing the darker of his two suits, a muted tie and a mournful expression, and carrying the at-the-last-minute remembered bouquet of flowers hurriedly purchased from a gas station on the way, the bright wrapping dumped at the first refuse bin he'd come upon as he'd begun his search for David's grave. The cemetery was landscaped with trees and shrubbery to create a parkland rather than a flat, regimented burial place. There were places where an assassin could safely hide at virtually every meandering twist and turn of the path he followed to locate David Slater's grave. It was still covered with bare earth, the grass around it still marked with the tread of feet from the funeral. There was a simple naming marker in place of the eventual tombstone and Ann and Slater's wreath – 'in memory of our darling, beautiful son' in Ann's recognizable handwriting – dominating the floral tributes that included a tasteless reproduction of a basketball, the dedication card of which Mason didn't bother to read.

David's grave was at the top of a small knoll, which isolated it from its three immediate, lower-level neighbours. The outstretched branches from a long established beech tree, its thick trunk almost three yards away, came close to shading the spot, and slightly closer a bordering privet hedge provided a perfect sniper's nest. As he'd wandered the cemetery trying to locate the grave, but unable to ask because of the risk of identification, Mason had, professionally again, counted only three mourners, one dog walker and three groundsmen, one driving a grass cutting machine the noise of which would have drowned any gunshots, even if they had been audible so far away, which he doubted. He thought about the Glock, securely hidden in the First National safety deposit vault in Washington, but more so about his limited ammunition. He had to get more as soon as possible. Wonderful though it would be for them to die in some exotic way – the rattlesnake fantasy still his favourite – it was going to have to be the gun.

At the moment of their killing, it was essential that they knew he had found them – in fact, as long before as possible, without giving them any chance of defence or escape. And he couldn't achieve that skulking in bushes or behind trees. He could, though, conceal himself behind bushes and trees to wait for them to visit and become engrossed in their mourning and flower-laying before approaching unseen. Their awareness had to be longer, their suffering greater, than mere seconds. He'd have to injure both of them sufficiently to subdue and incapacitate them for the fantasized torture without fear of Slater being able to fight back, or of being disturbed by another passing, uninvolved mourner.

Mason had actually turned from the grave and started to move away before he became aware that he was still carrying the flowers. He looked around for a garbage bin but abruptly stopped, held by a thought. He carefully wrapped the stems in his handkerchief, transferred them to his other hand and even more carefully wiped with as much cloth as remained every stem, from flower to base, where his hand and fingers might have come into contact. And then tossed the bouquet on the boy's grave, on top of the wreath from Slater and Ann.

Which was where Slater and Ann found them, an hour later. Ann, who'd left the path slightly ahead of Slater, saw the flowers first and said, 'Where are they from? Who?'

Slater passed his wife, who'd stopped abruptly, and leaned over the mound. 'There's no card.'

'They weren't there before!'

'I know.'

'And they're fresh.'

'Yes.

'It's him! Jack! Taunting us!'

Slater shook his head. 'We can't say that.'

215

'Who are they from then?'

'They could be from anyone. Put there by accident even.'

'They've been deliberately put on top of ours.'

The placing seemed contrived, conceded Slater. 'Let's not build this into something it's not.'

'What is it then?'

'I don't know! There's no indication who they're from but you mustn't, we mustn't, make a big thing out of it. Like I said, they could have been put there by accident.'

'Call him back on your cell phone! That man, Peebles.' At Ann's insistence they'd detoured to Slater's office to arrange the following day's meeting with the records clerk in Washington. If they'd driven directly from Hillary Nelson's office they would have come upon Mason at the graveside.

There was something he could do, Slater decided, ridiculous though it would seem to anyone but to Ann and hopefully to the facility who knew him as a security consultant who had in the past approached them with unusual demands. 'There's nothing to talk to Peebles about, not yet. But I know a laboratory where I can get the stems checked out, for fingerprints. I could ask him then to get a comparison made.'

'Can we do it now?'

'I could try.'

'Try,' insisted Ann. 'We can come back here later.'

Peebles would dismiss him as mad, Slater guessed. Maybe he'd have to identify himself to whomever he'd spoken to at Langley after all. Who'd probably think he was mad too.

Twenty-Four

This time John Peebles had remembered to record the incoming telephone contact and Slater's identity had been confirmed by Langley from the extensive voiceprints on file from the former KGB colonel's defection debriefing. Upon Langley's instruction the meeting had been fixed at the site of their previous encounter and Peebles assured the second meeting would be monitored by a CIA headquarters-based field agent who came early to the man's Justice Department covert office to identity himself and to fit Peebles with automatic voice-activated recording apparatus.

'He didn't give any indication what he wanted?' asked the field agent, Peter Denver. He was a bespectacled, nondescript man coincidentally undergoing the same sort of reassignment training for which Mason had been withdrawn from Moscow so many years earlier.

'Just that it was about the same thing as before but he didn't say what, precisely.' Today Peebles wore a suit, with a collar and tie. He felt restricted, fitted with the wire, the self-consciousness increasing when he followed Denver's instructions to move about the office to become accustomed to the equipment. He was aware of Barry Bourne smirking. Aware, too, that he was leaking sweat, despite the air conditioning.

'There's no cause for you to worry,' soothed Denver, aware of the perspiration too. 'We're just being ultra-careful, after the first approach we weren't able to supervise.'

'I'm not responsible for faulty equipment,' said Peebles, defensively, remembering the excuse he'd made for forgetting to tape Slater's initial call.

'This time everything's going to work,' assured Denver, who'd tested three times what he'd fitted to Peebles. 'You'll have back-up every step of the way.'

'Why hasn't this ever happened before?' demanded Peebles.

'Because it's never happened before – at least not for a long time,' said Denver, unhelpfully. 'It's most likely to do with the death of his kid, but we can't second-guess it. That's why you're wired and I'll be in the park with you. All you do is listen to what he tells you, say you'll get back to Langley and fix another meeting at his convenience. Just build in a couple of days in case we have to set anything up.'

'What happened to his kid?'

Denver kept any surprise from his face, but then thought why should Peebles have known? Langley probably wouldn't if it hadn't been for the publicity in the local newspaper and a chance recognition of the name by a retired Burt Hodges, who'd handled Dimitri Sobell's defection. 'He got killed in a traffic accident. A hit and run.'

'They get the guy?'

'No. Someone else got killed, too. Separately the police think. It's a murder enquiry.'

'Jesus!'

'You're not in any danger. I told you you're going to be covered, all the time.'

'What should I ask him?'

Denver looked curiously at the younger man. 'Whatever you think is necessary to ask him. We don't know what he wants, do we? Just keep it going. Listen to him.'

'I'll give it my best shot.'

'That's all we can ever do,' said Denver, who was uncomfortable having to rely on someone he considered an amateur and could never understand the Agency putting out low level jobs to untrained people, not even contract employees. 'You got any other questions?'

'I don't think so.'

'It'll be fine. Trust me.'

Peebles walked to the park, as he had on the first occasion, unable to lose the self-consciousness. By the time he got as far as the Treasury Building the transmitter at the hollow of his back was beginning to chafe. He hadn't been able properly to see in the washroom mirror before he'd left but he was sure it would be visible beneath his jacket, despite Denver's insistence that it wasn't. Denver had left the Justice Building thirty minutes ahead of him and Peebles was disappointed not to see the man already in place when he crossed from the Treasury into the flower-bordered park. Not one bench was occupied. Peebles chose the one that had been designated by Denver, in the very middle, looking directly at the White House. One of the bench struts was directly against the top of the transmitter, driving it into his back and Peebles groped behind him, pushing the waistband of his trousers down. He wished he could stop sweating. The stupid son of a bitch was probably playing spy games, like he had before. Where the fuck was Denver? If he was going to be fully protected the guy should have been here, prepared. Prepared for what? Peebles felt a fresh flush and tried to mop the perspiration under the pretext of blowing his nose. He wanted to piss, despite having done so trying to locate the bulge at the back of his jacket. Where the fuck was Slater? Denver? Anyone?

'Thank you for coming.'

Peebles jumped at the voice directly behind him, not having heard Slater's approach. 'That was the arrangement, wasn't it?'

Slater came around from the back of the bench and sat with his leg crooked between himself and the other man, one arm along the back rail, so that he could look directly at Peebles with a view as well of two thirds of the open space around them. 'I want you to do something for me. Or have Langley do it, through whatever links you have.'

Peebles himself twisted towards Slater, better to position the receiving microphone, which was taped in the middle of his chest. The movement relieved the discomfort of the transmitter but made the securing tape of the microphone pull the hairs on his chest, which was even more discomfiting. 'What?'

'Tell me where Jack Mason is. I don't mean an actual address. You told me before you didn't think you could legally do that. I just need to know whereabouts he is in the country.'

'Why do you want to know that?'

Slater breathed in deeply. 'My wife has a business, an art gallery. With protective CCTV. She thinks Jack Mason was caught on it, within days of your letter. Within days of him being released from the penitentiary.'

Peebles groped for a response, glad to see Denver coming at last into the park off Pennsylvania Avenue. Behind him, on

219

the avenue itself, an unmarked covered truck had pulled up. By the time the driver got out and raised the popped hood, a policeman from the White House protection detail reached it to talk to the now partially concealed man. Denver opened a copy of the *Washington Post* but sat twisted on the bench too, keeping Peebles and Slater in perfect view across the small, pebbled oval broken by a circular flower bed. Ironically the predominant flowers were tulips.

Peebles said, 'You got the loop?'

Slater gradually released the indrawn breath. 'No. I'd convinced her it wasn't possible for Mason to know where we were, after the first conversation you and I had. And she hadn't rewound the tape, as she should have done, so she only saw a limited back view of the man she thinks was Mason. I was out of town and she didn't tell me immediately.' It sounded empty, facile, an invention of an hysterical woman. It *was* empty and facile, even if Ann wasn't an hysteric! There hadn't been any fingerprints on the smooth stems of the tulips either, but he'd decided against mentioning yesterday's bouquet on David's grave. Peebles wouldn't think that made any more sense than everything else he was telling him. Slater didn't think that made sense, either, although not for the reasons Peebles would question. It was inconceivable that the bouquet of tulips could have been placed on David's grave without some physical trace being left upon them. So who'd gone to the trouble of wiping every stem? And why?

'She didn't keep the tape?'

'She was under a lot of stress. Not thinking.'

'I'm sorry about your son ... the accident,' stumbled Peebles.

Denver's back was to the White House and the stalled truck. The police officer was walking away now, his radio close to his mouth, leaving the driver engrossed under the hood.

'Thank you.' Slater shifted, straightening more naturally on the bench. 'I want to be able to convince my wife that it wasn't possible for her to have seen Mason. That's why I'm asking what I'm asking.'

'I don't think it could possibly have been Mason,' insisted Peebles. He wished Denver, seemingly intent on his newspaper just a few feet away, had given him an estimate of how long he wanted the exchange to be stretched out. And that he could stop sweating. His chest was positively aching where the tape was pulling at him. He put himself straighter on the bench, to ease the discomfort.

'I just need some idea of a location.' Slater supposed he could invent somewhere sufficiently far away. But after Hillary Nelson's verdict, and the unmarked flowers, Slater wanted the reassurance, as well.

'I double-checked when I got back last time,' said Peebles, anxious to end the encounter. 'It's way beyond my authority, which I told you it was. But I can pass the request on to Langley. Which I will do. I can't promise a quick answer, though. You've got my number. Why not give me a call in a couple of days, so I can tell you what they say?'

'You hot, Mr Peebles? I don't think it's particularly warm today.'

'I don't . . .' started Peebles, but stopped. 'I'm not feeling so good . . . feverish . . . I think I might be coming down with something.'

Slater's movement from the bench was very quick but smooth and he was halfway across the oval, skirting the flower bed, before Peebles properly realized Slater had got up. Denver moved, slightly, but didn't look up from his paper until Slater reached him.

Standing over the man, Slater said, 'Perhaps you can help me?'

Denver's face creased. 'What the hell . . .?'

Slater said, 'You've been on that same page for a full ten minutes. David's death wasn't reported in the *Post* – I know because I checked – so there was no way Peebles could have known and told me how sorry he was unless he'd been briefed. You were far too jerky getting your ear piece out when you heard me ask Peebles why he was sweating so much and he spent most of the time we were talking looking not at me but at you, as if he was expecting some guidance. And with the amount of terrorist security there is around the White House these days do you really think they would have let a potential car bomb stay that close unless there hadn't been a positive Langley guarantee that it was a communication van? I really would have expected things to have got much better, more professional, over the years.'

'Buddy, I don't know what the hell you're talking about,'

said Denver. 'And what's more I don't want to know. Why
don't you go back to your friend and both of you fuck off
back to whatever hospital you're on release from?'

'You heard the conversation we had. Can you help me?'

Denver stood up, crumpling his newspaper. 'I told you to
fuck off.'

'You fucked up,' accused Slater, conversationally. 'You
know it and I know it. You had a receiver in your ear, to listen
to everything I was saying to Peebles. So if you're not wired
to a two-way transmitter as well – and you shouldn't be
because they always cross-wire and interfere – your truck over
there don't know it yet. Which means Langley don't know it,
either. Not yet, that is. Not until I make contact with the
numbers I still have – numbers that still get answered – and
give them your description and tell them it was more like a
vaudeville show than a proper, professional intelligence operation. So, can you help me?'

Denver remained where he was for several moments, the
crumpled paper still in his hand. Finally, so quietly it was
difficult to hear, Denver mumbled, 'You heard what he said.
Call in a couple of days.'

'In two days I call Peebles,' stipulated Slater. 'If I don't
get help on the third day I call Langley.'

'Who the fuck do you think you are! You're —'

'A Russian defector who brought in one of the worst spies
ever to operate from within the CIA,' stopped Slater. 'Let's
not fall out . . . buddy.' He looked across the flower bed. 'Why
don't you go and put Peebles out of his misery?' He'd probably taken the sneer too far, Slater acknowledged. But he was
buoyed up, excited even, by how quickly and easily – how
professionally – he'd realized what was going on, his satisfaction undiminished by their incompetence. He was glad,
too, that he'd wired himself to record everything that had been
said, both to Peebles and whoever this amateur, very badly
posing as a supposed professional was.

Despite the quick insistence to the psychiatrist, Slater still
wasn't sure – didn't know how he ever could be – that he
could kill Jack Mason, not until the moment came. If push
came to shove he knew, though, that he could – and would
– do everything else and whatever else to keep Ann and himself
safe. He couldn't be sure about killing another human being

until the moment came. But if there were the slightest proof Mason had anything to do with David's death he wouldn't have any uncertainty. Then it would be exactly what he'd told Hillary Nelson. He'd *want* to kill him.

'Where are you?'

Always the same fucking script, thought Mason. 'My flight leaves in two hours; I'm already at the airport.'

'Which airport?' asked Beverley.

'Los Angeles.'

'How's it gone?'

'I think I've got a chance in San Diego. The second agency I told you about. San Diego's good. You ever been there?'

'No.'

'You'd like it. I didn't try, obviously, because I couldn't without a passport, but Mexico's less than an hour away.' Once more Mason felt like a conjuror, needing to keep so many balls in the air at the same time and, although it was necessary, he was becoming increasingly irritated that one of them had to be Beverley Littlejohn. Virtually at once the anger transferred towards himself; she *was* necessary, and he had to stay focused, keep juggling. Beverley was a bonus, essential to his evolving plan, and she couldn't at this fast-approaching conclusion become an irritant.

'LAX doesn't sound very busy from here?'

'I got a booth, not an open pod.'

'You spoken to the lawyer?'

'Told him I was coming back to settle everything. Got a meeting the day after tomorrow.'

'Then you're back here?'

'I'll be back when I'm back,' said Mason, putting the edge into his voice.

'I wasn't—' Beverley started at once but he interrupted her.

'You were. Don't.' It really was going to be a relief, getting rid of her. There was silence from the other end. 'Beverley?'

'I'm sorry. I miss you.'

'If it's like this every time I shan't call so often.'

'Don't say that!'

'There's just been a change on the indicator board, but I can't see it from where I am. They might have switched the pier.'

'Don't go! Not when you're mad at me.'

'I'm not mad. I just don't like these sorts of conversations, like I'm wrapped up. Hog-tied.'

'I'm sorry.'

'And for Christ's sake stop saying you're sorry!'

'I'm . . .' she started then stopped.

'I've got to go.'

'OK.'

'I'll call when I'm settled.'

'Soon?'

'When I'm settled.'

'I love you.'

'I love you, too . . .' Mason timed the pause. 'When I'm not hog-tied.'

He only just managed to stop himself slamming the phone down, irritated by the delay of the facile argument. It would be good, a relief, to be rid of her. Why did women imagine they had some God given right to pussy whip a man in every situation? He'd beaten that out of Ann but couldn't be bothered to do the same with Beverley. She was history now.

Despite the delay her whining had caused, Mason stuck to his prepared schedule, driving the short distance from the post office to the Annapolis mall with which he was most familiar, managing to park close to his already isolated weapon emporium, experiencing a jump of physical excitement the moment he entered the Aladdin's cave of potential carnage, allowing himself the briefest, new fantasy of the lingering agony he could inflict upon Slater and Ann with the ordnance set out all around him.

It was practically deserted and at once a man Mason guessed to be little older than twenty, blond hair in a long ponytail, detached himself from a group of waiting salesmen and hurried towards him, a smile clipped into place.

'Hi there!' he greeted. 'How ya doing?' The ID on his shirt named him as Rod Redway.

'Good,' said Mason. 'Impressive looking place.'

'With the stuff we've got available here we could have won the war in Iraq in half the time,' said the salesman, smiling at his own overly rehearsed joke. 'Means we got whatever you want.'

224

'It's not going to be a great sale,' apologized Mason. 'I just need a box of handgun ammunition and some cleaning material: oil and a brush and cloths, stuff like that.'

'Why don't I run past you some of the stuff we got?'

'Maybe another time,' answered Mason. 'I'm on a tight schedule today.'

'Wouldn't take all that long,' pressed the man.

'Another time,' repeated Mason. 'I'm looking for some ten-millimetre shells.'

'Hey!' said Redway. 'Serious *Dirty Harry* stuff. What you got?'

'A Glock.'

'No problem,' assured the man. 'I'll need your licence.'

Fuck! thought Mason, sure the inward jolt didn't show as hesitation. He groped into both inside pockets of his jacket, putting on the frown, then both on the outside, shaking his head as he did so. 'You're not going to believe this!'

'What? said Redway, frowning.

'I've come out without the damned thing. I didn't set out today to get it – just came in when I saw your store.'

'Can't let you have any ammunition without it,' said the salesman.

'Of course you can't,' said Mason. 'I know that well enough. I'll have to come back some other time. I could still do with the cleaning stuff.'

There was almost an imperceptible tightening of irritation in the other man's face at the smallness of the sale. 'That I can let you have.'

Mason bought the first of everything he was offered, uncaring at knowing it would be the most expensive. As he paid, he said, 'This is the sort of thing that makes you feel a total jerk.'

'It happens,' said Redway, in a tone showing that was exactly what he thought Mason to be. 'Come back again soon, you hear.'

'I will,' promised Mason, hurrying out of the store hot with embarrassment, never to know the irony of another encounter just a few miles away.

Slater had expected the gunsmith to be a work-shirted cowboy, maybe complete with Stetson. However, the man who confronted them wore a collar and tie and a subdued brown suit, the only inconsistency a droop-ended moustache that bracketed his mouth. There was a comprehensive and computer-consulted ID check, which established his business, after which the formality lessened and the man, whose quickly offered card named him as William Jackson, smiled in colleague-to-colleague understanding and said, 'What have you got already? Surprised we haven't met sooner.'

'I'm not,' said Slater. 'I don't have a gun.'

The man pushed himself back from his computer station and said, 'A security consultant who doesn't have a handgun – a selection, even!'

The genuine incredulity was almost amusing. Slater said, 'I advise on property, burglary protection, stuff like that.'

Jackson nodded back to his humming computer. 'Well respected, too. Still would have expected you to already have something.'

'That's why we're going to need your advice. I want something for my wife as well as myself.' Looking around him, from the barred and presumably locked handgun display cases to the wall-chained ordnance and rifles with their triggers removed, Slater decided there was enough weaponry in this warehouse-sized emporium less than half a mile from Ann's gallery to start a small-sized war. There were at least five other salesmen attending to customers: two, presumably husband and wife couples, had children with them, one boy, whom Slater guessed to be about the same age as David had been, had his nose literally pressed against a display case. Slater was conscious of Ann turning positively away from where the children were.

'I've got the name!' the man suddenly announced. 'Didn't recognize it before but now I remember. Sorry. Sorry about your loss, too.'

Slater felt Ann stir awkwardly beside him. 'Thank you. Like I said, something for both of us.'

'The paper said—'

'I know what the paper said,' stopped Slater. 'I don't want to talk about anything they said, OK?'

'Sure. Sorry again.' Jackson nodded once more to his computer. 'Know you're kosher with what the paper said, but I've still got to go through the system, you understand?'

'Of course you have,' accepted Slater.

'What's the system?' demanded Ann, impatiently.

The gunsmith got up from his computer station. 'You can't take what you buy away with you today. You've got to wait seven days, before you can collect it. That's to allow a full background check by the police, who have to approve the issuing of a licence.' The man shrugged, apologetically. 'It's into criminal records and mental stability. I've also got to fire a sample round from whatever you buy and send the spent cartridge to the police, to create a ballistic record to attach to your file, in case the weapon is ever involved in a shooting of any sort.'

'I can't carry a gun for seven days?' pressed Ann.

'You can't *carry* a gun at all,' insisted the dealer. 'You want to do that, you need to apply for a concealed gun licence and to get that the police need to be convinced you're doing so in the interests of public safety.'

'What about . . .? started Ann, indignantly, but stopped.

Jackson shrugged. 'I don't make the rules, Mrs Slater. I'm a believer in the Amendment that it's the right of every American to bear arms, but there's been too many nuts and now there's terrorism, as well.'

'Thanks for explaining things,' said Slater, who'd already known the regulations but wanted Ann to hear them separately, from an independent expert, to avoid her suspecting he was inventing obstacles. She'd again remained locked in the house while he'd been in Washington the previous day, only finally opening the door that evening when he'd presented himself in front of the monitoring porchway television. He wasn't totally sure she'd believed his lie that fingerprints found upon the tulips weren't on record and therefore couldn't have been those of Jack Mason. The impossibility of the stems being completely unmarked was the most pressing of all the illogicalities troubling Slater.

'So let's get down to business!' said the dealer, enthusiastically. 'You got any idea what you want?'

'We're relying on your advice,' reminded Slater. His recollection of his KGB firearms training was of a cumbersome Makarov revolver, with a kick virtually impossible to hold down or guarantee any accurate aim, and of being deafened for hours after range practice without ear mufflers.

'I think I might have something special for you,' offered Jackson. 'It's a .45 Hechler and Koch LAM – that's laser aiming model – known in the trade as a SOCOM from it being the choice of the US Special Forces Command. It actually beat the Colt company, although it's adapted to use the Cold-manufactured Knight suppresser if you want a noise and flash silencer. It's got a twelve round magazine and is one of the most accurate – if not *the* most accurate – handguns on the market.' The man had been moving among his display cases as he spoke, finishing the pitch at the exact moment of producing the gun. He offered it to Slater and said, 'How's that feel?'

Certainly far lighter and more manageable than the almost forgotten Makarov, thought Slater, hefting it in his hand. 'Pretty good.'

'You done much handgun shooting?'

'Not much. We're going to join a club, get some practice, obviously.'

'I got a range out back, where I fire my police records shot. You can pop a few to check it out, before you decide. I'm not trying to press this on to you, I just think it's the best.' The man turned to Ann. 'But it isn't for you, ma'am. Too heavy. For you I'd recommend a Walther TPH. It's a seven round weapon, .25 calibre, remarkably accurate for up to 100 yards and as light as a feather at three kilograms.' He'd been moving among the display cases again, producing the gun the moment he finished talking.

Ann held it awkwardly, looking down at it as if it were something prehistoric or from outer space. 'It doesn't look as if it could do much harm.'

'Let's hope you never have to put it to the test,' said Jackson. 'But believe me, you learn properly how to use it and you can bring down an attacker before he gets anywhere near you. Which is what you need. Why you're buying it.'

'It feels OK,' said Ann, uncertainly.

'Maybe we could both try them on your range?' suggested Slater.

Jackson preceded them, familiarly managing both weapons in one hand and keeping the two boxes of individual ammunition separately in his other. The range was divided into six separate booths, with varying sized targets set out in front that could be adjusted for distance by hand-operated pulleys. Slater thought the bullet-receiving butts at the back were made from a mixture of cork, sand and coiled rope but wasn't sure. Only one booth was already occupied, an assistant behind a testing customer almost completely enclosed in the booth. The attendant saw them and gestured, the movement acknowledged by Jackson, who stopped them going any further. He put what he was carrying on a bench to pick up ear mufflers. He handed one set to Slater and adjusted Ann's for her, before putting on his own and waving to his colleague. Despite the protection and her anticipation of it, the noise from the occupied booth was loud enough to make Ann jump. As they passed Slater saw the target was punctured dead centre. The large, bearded man holding the weapon wore the sort of check shirt and jeans Slater had expected the gunsmith to be dressed in.

When they reached their place, the mufflers dropped around their necks, Jackson nodded behind them and said, 'One of our best customers. Looking to buy his third Magnum, now his son's of age. Drop a buffalo at fifty yards with a gun like that. Got a kick like a buffalo, too.'

The man ushered Ann into the booth first, making a further adjustment to her ear protection and explained how to line up the fore- and backsights and pointed out the hammer safety catch before loading the Walther. He winched the target towards her to the twenty-five yard mark and positioned her left hand to support her right wrist. Slater saw the target flicker to Ann's shot but couldn't see a hole in it.

Jackson looked between the two of them, smiling. 'You did say you were going to get some training, didn't you?'

'Of course,' said Slater.

To Ann the man said, 'You're going to stand more chance of hitting your target if you keep your eyes open, Mrs Slater. Take another shot, to get the feel.'

This time Ann caught the outer circle. When they wound the target in they saw her first shot had nicked the top right hand corner. Ann said, 'I like it. This is the one I want.'

Slater fired three try-out shots, at twenty-five yards. Two hit the outer circle, the third the next in towards the bull. The difference between the SOCOM and the remembered Russian regulation Makarov was immense.

Jackson said, 'Pretty good for someone who hasn't shot a lot.'

Back in the store Jackson produced the suppresser and actually clipped it on, pointing out how it did not interfere with the sighting, but Slater rejected the addition. They made a collection appointment and left with Jackson's promise to get in touch if there were any problems, which he didn't anticipate.

As they drove away Ann said, 'There's no point in my having it without a carrying licence.'

'You heard what the regulations are.'

'For Christ's sake!' exclaimed Ann. 'The police are running a murder enquiry parallel with their investigation of David's death, which I know was murder too. Doesn't my need to protect myself and for you to protect yourself qualify as public safety: *our* public safety!'

'Let's get the initial permits first.' She was right, Slater accepted. He couldn't move until the following day's result of his CIA confrontation in Lafayette Park – didn't at that moment know what other moves there were to make – but their being able to carry a gun at all times was one of the most obvious. Another was Ann sufficiently learning how to use the gun to hit whatever she was pointing at.

'Let's start working on whatever needs to be done now, so we're not looking at another seven or however many more days' delay,' insisted Ann.

'I'll find out what it is . . . whatever it is that needs to be done,' emptily promised Slater. 'I've got to go back to the office. I'm not doing enough there to keep on top of the contracts. You want me to drop you off at the gallery or the house, before we go to the cemetery?'

'The gallery's closed, you know that. I'm going back to the house until you pick me up.'

'I'll call to give you an idea when I'll get back there this evening.' Without needing to discuss it Slater drove into the garage, remaining with Ann in the locked car until the automatic door was fully closed behind them, before entering the house ahead of her to check every room and then rerun that day's CCTV loops before resetting every alarm behind him to re-enter the garage and relock the car before reversing out. A traffic accident delayed him getting back to the office by ten minutes. During those extra ten minutes Ann had twice telephoned Mary Ellen to find out where he was.

Jack Mason was on the point of quitting the cemetery where he'd waited for more than two hours, when he saw Ann and Slater approaching along a path towards him; he hurriedly pulled back into the concealment of the privet thicket about twenty yards from the grave. So complete was his surveillance that Mason was sure he knew the elevation they needed to reach in order to fully see David's resting place, nodding in satisfaction when they halted precisely at the spot he'd predicted to establish there were no more unidentified floral tributes. The tulips he'd left the previous day had no longer been there when he'd arrived and he'd examined every refuse bin, some half filled with decaying blooms, in a 100 yard radius without locating them. Had it been such a good idea after all, leaving them as he had? Yes, Mason decided, as Slater and Ann resumed their approach. The flowers amounted to his first taunt – although no one but he and they would know it – and it was simple imagery but very effective to use again if he chose to do so.

They were very close to the grave now, almost upon it, and both were looking around them; Ann was talking to Slater in short, head-jerking burst, to which Slater was responding with head shakes and shrugs. Mason remained crouched and completely hidden behind the thicket, through which he could see every gesture and movement they made. There was a convenient burial place to his left and he was confident that anyone approaching from the opposite direction or from behind would believe it to be that of a loved one he was tidying. Ann was kneeling, as if in prayer, with Slater on one bended knee, a comforting arm around her shoulders. Mason turned, ensuring no one could see him, before extending his arm and outstretched finger through the entwined branches, sighting along an imaginary barrel and very quietly saying,'Pow. Pow,' as he pressed the trigger for two unmissable shots.

That evening Ann and Slater stayed almost forty-five minutes before leaving, each looking intently around as they went back along the most direct path to the car park. Mason straightened, to ease the growing cramp from his legs, in no hurry to follow. It would be so easy, with a rifle: absolutely and totally unmissable. It hadn't been possible to decide upon a method until he'd seen them in the location and established the possibilities, Mason once more reassured himself. But he wished now that he'd given more thought to the alternatives when he'd still been in the penitentiary.

Mason made his way out of the cemetery, turning away from the main entry and exit with its adjoining car park to a pedestrian side gate. At the junction of the two paths he paused for the last time, satisfying himself that neither Ann nor Slater's car remained in the car park. Mason's own was two streets away. As he got into it and set off towards Chesapeake he decided it was time to change to a different colour and model of car.

Back at the fishing cottage Mason at once changed into his running kit and pounded the beach for at least three sand-sucking miles, enjoying the satisfaction of toning himself up again. He showered upon his return and carried a drink with him to his laptop. There was a new email saved on Glynis Needham's computer. It was addressed to Beverley Littlejohn and read: I'LL CALL AGAIN AT YOUR TEN TOMORROW TO EXPLAIN THE MASON SITUATION.

Twenty-Five

Jack Mason's mind was momentarily blocked, the message frozen before him, two words – *call again* – echoing in his mind like a stuck record. They were telephoning each other! Why? Why the fuck weren't they using email, as they were supposed to do, as he was relying upon them to do for him to read and know what was going on? Why hadn't the bitch told him when he'd telephoned that morning? That's what he was calling her for, for Christ's sake, to make sure he was still safe. Still unsuspected. Never to be suspected. Concentrate! He had to concentrate harder, properly, not fall apart. No reason to panic. It was obvious why Beverley hadn't told him of the contact from her dyke predator. He'd calculated his call to Beverley for 9.30 a.m., which was 12.30 p.m. East Coast time; it was why his day had been knocked off schedule, because of how long she'd kept him with her where-are-you whining. Glynis Needham's email was registered on the screen in front of him at 2.30 p.m., 11.30 a.m. Californian time. He refocused on the two hovering, eroding words: *call again*. So they'd already had one conversation and needed to talk some more.

It had to be about the fucking CCTV outside Ann's gallery on Frederick's Main Street and him being shown up on it. But *what* about it? And why suddenly by telephone, not via email how they normally communicated?

He wasn't thinking fast enough, properly enough! There had to be something in his other electronic trawl nets. Mason hedge-hopped between his other illegally embedded sites, refusing with growing frustration to accept or believe that there wouldn't be some other reference, some exchange that would give him the steer. *There had to be something!* Slowly, thinking smoothly, objectively, Mason moved through every communication in his separate cuckoo's nest logs, even exchanges before he'd been released from White Deer. Once more, nothing.

He could call her again, invent some reason – he didn't need a fucking reason! – for doing so. No he couldn't. All the conveniently available post offices were already closed and the only other telephone was here, at the cottage. And he didn't want to risk registering a phone card call on it.

He had a choice, Mason decided. He could wait until tomorrow – until beyond noon tomorrow, to give the two probation officers the time to talk – or drive right now, tonight, into Washington where Beverley believed him to be, find an hotel and telephone Beverley either at her office or at the apartment to find out what 'the Mason situation' was. It was eight o'clock, he saw, checking his watch. To compensate for the time difference between east and west he couldn't call Beverley for another nineteen hours – virtually a whole day – if he stayed where he was and rang from Annapolis. Whatever the exchange involved between the two women, it wasn't complete. Was there any point contacting Beverley until they'd talked again? Could he chance calling her tomorrow, even? She was the only person who could lead a CIA or police investigation to him, the only person still to have the slightest idea where he was, which he'd confirm the moment he telephoned the following day.

He could run, Mason told himself, just adopt his new identity as Adam Peterson, not bother to contact Patrick Bell again and dump Beverley and . . . Mason stopped the mental litany. He wasn't thinking straight, as he should be thinking. He had to *know*! Until he knew, knew what 'the Mason situation' was and whatever possible danger to which he might be exposing himself, he couldn't go on with the killing of Ann and Slater; conceivably, although he was sure he would have detected it, they could be under protective surveillance. Only when he knew could he decide if he had to run. And he wouldn't do that – wouldn't walk away from what he'd promised himself for the last fifteen years – until he was convinced the odds were stacked a mile high against him. Eighteen and a half hours to go, Mason calculated, checking his watch again. It was going to be like counting off the days and weeks and months as he had in the penitentiary.

The address relayed by John Peebles, in a voice discernibly relieved at no longer being personally involved, was on Tennessee

Avenue, close to Lincoln Park, and Slater was there more than thirty minutes before the appointed time, surveilling the surrounding streets before locating the actual building itself, isolating the observation points to confirm it was a CIA safe house. There was the inevitable CCTV. That it was a safe house was on the one hand encouraging, because it showed they were taking his concerns seriously, but unsettling on the other. For the Agency to disclose a safe house could indicate that they had confirmed – although he couldn't yet imagine how – that Jack Mason was in the Frederick area and that he and Ann were being stalked.

Denver himself opened the door to Slater's summons, smiling affably. Nodding beyond Slater, the CIA man said, 'You were very thorough, checking the place out. Think you got everything?'

'I hope not,' responded Slater. 'I'd feel safer if there were some I missed.'

Denver stood aside, gesturing Slater in. 'There were. You didn't have a tail.'

A meeting of equals, thought Slater, starting to follow the other man but stopping abruptly at the door of a room overlooking the park at the sight of someone else already there. The man was so fat he overflowed the chair from which it would have been an effort to rise, which he didn't attempt. He smiled instead, raising a hand in greeting.

Denver said, 'Dave Potter. FBI.'

'How you doing?' said the man, his voice an ole-boy Southern drawl.

'I'm not sure?' said Slater, questioningly. 'I don't remember a lot of friendship between the CIA and the FBI?'

'There isn't,' confirmed Potter, hands linked over his expansive belly, as if it needed support. 'You were a shared case, remember? Everyone wanting to feed off you, make sure we got it all. And if there's any foundation at all in what you're telling us – telling Pete here, who's told me – it's more an FBI problem than CIA.'

'I guess I'm holding a watching brief,' supported Denver.

But not the supervisor left holding the can if anything goes wrong, thought Slater, understanding the doorstep affability. He certainly remembered the combined attention of both Agencies. The debriefings weren't shared, although he accepted that the interviews would have been, so the separate agency interrogators could peck at the efforts of their predecessor to ensure they did get everything; picking the carcass – his carcass – clean. If the FBI were in charge it meant it was a Bureau safe house. 'It's good to know it's still shared and that you're taking it seriously.'

'You want something to drink?' invited Denver. There was a half-filled coffee percolator, with cups, on the table between him and the FBI agent.

Slater sat in the nearest chair, keeping the separation, and said, 'No thanks. I'd like to know about Mason?'

Denver took the third chair, helping himself from the jug. 'California. Got his parole supervision switched and is trying to get something in the computer industry.'

'When?' demanded Slater.

'When?' echoed Potter.

'When – what was the exact date – that he went to California?'

'May eighth,' said Denver.

'Ann thinks he was outside her gallery on April twelfth.'

'*Thinks*,' qualified Potter, heavily. 'Caught on a CCTV spool you didn't keep.'

'You heard the recording from Lafayette Park?' This encounter would be automatically recorded, too, Slater knew. Probably videoed as well, although he hadn't detected a lens.

'You know your meeting with Peebles was being recorded,' said Denver, unapologetic.

'Then you know why we didn't keep the recording,' said Slater. 'She made a mistake. People do.'

'We're surprised she made a mistake about something like that,' said Potter. With obvious and heavy breathing the man came forward in his chair to pour himself coffee.

'So am I,' admitted Slater. 'That's just how it was. And if she was right it could have been him, according to the dates.'

'What's convinced you she's right?'

Slater hesitated, the reservations colliding in his head. 'I thought she might have been close to a breakdown, after David's death. We saw a psychiatrist, in case Ann had become ...' He paused again. 'Become confused. The psychiatrist is convinced she isn't; devastated, certainly, but not suffering from any sort of delusion or mental imbalance.'

Potter was slumped back, the coffee supported on his stomach. 'You convinced, too, that Mason wants to cause you some harm . . . that he killed David even?'

Slater's hesitation continued. Then he blurted, 'Yes!'

'David died May nineteenth,' gently reminded Denver. 'Mason was in California, 3,000 miles away, on May nineteenth.'

'Who says?' challenged Slater.

'His probation officer.'

'Does he have to report to her every day?'

'I don't think so,' said Denver.

From the look that passed between the two men Slater knew it was a requirement they hadn't asked about. Shouldn't lose his temper, he told himself; he hadn't expected to get this degree of consideration and he didn't want to lose it. 'He could have flown back, ran David down and been back in California in two or three days, without the probation officer knowing he'd left the West Coast.' Emotion had started to rise as he spoke and he finished thick-voiced, coughing to clear the difficulty.

'Mr Slater,' said the obese man. 'We've all three of us got experience of things, the sort of things we're talking about. You can't plan intentionally to kill a person like that, like it's a day trip. It takes time, preparation. In your specific case, how could Mason have known that on May nineteenth David would have been going to school on his bicycle and not as he normally did on the school bus?'

Slater felt the exasperation growing but then punctured it with a sudden awareness. 'You've spoken to Frederick police . . . to the people investigating David's killing. And the murder of the man in the underpass gully?'

There was another exchange of looks between the two other men. Potter said, 'Yes, I have.'

'I didn't tell them who I really am.'

'Neither did I,' said Potter.

'How did you explain your interest?'

'That there could be a pattern, with other car incineration murders in other states. They'd be quite happy for the Bureau to take the investigation over. They're getting nowhere.'

'Which means they're getting nowhere investigating David's killing?' seized Slater.

'I'm afraid it looks that way,' said Potter.

'*Are* you taking it over, the death of the man in the underpass as well as David's? pressed Slater.

'It was a cover story, Mr Slater. It doesn't – can't – come within FBI jurisdiction.'

'If you can't take it over, why make the approach in the first place?' persisted Slater.

'Because we want to know everything to satisfy ourselves that Mason hasn't found you,' said Potter. 'I'm going to be honest with you, Mr Slater. And I apologize in advance if I offend you. The Witness Protection Programme, tidied up with all the various amendments over the years, works remarkably well. We snared a real son of a bitch in Mason, because you knew you'd get protection. We've made some big hits against organized crime with the same guarantee.' The smile did become apologetic, as promised. 'Here comes the honesty. If, in some way we can't work out, Mason has found you and is planning some half-assed revenge, we want to stop him. Because if he managed to cause you or your wife some harm the protection programme goes to hell in a handcart and people stop coming forward and telling us things we need to hear. I'm sorry but that's the reality of it.'

'So what is the reality of it?' Slater threw back. 'You think he's found us?'

'The jury's still out,' clinched Denver, awkwardly.

'There's something else I haven't told you,' admitted Slater, anxiously, needing to keep them with him and not dismiss everything that seemed so easily dismissible. 'Something that might sound ridiculous – why I held back from mentioning it – but could be the opposite—'

'You're not doing a great deal to help yourself, let alone help us,' broke in Denver, accusingly.

'What is it, Mr Slater?' demanded Potter.

'My wife and I go every day to David's grave,' explained Slater, avoiding the looks of both men. 'We did, after the confrontation in Lafayette Park. When we got there, there was a bouquet of tulips very definitely placed on top – taking precedence – of our own wreath. There was no card. I took them to a laboratory I've occasionally used and had them checked for fingerprints; tulip stems are very smooth, a good surface—'

'What did the laboratory get?' interrupted Potter.

'Nothing,' said Slater. 'They were absolutely clean. Which they shouldn't have been. No one could have touched those stems without leaving a trace ... unless they'd been very carefully and individually wiped. Or whoever put them there wore gloves.'

'Which whoever laid them there could have been doing,' said Denver. 'Why'd you think it could be Mason?'

'Goading us. Letting us know he's found us.' Slater looked up at last, tensed for the ridicule. Instead of which Potter said, 'Where are they now, these flowers?'

'I left them at the laboratory.'

Potter went quickly to speak but didn't. More slowly, gesturing towards a side table upon which there was a telephone that Slater hadn't seen before, the FBI man said, 'Call them! Make sure they haven't disposed of them!'

'They will have done by now,' said Slater. 'Why should they have kept them?'

'Call them!' insisted Potter, making a vague hand movement. 'At the Hoover Building downtown we've got state-of-the-art laboratory facilities no commercial laboratories could afford or dream of.'

Slater knew he shouldn't feel self-conscious, the object of their attention standing at the telephone, but he did. There was a delay locating the man through whom he usually dealt and to whom he posed the question, and he was kept even longer on hold while the man tried to find the answer. Almost ten minutes elapsed before he was able to turn back to the two intelligence agents, the relief surging through him. 'They've still got them! They were my property that they didn't have authority to dispose of. They're holding them, for me to collect.'

'Something that's been saved at last,' said Denver, critically.

'There's something else you haven't told us about, isn't there, Mr Slater?' accused Potter.

Slater shook his head, confused. 'No!'

'You haven't told us that you and your wife have bought handguns.'

239

'It hasn't come into the conversation,' protested Slater. 'We only made the purchase and went through the formalities a day or two ago!'

'The local PD have set up a computer base on their combined enquiry. Your name registered automatically, with the application and confirming address,' said Potter.

'I've already told you that my wife has been diagnosed without any mental problems, which I know would have precluded a licence being granted,' said Slater, knowing it was important to cover every prohibition. 'We're going to join a club, take lessons. I said earlier that my wife is devastated by David's death, as I am. She's also terrified, as well as convinced, that who she saw on the CCTV was her ex-husband. She's at home now, refusing to go back to her gallery, every alarm and protection on until I get back.'

'What do you think she'd do, if she saw someone on the street she identified as Jack Mason?' asked Potter. 'Do you think she'd wait, to be sure? Or shoot and wait until afterwards to find out if she was right?'

'Are you going to block the licences?' said Slater.

'That isn't an answer to my question, Mr Slater.'

'I don't have an answer to your question.'

'What would you do in exactly the same circumstances?' came in Denver.

'Ensure I'd properly identified the man.'

'And then what, after you had properly identified him as Jack Mason?' said Denver. 'Would you try to kill him?'

It took a long time for Slater to reply, convinced as he was that the gun application depended on his response. 'If I thought he was going to try to kill Ann or me, harm us in any way, I'd have every legal right to defend both of us.'

'If you genuinely believed your lives to be in danger,' agreed Potter.

'Do you think they could be?' asked Slater.

'I told you we don't have any positive evidence or reason to believe they might be,' reminded Potter. 'More immediately I think we should go and retrieve those flowers, as soon as we can.'

'I would have imagined there's good enough reason for my wife and I to get handguns,' argued Slater.

'Maybe,' conceded Potter. 'It's evidence we're short of, not reasons. We'll all go,' decided Potter.

'What about the gun licence application?' said Slater.

'Something else that's out of my jurisdiction,' said Potter. 'That's something for the local PD.'

They hadn't laughed or ridiculed him, Slater realized. He hadn't felt they despised him as a defector, either. There was, in fact, a lot about the encounter that he hadn't expected. Some, indeed, that he hadn't fully or properly understood.

'Sorry I was irritable when we last talked,' said Mason. 'That's why I'm calling so soon, to say sorry.'

'You said you weren't mad,' reminded Beverley.

'I'd had a bad day.'

'How come?'

'Now I've decided to settle out there I'm transferring banks,' said Mason, the lie one of several he'd rehearsed during the interceding and unsettling nineteen hours.

'You didn't tell me you were doing that.'

'I hadn't thought about it until I got here, which was stupid.'

'What's the problem?'

The problem is that you haven't already told me what you and Glynis Needham are talking about, thought Mason. 'I imagined it was going to be easy but it isn't. I've got to go back tomorrow and sign some more forms.'

'How's it going with the lawyer?'

He had to switch this fucking conversation! 'Slower than I expected there, as well. I miss you.'

'I miss you, too. What—'

'I don't want to talk about me,' Mason cut across her. 'I want to talk about you. What are you doing?' Mason felt hot, stifled, and wished he could open the door of the booth at the Annapolis main post office.

'Working, what else?'

'Busy?' Why was she holding out on him?

'I heard from Glynis.'

At last! 'She planning to come out again?'

'About you.'

'What about me?' Mason hadn't intended the question to be so sharp and bit angrily at his own lip.

'Wanted to know if you'd got fixed up with a job yet.'

'What did you tell her?'

'That your interviews were going well. That's what you told me, wasn't it?'

That wouldn't take two telephone calls. 'Why's she so interested? I thought you were my case officer now.'

'She also wanted to know about the compensation claim. She was glad you weren't going to go ahead with it.'

'That all?'

'What else could there be?'

'I don't know,' said Mason, in rare honesty. The damned dyke *had* kept on about the penitentiary case, he reminded himself.

'She did talk about coming out again,' conceded Beverley. Getting there! Mason said, 'What did you tell her?'

'She didn't talk dates. I told her to call me again when she was more definite.'

'You think asking about me was just an excuse to make plans to come out and hit on you again?'

'That's exactly what I think.'

'Is that why you're sounding so down?' There wasn't a problem, Mason determined: no cause for him to re-plan or reschedule anything. Just one thing, he corrected himself. He didn't think he'd bother to go back to San Francisco, convenient – and pleasurable – though it was to have his very own sex slave.

'I've got my period. It's a bad one.'

'We'll think of something to put Glynis off.'

'You going to give me your number?'

'That's another pain in the ass,' said Mason, coming to another rehearsal. 'I checked out this morning from where I've been for the last couple of days: you could have thrown a saddle on the cockroaches and ridden in the Kentucky Derby. I'm going to try a Marriott, downtown. I'll give you a call later, with the number. You going to be in the office all day?'

'All day,' she said.

'I hope the period gets better.'

'So do I. When do you think you'll get back?'

'It's difficult to say. Not much longer.'

'You promise?'

'I promise.'

'I love you.'

'I love you back.'

'Goodbye, darling.'

'Goodbye Beverley,' said Mason, meaning it.

'What do you think?' asked Denver.

'It's definitely Dimitri Sobell,' said Burt Hodges, the original CIA debriefer, whose retirement home was at Harper's Ferry, and who'd recognized the Russian's assumed name from the *Frederick News-Post* and watched the entire interview on video link to an upstairs room. Hodges was a trim, upright man, the only hint of him passing seventy years his almost total baldness.

'We'd confirmed that from the voiceprint,' reminded Potter.

'You think your guys will be able to pick up anything from those flower stems?' asked Hodges.

'If it's scientifically possible they'll get it,' insisted Potter. The coffee had been replaced at the Tennessee Avenue safe house with a bottle of Wild Turkey, the video turned off. All three men were drinking.

'It would be a hell of a confirmation,' said Denver. 'What did you think of Slater?'

'Pretty good,' judged Hodges, who'd spent virtually every day for three months with the man during his defection debriefing. 'Not as rusty as I'd expected. His story sounds genuine by its very weakness. If they were fantasizing they'd have made it a hell of a lot better than that.'

'I'm not happy about the handguns,' cautioned Potter. 'If some innocent gets shot it'll be my tit in the wringer.'

Denver smiled at the thought of the physical impossibility of that being inflicted on a man of Potter's size. 'It'll work out. There's not a lot of options.'

'There never is,' said Potter. 'So far I've been lucky. I keep worrying it can't go on without breaking.'

Twenty-Six

S later hoped that Ann's conviction would be allayed by knowing that both the CIA and FBI were jointly involved, but it wasn't. Since the discovery of the bouquet on David's grave, she'd become more adamant than ever that Mason was stalking them and it remained the only all-consuming subject of every conversation between them, not discussed as a possibility but as an indisputable fact. She even argued that the intelligence organizations' interest was confirmation of their having been found by her ex-husband, continuing to refuse to leave the house except for their mourning vigil at the cemetery, where the nervousness shivered through her. Her only slight recovery had been to re-open the gallery, although at a distance, liaising by telephone several times a day with Jean, whom she officially appointed manager, with a salary increase. The day of Slater's safe house encounter she agreed to her former PA employing a recently graduated art student who applied for a work-experience position and had Slater drop off some pre-signed cheques for Jean to keep the finances up to date. She also had him reiterate her refusal to stage any further exhibitions. Among the accumulated mail had been two enquiries, one at the international level for Andre Worlack. There was no one resembling Jack Mason on the CCTV footage Slater examined and reset, as he had done in yet another effort to reassure Ann since her self-imposed imprisonment.

Slater kept to the arrangement he'd agreed with David Potter after the flower retrieval, despite Ann's demands that he call the FBI supervisor earlier, using the intervening time to fully catch up with everything outstanding at his own office. He, too, declined two overdue enquiries, although he could have fitted them into his existing schedule. In reply to a letter from the San Jose company, he promised to let them know as soon as possible when he would be able to return to New Mexico to discuss the further, promised work. He enclosed with that letter the provisional plans for the first two already agreed contracts. On his way home to collect Ann for that evening's cemetery visit, he enrolled them both in the gun club with which he'd so far only had telephone conversations, despite not having received their handgun permits. The senior instructor warned that it was extremely unlikely either of them would be granted a gun carrying licence.

Slater hadn't told Ann of the discussion with Potter about the guns, knowing it would increase the tension that seemed to be permanent between them and which quickly surfaced when he refused to make the scheduled telephone call to the FBI man before noon.

'You told me he fixed today!' she flared.

'Because today he might hear something but it won't be yet, not nine o'clock in the morning. People have to get to work, look at and assess whatever experiments they've carried out before they can tell him.'

'So now you're a scientist! Know how it's done!'

'Stop it, Ann. It's wrecking us,' said Slater, a familiar plea.

'We're already wrecked!'

'We could stop it happening if we tried.' He was coming more and more to believe that she was right.

'If I tried, you mean!'

'I mean we're not going to achieve anything if we go on fighting . . . making things worse than they already are. We could today get the results of the Bureau tests that prove Mason didn't put the flowers there.'

'He did!' insisted Ann, irrationally.

'What if they find fingerprints that aren't Jack's? Are you going to believe the findings of the best scientific criminal investigation facilities in the world? Or yourself?'

'Call them!' Ann insisted, refusing the logic as she customarily did.

'Not before noon,' refuted Slater, just as insistently. 'I'll come back from the office, do it from here. You'll know the moment I do.'

Would they know, one way or another? Slater asked himself, on the first of his journeys that day into the town, the routine automatic now to stop at the gallery to go through the overnight CCTV film as he had at the house before leaving. Abruptly,

245

unable to stop it, Slater sniggered, immediately conscious of the curious look from a commuter next to him in the momentary traffic jam, hurriedly and visibly putting his hand out to the radio, which he wasn't playing, as if turning a programme up. It was surreal, absurd, to realize so much depending upon a dollar's worth of flowers! Except that it wasn't funny. Neither Denver nor Potter had laughed, thought it ridiculous. This was how things were in real, serious life: situations being resolved or exacerbated by the unreal, the unexpected. He was as uncertain and worried as Ann, just better able to control it – conceal it – because of his ingrained professional training. Perhaps not as easily able to control it, though. There was a tinge, maybe more than a tinge, of hysteria in that giggling outburst. He'd been so quickly aware of the curious frown from the guy in the next car because he was constantly alert to everything around him, relieved that the traffic was moving again, as anxious as Ann to pick up their handguns and undergo the lessons.

Would they get a carrying licence if it were proved Mason had handled the flowers? But this wouldn't be enough, even if it were granted ahead of their becoming competent gun handlers. They'd have to be given protection, as they had when he'd defected. Then, he remembered, it had been virtually protective custody, he and Ann separated, able only to talk on the phone which would inevitably have been bugged. Then the CIA and FBI had needed him, to learn everything he could tell them – and maybe things he might try to conceal – for his evidence against Mason at the trial. Would the need to keep the Witness Programme intact, as Potter had insisted, be sufficient this time? Running ahead of himself, Slater mentally cautioned. He shouldn't speculate ahead of learning the scientific results. He could, in one respect though, perhaps the most important: he was quite sure Ann wouldn't accept that her ex-husband wasn't hunting them even if the FBI produced irrefutable evidence to the contrary; no more than he would, not completely.

There was nothing on the gallery CCTV and it only took ten minutes to reset but Ann had already called the office once before he got there.

'They might have called you ahead of you calling them,' she said.

'They haven't.'

'You are coming back?'

'I promised, didn't I?'

'If they've found anything . . . that it's him, I mean, I don't want you to go back to work. I want you to stay here, with me.'

'All right,' agreed Slater. Could Hillary Nelson be wrong? Too many questions, too much uncertainty, he thought, one nagging at him more persistently than all the others. He shouldn't make monsters out of shadows, as Ann was doing, he warned himself.

'It can only mean that they've confirmed it's him!' insisted Ann, hunched in the seat beside him as he drove towards Washington and the safe house on Tennessee Avenue.

'It doesn't mean that at all,' refuted Slater.

'What did this guy . . . Potter . . . say?'

'You were close enough to hear when I called him from the house. Just that he thought it would be best if we met personally rather than talked on the telephone and why didn't we both drive in to where I met them before.' Slater was as bewildered as Ann by the suggestion. David Potter and Peter Denver would both be cover names but neither the CIA nor the FBI casually surrendered the location of safe houses without good reason. Slater had been surprised at Tennessee Avenue being identified to him for his first encounter, despite his long absence from Russian intelligence. He'd never before heard of it being done with anyone so peripherally involved as they would consider Ann to be. Perhaps they didn't consider her to be peripheral. Or maybe they intended abandoning Tennessee Avenue. Safe houses weren't maintained indefinitely.

'They know it's him,' Ann continued to insist, slumping lower in the passenger seat but at the same time looking anxiously around her, as he had been doing since they'd left Frederick, although not so obviously and despite knowing that locating a following car on a traffic-thronged interstate was virtually impossible.

Slater actually, very positively, hoped Ann was right. It would throw their lives into utter turmoil – turmoil neither of them could begin to imagine – and could conceivably result in the destruction of both their businesses and their having to relocate to some other part of the country; some other part of the world even. But at least they'd *know*! The ghost-generating limbo in which they were suspended now *was* wrecking anything there was between them as effectively as any physical harm Jack Mason might have contemplated or tried against them. Slater couldn't remember – this fact the very proof in itself how bad things had become – the last time he and Ann had made love or even felt or shown any affection whatsoever towards each other. He was sure Ann couldn't have remembered, either.

'Let's wait until we hear what they have to say.'

That afternoon Slater didn't reconnoitre the house as he had before, although he had to drive around two connecting streets before he found a parking space. It was almost over a hundred yards from the house and Ann clung to his arm as they walked, her head hunched. As before, Denver opened the door at the first summons. Potter was respectfully on his feet when Ann entered the room with its view of the park, additional cups for either the offered coffee or afternoon tea, neither of which Slater nor Ann accepted. There was an additional chair for Ann, too, and as she took it she said, 'It's him, isn't it? Jack? You've established that he handled the flowers.'

'No, we haven't, Mrs Slater,' said Potter, settling gratefully back into his inadequate chair. He was short-breathed by the effort of standing.

The denial silenced the already convinced Ann. Slater's reaction was mixed, the predominant – although there was a mix in that, too – one of relief after all. He said, 'What *was* found?'

'It was inconclusive,' qualified Denver, sparring his colleague. 'There were marks, under high definition spectro-analysis, but they weren't definable as prints.'

'What were they then?' said Ann.

'Smudges.'

'Fingerprints that had been wiped,' she said.

'Or imposed by someone wearing gloves . . . like a mourner who might wear gloves taking a belated tribute to a grave and getting confused which grave it was,' said Denver.

'It's identified by David's name on the temporary marker,' refuted Ann. 'You go to the trouble of laying a tribute, you go to the trouble of finding the right grave.'

'What's your judgement?' interceded Slater, wanting to move on from the predictable exchange, judgements of his own to make. Or try to make.

'The only one we can reach,' said Potter. 'The scientific examination was inconclusive and hasn't taken us one step closer at this stage.'

'So what happens now, to your involvement and Frederick PD's investigation?'

'We don't know about Frederick; we're not working with them,' said Potter. 'There's still some more scientific tests for our guys to make.'

'More?' queried Slater.

'I told you the Bureau have state-of-the-art facilities at the Hoover building.'

'Why are we here, if you've found nothing but there's still more scientific tests to be carried out?' questioned Slater, with rising uncertainty.

Potter made another difficult, wheezing stretch to pour himself more coffee. 'We made an arrangement. I thought you'd want to know how we were getting on.'

Before Slater could speak Ann said, 'What about giving us protection?'

'What?' said Denver, frowning.

'Protection,' repeated Ann. 'We wouldn't be here, talking like this, if either or both of you didn't think there was a genuine reason. You want to keep your protection arrangements alive, why not ensure that we're kept alive?'

Slater decided against saying what he'd intended.

Potter said: 'We're a long way from believing you're in any physical danger, Mrs Slater.'

'When Daniel came to you a long time ago we were given total protection. Daniel was kept on an army base, for Christ's sake!' Ann said. 'And then Jack was already under arrest and in jail! He's not in jail any more. He's out there, watching. Waiting.'

'Then we weren't protecting you and your now husband from Jack,' said Denver. 'We were protecting you from KGB retribution.'

'Daniel maybe,' argued Ann. 'Not me.'

'Very much you, Mrs Slater,' said Denver, uncomfortably. 'I'm afraid you're not making this conversation easy, but

Daniel came to us *because* of you. And his continued co-operation with us then depended entirely upon your safety.'

'And now it doesn't!' she demanded.

'No, it doesn't,' agreed Denver, honestly. 'But the CIA and the FBI are listening to what you and your husband are telling us and FBI facilities are being used to check out what we're being told as far and as well as is possible . . .' The man paused. 'Please understand that I am not trying to be rude or critical, Mrs Slater. But we wouldn't be here today, talking like this, if you hadn't, for reasons we still find inexplicable, destroyed the CCTV tape upon which you insist your ex-husband was shown.'

Ann jerked her head towards Slater. 'You think I imagined it, like he does.'

'We wish we'd had the opportunity to see it, as I'm sure your husband does,' said Potter.

'We're grateful, both of us, for what – and how much – you're already doing,' hurriedly intervened Slater. 'And thank you.'

'Give me another call, in two or three days' time, to see where we are,' suggested Potter. 'If anything comes up in between, I'll call you.'

'I'll do that,' promised Slater.

'That was a complete and utter waste of time,' complained Ann, on their way back to Frederick. They were going direct to the cemetery.

'I'd hoped you'd be reassured at meeting them, knowing they were involved.'

'You told me they were involved. I would have been re-assured if I believed they were actually doing something. And that they'd agreed to the protection I asked for.'

Slater was a long way from being reassured by the meeting, too.

Although it had all turned out OK, Mason acknowledged that he had been unnerved by the renewed contact between the two probation officers, which was why he hadn't gone anywhere near Frederick for the past three days. Now, thinking it through as he jogged along the sand strip and after that sat, drink in hand, on the outside deck of the cottage overlooking the bay, he faced further reality. As much as he wished he could have taunted them further, for them to know he had trapped them, it had been part of his fantasy. Just as he'd fantasized about killing Ann and Slater with some exotic reptile, particularly a rattlesnake as in the Capote book he'd liked so much when he'd been the penitentiary librarian, or with one of the Internet formula bombs. It was, mundanely, going to have to be with the untraceable Glock. Restricted as he was by the number of rounds available, he'd have to get very close to them to ensure they both died, close enough for him to be the last person they saw. He'd wanted more, so much more. But he had to be practical. That would have to do. Determined upon reality he accepted that Beverley might do something stupid before he could make the hit. And he needed to speak just once more to Patrick Bell; he didn't have any practical reason for doing this except to time it within hours of the two deaths, to establish that he was supposedly in California and therefore couldn't possibly be responsible, even though Jack Mason no longer officially existed. And then he had to move on to Peter Chambers. That killing was going to be a lot easier, once he'd manoeuvred access to the hidden millions.

The killing of Ann and Slater had to take place at the cemetery, where they were most obviously and easily vulnerable. There was nothing more to add to what he'd discovered from his surveillance there. He knew how sparsely populated the cemetery was during their regular pilgrimages, that they always knelt and prayed with their backs to the thick privet from which he could get to them unseen, unable to miss. Head shots, facial shots, but not until after they'd seen him, recognized him. He was discarding all the fantasies, all the daydreams but they had to know it was him – that he'd won, not them – before they died. Maybe there could be a final humiliation. Holding them, literally on their knees, at the point of a gun, he'd make both of them say sorry. And then plead. Mason knew they'd do it. Kill me, for what I did to you, but spare her. Kill me, for what I did to you, but spare him. That would be enough, letting them think they had a chance – an escape – before blasting their faces off. That's how he'd do it! He only had eight bullets in the magazine. Enough. One each in the face, after they'd begged and pleaded, one left for each, to make sure. Leaving both of them symbolically lying – dead – on the grave of their son. More than good enough. Stupid to have fantasized for as long as he had. The timing was perfect. Just three weeks before the always-trembling, always-apologizing Peter Chambers was due to walk – shuffle, as he always hesitatingly shuffled, never walking like a man – into their rendezvous hotel.

Mason hoped it wouldn't take too long to get access to the three million dollars. So far it hadn't gone as smoothly as he'd expected it to go. He was anxious to finish everything and get out of the fucking country forever. Tomorrow he'd get the Glock out of the safe deposit box. And make all the other necessary arrangements.

'It was definitely Jack Mason's wife,' confirmed Burt Hodges, who'd debriefed Ann as well as Slater, comparing the stories of each. 'But then we knew it was from the newspaper photographs. I was disappointed this time that Dimitri – I'm sorry, I still automatically think of him by his Russian name – seemed to have lost more of his edge than last time.'

'You think so?' queried Denver.

'Didn't you?'

'I didn't handle him during the defection,' reminded Denver.

'Which makes it even more difficult for us,' said Potter, adding to his glass. They were drinking Wild Turkey again.

'You should do what she asked, take her into protective custody,' said the retired CIA man.

'To achieve what?' demanded Potter.

'You know what I mean,' protested Hodges.

'She certainly didn't strike me as being mentally unbalanced,' said Denver.

'Because she isn't,' said Potter. 'Just shit scared.'

'Easy to be,' said Hodges.

'Don't tell me about it,' said Potter.

'I hope I don't have to,' said Hodges. 'This is the sort of situation that makes me glad I'm retired.'

'This is the sort of situation that makes me wish I was,' said Potter.

'You might well be, soon,' said Denver. 'We both might be.'

'You sure the tape's off!' suddenly demanded Potter.

'Of course I'm sure,' said Denver.

Twenty-Seven

They went directly from collecting their handguns and permits to the gun club.

Ann shot first, at twenty-five yards on a points system and scored thirty-five out of a possible one hundred. Slater achieved fifty-five. Ann wanted to extend their allotted time but the instructor said that was inadvisable on her initial session: she was unaccustomed to the straight-armed stance and despite the apparent lightness of the weapon, she'd be tired. He didn't want her confidence affected by a lower score.

'Let's build up, gradually.'

'Let's,' agreed Ann. 'I want a lesson each day. Next week we'll build it up to one in the morning and one in the afternoon.'

'You're going to get very good,' predicted the instructor.

'I intend to be better than very good,' promised Ann.

'You go on using your own weapon, you're going to need a carrying licence.'

'We're getting them,' said Ann.

On their way back to the house Ann said, 'We are, aren't we? You've applied or done whatever you have to do?'

'I said we'd take it a step at the time,' reminded Slater.

'I want to carry it *all* the time! You know that!'

'I'll sort it out.'

'Right away,' she insisted.

'I'm not sure I can spare the time for two sessions a day.'

'You don't seem to need the practice I do. Were you trained, before?'

'When I was in Russia.' They'd never talked about the KGB or anything he'd done during any of his postings. When he'd mentioned it after they'd entered the programme and settled in Frederick, she'd told him she didn't want to know anything about it or what Mason had done beyond what she'd read in the newspapers or heard on television during the trial. She'd stopped doing that before he was sentenced. Until Peebles' letter it had been years since they'd even spoken of Mason.

'When we get the licences I'll start going back to the gallery,' Ann announced.

'I'd hoped you would. I'm going to have to go back to San Jose soon.'

'*What?*' she demanded, the alarm immediate.

'They're offering more work.'

'Turn it down!'

'I've already turned some stuff down. I can't go on saying no. I thought you could come with me.'

'I don't know.'

'What's to decide? Jean's running the gallery. It would do you good to take a trip. We could go on somewhere, make a vacation out of it.'

'I don't know,' she repeated. 'We haven't sorted out the headstone yet. And I like going there as we're doing.'

'Ann, we can't go on visiting every night for the rest of our lives. Any more than you can stay locked up in the house.'

'I told you I'm going back to the gallery!'

'If you get a carrying licence.'

'We'll . . .' started Ann but stopped, fear mewing from her. She was scrabbling into her handbag, talking at the same time. 'There's a car in the driveway! What . . . ? Who . . . ? What?'

'Leave the gun!' ordered Slater. 'Don't bring it out . . . it's all right.'

'It's not!' said Ann, the weapon half free of her handbag.

Slater snatched across, grabbing Ann's wrist. 'It's Stone, the homicide detective. And Hannigan.'

The two police officers got out of their car when Slater came in behind, reaching them before they opened their doors. Stone said, 'We've been waiting a while.'

'You got him!' demanded Ann.

'No, Mrs Slater. We haven't made much progress I'm afraid. You picked up your handguns and permit today.'

'That's where we've been, picking them up.'

'Three hours ago,' said Hannigan, pointedly.

'We've joined a gun club because—'

'Let's get into the house,' interrupted Ann. 'We're in the open here in the drive.'

Inside the house Hannigan said, 'You're not licensed to drive around with the handguns.'

'We had to get them home,' said Slater.

'And we're going to get a carrying licence,' said Ann.

'That's what you should have done, got them straight home,' said Hannigan. 'Not stopped on the way.'

'We know the rules,' said Slater. 'And we *are* going to file the application.'

'We're prepared to let it go this time but let's not have either of you driving around with a gun on board,' cautioned Stone. 'The State of Maryland keeps a pretty tight gun policy.'

'We both just told you we're going to apply!' insisted Ann, in a voice that Slater considered too loud and too indignant. She went on: 'You're on a homicide investigation, not monitoring handgun licences.'

'People who suffer a loss like you suffered often buy guns,' said Hannigan. 'We like making sure it's for the right reasons.'

'You think you can satisfy the public safety provisions?' asked Stone.

'I know you've spoken to the FBI about a possible connection with car burn killings in other states,' said Slater, remembering the conversation with Potter. 'I would have imagined that's a pretty convincing argument.'

'We don't think there's a direct connection with the body in the underpass,' said Stone. 'If it was the same car that struck David we think it was an accident.'

'*Think*,' qualified Slater, nodding to the outside drive. 'You told us out there you haven't made much progress in the case. What positive evidence have you got that there's definitely no connection?'

'The FBI have spoken to you!' said Stone, frowning.

'Yes,' said Slater, conscious of Ann's attention.

'They haven't told us they think there's a hard link,' said Hannigan.

'They haven't told me, either,' said Slater. 'But I think it's a strong supporting reason, don't you?'

'I'm not the licensing authority,' avoided Stone.

'The point that Ann's just made,' said Slater. 'I'm certainly going to spell it out in as much detail as I can in the application. Which will obviously require naming you both as the

255

investigating officers. I was going to tell you, of course. It's good that you came by.'

'Thanks for the warning,' said Hannigan.

'I'll set out the meeting with David Potter, too.'

'When are you making the application?'

'Tomorrow, first thing.'

'You will remember what we said, though, won't you?' said Hannigan. 'About not driving around with the guns on you, until you get the proper licence?'

'And you'll remember how anxious we are to know the moment you arrest whoever killed David, won't you?' said Ann, again too sharply in Slater's opinion.

'What car burn killings!' demanded Ann, when Slater came back into the house from moving his car for the policemen to back out and finally garaging his own vehicle.

'Potter needed a reason to talk to Frederick PD. The FBI don't have any local jurisdiction.'

'Why didn't you tell me?'

Slater sighed. 'It was a cover story, Ann. To avoid having to tell them who I am.'

'What else haven't you told me?'

'Oh, for Christ's sake, Ann!'

'What else haven't you told me?' she repeated.

'There is nothing else I haven't told you.'

'What would you say if I told you I didn't believe you?'

'I'd say that our marriage is breaking up,' replied Slater, exasperated. That's what David had thought was happening, he remembered.

Jack Mason decided to avoid Frederick until the evening he chose to ambush Ann and Slater, believing he had the schedule for everything he had to do sequenced in his mind and that he had overlooked nothing except a place to dump the incriminating weapon and laptop. He drove along his intended escape route to within ten miles of the town before turning off the main highway but staying roughly parallel to it, not wanting the deviation to hinder him more than a few minutes after the killing. It had to be water, he supposed: a reservoir or a river. A quarry or a landfill site was another possibility but deep water would definitely be better. It took him an hour to find the creek, isolated in thick woodland

256

and crossed by an echoing wooden bridge, on one side of which a path led down to the bank. Mason clambered down, searching for a marker to gauge the depth. There was no tidal or high water marker but he couldn't see the bottom. It appeared to flow comparatively fast when he tested it by tossing in some fallen tree debris. The idea came to him as he was collecting up the twigs. He found the branch for which he was looking just beyond the tree line. It was about six foot long and necessarily straight. He clambered back up to the road, checking that it was empty before emerging on to it and walked to the centre of the bridge, testing the balance in his hand before stepping up to the bottom rung of the bridge support, to give himself leverage. He hurled the branch like a spear, guessing it plunged in by at least two feet before being caught up by the water flow. Deep enough, Mason decided. And secluded enough. Testing further, Mason timed the drive to and from the main highway, gauging that the detour would only delay him for a maximum of thirty minutes.

He'd been dissatisfied with the strength of the first bag he'd bought to carry the Glock in, worried that the vague shape of the gun might actually be visible through the thin plastic. He took his time finding the sports outlet store conveniently close to the First National Bank when he got back to DC. He examined several before buying a stiffly reinforced canvas carrier through which nothing inside would be discernible. The safe deposit ritual went as smoothly as always, and as he walked back to where he'd parked the car, he hefted the bag containing the Glock and the separately bagged ammunition; the weight felt good, comforting. But he was at his most vulnerable, Mason reminded himself, as he had been when retrieving the weapon from New York. He had to drive carefully again: couldn't risk becoming involved in a traffic accident or being stopped for some idiotic traffic infringement.

He was close to fulfilling the dream that had sustained him for fifteen robbed years! Mason thought, letting the excitement surge through him. A ten-millimetre bullet could blow a fist-sized hole exiting a body, according to everything he'd read on the Internet during those years in the penitentiary. The imagery of that was exciting, too. He still wished he'd been able to play cat-and-mouse with them longer, terrified them, but that couldn't be helped. He couldn't change the schedule now. Everything was arranged in his head, step by step, stage by stage, shot by shot; the anticipated shots most of all. Slater first, for Ann to see him die. Slater was the son of a bitch who'd stolen her from him and got him slammed up. Definitely blow Slater's face away. Make sure with a second shot. Then Ann, the same way.

Mason considered stopping at the Old Ebbitt or even one of the 14th Street hooker bars, for an early celebration drink, but just as quickly changed his mind. Step one was to clean, oil and prepare the Glock, a handgun with which he was not familiar and for which he didn't have a manual to follow the cleaning and reassembly instructions. Too early to celebrate. He could do that later when he was in New York, waiting for Chambers. He'd be there several days before they were due to meet. Might even include Miriam in the celebrations. Fuck her brains out this time, to prove that the problem the first time had been her fault, not his. Yes, he'd definitely do that. And not give her the fifty bucks bonus, either.

Mason got back to the Chesapeake shore by four and boiled some hot dogs to eat on the outside deck. He limited himself to two glasses of Napa Valley claret, taking his time about everything. He wanted to be able to remember it all, even something as inconsequential as what he had to eat and how many glasses of wine he drank. Maybe write it down in a diary, set it all out to read, over and over again.

There was scarcely any wind off the bay, calm enough to clean and prepare the gun outside. He laid out a clean white towel for the gun and the few bullets he had and set out the cleaning material in the order in which he'd need it, deciding against too much dissembling. He released the magazine catch on the left of the butt and pulled back the slide to eject anything in the chamber, which he inspected through the ejection port, surprised how clean it appeared to be. He gently brushed and cleaned the chamber with a clean cloth before following the same procedure with the magazine. He rotated the brush as he gradually entered it the full length of the barrel, anxious to remove the slightest debris or dust from either side of the rifling. Completely satisfied the gun was empty, he released the automatic trigger safety bar before further depressing the trigger to free the hammer and striker pin, blowing and brushing to ensure its unimpeded cleanliness. Without a manual he didn't know where or by how much to oil. He concentrated on the firing and striker mechanism but only minimally lubricated the barrel. He cleaned and polished the eight bullets that he had, acknowledging as he did so that he had to sacrifice one, maybe more, in test shots, which he could do without attracting any curiosity: ever since he'd been in the cottage there'd been almost a daily sound of waterbird shooting. He'd oiled by instinct and hopefully common sense but there was every chance of his having missed some of the mechanism and he couldn't risk it jamming.

He divided his minimal ammunition stash, leaving himself five for the kill and three to guarantee that the Glock operated smoothly. He put the test shots in the magazine and slammed it home and retrieved from the refrigerator two cloves of garlic that he wiped liberally over those that remained, carefully picking away any sticking fibres. He didn't intend either of them to survive, but he knew from his research that garlic guaranteed fatal blood poisoning and the intended facial shots would make it impossible for either of them to name him if by some miracle either of them survived. As he returned the bullets to their glassine envelope, Mason determined to apply a second garlic coating before loading them into the magazine. And to oil everything again, too.

He chose for a target the cardboard wrapping of a yoghurt six pack, wedging it against what remained of a grey-weathered, long dead tree stump. Mason carefully scrutinized the shoreline and the scrubland beyond before scouring the lake to establish that all the visible boats and yachts were sufficiently far away and positioned himself about five feet from his target, the distance he estimated he would be from Slater and Ann before they'd be aware of his approach from behind. He dropped into the remembered crouch, aimed and fired. The explosion was deafening, even in the open, and the kick jarring, actually hurting his wrist even though he had it supported by his free hand. Mason missed the cardboard entirely but blasted away almost a foot of the atrophied trunk above. He looked anxiously around, and waited several minutes for any obvious movement, all the time stretching and making a fist of his aching hand and wrist to ease the discomfort. Mason made a far greater allowance for the kick on his second shot, which still wasn't sufficient, but on the third attempt he blew what remained of the cardboard into confetti and match-sticked the stump down to its protruding roots.

He wouldn't bother with the second coating of garlic, he decided. It wouldn't be necessary.

'The bastards are trying to cover their backs,' complained David Potter.

As you've been trying to do by involving me, thought Denver, as worried as the FBI supervisor that he risked being identified by the official enquiry from the local PD about a gun carrying licence for Ann and Slater. 'The whole idea was always too uncertain.'

'I don't remember you voting against it until now,' retorted Potter.

'So now I am,' snapped Denver.

'Perhaps I was wrong,' said Burt Hodges, anxious to support a former CIA colleague. 'Perhaps Sobell – sorry, Slater – hasn't lost the edge after all. He was clever, putting on the pressure like that.'

The three men were in Potter's room at the FBI Washington field office, convened by Potter after the approach from Frederick PD. Potter said, 'I don't think we've got any alternative but to support the issuing.'

'That puts our asses on the line,' said Denver, alert to Potter's use of the plural to bind him into the responsibility.

'They always were, if anything went wrong,' said Hodges, the only one against whom there could be no official censure. 'According to Harrigan and Stone the guy at the gun club says Slater's not bad.'

'After one session at the range, not under any pressure!' rejected Denver. 'What about the wife?'

'We've got it covered,' insisted Potter, defensively.

'If you've got it covered then support the application,' said Denver, stressing the singular.

'You could always tell Harrigan and Stone.'

'Who'd object, say we should have told them from the start, probably get in the way and fuck everything up. It's got to stay tight.'

'It's your decision,' insisted Denver. It had been fucked up from the beginning, with that asshole Peebles making it easy for Slater to identify him and the recording van in Lafayette Park. 'We don't get it right soon we're going to have to wrap everything up, anyway.'

'We do that our asses are even more on the line,' judged Potter, miserably. 'We're sure as hell between a rock and a hard place.'

More so you than me, thought Denver. As an ex-CIA professional Hodges would testify that he'd argued against it.

Twenty-Eight

J ack Mason was ready an hour before the realtor's arrival, his cases and laptop packed and in the trunk of the waiting Ford, alongside the re-oiled and now fully loaded Glock. The precaution of collecting up and bagging a lot of the cardboard target debris occurred to him as he sat on the deck, waiting, and as he did so he scattered more widely some of the blown-apart tree stump, which prompted a reflection. The gun had a hell of a kick. And he only had five ten-millimetre bullets left. He had to get closer than five yards. And switch the intended shots, the body first, then the face. Even then it would still be possible to miss. He needed more, another weapon, unable as he had been to buy more ammunition in the Annapolis store. There'd been a selection of hunting knives there, he remembered, as there had been in the sports outlet in Washington where he'd bought the canvas bag. He could easily fit in a shopping call without upsetting his carefully worked out schedule. He had time to spare, in fact, so he wouldn't even have to hurry the choice.

The realtor saw him sitting on the deck and tooted his horn in greeting, striding up with his hand outstretched. 'As good a trip as last time?'

'Better,' responded Mason. 'Didn't get summoned back early.'

They toured the house and went through the inventory and the man produced the telephone account he'd obtained the previous day. He said, 'Just the short rental. You're not a tele-phone person, are you?'

'I came here to get away from telephones.'

'We going to see you again?'

'You might well,' lied Mason. 'I've got your number.'

'Look forward to hearing from you,' assured the realtor. They drove in convoy along the dirt slip road until they connected with the first black top, where Mason held back from overtaking, letting other cars come between them. By the time he got to the Annapolis turning the realtor had disappeared.

Mindful that he was travelling with a loaded, unlicensed gun Mason kept well within every speed limit and driving restriction, aware of the Highway Patrol vehicle long before it overtook, the driver seemingly oblivious to him. He reached Annapolis by eleven, five minutes earlier than he'd estimated and went directly to the mall in which he remembered from his initial unsuccessful visit the hunting store to be.

Mason at once recognized the sales assistant approaching him as the one who'd demanded a licence when he'd tried to buy the ammunition before, but felt no immediate concern: the unremarkable incident, which hadn't lasted more than a few minutes, had been long enough ago.

And then the man said, 'Hi there! Remembered your permit this time?'

'You've got a good memory,' said Mason, his stomach lurching. Rod Redway, he read from the name tag.

'Never forget a face,' Redway boasted. 'Kind of a knack.'

He had to keep calm, Mason knew, not try to hurry away. 'It must be useful.'

'Certainly is. You come back for ten-millimetre shells?'

'You even remember that?' said Mason, inwardly in turmoil.

'It's a heavy calibre, like we talked about then. Don't get asked for them often.'

'I got them elsewhere,' hurriedly improvised Mason. 'Guy I know, sometimes go hunting with, he's got a birthday coming up. Likes big game. I'm looking for a skinning knife. You got anything you could show me?'

'Gotta good selection,' guaranteed the man. 'You get your other stuff locally?'

'What?' stalled Mason.

'Your ammunition. You get it somewhere here in Annapolis?'

Mason shook his head. 'Alexandria, I think. Can't rightly remember. Passed a gun store by chance and dropped in.' Perspiration was making its way down his back, creating an irritation.

'Don't know a gun shop in Alexandria. Try to keep up with the competition.'

'Don't recall its name,' said Mason, in hopeful dismissal. 'Let's look at some knives, shall we?'

The assistant arranged his display on a green baize with the flourish of a jeweller offering priceless diamonds, going at once into a well rehearsed sales spiel that Mason became anxious to stop. 'I'm going to need your advice. I don't shoot big stuff with him – certainly don't know anything about butchering.'

'He a good friend of yours, this guy?'

'Known him a long time.'

'Then I guess you'll want the best,' said the man, offering what Mason expected to be the most expensive. It was thick bladed, about twelve inches long, one edge honed, the other serrated. 'You got the blade to open the skin and peel, the saw to cut through any bone. It's the one I'd recommend.'

'I'll take it,' accepted Mason. Forcing himself on, he said, 'I don't suppose there's a presentation case. It's a gift, like I told you.'

'I could box it, with the sheath.'

'Would you do that?'

Mason began to relax when the man moved away. It was annoying – he'd been stupid coming back to the same place, a mistake he'd consciously avoided with bars and restaurants and for the last five days even Frederick itself – but that was all it was; by this time tomorrow he'd be far away in New York, beyond recognition by any fucking idiot with a quirky memory. Beyond identification or discovery or arrest, moving on to the next part of a plan so perfect it couldn't be prevented or stopped.

'Here you go,' announced the returning salesman, the knife boxed and wrapped. He held a ledger as well as a sales slip in his other hand. 'Why don't I take your name and address, so I can send you information on our new stuff as it comes in? Don't like losing potential customers to other stores.'

Fuck you, thought Mason, finding an immediate rejection in his anger. 'Give me a card or whatever. I'm between relocations at the moment. When I get a permanent place I'll register. I like the personal service.'

'Personal service!' seized the man. 'That's what we give here, personal service, Mr . . . ?'

Mason's mind filled and became overcrowded by names

unconnected with his own. 'Jefferson,' he gabbled, snatching at the first with no obvious link. 'Josh Jefferson. I'll be in touch very soon.'

'I'll look forward to that, Mr Jefferson,' said the man. 'We'll really take good care of you here. Personal service.'

Mason was physically shaking as he emerged back out into the mall, wanting to stop and recover but instead forcing himself on, realizing almost at once that he was walking in the opposite direction from where he'd parked the car but not turning back to pass in front of the store. Easy, he urged himself. Take it easy. Relax. A ridiculous episode. Stupid, as he'd already decided. Wrong to overestimate its importance, though. It had happened, he'd outwardly handled it and now it was finished. It might have seemed like hours but it hadn't been. Less than half an hour, everything he still had to do still well within schedule. Just needed a little time to settle down, get his priorities back in order. He walked out of the mall, leaving the car where it was, and found a bar on a bordering street.

He got a stool at its back corner, keeping his twitching hands out of sight when the barman reached him, and ordered a double Jack Daniels.

'Time for a pit stop?' greeted the barman, professionally.

'It's been a difficult day already,' said Mason.

'You said to call in two or three days,' reminded Slater. 'It's been two days.'

There was a wheezed intake of breath from the other end of the line. 'Spoke to our guys at the Hoover building this morning,' said Potter. 'It seems that these deeper scientific tests take longer than I thought.'

'So there's still nothing?'

'Not yet,' said the FBI man. 'How's Mrs Slater?'

'A lot better since we got the carrying licence.' That morning Ann had gone into the gallery for the first time, although insisting he follow in his car until she'd parked and actually got into the building. She was going to wait there until he collected her for their afternoon practice at the range, before picking up her own car to follow him to the cemetery.

'How about you?'

'I'm OK,' said Slater, which was a lie. He was becoming

265

increasingly uncertain, worse even than the unexpected shock of Mason's release. 'You have anything to do with our getting the licences?'

'Frederick PD came on to me, sure.'

'You tell them who I really am?'

'Of course not.'

'But you supported our application?'

'I knew from our meeting how important it was to you . . . particularly to your wife.'

'Even though there's no proof that Mason knows where we are?'

'We've had this conversation, Dimitri.'

'Daniel! The name's Daniel!'

'That was a bad mistake. I'm truly sorry.'

'How come you made it?'

'Been going through a lot of trial material . . . things that came out. Guess I got it stuck in my head. You didn't have a new identity then.'

'How long you going to keep the investigation going?' The answer might give him a steer.

'We've had this conversation, too. Until we decide there's no need to continue it any longer.'

'When do you think the results of these new tests will be through?'

'Maybe another couple of days.'

'I'll call you then.'

'You do that,' encouraged Potter. 'You and your wife still going to the cemetery most evenings?'

'Every evening.'

'There hasn't been any more tampering with the grave?'

'No, thank God.'

'Grieving is a long process.'

'I guess it is.'

'You take care now. Both of you.'

'We will,' said Slater. He was right! he thought. He *had* to be right!

Mason didn't hurry over the second Jack Daniels and it was gone twelve thirty before he called Patrick Bell from the central post office, his schedule running more than thirty minutes behind now. Still not a problem. The secretary said he'd only just missed the lawyer but the man wasn't due in court that afternoon and should be back by two thirty. Mason said he was moving around and didn't have a cell phone upon which he could be reached. When she suggested he stop by the office to be ahead of Bell's next appointment Mason said that would be difficult as he was in California.

Mason stayed with water at lunch, although he would have liked a drink with the rib eye steak, promising himself a start to the intended celebration later that night in New York. With enough slack still in his timetable and prompted by the thought of New York, he stopped at a travel office on his way back to the post office and as well as confirming the times of the last three shuttles, he confirmed a reservation at the UN Plaza hotel, endorsed for a late arrival although from his meticulous surveillance of the cemetery visits he was sure he could get the seven thirty flight from Reagan airport after the killings.

He called precisely at two thirty and was connected at once. Patrick Bell said, 'I've been wondering where you were.'

'You knew I was in California,' said Mason, immediately curious.

'Had it in my mind that you were coming back east?'

'I thought about it. Then I changed my mind.'

'So you're still out there?'

'I just told you I was.'

'I must have misunderstood.'

Asshole, thought Mason. 'Is everything settled?'

'It hasn't been easy.'

'You know I'm good for the bill,' said Mason, pushing the weariness into his voice. Except this time he wouldn't be, he thought. Serve the son of a bitch right.

'I'm not jacking up the fees,' protested the lawyer, indignantly. 'They tried to renege on their original offer when I offered to withdraw. They only restored it two days ago.'

'But now it's settled?' He didn't believe the man. It was becoming the second awkward conversation that day.

'Not quite. There are things for you to sign. That's why I'd hoped you were back here ... that you could drop by and wrap everything up.'

'You'll have to send it. You've got the San Francisco box number.'

'You're not coming back then?'

'I just told you I'm not,' said Mason, impatiently.

'I can't send the settlement cheque without your signed receipt.'

'Post the acceptance for me to sign ahead of the cheque.' Only three weeks until Peter Chambers' release, Mason calculated. He'd be glad to be free of this shit, his mind cleared to move on to the final plan. It was going to be much easier, the next time.

'I don't like sending cheques through the post.'

'What other way is there?' said Mason, frowning.

'I could courier it to you if you gave me a San Francisco address.'

'For eight thousand lousy bucks!'

'You're right,' agreed the lawyer. 'I'll wait until I get the signed receipt back.' He paused. 'Guess we won't be seeing each other again.'

'Thanks for everything.' And kiss my ass, Mason mentally added.

He went uneasily back to his car, still in the mall parking lot. Easily concealed within the boot he unwrapped the hunting knife and took it out of the box, leaving it ready in its sheath, and took out the laptop. He squatted in the back of the car, running it off its battery, and accessed all his Trojan Horses, leaving the penitentiary and Patrick Bell until last. There was nothing new, as there hadn't been when he'd gone through his daily exercise regime that morning, before the realtor's arrival at the cottage.

For several moments he remained hunched where he was, after closing the machine down, going through the conversation with the lawyer in his mind. And then he smiled. Of course the exchanges between the lawyer and the state authorities wouldn't have been by email. There were documents that needed to be signed so it would have been by ordinary letter mail. He was still unsettled by the nonsense in the hunting store that morning.

Mason returned the laptop to the trunk but again sat for several moments at the wheel, breathing deeply, preparing himself.

Showtime, he thought.

Twenty-Nine

Jack Mason began ticking off his mentally prepared list as soon as he left Annapolis. The car was first. He stopped at a designated gas station, not only filling the car for the escape drive to DC and the New York shuttle, but to check the oil, water and air, determined against any unforeseen setbacks. In the gas station shop he bought the necessary pack of latex gloves and, as an afterthought, two bunches of tulips He approached Frederick with sufficient time to spare to make the detour to the creek in which he intended to dump the Glock and the laptop and turned off the main highway at the same spot as before. He drove slowly over the echoing bridge, satisfying himself the banks were deserted, and stopped in the same lay-by as before on the opposite side. He was actually on the bridge, crossing to where the path sloped down to the bank before he saw the man and boy, presumably father and son, fishing together. The boy looked up and gestured. With no alternative, Mason waved back. The weak sun in their eyes would make it difficult for them to see him clearly.

'Caught anything?' Mason called down.

'Couple of trout,' said the boy. 'Not very big.'

If he hadn't made the detour he might have come upon them with the Glock, empty, openly in his hand, ready to throw into the river, Mason thought. 'One of your favourite spots?'

'Pretty much,' said the man, squinting up.

'We usually get more,' said the boy.

'I promised you six and that's what we'll get,' said the man, not talking to Mason.

'Best of luck,' said Mason, turning away.

He'd lost his hiding place, Mason accepted, putting the Ford into a u-turn to recross the bridge, sounding his horn in farewell as he did so, to rejoin the Frederick road. The danger wasn't from recognition but from being stuck with the incriminating Glock after the killings. What about the deserted area by the canoe club from which he'd thrown the first laptop into the Potomac beneath the Key Bridge? It would involve a time-consuming route change to Reagan airport and . . . no it wouldn't, Mason stopped himself, turning on to the blacktop. He'd be on the right side of the city, descending from the Beltway. He could simply continue on into Alexandria and discard the gun in the Potomac from one of the convenient roads leading down to the river there. He could easily carry the laptop up to New York to dispose of it there.

As he drove into Frederick Mason saw from the dashboard clock that he was still conveniently ahead of the cemetery ritual, which gave him more than sufficient time to take more precautions. He chose the house first, taking the familiar turn. Hill Street SE was, as always, pristinely empty, unsullied by any tree or hedge litter, unmarked by a single discarded toy or child's bicycle or play cart. The Slater's driveway was empty, the garage doors shut. For the first time Mason allowed himself a direct look as he passed, seeing immediately that the basketball hoop had been dismantled. Well before he reached it, Mason knew Ann's gallery was open: two women, one carrying a picture-shaped package, emerged as he went by. This time he didn't turn his head to look, apprehensive of the CCTV. He did try to locate Ann's recognizable car in the adjoining parking space but couldn't.

Mason approached the now familiar cemetery by the circuitous route that would position the car in the direction he needed to drive directly to the Beltway link road, slowing as he went by the church at the front. There were more cars than he expected, making it difficult to be absolutely sure, but Mason didn't isolate the memorized licence plates of either Slater or Ann's car in the carefully avoided parking area. Mason left his car in the chosen road separated by two streets from the cemetery. He painstakingly fitted each finger into its designated stall of the latex gloves, which he'd left lying on the passenger seat beside him, before intertwining his hands to ensure they were perfectly snug, shrugging the sleeves of his jacket down to test that they were totally concealed. Satisfied, Mason reached beneath the passenger seat to retrieve the Glock and the serrated hunting knife and wiped every surface of the gun, the trigger particularly, with what remained of the unused cleaning rag. After that he did the same with the knife. Even though he had only touched their outer plastic wrapping, which he now removed, Mason also wiped every stem of the two bunches of tulips, very aware that there was not the slightest shake in his hands as he worked. He felt completely calm, too, although very eager. He wedged the gun into the front waistband of his trousers, to the left. He put the knife, unsheathed, into the left inside pocket of his jacket and got awkwardly out of the car so that the door and its window would hide the Glock until he could button his jacket over it. There was a discernible bulge but it was completely covered when he positioned the flowers in front of him. The flowers also hid the gloves.

'Ready,' he said, aloud, turning back towards the cemetery.

Now that she had a carrying licence Ann was insisting on practising twice a day at the gun club range. Her slot that afternoon was later than usual so the arrangement was for Slater to pick her up from there and then for them to continue on to the cemetery in his car and collect hers on the way back. He drove badly and knew it, too tensed to everything around him, his speed fluctuating sometimes so widely to bring protesting horn blasts from other cars, which heightened his tension.

He had to bring things to a head, Slater determined, resentment adding to all the other conflicting emotions, anger the most predominant. The risk of failure – which inevitably meant disaster – was appalling and couldn't go on any longer, no matter whatever threats or denials there would be. Despite his earlier conviction to the contrary, Slater was increasingly coming to believe that the turmoil of relocation – of their having to adopt new identities and start new lives again – was their only escape. He knew Ann would be reluctant to the point of outright refusal to any suggestion of their no longer being near to David's grave. He'd call Potter or Denver or both tomorrow. Openly challenge them – how much he wished he could threaten legal action! – and demand the official help he would need. The hovering uncertainty hardened in his mind. What if they refused, now that he was no longer of any use or value to them? But they did need him, he tried to reassure himself. He might not be any longer professionally important to them, but their precious Witness Protection Programme was. And it provided him with his necessary pressure point, one he'd impose as hard as he could when he spoke to Potter tomorrow.

He had to wait for Ann to come off the range and when she did she said, 'I took an extra fifteen minutes. The person after me was late.'

Slater kept protectively behind her as they emerged into the parking lot, not looking at her but all around, releasing the automatic lock to avoid any delay in her getting in when they reached the car. 'How'd you do?'

'Two bulls at twenty-five yards, one at thirty. Almost all of the rest in the next ring.'

'That's pretty good,' he said, as they gained the cemetery road.

'That's pretty *damned* good,' she corrected. 'John says I'm one of the best he's ever trained.' John Bristol was their permanent instructor.

'What's wrong with your wrist?'

'Nothing!'

'You've been holding it – nursing it – ever since you got into the car.'

Ann took her left hand away from her right wrist. 'I told you nothing was wrong with it.'

'You've done too much. It won't be bulls tomorrow.'

'We'll see. Why are you driving so slowly?' she fought back.

'I wasn't aware that I was.'

'You are! We're going to be late if you don't hurry.'

'We'll be there at the same time as we always are,' insisted Slater, increasing his speed. 'We don't have a time schedule.'

'You got the cleaning things?'

'You saw me pack them this morning, before we left the house.'

Ann's hand was back supporting her wrist, Slater saw. He'd definitely make contact with Potter tomorrow. This really couldn't go on any longer. 'I'm going . . .' started Slater, but then stopped.

'What?'

'Nothing,' said Slater. He'd gauge the FBI supervisor's reaction before beginning the battle with Ann about relocation.

272

'There's the cemetery up ahead,' she said, unnecessarily.

Battle was very definitely going to be the apposite word, Slater knew.

Surveillance – remaining invisible while always keeping a target in sight – had always earned the highest grades in Jack Mason's tradecraft training; he'd never blown a genuine field operation, which was how he regarded the killings he was about to carry out. He'd be unseen in the most perfect ambush position at the precise moment Slater and Ann were at their most vulnerable, emerge, strike and be gone, the contemptuous flowers strewn about them, the perfect, unsolvable crime committed. It would probably be listed as that in crime text-books, as he knew both from his Internet surfing and time as the penitentiary's librarian that his treason was listed as one of the most serious as well as the most humiliating spying episodes in the CIA's history. He wished he could be publicly acknowledged for the second as well as the first memorable acts.

Mason used the discreetly small side gate from which the boy's grave was completely hidden and approached the privet hiding place along a path that gave him the most extensive view of the area beyond it. There was a scattering of mourners, all of whom he judged far enough away not to connect his firing of the Glock with bullet shots. If Slater and Ann were on time, the funereal tolling of the church bell would help cover the noise, as well. Much closer, though, were two separate gangs of cemetery gardeners, weeding and border edging and grave tidying. Slater and Ann always knelt, as if they were praying, which they probably were. That's what he had to do, come in low like someone else praying with them in a grieving huddle if any of the workers abruptly looked up, attracted by the sound. That was the trick of being invisible, merging in with the background. Slater and Ann would be prostrate by death, not grief by then, unable to shout for help. It was a delicious irony that briefly, as he stayed crouched low over them, they would be providing cover for him. They'd deserve their flowers.

They were coming! He could see them, walking as they always walked, Ann leaning heavily upon Slater's arm as if she needed his physical support, her head bowed. In her free hand she carried a bouquet of red flowers the names of which Mason didn't know. Slater, by comparison, was not bow-headed, but gazing about him, once even turning to look behind them. Slater was carrying a bucket, a broom handle protruding above its rim. At a standpipe faucet about five yards from the grave they separated. Ann took out the broom, as well as a trowel and a dust tray. Slater splashed some water into the bucket, which Mason saw had a funnelled rim. Perfect, Mason decided; they'd be distracted, engrossed, in their grave tidying. They wouldn't be aware of him until he was upon them, too close – too ready – to miss.

Momentarily they went out of Mason's view, obscured behind his protective hedge. Mason gently parted the thicket, giving himself a disguised peephole, breathing in sharply at what he immediately saw through it. They were at the grave-side, Slater brushing and sweeping, Ann changing old flowers for new and adding fresh water from the bucket. But not positioned as he'd expected. Always before they'd knelt side by side, their backs to the privet hedge from behind which he'd approach. Today they were either side, Ann with her back to him but Slater opposite, facing him. He had to go ahead, couldn't put it off. Slater *was* engrossed, head bent. He had to move slowly, Mason knew, do nothing to attract Slater's attention. Do it now, while Slater was hunched forward! Move now!

Gently Mason squeezed the trigger, unlocking the bar, as he rose and stepped from behind the hedge, treading as lightly as he could, needing to concentrate upon them and not able to look down to avoid any twig-snapping alert. He could hear the thump of his own heart, sounding in his ears, glad that the gloves stopped the butt feeling slippery in the sweat of his hands.

The other noise was startling, stopping him, although he couldn't distinguish the megaphone words. He only heard his own name when it was repeated but heard it all the third time.

'MASON! DROP THE GUN! ON YOUR FACE! ON YOUR FACE OR WE'LL SHOOT! NOW! ON YOUR FACE NOW!'

Everything kaleidoscoped. Mason saw some of the cemetery gardeners running towards him, although they had guns in their hands. Beyond them three marksmen were spread out, sight-fitted rifles trained upon him. At the grave Slater was snatching inside his jacket and as he did so Ann screamed, throwing herself forward but turning at the same time to look behind her. Mason ran at them, firing as he did so, crying out at what felt like a punch that abruptly stopped him, and at not seeing Ann, at whom he'd fired, crumple forward. Mason tried to bring his arm over, to steady his right wrist but he couldn't move it because of the numbness. Slater had a gun in his hand now and was crouched but when he tried to fire nothing happened. There was the noise of two faraway shots, from the marksmen, but again Mason didn't feel any immediate pain at the punch of impact.

But then he did, taking his breath, and saw Ann, still on the ground but with a gun now and as he tried to train the Glock on her she fired again and he was falling, not able to stop himself but still not feeling any pain, and then she was standing over him shouting words he couldn't hear. The jerk of the gun as Ann fired for the third time was the last thing that Mason ever saw because she shot him full in the face.

Thirty

'**Y**ou pig fucking son of a bitch,' exploded Slater, the fury as well as the lingering terror shuddering through him. 'Ann could have died, set up as bait like that! I could have died!'

'But you didn't,' said Potter, dismissively. 'We had everything covered and my guys stopped him.'

'Ann stopped him after your guys missed him being anywhere near the cemetery because you had fuck all covered. You didn't even know he was here until he came out from behind the most obvious concealment so close to David's grave; the most obvious place to watch, not the main entrance where you all were,' accused Slater, sweeping his hand around the large cemetery administration office which the FBI had taken over for what had clearly been a long established surveillance operation. There were two scope-equipped sniper's rifles mounted on stands overlooking the parking area and three still flickering screens connected to temporarily installed CCTV cameras showing the three major paths leading to David's resting place. Incredibly the actual grave was only shown in the top left-hand frame of one. Even more incredibly the hedge behind which Mason had hidden wasn't shown at all. Mason's body had been removed but the grave was trampled and a lot of earth scattered by the stampede of agents that had followed Mason's sudden appearance. The doctor who had given the near hysterical Ann the calming sedation had gone and only Denver and Potter remained with them in the room, Ann seemingly oblivious to the argument.

'What are you more pissed off about, the fact that you lost your professional edge and didn't see what was going down or that you forgot to slip the safety on the gun we fast tracked a carrying licence for you?' demanded Potter, belligerently.

He *had* realized what was going down, thought Slater, had

intended confronting Potter the very next day. They wouldn't believe him if he admitted that now. And he didn't want to anyway because it made him look a wimp and destroyed his own argument against them. And he was pissed off, totally humiliated, by his ineffectiveness at the very moment he'd been called upon to protect Ann. He said, 'I'm pissed off at being treated like an idiot,' and knew he sounded like one.

'It all turned out fine, no one hurt except the guy who was intended to be,' intruded Denver, the peacemaker. 'You and your wife have nothing more to worry about, ever again.'

Except rebuilding their lives and spending the rest of it without David, which Slater knew they could never completely do. 'How'd you know for sure that Mason had found us?'

'He wore latex gloves when he torched the stolen car with which he killed David; tossed them in after soaking everything in gas. The explosion blew one of them a long way from the car. The FBI wonder men at the Hoover building found enough of a print *inside* one of the glove fingers to match with Mason's records. And the sap, or whatever the hell it is in a tulip stem, held enough under a scientific test too technical for me to understand to confirm another print. And we got a little help from California, where he tried to set up an alibi.'

'So what happens now?' asked Slater.

'We did have the scene covered,' insisted Potter. 'We controlled enough of the cemetery to keep everything totally under wraps. David's murder, which it really was, will officially remain an unresolved accident, never to become public knowledge as a planned killing. You'll never be identified for whom you really are. Like Pete says, you and your wife can get back to living your lives.'

'It was the Witness Protection Programme, wasn't it?' demanded Slater, disgusted by the cynicism. 'You really didn't give a fuck about Ann or me, did you? You'd have covered up who I am, if we'd got killed, just as long as you'd got Mason to keep everything tidy.'

'You might have forgotten most of them, but you know the rules, Mr Slater,' said the fat FBI man.

'Motherfuckers!' said Slater.

'On behalf of the United States Government, the CIA and the Federal Bureau of Investigation I have to thank you and your wife for your co-operation,' said Denver. 'I can't imagine you having the need again, but if you do, you have the numbers.'

'No,' said Slater. 'I won't ever have the need to speak with you again.'

'You didn't shoot when he came up behind me!'

Slater jumped, startled by the quiet-voiced accusation. Ann had slumped against him, needing his support to get from the cemetery office to his car. 'My gun jammed.'

'He said you forgot to release the safety catch.'

'It jammed,' lied Slater. In his terror of Mason he'd frozen, like a rabbit caught in headlights. And Ann knew it. She was established with the gallery; had a reputation. She could survive on her own, now that Jack was dead, now that he didn't have a face any more. 'It was me . . . me who stopped him. Killed him. Not you.'

'Yes.'

'Didn't protect me, as you should.'

Slater didn't have a response.

'That's why I stopped drinking again. I knew I had to stay sober, to look after myself. That no one else would.'

'My gun jammed!' persisted Slater.

'Jack's face will never haunt me again. I shot his face off. He always said that's what he'd do to me, if I tried to leave him, take away my face. I took his off instead.'

'We're almost home,' said Slater. Ann was definitely going to need help now. He'd call Hillary Neslon in the morning.

'We won't be able to, will we? Go on living our lives. Not now.'

'Yes we will,' said Slater, knowing she was right.

'No,' refuted Ann. 'It's changed now. Nothing's the same. All over.' She was established with the gallery now, had a reputation. She could survive now that Jack was dead, now that he didn't have a face anymore.

They lay naked and uncovered on the bed of the Santa Barbara cottage as Beverley remembered she had twice lain with Jack Mason, the perspiration of their lovemaking drying on them. She said, 'That was wonderful.'

'It always is, with you. It's going to be a great vacation,' Glynis Needham answered.

'I'm glad you're here.'

'I want to be here a lot more,' said the DC-based parole officer, stretching out a hand to touch Beverley. 'You know what I'd like?'

'I thought you'd just shown me,' Beverley sniggered.

'I'd like to show you a lot more often. Settle in together. Either I relocate out here or you come east.'

'It's something to think about,' hedged Beverley.

'You've got a whole lot of federal brownie points over the Mason case. How'd you get on to him like you did, realize things weren't right?'

'A hunch, I guess. He told me he wasn't surprised his wife divorced him and that he hoped she was happy, that he still loved her in some ways. But in all those documents you sent me there was her statement that was never produced in court that he beat her a lot. And when he was here in California, he kept moving around, claiming to be trying to get work but nothing ever materialized. When you called and told me of the FBI enquiry I checked at the firms he told me he'd approached. Some had never even heard of him.' She'd been lucky, getting away scot-free. She was sure now that he'd have done his best to destroy her if he'd been caught, not killed.

'He was a cheating, lying motherfucker,' said Glynis.

'And then some.' The sex had been fantastic and she'd actually thought he was the man with whom she could have gone straight, after swinging both ways for so long and failing with the man she'd married. Maybe setting up home with Glynis wasn't such a bad idea. It would settle the uncertainty.

'I want you to kiss me, like you did just now.'

'I want to, as well,' said Beverley.

Postscript

'You sure you had the right date?' asked the New York parole officer.

'Positive. And the place.' Peter Chambers hadn't told the other man it was Jack Mason for whom he'd been waiting to set up a business arrangement and was glad now that he hadn't. He felt stupid, worried the guy would think he was a fantasist, weak in the head.

'Guess he's not going to show, Pete.'

'I guess not,' said Chambers, who hated being called Pete. Mason had never shortened his name. Always properly, Peter. Why hadn't he been there at the hotel, like he'd promised? He'd have abandoned New Orleans for California, if Jack had demanded it.

'Guess that puts you on your own.'

'Yes,' conceded Chambers, confronting the loneliness that terrified him.

'You know the conditions of your release?'

'All of them,' assured Chambers.

'What are you going to do?'

'I'm not sure, now that I've been let down like this.'

'We need to keep in close touch. Your conviction isn't going to make it easy getting anything like a bookkeeping job.'

'I might look at something else. As I said, I don't have anything definite in mind, not now.'

'You've got to find some gainful employment,' said the parole official, formally.

'I know, sir,' assured Chambers. Why hadn't Jack been waiting for him! Maybe, Chambers thought, he should have told Jack he definitely had three million dollars squirreled away, instead of implying it. He'd go on living at the Sheraton, Chambers decided, just in case. There could be all sorts of reasons why Jack was delayed.